FAR WORLD

FOREST OF
BEFORE TIME
Ice Hold
Borderlands
WINDLASH MOUNTAINS
RUINS OF
WINDSHOLD
Westland
Woods
TWO PRONGS RIVER
ALTARIAN
MOUNTAINS
Air
Keep
Westland
Terra ne
Staric
UNCHARTED
TERRITORY SOUTH

FIRE KEEP

BOOK FOUR

J. SCOTT SAVAGE

Savage, J. Scott.
    Fire Keep / J. Scott Savage.
        p. cm. — (Farworld ; bk. 4)

Summary: With no word from Kyja, the people of Farworld are
beginning to face the possibility that she is truly dead, and the quest to
save Farworld and Earth has failed. In an effort to find a way to bring
Kyja back, Marcus must enter the most dangerous place possible the
realm of shadows. Meanwhile, Kyja wakes up in a world of lost souls
and memories. With no idea who she is, she wanders Fire Keep, home
to the most quick tempered of the elementals. The other spirits around
her have given up hope. But Kyja is driven by a strong sense that
something is wrong and getting worse. A familiar voice warns her that
time is running out. To recover her memories, she must face a literal
trial by fire. Can Marcus survive the realm of shadows to reach Kyja?
Can Kyja survive Fire Keep in time to regain her memory? Time is
running out for Kyja, Marcus, and their worlds and the Dark Circle's
real plan is only now beginning to be revealed.

ISBN: 193999358X
ISBN-13: 978-1-939993-58-8
[1. Foundlings—Fiction.   2. People with Disabilities—Fiction.
3. Magic—Fiction.   4. Fantasy.]   I. Title

To Lu Ann Brobst Staheli:
mother, author, teacher, friend. You inspired so many
people and will be missed by everyone who knew you.

See the Lords of Water—
Beyond the waves they leap

∞

See the Lords of Land—
Beneath the ground they sleep

♁

See the Lords of Air—
Above the clouds they creep

♋

See the Lords of Fire—
Around the flames they reap

∞

Water. Land. Air. Fire.
Together, the balance of Farworld they keep.

CONTENTS

CONTENTS

PART 2: FIRE KEEP

PART 3: THREE WORLDS

CONTENTS

PART 4: THE DRIFT

TREACHERY

The black water rippled and stirred, but the only things reflected in its surface were the sputtering torches around the room and the frustrated face of the portly water elemental standing above the pool as the other elementals watched nearby.

Leaning against a wall, his body currently composed of glittering diamonds and gold coins, Calem snickered. "The vision of the Fontasians is indeed impressive. If only I, a poor air elemental, could look into a puddle of water and see my own befuddled face."

Tide glared at him. The water elemental snatched a fish from the school circling slowly around his head and crunched it viciously between his teeth. "Watch your mouth, Aerisian," he growled around the food, "or I'll show you that a Fontasian is capable of much more than vision."

Calem guffawed, his diamonds catching the torchlight and reflecting it into Tide's face.

The land elemental pair Nizgar-Gharat flapped their wings lazily, stirring the smoke-filled air around them. Nizgar's green-striped lizard head studied Tide, while Gharat's purple lizard head looked at the dark pool of water. "You said you could see through mountains," Nizgar hissed.

"I can!" Tide snapped. He waved his hand at the pool, and at once a dizzying vista of open forest blurred by. He gestured again, and the trees were replaced by mountains. The image in the pool zoomed in to focus on a single flower then back out to reveal thousands of them. "Anywhere there is water, I can see."

Focusing intently, the Fontasian changed the image to an army of undead creatures. Swarms of two-headed dogs, rag-clothed humans, and the corpses of nearly every animal imaginable paced the ground like insects drawn to a pot of honey. Watching over them were at least a hundred Thrathkin S'Bae—the Dark Circle's wizards. In the distance beyond, a tower was barely visible, surrounded by what might be a city wall.

"Closer," hissed the land elementals, tongues flicking.

"What do you think I've been trying to do?" Tide asked. He moved his hand; the image in the pool flew over the army and toward the tower. For a tantalizing moment, the tower began to come into focus, and all of the elementals leaned forward. Then, just as the city began to grow clear, it disappeared into a white haze of mist.

"What's wrong?" Gharat demanded. "Why can't we see anything?"

Calem waved his arms and gold coins clinked merrily against one another. "Because the king of the water elementals is king of no one. His Fontasians have turned against him, and the boy Cascade makes a fool of him. Perhaps I could lend him a few of my loyal Aerisians?"

Tide spun around, face cold and purposeful. "I warned you!" He waved his hands, and water rose from the pool in the shape of a swirling serpent. Before Calem could react, the water serpent wrapped itself around him and clamped down.

"Get . . . . off . . ." The Aerisian gasped. He tried to change form, but the water bound him tight, squeezing his body in its powerful coils.

"Stop!" a commanding voice filled the chamber, echoing off the walls and filling the air as if it had physical substance. A robed figure raised his hand, and the Summoner chained to the wall shot a stream of molten fire across the room.

Tide howled in pain as the flames encased his body. Steam billowed from his hands and feet, and the tiny fish circling his head dropped to the ground, charred and curled. The water serpent he had been controlling splashed to the floor, and Calem gasped for breath, his body now a swarm of angry black hornets.

"I'll teach you to attack me, you fat—"

The Aerisian's voice cut off as the robed figure strode toward the elementals. The figure's face was entirely hidden beneath his dark hood except for a pair of glowing red eyes. Although the master was hunched, and shuffled like an old man, all the elementals stopped speaking and bowed their heads.

"Tell me what you've learned," the master said, his voice raspy like the buzz of a wasp or the warning of a rattlesnake.

The three elementals looked at one another, none wanting to be the first to speak.

Finally, Tide cleared his throat. "The land elementals have closed off all entrances to Land Keep."

"Show me," the master said.

The pool glowed, and a moment later, the four of them were staring at a swamp on the edge of a bay. Positioned strategically around the swamp were hundreds of winged creatures, each consisting of a pair of animals combined into a single body. Tide zoomed in on a creature that was part dragon, part lion, and Nizgar-Gharat's heads growled deep in their throats.

"What are they protecting?" the master whispered almost to himself.

"The wizard has been there several times over the last few days," Nizgar-Gharat's two heads said together. "We believe he is seeking a way to bring back the girl."

"Have they discovered such a way?" The master enunciated each word carefully—a knife blade waiting to slice through the wrong answer.

The land elementals lowered their heads. "We do not know," Nizgar said.

"The library is immense," Gharat added. "It's impossible to know everything it contains."

The master snorted. "If he'd found an answer, Therapass would be doing something about it." He threaded his fingers together, the ring on his right hand glittering. "What of the Windlash Mountains?"

Calem spoke up quickly. "The humans have been beaten back, and we—that is *you*—hold all entrances to the Unmakers' cavern." The image in the pool shifted into a black opening above of an icy mountain ledge.

Dozens of bulbous creatures flew around the entrance. Their purplish bodies pulsed, deep blue veins clearly visible in the tentacle-like legs hanging from their torsos. Their wispy black wings seemed far too small to keep them aloft, but the dead bodies spread below them on the mountainside were clear evidence of their powers.

Higher up the mountain, twenty or more Aerisians loyal to the Dark Circle flew their mounts through the air, scouting for any signs of attack.

The master chuckled and smacked his lips wetly. "Very good. Now I need to see what is happening in Terra ne Staric."

Tide wiped the back of his hand across his mouth. "That is a . . . *problem* at the moment. The other Fontasians have created an unnatural mist around the city, blocking me from seeing in."

The master's glowing red eyes fixed on him. "Do not tell me what you cannot do. Tell me how you will obey my command. Do you not rule the very oceans themselves? Perhaps you are not a worthy ruler for Earth after all."

"N-no, master," the water elemental stammered. "Of course I will obey your command. I only . . ." He stared down at the pool, deep in thought, and a smile stole slowly over his face. "Yes."

He waved his hands, and the image in the pool showed a placid ocean—waves rolling gently across the surface. He turned to Calem. "I need wind. A lot of it."

Calem nodded. He placed his palms together, hornets buzzing angrily and stinging one another. Immediately the calm surface of the ocean began to change. Whitecaps grew and crashed—first the height of a man, then a tree, and finally a small mountain. Sky and water roiled and spun until a huge spout rose out of the waves, filling the blue sky with dark green clouds.

"Yes," Tide said. "Now, push it inland."

The clouds raced toward the shore, across the land, and directly over the undead army stationed outside Terra ne Staric. Thrathkin S'Bae glanced up uncertainly as the creatures under their command howled and bit one another.

As the dark clouds pushed through the mist, the city came clear.

"There," the master said, pointing a finger at a glass coffin lying above ground at the base of the tower hill. Sparkling gold light surrounded the coffin, but the girl inside lay unmoving. The master nodded. "Her time grows short."

The cloud, forming a salty mist, pushed through the doors and windows of the tower.

"Find me the boy," the master commanded.

The pool showed a series of winding stairs, and a moment later, a single prison cell, where a dirty-faced boy and a skyte sat miserably side by side.

"They've locked him up?" the master whispered incredulously as if he couldn't believe his own luck. "This is too perfect."

The image began to blur, and Tide's brow furrowed. "They sense an outside presence. I won't be able to see for long."

"Quickly—the wizard," the master said. "Show me Therapass."

Tide pushed the mist up the stairs, higher and higher into the tower as the picture grew increasingly fuzzy.

"There!" the master shouted, pointing at a closed door.

Tide forced his mist under the door, and for a brief moment, the image of Master Therapass appeared in the pool. The wizard was heating a dark-gray solution in a beaker over a flame. As the mist blew into the room, he spun around, hiding the beaker behind his back, and shouted something.

Cascade and Divum charged toward the door. Cascade reached his arms into the mist as the air elemental put her hands to the sides of her mouth and blew. Instantly, the picture disappeared.

Tide spun around. "I'm sorry, I couldn't . . ."

The master waved his pale hands. "It is enough." He stared at the black water and whispered, "What are you up to, old man?"

At the far end of the room, a door opened, and a small, misshapen creature shuffled in. It bowed its twisted torso and turned its owl-like head in the master's direction. "The traitor is in place. He has your item and is waiting to use it."

The Master's eyes flashed red. His hand went to the pale line on his finger. "Very good."

PART 1
The Waiting Game

CHAPTER 1

COUNTING
THE DAYS

Water leaking from the narrow crack in the stone ceiling made a rhythmic tapping on the cell floor—two quick plinks, followed by a heavier splat. After the splat came a pause so long, you might actually think the water had stopped falling altogether—if you hadn't been listening to it for so long that the sound of the drips were as familiar as your own heartbeat.

Marcus knew the pattern well enough that he could anticipate exactly how long the pause would last before three more drops splashed into the puddle in the corner—*plink, plink, splat*—like keys on a piano.

Exactly twenty-seven drops per minute. One thousand six hundred twenty drops per hour. Thirty-eight thousand eight hundred eighty drops per day.

Or was it thirty seven thousand seven hundred seventy?

Math was never Marcus's strong suit. And he was almost positive the water dripped faster at night than in the morning. So it could have been as many as forty thousand.

He'd tried calculating how many drops had fallen since Kyja's . . . He refused to call it *death*, even though it was beginning to feel more and more like that after ten days with no sign from her. Instead, he tried to think of it as her *departure*—as if she'd gone on a long trip, and any minute now, he'd get a letter, or the magical equivalent of a phone call.

But the numbers had started to jumble in his head until he was pretty sure he was going crazy.

Riph Raph, perched on a rock outcropping above Marcus's head, waggled his ears. "Well?"

"What?" Marcus pulled his gaze away from the puddle and blinked.

"Your question," Riph Raph snapped—although with far less snarkiness than he would have used back when Kyja was still around. "You're on seventeen. You have three more to go."

Marcus rubbed his grimy hands across his face, remembering that they were playing twenty questions. It was one of the games he'd taught the skyte in the days they'd been locked together in the dungeon—along with I

Spy (which had gotten old quickly when the only things they could see outside the cell were a hallway, a torch, and the occasional beetle), a rhyming game called Pink Stink, and enough games of Tic-Tac-Toe to cover one entire wall.

"Right. Okay." Marcus tried to concentrate—something that was getting harder and harder to do, as though his mind was wearing away with each drop of water that fell. "Are you thinking of Kyja's laugh?"

"How did you guess?" Riph Raph asked.

Marcus gave a ghost of a smile. "We already did her hair, her robe, her slippers, her eyes, her hands . . ."

"Don't forget her smile," the skyte said.

How could he, when all he had to do was close his eyes, and it was right there in front of him? Marcus's hands clenched as he wondered for at least the thousandth time why she'd done it. How could she have left without him? How could she drink some unknown potion on the word of an *air elemental*? For all she'd known, it was another of their stupid jokes.

Look, I got a human to drink poison.

Riph Raph glided to the floor and placed a wing on Marcus's knee. "She'll pull you over any time now."

"I know." Marcus sighed.

The skyte blinked his big yellow eyes. "And when she does, you won't forget to bring me with you?"

Marcus scratched the back of Riph Raph's head in the

same spot Kyja always had. "Of course not."

From around the corner of the hall came the sound of footsteps descending the stairs that led from the tower to the dungeon.

"Breakfast," Marcus grunted with a frown.

It wasn't that the food was bad. Bella made all of their meals personally, and she was the best cook Marcus had ever met. The meals weren't the problem. It was the two guards who brought them.

"Maybe it's someone new," Riph Raph said. "Maybe the dumb one finally killed the noisy one. Or maybe someone pushed them both off a wall. People that annoying must have enemies."

Marcus wished. At first the guards watching him had rotated in and out. But the last few days it had been the same annoying pair. He'd asked the warden for new guards at least ten times. But every meal, the usual two came—a fat, stupid man with a bad attitude, and a skinny one that Marcus was almost sure was crazy. Personally, he couldn't understand how the two of them had gotten their jobs in the first place. The city had to be desperate to hire them.

The footsteps grew louder, accompanied by the clanking of badly fitted armor. With them came the sound of off-key singing.

I met her in the market square,
a lovely little flower.

I raised my wand above my head
to demonstrate my power.

I thought to place into her hair
a pleasant scented blossom.
Alas, my magic went awry.
And now she is a possum.

Marcus looked at Riph Raph, and the skyte flapped to the farthest corner or the cell.

"What kind of a song is that?" a deep voice bellowed. "Who ever heard of a love ballad for a possum?"

"Tain't *for* a possum," answered a squeaky voice, which grated on Marcus's ears like the tines of a fork dragged across a tin plate. "It's a song for a woman. A lovely woman with eyes like those blue gems. What are they called?"

A huge belch echoed down the corridor, and Marcus could only hope it hadn't been pointed toward his plate. "Blueberries?"

"That ain't a gem. It's a vegetable," the squeaky voice said.

The two guards came into view and stopped. The fat one shook his greasy red hair out of his face and scratched his rear with the hand not holding Marcus's plate. "You're right. He's still there."

The skinny guard, who had a long, curved nose that

came down past his mouth, cackled. "Told you so. Pay up."

Marcus, didn't want to talk to either of the guards, but he couldn't help himself. "Where did you think I'd be? I'm locked in a cell."

The fat guard rubbed his doughy cheeks, a stupid expression on his face. "Hmm. Never thought of that."

Each man carried a plate—one for Marcus and another for Riph Raph—to the cell door and slid them under the bars.

"You know," the skinny guard said, squeezing a wart on the tip of his chin, "when you first demanded to be locked up here, I thought you was suffering from depression or obsession or some other *-ession*. But now your strategy has become all too clear to me. You realized with all the cleaning up going on in the city that you would never be able to get any serious thinking done." He tapped the side of his helmet and gave a sly wink. "But down here, you got no distractions at all. Good planning, young man. Ought 'a see if I can get a room in the dungeon myself."

"That's about the dumbest thing I've ever heard," Marcus said, sliding a plate to Riph Raph. "I'm here for a crime I committed, like everyone else in the dungeon."

"*Crime?*" The fat guard gasped as though the thought had never occurred to him that someone locked in a dungeon might have done something to deserve it. "What did you do? Swipe someone's gold? Kidnap their children?" He shivered. "The very thought gives me the willies."

Marcus stared at his hands. "I'm guilty of murder. I killed my best friend."

The skinny guard's eyes opened wide. "Spells and curses! You didn't!" He arched a bushy eyebrow. "Put a knife in his heart, did you?"

Marcus glared at the old buffoon. "My best friend is a *she*, not a *he*. And I might as well have stabbed her. I gave her the poison that . . ." He hated the word, but it was time to face the truth. "I gave her the poison that killed her. Then I let her drink it."

The fat guard clapped both hands to his mouth. "He's talking about Kyja." He placed his lips to the skinny guard's ear and whispered so loud that Marcus could have heard it from the top of the stairs. "I was there too. I seen her drink the poison straight down. And I dint do nuffin to stop her. Think they might throw *me* in a cell too?"

The skinny guard smacked him on the front of his breastplate. "Don't strain what little brains God gave ya. I heard tell the girl was determined to take the poison no matter what anyone did. If letting a person do what they are determined to do is a crime, half the people in this city are guilty." He leered at Marcus. "I know what you *are* guilty of, though."

Marcus shoved a forkful of eggs into his mouth, barely tasting them. "What?"

"Of being so arrogant as to think you are the only one who feels the pain of the dear girl's loss and the guilt of not realizing what she was up to."

Marcus slammed his fork on his plate. "That's the lamest thing I've ever heard. Who told you that?"

"I know! I know!" The fat guard danced around, waving his hand like a kid in school. "It was the crazy old wizard you're always talking to. Ther-a-puss."

Marcus jumped to his feet and grabbed the bars. "Master Therapass is *not* crazy." He turned to the skinny guard. "Is it true? Did he say that to you?"

Master Therapass had come down to the dungeon once, trying to convince Marcus and Riph Raph that they didn't belong there. It didn't work, and he hadn't returned.

The skinny guard bobbed his beak-like nose. "That's exactly what he said. Also that you are guilty of the crime of stubbornness, the crime of ignorance, and most damaging of all, the crime of pride."

The words cut deeper than Marcus wanted to let on. He dropped to the floor. "He can say whatever he wants. I'm not leaving."

"Neither am I," Riph Raph said. "We're waiting right here until Kyja pulls us to Fire Keep."

The fat guard rubbed the back of his thick neck. "What if she *never* pulls you over? What then?"

That was what Marcus was most afraid of. If Kyja

didn't pull him over soon, it could mean only one thing. That she was dead.

The fat guard stared down at Marcus, his face surprisingly serious. "I hear that batty old wizard has been working night and day on a way to get her back."

"Really?" Marcus asked. Riph Raph, who had been pecking at his food, flew to Marcus's side and nuzzled under his hand.

The skinny guard moved close, his eyes oddly familiar. "Do you think for a minute that every man, woman, and child in this city wouldn't do anything they could to bring Kyja back?"

Marcus shook his head silently.

The fat guard rubbed his jowls. "Don't you think she would do anything in her power to bring you to her if she could?"

Marcus's vision blurred as tears leaked from his eyes. "I know she would."

The skinny guard stepped back from the cell and straightened his ill-fitting armor. "Then we must assume she is not able to summon you to her at this time. The way I see it, you have two choices. You can sit here wallowing in your own guilt and feeling sorry for yourself, which seems as dull-witted as my large-bellied companion—"

"Or you can do something useful by figuring out how to reach her," the fat guard added. "Become a man of action." He pointed to the skinny guard. "Unlike this cowardly excuse for a human being."

"Reach her?" Marcus had spent the first few days here thinking about that exact thing before deciding it was impossible. "How can I?"

"You could join that *brilliant* wizard, Master Therapass, and his bullheaded, bumbling, act-first, think later, excuse for a warrior, Tankum," the skinny guard said. "I hear they're leaving for Land Keep to search for an answer."

Marcus jumped to his feet, feeling the first hope he'd had since Kyja's eyes had closed for the last time. "When are they leaving?"

The fat guard counted on his pudgy fingers. "I'd say . . . right about . . . now."

"Let us out," Riph Raph yelped.

"We're going with them," Marcus shouted.

The skinny guard reached under his armor and pulled out a wand. He glared at the fat guard. "It's about time. If I had to spend another day listening to your ridiculous fake accent, I would have gone crazy."

"Trust me," the fat guard said. "Based on your singing, you went there a long time ago."

The guard waved his wand and the men's costumes disappeared, revealing Master Therapass and Tankum. The cell door clicked and swung open.

"Well?" the wizard asked looking back with a sly grin. "Are you two coming or not?"

CHAPTER 2

THE POWER OF HOPE

Marcus leaned against the wall, trying to catch his breath. After sitting in the cold, damp cell for more than a week, his legs wobbled with each step, and every few minutes, a raspy cough tore at his chest. His joints felt as if they'd been filled with crushed glass.

The pain wasn't only from his time spent in the dungeon, though. His health was still mysteriously tied to the health of Farworld, and right now it felt as if Farworld was in danger—maybe the worst danger it had ever seen. But what did that mean? That the Dark Circle had grown in power? Or was it because Kyja was in trouble? Or *dead*?

Tankum reached out one of his large stone hands. "Let me help you."

"No." Marcus wiped the sweat from his face and made himself climb another step, trying to stifle the groan that forced its way from his mouth.

"Punishing yourself won't help Kyja," Master Therapass said.

Marcus stopped, nearly falling backward. Riph Raph grabbed the front of his robe and flapped furiously until Marcus regained his balance. "You think I'm punishing myself?"

He'd been warned more than once that he would kill Kyja. He should have been on guard. But that night, he'd been so busy stuffing his face with food and drink—and congratulating himself on stopping the Dark Circle—that he hadn't noticed something was wrong with Kyja until it was too late. The only reason he wasn't in his cell paying for that anymore was the small sliver of hope that he might be able to find a way to bring her back.

"Maybe I am."

Tankum turned, the metal of the crossed swords on his back reflecting the sunlight shining through a nearby window, and started up the stairs. "Good."

Marcus thought he must have misheard. "You think I *should* be punishing myself?"

Riph Raph launched himself into the air and circled the warrior's head. "Who asked you? I say he should be giving himself a break. No one could have stopped Kyja."

"Doesn't matter what I think," Tankum said, continuing up the circular staircase. "But you might as well get used to it."

"Get used to what?" Marcus panted, trying to keep up. He coughed again, his lungs and throat burning. He deserved everything he was putting himself through and worse. But part of him hoped that Therapass and Tankum would find a way to convince him differently.

"Get used to doubting yourself." Tankum turned and folded his arms across his broad chest. The cold expression on his face matched the granite he was made of. "You've got a whole lifetime of *what ifs* ahead of you, lad— assuming you live that long. Trust me. I've had enough myself. What if I'd told my troops to retreat instead of charging the day I lost half my regiment in an ambush? What if I'd been there the day my friends were slaughtered? What if I'd asked the girl I loved to marry me before she chose another man? What if I'd opted for a life of peace instead of war so I could have been there when she needed me?"

Marcus thought that the warrior's eyes glistened for a moment. But it had to be a trick of the light; statues couldn't cry.

Tankum clenched his jaw before growling, "You have two choices in life. You can spend your time stewing over what you could have done differently and beating yourself up for decisions you can't go back to change. Or you can look forward, learn from your mistakes, and keep doing your best."

Marcus opened his mouth, but the warrior held up a

flat, gray palm.

"You have the weight of an entire world on your shoulders, lad. You didn't ask for it, but it's there. And the fact of the matter is, you'll probably fail. Your chances of success were never good, and they're worse now than ever. If you're going to wallow in guilt over everything you could'a done differently, you might as well get used to it. Because this won't be the last time you have regrets."

Marcus collapsed against the wall, his face hot with sweat and anger. The backs of his eyelids prickled. "If . . ." He gasped for breath. "If you think I'm going to fail, why did you bother coming to get me?"

Tankum stopped short of the door at the top of the stairs, where he and Master Therapass shared a look Marcus couldn't read.

"Not *everyone* believes you will fail," the wizard said. "But as Tankum so aptly stated, it doesn't matter what we think. If you've already quit, you may as well return to your cell."

Marcus snapped his head up. "Who said I quit?"

"Haven't you?"

"Of course not," Riph Raph said, ears waggling furiously. "I know Marcus. He'd never give up. *Never.*"

The wizard nodded slowly. "Then it's time to stop acting like a quitter. And that means accepting all the help you can get."

Marcus swallowed. He'd never been good at accepting

help, and he was even worse at asking for it. But if that's what it took to get Kyja back . . .

He tucked his staff under his arm and held out one hand. "Could you help me up?"

<hr />

"I don't understand why I have to take a bath," Marcus called over the screen that shielded the brass tub he was soaking in from the rest of the room. "The sooner we get to Land Keep, the sooner we can find a way to save Kyja."

"For one thing," the wizard called back, "you smell like a dung heap." Therapass had brought Marcus to a room high in the tower to wash and change clothes while Tankum checked on their transportation. "It makes my eyes water to be in the same room as you."

"He's right," Riph Raph said. The skyte perched on the top of the screen, looking the other way to give Marcus some privacy. "I wasn't going to say anything, but I've smelled three-day-old fish rotting in the sun that weren't as stinky as you."

"You haven't bathed either," Marcus said, shoving away the magical scrub brush that was flying through the air attacking his ears, back, and hair.

Riph Raph rolled his golden eyes and clucked. "Skytes don't need baths. We are some of the most naturally clean animals in the world."

As if hearing his words, the scrub brush ducked under the water and flew straight at Riph Raph's stomach.

"Stop that," the skyte yelped. "It tickles." Dirty gray water streamed from his scales as he flew into the air, and the scrub brush stayed right with him, darting up under his floppy ears.

"For another thing," the wizard said with a chuckle, "it wouldn't do to have the city see you looking like a mud-caked sewer rat." He reached over the screen and draped a freshly cleaned robe across the top.

Marcus climbed out of the tub, dried off, and began getting dressed. The robe was thick wool, with the crest of Terra ne Staric on the front and what looked like gold leaves on the collar and sleeves. It seemed way too fancy for a trip to Land Keep. "Why do they have to see me anyway? Wouldn't it be better if we snuck out so the Dark Circle doesn't know what we're up to?"

"The Dark Circle has the entire city surrounded," Master Therapass said. "With the largest army of Fallen Ones I have ever seen."

The Fallen Ones were undead creatures and humans brought back to life by a Summoner.

Marcus limped around the screen, still barefoot. "They're here? Since when? Why didn't you tell me?"

Master Therapass rolled the map he had been studying into a tube, which disappeared up the sleeve of his robe. "They arrived the day after Kyja went over. Either they had spies in the city, or they have . . . another way of tracking what goes on here."

"But how are we supposed to get past them?" More than once, Marcus had nearly been killed by a Summoner; he had no desire to meet one again if he could help it. "That makes sneaking out an even better idea."

"I vote for sneaking too," Riph Raph called from the back of a chair, where he was keeping the scrub brush at bay with a volley of small blue fireballs.

Master Therapass handed Marcus a pair of leather boots embroidered with gold thread, then inspected his robe. "Over the last ten days, word of Kyja's 'death' has spread to all corners of Farworld, along with the fact that you have been holed up here inside the tower, planning a rescue."

"But I haven't." Marcus felt his face flush. "I've been sitting in the dungeon feeling sorry for myself."

"The only person other than Tankum and I who knows that is High Lord Broomhead, and we have sworn him to secrecy." Master Therapass tugged one sleeve of Marcus's robe even, then wrapped a blue and gold scarf around his neck.

"Why?" Marcus asked, sitting down. "Why would you let them think that I was doing something I wasn't?"

The wizard picked up one of Marcus's boots. "At this moment, Farworld is on the brink of panic. When Kyja brought you here from Earth, most people doubted that a boy and girl as young as you two could defeat a group as powerful as the Dark Circle. But as they have watched the two of you find and gain the help of first the water elementals, then the land elementals, and finally, the Aerisians, their trust in the two of you has grown."

He pushed the boot until it slid over Marcus's foot. "When the two of you managed to defeat the golems here, and the Summoner in Windshold, people discovered a hope they hadn't felt for years."

Marcus ran his hand along his crooked right leg. "We didn't do it alone."

"The two of us know that," the wizard said, holding up a pair of knobby fingers. "But the people see you and Kyja as proof that victory against an evil that grows more powerful every day is still possible. At least, they did until—"

"Kyja drank the poison," Marcus interrupted. "So *they* blame me too." It made sense. He'd have done the exact same thing in their position.

"No!" Master Therapass closed his fist, and everything in the room jumped—the screen fell over, the tub splashed water, and Riph Raph leaped from the back of his chair. "They don't *blame* you," the wizard said. "They *trust* you. They trust that you will find a way to reach Kyja, and that the two of you will find a way to defeat the Dark Circle. That trust is the only thing keeping them from panicking. It's the only thing keeping the Dark Circle from complete victory."

Marcus ran his tongue across the front of his teeth. He'd never looked at it that way. "I'm . . . I'm sorry."

Master Therapass gripped Marcus's shoulder. "I don't need you to be sorry. I need you to be brave."

Marcus studied the wizard's face. "Tankum thinks I'll fail, doesn't he?"

"Tankum looks at the world from the viewpoint of a general. When I sent out the stone wizards and warriors, I told them they were looking for any remaining Keepers of the Balance. But the truth is that Tankum was scouting the land, looking for potential allies in the event we need to raise an army to fight the Dark Circle."

"Did he find them?" Marcus asked.

Master Therapass sighed. "We are hopelessly outnumbered. For every soldier we recruit, the Dark Circle creates a dozen undead warriors. We've managed a few victories here and there, but at a cost. When we lose soldiers, they're gone. When the undead are destroyed, the Summoners simply create more. Yes, we have the elementals on our side—at least some of them. But it's not nearly enough. "

"I *have* failed," Marcus whispered. No wonder his body felt like it was falling apart. "Everything we did was for nothing."

The wizard's hand tightened on his shoulder. "Never

think that. Never. I told you that Tankum looks at the conflict as numbers on a field. That's the only way he can see it. War is all he knows. But there's something more. Something that doesn't show up in a headcount. Outnumbering us the way they do, why do you think the Dark Circle hasn't already attacked?"

Marcus shook his head and shrugged.

"Because they're afraid—afraid of the same thing that gives our people hope." He reached into the sleeve of his robe and pulled out a scroll.

It was the prophecy that Master Therapass had told him about the first time they'd met. Marcus still remembered the words by heart.

He shall make whole that which was torn asunder. Restore that which was lost. And all shall be as one.

"It's *you*, Marcus. You are what stands between the people of Farworld and oblivion."

Marcus didn't think he'd ever felt more overwhelmed and alone in his life. "Do *you* think I'll fail?"

The wizard smiled. "As long as you are alive and well, I have hope. Now, let's go to the top of the tower and share that hope with the people of Farworld."

CHAPTER 3

MISDIRECTION

By the time they reached the top of the tower, Marcus was grateful for the heavy robe and scarf. The late fall air, which had been cool only a week earlier, was freezing now, and the thick, icy fog found every inch of his exposed flesh.

Tankum stood at the top of the tower next to Breslik Broomhead. As Marcus approached them, a giant face, which looked like a dragon made completely of ice, peeked out of the fog.

"Zethar," Marcus called with a grin. He should have realized that the frost pinnois would be their transportation to Land Keep.

The ice creature, who normally as talkative as Riph Raph, nodded silently and winked.

As Marcus started forward to climb onto the frost pinnois' back, Tankum motioned him toward the tower wall, where Master Therapass was standing. A small section of fog rolled away, and a roar arose from ground below. Marcus leaned over to see a huge crowd gathered at the base of the tower. Despite the cold, the entire population of Terra ne Staric appeared to be down there waving flags, scarves, coats, and even a few babies.

"What's that all about?" Marcus asked.

"They're here for you," the wizard said. He had to be joking, but there wasn't a trace of humor on his face. "Are you going to say something?"

"Like what?" Marcus stared at him, completely stupefied.

"I'll handle this," Riph Raph said. He swooped out over the crowd. "Thanks for coming, everyone. I hope there's refreshments!"

The people below roared with laughter, and one of them shouted. "How about a fresh fish?"

"Remember what I said about hope?" the wizard whispered, raising an eyebrow.

Marcus called Riph Raph back and moved to the edge of the wall. His whole body shook, only partly from the cold. He cleared his throat twice.

"I, um . . ." He glanced at Master Therapass, but the wizard seemed to be studying the fields outside the city. "I really . . . um, thanks for coming."

"Down with the Dark Circle!" a woman shouted.

"Right," Marcus said, feeling a little more confident. "We're totally taking down the Dark Circle." The people below howled with pleasure. "And we're going to get Kyja back." The roar of the crowd was deafening even from the top of the tower.

"Do you still think they blame you?" Master Therapass whispered, a half-smile on his wrinkled face.

Marcus shook his head. He hoped he wouldn't let everyone down. "Okay, so thanks for your support, and I'll see you soon." He thought he sounded totally lame, but no one seemed to mind. When he waved, they all waved back and cheered.

As he stepped away from the wall, he noticed Tankum had his swords out. Master Therapass was gripping his staff tightly. The wizard looked at the warrior and raised a bushy white eyebrow.

"All set?" Tankum called.

"Everything is ready," answered a male voice from somewhere in the mist.

"Who is that?" Marcus asked. The voice sounded so familiar, but he couldn't quite place it.

Therapass looked at Tankum and nodded. Marcus started toward Zhethar, but froze when he saw a figure wearing his exact same robe and scarf, clinging to the creature's back. The frost pinnois flapped its wings and burst forward over the side of the tower. Zhethar soared above the crowd before banking gracefully left toward the open field Master Therapass had been studying.

"What's going on?" Marcus asked. He started toward the wall again, but Tankum reached out and pulled him into the fog. "Who is on Zhethar's back?" Marcus demanded. "And why—"

His words cut off as a huge red shape exploded out of a distant grove of trees and headed straight for Zethar. Marcus barely had time to register that it was a Summoner before a jet of flame hit the frost pinnois dead on. Zhethar shattered into a million shards of ice, and the figure on its back burst into flames before plummeting toward the ground.

"No!" Marcus screamed struggling to escape Tankum's grip. Had they known this would happen?

"Now," the warrior called, waving a sword over his head.

Dozens of air elementals burst through the fog mounted on their strange seahorse-looking creatures. At the same time, Master Therapass raised his staff and shot bolts of ice at the Summoner. Outnumbered, the winged monster turned in retreat.

At the same time, three more frost pinnois rose out of the fog, heading in different directions. Each of them had a robed figure on its back. Marcus pulled his silver wand from his belt, but before he could use it, a hand took him by the sleeve.

"This way," said the familiar voice. Marcus turned to find a blue face looking at him through the fog.

"Cascade?" Marcus asked.

The water elemental tilted his head as though wondering who else he might be, before nodding. "It is I." He led them through the mist until Marcus touched ice-cold scales.

"A pleasure to be seeing you again," said a second frost pinnois. "Climb aboard."

"Zhethar?" Marcus asked, as Cascade helped him onto the creature's blanket-covered back. "But then who . . . ?"

"It was water magic," Cascade said. "We made a dummy pinnois to deceive the Dark Circle."

Zethar flicked his tail with a sound of chattering icicles. "Did you really think I'd let myself be fried by that lizard in snake's clothing?"

Marcus shook his head, thoroughly confused. "And the person on his back was . . . ?"

Mist, the water elemental who controlled fog and clouds, appeared from behind the frost pinnois, a haze of sparkling light hovering over her. "More water magic." She pointed toward Zhethar. "I can give you some cover, but for your best chance of success you must leave now."

"Where are Master Therapass and Tankum?" Marcus asked. "We're going to Land Keep." He tried to look for them, but it was impossible to see anything through the fog, which was growing thicker by the minute.

"No time to explain," Cascade said.

The frost pinnois spread his massive wings as Marcus climbed onto the thick blankets strapped to his back.

"Riph Raph!" Marcus called. The skyte flew through the fog, tumbling head-first into the blankets.

Before Marcus could ask another word, Zhethar launched himself into the air, forcing Marcus and Riph Raph to burrow under the covers or risk frostbite.

Marcus had no idea how long he and Riph Raph rode on the frost pinnois' back. Every time he pulled down the blankets to see where they were, he found himself buffeted by thick, gray clouds, which quickly formed ice crystals on his nose and cheeks.

Where were they going? And why hadn't Therapass come with them? Trapped in the dark, he kept replaying the scene on the tower—the cheers of the crowd, which had turned to screams as the Summoner rose, dragon-like, into the air and blasted the decoy Cascade and the other Fontasians had created.

Master Therapass and Tankum must have known about the plan, or at least suspected it. So why hadn't they warned him? Why had they tried the escape so publicly, instead of sneaking out like he'd suggested? No matter how many angles he considered, the situation didn't make any sense.

Riph Raph was no help either. After the first time Marcus peeled back the blankets to look around, only to discover it was impossible to see where they were, the skyte had curled up, tail wrapped around himself, and was soon snoring.

Marcus worried about whether Therapass and Tankum were safe—whether they had managed to fight off the Summoner. Even if they had, the terrifying creature might still be chasing after him and Riph Raph at this very moment.

A million possibilities raced through his head, but eventually, the steady up and down of the frost pinnois' wings, the rushing whoosh of the air outside, and the warmth of the thick blankets rocked him into a terrifying dream in which Kyja was slipping over the edge of a cliff. No matter what he did, he couldn't quite reach her.

It wasn't until something nipped the tip of his nose that he realized he'd fallen asleep. "Wake up," Riph Raph hissed. "I think we've landed."

Marcus sat up, trying to worm his way out of the blankets. "Where are we?"

"No idea," the skyte said. "I was going to check, but . . ."

"You were scared." Marcus flung the blankets off him with a grunt and blinked at the bright sunlight which had replaced the fog.

"I wasn't scared," Riph Raph said, peeking around Marcus's shoulder. "I was *cautious*. A careful skyte is a live skyte."

As his eyes adjusted to the sunlight, Marcus looked around to see they had landed in a narrow mountain pass. The air was a little warmer than it had been at the tower, but he couldn't tell if that was because they were finally out of the fog, or if they had flown south. They'd landed in a grassy meadow, but the trees on both sides of them were filled with colored leaves, so it had to still be fall.

"This isn't Land Keep," he said. "Where are we?"

Zhethar looked back, blinked his big silver eyes, and yawned. "Somewhere in the mountains, would be my guess."

"Your *guess*?" Marcus leaped out of the blankets and clambered over the side of the pinnois before realizing he was still twenty feet above the ground. He tried to catch himself, but the icy scales were too slippery.

"Look out!" Riph Raph called, yanking at his robe. But it was too late. Wheeling his good arm, Marcus slid off the creature's back and would have taken a bad fall if Zhethar hadn't put out a wing to catch him.

The frost pinnois had probably saved him a broken bone or two, at the very least, but Marcus was still angry. He glared at Zhethar. "I want to know where we are, why we're here, and where Master Therapass is. Then I want you to take us straight to Land Keep."

Zhethar lowered his wing until Marcus could reach the ground. "Under less, shall we say, *demanding* circumstances, I would be extraordinarily offended by your lack of gratitude, considering that I have now saved your life twice."

"I'm sorry," Marcus grumbled, balling his fists.

The frost pinnois waited.

Riph Raph leaned toward Marcus. "I think he wants you to say thank you."

Marcus sucked in a frustrated breath. "I know what he wants." He turned back to Zhethar, trying to keep his temper. "Thank you for saving our lives. And thank you for bringing us here—wherever *here* is. Now, will you *please* tell me where we are?"

Zhethar gave him a big grin, his icy-blue fangs flashing in the sun. "See? Isn't conversation much more pleasant when we speak civilly to one another?"

Marcus stomped.

"Unfortunately," the frost pinnois continued, "I am under strict orders not to tell anyone where I have brought you. In fact, as soon as I leave, I will forget I was here. It's a shame; this looks like a very nice place—shady trees, babbling brook, green grass." With that, he flapped his wings and rose into the air, turning toward a thick bank of clouds.

"Wait!" Marcus yelled, leaning on his staff. "You can't leave us here. What are we supposed to? Where are we supposed to go?"

"Your ride awaits," the pinnois called back, growing smaller and smaller as he flew farther away.

"Ride?" Marcus yelled. "What ride?" He heard a snort behind him and turned to see a gray and white horse trotting in his direction.

The horse shook its thick mane and asked, "What is long, brown, and sticky?"

When neither Marcus nor Riph Raph answered, the stallion pulled back its lips, baring its large teeth in what looked like a grin, and said, "A stick."

CHAPTER 4

JOKES AND ILLUSIONS

Clinging to the reins and saddle horn with his good hand, Marcus shook his head. "This is so dumb."

The horse he was riding looked back at him, champed at the bit in his mouth, and asked, "What did the little tree say to the big tree?"

"I don't care," Marcus growled. "I want to know where we're going." At first he'd been excited to discover that the stallion was Chance, the horse he and Kyja had ridden to the Westland Woods when they'd first met. It was good to know that Chance had made it home safely. But then Marcus remembered that while the horse could talk, all he did was tell dumb jokes.

If Chance understood Marcus's words, he didn't seem to care. "The little tree said, 'Leaf me alone,'" he said, answering his own question.

Marcus had been riding for over an hour, and his legs and rear were aching. "How do we know we're going in the right direction?"

Riph Raph, who had been staring at the quietly burbling creek on their left—no doubt imagining all of the tasty fish in it—waggled his ears. "You could try going another way."

"That doesn't seem to be an option." Marcus pulled the reins as hard to the right as he could. He might as well have been pulling on a brick wall. Chance kept walking straight up the valley, the same way he'd been going since Marcus had climbed onto his back—all the while cracking his dumb jokes.

"What does a storm cloud wear under its clothes?"

"Thunderwear," Marcus said, gritting his teeth. "That joke was old when I was a little kid."

"Thunderwear," Chance agreed. The stallion paused briefly to go to the bathroom, then continued up the mountain pass, which was growing narrower the farther they went.

Trying to ignore the constant stream of jokes, Marcus studied the passing scenery. "Have you noticed anything strange about the air?"

Riph Raph tore his gaze from the stream and sniffed. "Smells kind of like horse poop."

"Not that." Marcus glanced at the trees to his right. "Up close, everything looks clear."

Riph Raph squinted before nodding. "It even looks clearer to my eyes, and Skytes have the greatest eyesight in the animal kingdom. Better than—"

"Now look behind us," Marcus said, cutting him off. "See how it's all hazy?"

Riph Raph peered down the way they'd come. "Maybe there's smoke in the valley?"

Marcus nodded. "That's what I thought at first. But the same thing happens if you look forward or straight up. The farther away things are, the more they get this weird kind of blurry look. Also, I've felt a strange tingling ever since we got here, like the hairs on my arms are standing up."

"Maybe you're sick," Riph Raph said. "I told you to stay under the blankets."

"That's not it." Marcus ran his fingers over the tip of his wand. "It's very subtle, but I think I'm sensing someone around here using air magic. It's like they're trying to hide something from us."

Riph Raph switched his tail back and forth like a cat preparing to pounce. "I'll fly around and take a look."

"Yeah, okay."

Riph Raph loosened his grip on Marcus's shoulder and raised his wings. But before he could take flight, Marcus reached up and grabbed one of his legs. "Wait. Maybe that isn't a good idea." He looked around, still feeling the strange tingling sensation running over his skin.

"What is it?" Riph Raph whispered. "Do you see something?"

Marcus pulled his wand from his belt. "No. But I have an idea. What if whoever is using air magic isn't hiding something from us, but is hiding *us* from something or some*one*?" He reached over to scratch Riph Raph's back. "If that's true, and you fly past the protective field, you could be putting us in danger. Or . . . if what I'm thinking is right, you may be able to fly away just fine, but when you turn around, you might not be able to find your way back."

"You think someone is trying to keep us hidden?" Riph Raph asked. "Who?"

"The question isn't who is hiding us," Marcus said. "But who are they hiding us from?" He could think of only one possibility. "The Dark Circle."

That made even more sense when he considered Zhethar's comments. Marcus had thought that the frost pinnois had been trying to keep from telling where they really were. But now Marcus was beginning to believe that Zhethar had not only been told to forget where he had gone, but that maybe magic had been used on him too—to erase his memory.

If that was the case, then someone had been planning on sending them here all along. And unless he was mistaken, that someone could only be the wizard.

"Do you think Master Therapass would intentionally lie to us?" He was talking mostly to himself, but Riph Raph nodded so vigorously, his ears flapped up and down like wings.

"I say, never trust anyone who can turn into a wolf. Especially a wolf with sharp teeth that could eat a skyte in one mouthful."

"But why would he lie to us?" Marcus asked. The answer came to him before the words had left his mouth. "He wanted to get us out of the dungeon."

So this was what, a trick? What about Land Keep? Something was going on that he didn't understand, and he now wished that he'd asked more questions instead of jumping as soon as the wizard had mentioned finding Kyja. But time was running out, and sitting in the dungeon wouldn't get them any closer to bringing her back.

"Look at that," Riph Raph said, staring straight ahead.

Startled out of his thoughts, Marcus glanced up the hill. Not a hundred yards away, the sides of the canyon, which had been drawing closer and closer together, met completely in a high, stone wall—a dead end. Running straight down the center of the cliff was a huge waterfall.

"Very pretty," Riph Raph said. "What do you want to do next? How about a picnic?"

Why would Master Therapass send them all the way here to see a waterfall? As they approached the falls, Marcus kept waiting for Chance to turn around. But the stallion walked straight toward the water. Soon they were close enough that he could feel cold mist on his face.

Marcus stared at the waterfall. Something wasn't right. All at once the narrow walls of the canyon began to feel like a trap. He yanked the reins, doing his best to get the horse to turn away from the falls. But Chance kept plodding straight forward, as if it were the most natural thing in the world for a horse to walk into a waterfall.

"No offense," Riph Raph said as Chance stepped into the pool at the base of the pounding water, "but skytes do not swim. We don't even like to bathe. It's one of those things—fire, and water, water and—"

They were almost to the falls now, and it was next to impossible to hear Riph Raph. The roar of the water was so loud that—

"That's it!" Marcus yelled. "The sound of the water! We should have been able to hear a waterfall this big for miles. But we didn't notice it until we were nearly on top of it." And how could a waterfall this big fill only a babbling brook that ran down the canyon?

"I. Have. No. Idea. What. You're. Saying," Riph Raph wailed. "But I'm not going into that." Riph Raph tried to fly away, but Marcus caught him.

"Hang on," he shouted, tucking the skyte under his arm. "I don't think—"

Then they were entering the waterfall. Marcus ducked, bracing himself for the pounding water, but it never came. One moment they were walking through a pool that nearly reached the horse's belly, and the next, they were in the middle of a grassy meadow.

"Don't let me drown," Riph Raph squawked before opening his eyes. He blinked twice and craned his neck. "Where'd the water go?"

Marcus looked behind him. The pool and waterfall were gone. The sound and mist had disappeared too. It had all been a trick. In place of the waterfall was only a narrow entrance and a couple of stone pillars.

"That was funny." A little girl's voice giggled, and Marcus turned to find Morning Dew grinning up at him. The Fontasian's long, green hair flowed over her shoulders like strands of seaweed. Cascade, Mist, and Rain Drop were there was well.

"A particularly effective illusion," Cascade said, with his usual serious expression.

"Don't get all big-headed on us," said a swirl of brightly colored birds that could only be Divum, one of the two air elementals Marcus and Kyja had met in Air Keep. "After all, it was only water. I could have made it look like falling diamonds or frogs, or tinkling silver bells."

Cascade wrinkled his forehead. "And how would falling silver bells have created an effective cloak for the entrance?"

"I didn't say it would have been effective," Divum said with a laugh, which sent the tiny birds fluttering. "But it certainly would have been amusing. I'd have given anything to see the look on their faces when they discovered the canyon ended in a wall of bells."

A shadow dropped over the two of them, and Marcus looked up in time to see a huge creature land softly to his right. It was half boar and half fox, with wings like the world's biggest butterfly

"I find your sense of humor to be more than a little warped," the fox said.

"On the other hand," said, the boar, "I don't know that I could stand living with the complete lack of humor the Fontasian displays."

Marcus nearly jumped off Chance's saddle with excitement. "Lanctrus-Darnoc! I was afraid I'd never see you two again. What happened in the cave of the Unmakers?"

"It's a story we will tell you all about," the fox and boar said at the same time.

Marcus couldn't believe it—all of the elementals were back together. "I thought you elementals didn't—"

"Get along?" finished a familiar voice. "Trust me; they don't. They've been bickering ever since they arrived."

It took Marcus a moment to make out the long-haired man standing in the shade of a nearby tree, but when he did, he scrambled off Chance's back and nearly fell as he threw his arms around the tall man. "Graehl! When you didn't come back from the Windlash Mountains, I thought something must have . . ." He pressed his lips together, unable to say anything more.

They were all back together—and safe. If only Kyja could see this. At the thought of her, he remembered why he was there and looked quickly around. "Where are Master Therapass and Tankum? We're supposed to be going to Land Keep. We need to find a way to bring—"

All at once, he remembered that Graehl had left before Kyja . . . Marcus dropped his head. "I have to tell you something."

"I know," Graehl said, hugging Marcus tightly against his chest. "I heard all about it. I also heard it wasn't your fault." He waited for Marcus to catch his breath before holding him at arm's length and looking into his eyes. "There's a lot we must tell you. Therapass and Tankum should be here soon. But first, let's get you fed." He nodded toward the passage Marcus had come through. "Besides, the guards get nervous when we stand too close to the entrance."

Marcus turned to follow Graehl's gaze and realized that what he had taken for stone pillars were actually living statues of warriors. Each of them held his weapons at the ready as though prepared for an imminent attack.

CHAPTER 5

A STRANGE WARNING

Marcus hadn't realized how hungry he was until he smelled meat and vegetables bubbling in the big stone pot and watched Graehl dish up steaming piles of boiled potatoes and baby peas with onions. Whipping up a meal with magic would be quicker, but even the best spells couldn't quite match the smell of freshly cooked food.

Maybe it was the fact that he hadn't eaten anything but prison food for two weeks. Maybe it was that he'd exercised more today than in the last ten days combined. Or maybe it was the fresh mountain air. Whatever it was, he ate two helpings of potatoes, three big piles of peas, and two helpings of meat, soaking up the last of the gravy with his fourth piece of bread.

Even Riph Raph appeared impressed. "My stomach hurts just watching you eat," he said, spearing a pea with one talon.

Graehl rocked back in his chair, carving a stick into what looked like a flute, and watched them eat.

When Marcus finally felt like he couldn't eat another bite, he leaned against the log wall of the cabin pulled his bad leg onto the bench, and took a deep breath. "How long has this place been here?"

The valley had nine log buildings, a fresh-water spring, and was surrounded on all sides by steep rock cliffs. It clearly wasn't something that had been set up recently.

Graehl stabbed the knife he'd been carving with into the table and shrugged. "No idea. I didn't know it was here myself until Therapass gave me directions a week ago."

"A week?" Marcus sat up. "You've been here that long?"

"More or less. The elementals were already setting up the protections when I arrived. It's some pretty impressive magic. From above, all of this looks like nothing but a bunch of forest. As you saw yourself, even if you walk right up to it, you don't see anything but a waterfall. By the time you're that close, the guards are aware of your approach. It would be all but impossible to attack unless you knew exactly where you were going."

Master Therapass must have started his plans to bring Marcus only a few days after Kyja's funeral. Had he known then that Kyja wouldn't be able to pull Marcus over? Graehl fiddled with something in his pocket and Marcus thought he saw a flash of gold.

"What's that?" he asked.

Graehl looked down and chuckled. "A good luck charm," he said, shoving the item back into his pants pocket. "We can use all the good luck we can get."

"So what's the plan?" Marcus asked. "Master Therapass must have told you something."

"Actually, he didn't. Between you and me, I've never seen the wizard so secretive. I'd like to know what he's up to myself."

Marcus couldn't wait until Therapass and Tankum arrived. They had a lot of questions to answer. He noticed a fresh scar on the back of Graehl's hand. "Did you get that exploring the Windlash Mountains?"

Graehl's eyes darkened as he flexed his fist open and closed. "It was terrible."

"Tell me about it," Marcus said, leaning forward. "I mean, unless it's too painful. Or a secret."

"It's no secret. But it *is* painful." Outside, the sun had almost completely disappeared behind the high cliffs. Graehl waved his wand, increasing the size of the fire in the stone fireplace and turning the flames from orange and red to a flickering blue green, which gave his face an almost sickly color. Graehl stared into the dancing colors and lines cut deep into the sides of his face. Marcus realized for the first time how much weight the man had lost and how old he looked.

"You don't have to tell me," Marcus said.

Graehl pulled his blade from the table and went back to carving. "The one thing Master Therapass did say is that we need to tell you as much as we can before he gets here. He gave us all a list. To prepare you."

"Prepare me for what?"

"He didn't say." Graehl feathered a long strip of wood from his carving and flicked it into the fire. "I took twenty men with me into the mountains. Therapass had this idea that there was something we'd missed in or near the Unmakers cavern. He didn't say what it was, only that he thought it might be important to the Dark Circle.

"Frankly, I didn't expect to find anything. I'd been through those caves more than anyone. Other than those disgusting creatures and their cages—but you know about those."

Marcus shivered. He and Kyja had nearly died in the Unmakers' caverns. He'd never experienced worse pain than when the nearly invisible creatures fed on him, sucking out his emotions.

Graehl turned the carving in his hands and grimaced. "Maybe I should have asked more questions before I left. Maybe I should have gone alone—done reconnaissance. But I was so sure I wouldn't find anything. We walked straight into an ambush."

Marcus remembered the vision the air elementals had shown him and Kyja. "It was the creatures, wasn't it? The things that looked like an octopus with wings."

"Don't know what an octopus is. But they had wings, all right. And ten legs with poisonous stingers all up and down each one. And magic so powerful, they could rip open the mountains themselves."

Marcus didn't want to ask the question, but he had to know. "How many of your men?"

"Lost?" Graehl stared into the fire. "How many of my men did I lose? Fathers, sons, brothers, husbands."

Marcus opened his mouth to tell Graehl he didn't need to go on. He knew the answer.

"All twenty of them." Graehl took a deep breath and tried to smile, but it came out looking like a snarl, a diagonal scar of pain across his face. "The worst part is, I don't know what they died for. But there *was* something up there; why else would they have protected it like that? And where did those monsters come from? I've never seen anything like them."

"How did you get away?" Marcus asked.

Graehl dropped his eyes. "I hid. Ran. Starved. Honestly, I'm not sure how I survived."

That made sense. What else could he have done? So why did Marcus have the feeling that Graehl wasn't telling the whole truth?

"Go talk to the Land Elementals," Graehl said, sounding more like himself. "They can probably tell you more. They got farther than I did."

"Sure." Marcus pushed his plate away. "You'll let me know when Master Therapass gets here?"

"Of course." Graehl stood. "In the meantime, you and Riph Raph are bunking in the northernmost cabin. Up on the little rise by the trees."

When Marcus stepped outside, he was surprised to see how dark it had grown. Although it wasn't that late, the walls acted as a natural barrier. Looking up into the sky was like looking up from the bottom of a well. Despite the protective spells around the settlement, the deep black sky was filled with thousands of pinprick stars.

Standing with his arms folded across his chest, staring up into the darkness, he tried to imagine what Kyja was seeing right now. Not stars—of that much he was sure. Was she alone? Afraid? Hurt? The idea that she might need him made him crazy. Why wasn't she able to pull him over? What could be in Fire Keep that would stop her from reaching out to him?

"We have to find her," Riph Raph said from a nearby tree branch.

"If I knew how to, I'd be there now," Marcus said.

Time was running out. He could feel it. For Kyja. For Farworld. For himself. No one had brought it up yet, but he couldn't stay in Farworld much longer without jumping back to Earth. Even with Master Therapass's potion, he could feel his body starting to sicken.

If Kyja didn't get back, if she couldn't jump him back

to Earth, he'd be dead in a less than a week.

"Come on," he said. "Let's go check out our room." As they walked up the small rise toward the northernmost cabin, they passed at least a dozen guards. Most of them were stone warriors and wizards, but a few were soldiers he thought he recognized from Terra ne Staric.

Riph Raph flapped ahead of him. "If it's a bunk bed, I get the top. Skytes don't sleep well in bottom bunks. They give us claustrophobia."

Marcus chuckled. "That's fine. But if you wet the bed and it leaks on me, I'm making you sleep outside."

"Wet the bed?" Riph Raph glared at him. "Skytes do *not* wet the bed. It's so unsanitary."

"That's not what Kyja said," Marcus teased. It had been too long since he and Riph Raph had really gone after each other, and he kind of missed the rivalry.

"She did not," Riph Raph squawked. "She would never." He flew up to the cabin door and glanced back with a scandalized look on his little blue face. "She didn't, did she?"

Marcus tried to hide a smile. "I'm not sure. I'll try to remember." He pushed open the door. Sure enough, half of the small room was occupied by an old bunk bed with sagging mattresses.

Riph Raph flew straight to the top bunk. "I'm not saying anything like that ever happened. But if it did, it would have been because I had a very bad bladder infection. Skytes are prone to bladder infections."

"Uh-huh." Marcus checked the drawers of the small dresser. Inside lay a number of robes—all his size—plus socks and underwear. Someone had not only been expecting him, but from the look of it they were also expecting him to stay several days. He clenched his jaw. He'd wasted enough time in the dungeon. He wouldn't spend more time hiding here while Kyja was trapped in Fire Keep.

Dropping onto his bed, he noticed something beneath the corner of the pillow. Pulling it out, he discovered a small, plain piece of paper. The paper was blank. He turned it over, but there was nothing on the back side, either. He nearly threw it away, when he noticed a red line on the front, where his thumb had been when he'd picked it up.

Squinting at the paper, he touched his finger to the line. Immediately a second line appeared, curved and connected to the first one at the top and bottom. A letter *D*.

He slid his finger to the right and more letters appeared as he touched them. *O—N— —T*.

Don't.

Quickly he ran his fingers across the rest of the page, and a message appeared as though written in magic ink.

Don't trust the wizard.

He's not telling you everything.

Marcus touched the rest of the paper to see if there was more. But that was it; there was no signature. He flipped it over and tried the back. Nothing there, either.

As he was trying to think what the message might mean and who had left it, the paper began to darken, first to brown, then black. The words disappeared, and a second later, the entire note turned to ash and crumbled in his hand.

Don't trust the wizard? What was that supposed to mean? It almost had to be referring to Master Therapass. What other wizard could it be? But who would tell him not to trust Master Therapass—and why?

He thought about telling Riph Raph but decided to keep the note a secret for now. He had no idea who'd written it or what their motivations were, and until he did, there was no point in getting the skyte all worked up.

Marcus turned off the lamp by the side of his bed and closed his eyes, but it was a long time before he finally drifted off. When he did, his sleep was filled with confusing and stressful dreams.

CHAPTER 6

TRAINING

Marcus woke to a steady banging on his front door. He vaulted out of bed, shouting, "Master Therapass!" before he was completely awake.

But when he threw open the door, no one was there. It was still dark outside, where a cluster of stars shined so brightly that it looked like he could almost touch them. He stepped through the door and looked around.

"Master Therapass?"

The stars moved, and he rubbed his eyes. They weren't stars at all, but brightly glowing insects. Sort of like the fireflies he and Kyja had seen in the Midwest, except much brighter—like electric diamonds. As he watched, the insects changed color from white to red to purple to orange. They danced though the chilly air in a ballet of ever-changing geometric shapes.

As Marcus reached for the insects, they swirled away, forming themselves into a face. A female voice laughed.

"No touching. Only looking."

"Divum?" Marcus said, backing up a step. "What are you doing here? Where's Master Therapass?"

The glowing insects disappeared, replaced by the air elemental, now made of leaves, flowers, and what looked like silver smoke. "He hasn't arrived yet. But I was instructed to begin your lessons this morning. The first thing you need to know is that air magic is the most powerful of all the magics. And the most difficult to master."

"Hang on a second." Marcus ran his hands through the top of his hair. "You're here to teach me magic? It's not light yet."

Divum giggled. "The sun is up. You just can't see it." The leaves and flowers changed into what looked like a bunch of squirming red pieces of spaghetti. "Besides, the worm that rises earliest avoids the bird's beak."

Marcus had never heard the saying put that way before and wasn't entirely sure it made sense. But he was awake now, so he figured he might as well see what the Aerisian wanted to teach him. "Okay. Let me have it. What's so great about air magic?"

Riph Raph, who had made his way sleepily out the door, eyed the juicy worms with suddenly bright eyes. "Breakfast!" But as he started toward the worms, part of them broke off and morphed into a spiked wooden club. Without warning, the club swung toward Marcus.

"Hey!" he yelled, ducking out of the way. Without his staff to lean on, his feet slipped out from under him on the dew-covered grass, and he slammed to the ground.

"You must do better than that, or the land elementals will have to teach you how to use magic to put your teeth back in," Divum called. The sweetness of her voice was offset by the club circling around and swinging at Marcus's face.

Panicked, he managed at the last minute to deflect the club with a blast of air. "Geez!" he howled. "You could give me a little warning."

"There is no warning in battle," Divum sang.

The club swung again, but this time Marcus was ready. Waiting until the spikes were inches from his face, he attacked the club with another blast. This time, instead of simply deflecting it with a single flow of air, he grabbed the air inside the wood itself and yanked in all directions. The club exploded into thousands of tiny splinters.

"How do you like that?" he said, pushing himself to his knees and doing a little victory dance with his arms.

Riph Raph bobbed his head in time with Marcus's dance. "Oh, yeah. Oh, yeah. You want any more?"

"Better," Divum said. "As long as people use only wooden weapons, you'll be fine. Let's see how you do with something a bit more difficult." With a flash of light, the club pieces turned into a shining metal blade.

Over the next hour, Marcus fought against a sword,

two swords in unison, a spear, arrows, and a throwing axe. Each weapon required a different kind of spell to be defeated. By the time he'd driven the axe so deeply into a nearby tree that even Divum couldn't pull it out, he was covered with sweat and bleeding from scores of nicks and cuts. The morning air, which had felt cold when he first woke up, was a relief to his burning skin.

"Can we take a break for a few minutes?" he gasped. "I think I can handle whatever you throw at me."

"Of course," Divum said, returning to what seemed to be her natural form, which looked mostly like a normal woman if you didn't pay attention to the fact that she was made of leaves, rocks, flowers, sticks, and anything else that might be handy. She lay back on the ground, watching the sky, which was quickly turning from purple to orange as the sun peeked above the cliffs surrounding the valley.

"Do you have any idea why Master Therapass is having me learn all this?" Marcus asked. He watched the Aerisian carefully, thinking about the note.

"I would assume he'd like to keep you from being chopped to pieces." Divum laughed. "That, or he knew how much I'd enjoy throwing swords at you. It's not as much fun as, say, teeth made of ice. But it suffices to keep me amused."

"Haha." Marcus groaned, remembering how close he and Kyja had come to being killed by the *Frost Bite*. "But seriously, don't you think this seems like a waste of time with Kyja still somewhere in Fire Keep? Maybe Master Therapass, has—I don't know—some other plan he isn't telling us about?"

If Divum had written the note, she didn't take the bait. Instead, she sat up and stared at him. "Knowing how to protect yourself, and others, is never a waste of time."

Marcus shook his head. "How about if you tell me what you know about Fire Keep? I can protect myself fine."

"Can you?"

Divum did something to the air that Marcus couldn't make out. He looked around for another weapon, but there was nothing in sight, which was a relief. Marcus leaned over, trying to catch his breath. "Yeah. I mean . . ."

The Aerisian stood, and a pair of small, gold blades flashed between her fingers. For some reason, as Marcus stared at the blades, a cold ball filled his stomach. As she walked toward him, he tried to cast a flow of air to push away the weapons, but stopping the Aerisian seemed nearly impossible. Had he really believed he could protect himself? Compared to the air elemental, he was nothing—a baby crying in his mother's arms.

Terror filled Marcus's mind as Divum walked slowly toward him. The blades were so small. But what if they were really sharp—like razors? Or poisonous? He tried one last time to summon an air spell as the realization came to him that Divum must not be on his side at all. She'd joined the Dark Circle, just like Calem. But he couldn't seem to focus. His skin, which had been burning up before, was ice.

The Aerisian knelt before him, her eyes glittering, her smile wide. She placed the blades against the sides of his neck, and Marcus knew he was about to die.

"One thing you might not know about air magic," she whispered, caressing the sides of his neck with her blades, "is that it can also control emotions. A strong enough spell can change the morale of an entire army. Would you like to learn how?"

All at once, his fear was gone—along with his doubts about Divum's being on his side. With the sleeve of his robe, he wiped a sheen of perspiration from his forehead then nodded. "Yeah, that would probably come in handy."

For the remainder of the morning, Marcus continued to practice air magic with Divum. Influencing emotions was much harder than blocking weapons, requiring a more subtle use of air that was more art than science. He couldn't control Divum's emotions at all, but he did manage to convince a soldier that he was hungry. And he made Riph Raph so giddy, the skyte got hiccups from laughing.

The air magic he mastered the quickest was extinguishing flames. The biggest fire could be put out easily by cutting off its oxygen. He wondered if he could use the skill to offset a Summoner's fire breath.

At some point, Riph Raph brought him his staff. By the time Graehl showed up with fruit, cheese, and sliced meat, Marcus was exhausted. He collapsed by a small stream, eyeing the food like a lion studying a grazing antelope.

"How goes the magic?" Graehl asked as Marcus piled several slices of beef and cheese on a piece of bread.

"Divum is a great teacher," Marcus said around a mouthful of food. "Even if she does seem to take a little too much enjoyment from my mistakes."

Divum chimed—she was now a series of small brass cymbals—and smiled. "What can I say? Humans are amusing."

"She's right," Riph Raph said, flying over to snag a likely looking piece of meat. "You were pretty funny the first time she sent a flame dragon your way. You should have seen yourself. *Helllllp me!*"

"Whatever" Marcus snorted. He stuffed his mouth with a handful of fruit that looked sort of like raspberries, but tasted like fruit-punch-flavored marshmallows. "Have you heard anything from Master Therapass?"

Graehl gave him a considering look. "Not a thing. I assume he's doing something important. Once you finish your lunch, you can continue your magic lessons."

"*Continue?*" Marcus looked at Divum and groaned. "I thought you said we were done for the day."

"*We* are," Divum said with a soft musical clattering.

"But *we're* only beginning," Cascade said, forming himself from the shallow water of the stream in a way that always freaked Marcus out a little.

Marcus turned to Graehl for help. "But I already know water magic. I can make a pretty good water creature, and my ice bolts rock."

"Water magic is much more than water creatures," Cascade said.

Marcus felt a sharp pain across the front of his right arm and turned to see that the Fontasian had sliced open the skin halfway between his palm and his elbow with a blade of sharpened ice. "What are you doing?" Marcus yelped. "That hurt." Warm blood oozed from the wound and dripped down the side of his arm.

"I imagine it does," Cascade said. "For your information, water magic is the most powerful of all magics. It will not be as easily mastered as air magic. One of the greatest strengths of water magic is healing. So you may as well get to work on closing that wound." He nodded thoughtfully as though reviewing what he had said and agreeing with it. "The cut won't hurt for long though. There was a mild poison on the blade. It won't kill you. But it will numb your body for several hours if you don't counteract it quickly."

Marcus didn't know if it was because he'd already spent all morning practicing air magic, or if water magic really was that much harder, but healing wounds was exhausting. And all of the practicing was done on himself.

Without any warning, Cascade held a burning stick against Marcus's hand and said, "Let's work on burns."

Then he snuck up behind Marcus, hit him over the head with a branch, and said, "Concussions are an interesting case."

He had never been as glad as when Cascade told him they were done with healing for the time being and they were moving on to seeing. But seeing proved to be harder than healing. When Marcus couldn't see through the stone cliffs outside their camp, Cascade gave him a befuddled look and shook his head. "You saw through the tree, easily enough."

"A tree's like *this* thick" Marcus said, holding out his hands. "That cliff must be a hundred feet of solid rock. Duh."

"I am not familiar with the word *duh*," Cascade said with a placid expression. "Does it mean *difficult?*"

Marcus rolled his eyes. "Yeah, that's exactly what it means."

"Well the more *duh* the task, the more important it is that you practice it. After you conquer seeing, we will work on invisibility. That, too, is *duh*, but you must not let it stop you."

Late that afternoon, Raindrop came by to work with Marcus on weather control, blocking curses, and visions.

Marcus managed to create a small, black raincloud, which chased Riph Raph around the valley floor, shooting him with tiny lightning bolts. At least half the time, Marcus was able to either block or cure curses, which covered his face with angry red hives, made him slobber uncontrollably, and caused him to bark like a dog.

"I'd rather learn how to *cast* curses," Marcus growled irritably.

Raindrop shook out her color-changing robe and smiled. "You have no need of curses at the present time."

Marcus wasn't so sure. "The next time I see Master Therapass, I'd like to try a couple of curses on that old wizard for putting me through this day of torture." Speaking of Master Therapass, where was he? Marcus looked over to where the sun was beginning to set. He'd been so busy practicing magic that he'd nearly forgotten he was waiting for Therapass and Tankum to arrive.

An unsettling thought occurred to him. Had the wizard distracted him on purpose? Was this entire day nothing more than a way to keep his mind off of Land Keep and recuing Kyja?

And if so, why?

CHAPTER 7

DOUBTS AND DECEPTIONS

As the sun disappeared behind the cliffs, Marcus made his way toward the building he'd eaten dinner in the night before. A pair of soldiers stood outside the door, eating roasted chicken from metal plates. They glanced curiously at Marcus and Riph Raph as they approached, then turned and wandered back to their stations.

Marcus yanked open the door, hoping for news on Master Therapass and Tankum, but Graehl sat alone by the fire. He shook his head. "Still no word." Reading the look of frustration on Marcus's face, he frowned. "I know. I'm concerned too. I'm starting to worry something might have happened to them."

Marcus dropped onto a bench and banged his fist on the wooden table. "Then let's go looking for them. If they're in trouble, they may need our help."

"We can't do that." Graehl reached into the fire with a pair of tongs and removed a whole chicken from one of the slowly turning spits. "Therapass made me promise we wouldn't search for him. He doesn't even want the water elementals checking up on him. Whatever he's doing, he wants it kept secret."

Marcus whipped his wand out of his belt and extinguished the fire with a single burst of air magic, which made his ears pop. "Listen to yourself! This doesn't make any sense."

Graehl nodded appreciatively. "Looks like you learned something today." He handed Marcus half a chicken and a fluffy biscuit on a metal plate. "Eat. You must be starving."

"I'm not eating anything until I know what's going on," Marcus said, pushing the plate away.

"If you're not going to eat that . . ." Riph Raph said, tentatively. "I'd hate to see it go to waste."

"Have it," Marcus said. He stared at Graehl. "There's something you're not telling me. What is it?"

Graehl waved his wand at the fireplace, bringing the flames back to life. "I don't know anything. And frankly . . ." He sighed. "Frankly, I'm as worried as you are. But I made a promise, and until I hear differently, I'm not comfortable breaking it. At least not yet."

Not yet. What did that mean? Again, Marcus

considered telling Graehl about the note. But it was clear that whoever had given him the message didn't want it to fall into the wrong hands.

"Answer me truthfully. Do you trust Master Therapass?"

Graehl blinked. "Do you know of any reason that I shouldn't?"

Marcus chewed on the inside of his cheek. "You mean besides the fact that he told me we were going to Land Keep, then dumped me here with no idea of what's going on? While Kyja could be hurt or trapped, for all I know?"

"There is that." Graehl fiddled with something in his pocket. "Just between the two of us, I'm beginning to wonder." Although they were alone in the room he glanced toward the door and lowered his voice to a whisper. "Don't say anything, but if he doesn't show up by tomorrow night, I'm planning on sneaking past the guards."

"How?" Marcus asked. "Take me with you."

The tall man seemed to think it over for a minute. Then shook his head. "It's too dangerous for you to leave. I wouldn't take you unless it was an emergency."

"It *is* an emergency," Marcus said. "We have to rescue Kyja. I don't know how much longer she's got."

Graehl grunted. "Eat your dinner and keep up your strength."

Marcus took his plate back from Riph Raph and

forced himself to finish his food.

As soon as they were outside the building and on their way back to the cabin, Riph Raph flew to Marcus's shoulder. "What was that all about? You really think the wizard's up to something?"

"Oh he's up to something," Marcus said. "I just don't know what." He weighed the pros and cons for a minute, then went ahead and told Riph Raph about the note he'd found under his pillow. "You and I are in this together," he said when he'd finished the story. "We both understand that the most important thing is finding Kyja."

Riph Raph peered around the dark valley, his eyes reflecting the silver moonlight. "Who do you think left the note?"

"I don't know," Marcus admitted. "I can't imagine Cascade or one of the other water elementals leaving that kind of message; they don't have the imagination. And if it was Divum, the note would probably have exploded in my face. She thinks that kind of thing is hilarious. That leaves Lanctrus-Darnoc or one of the soldiers."

The skyte licked a bit of chicken from his beak. "What about Graehl?"

Marcus had considered him, but what would have been the point of his leaving a note? "If he wanted to warn me, he could have done it at any time."

Eying each of the soldiers they passed—wondering if one of them might have written the note—Marcus made his way back to the cabin. The first thing he did when they stepped through the door was check under his pillow and beneath his blanket. But whoever had left the original message apparently didn't have any more information to pass along.

As tired as he was, Marcus fell asleep almost immediately, and what seemed like only a couple of hours later, there was a knock on his door. This time, Marcus had a pretty good idea who it would be. Aching and sore, he grabbed his staff and limped across the room.

Outside, the inquisitive faces of Lanctrus-Darnoc greeted him. "Good morning," the fox said. "Did you sleep well?" the boar asked.

"I have no idea," Marcus said, rubbing his bad leg. "I was too tired to notice. So what's it going to be today? Are you going to throw axes at me, scare me, poison me, or hit me over the head with a stick?"

The boar and fox looked at each other with what appeared to be genuine curiosity. "Why would we do any of those things? They certainly don't seem conducive to meaningful study."

Marcus sighed with relief. "Tell me about it."

It turned out that the land elementals were really quite amazing teachers. The first thing they taught him was the relationship between the elements.

"Each element needs one of the others to feed it," Lanctrus said. "But they also have the ability to cancel one another out. Fire evaporates water. Water washes away land. Land blocks wind. And water, land, and air, all extinguish fire."

"Which is a good thing," Darnoc, the boar, said. "Because of all the elements, fire is the most dangerous, the most unpredictable."

"This is so totally cool," Marcus said. "You guys are amazing."

"Well," Darnoc said, "we are trained in the transference of knowledge. But it's really not all that difficult when you consider that of all the magics, land is the most powerful. The most refined."

"Too true," the fox agreed.

Taking their time and making sure Marcus understood each step, they taught him how to dig deep holes and to create walls of rock and dirt. He couldn't bring stone to life the way they could, but he did manage to command a rock to fly several hundred feet.

"They key is to learn to think like whatever it is you wish to control," the two heads said together. "To command a stone you must see the world through the viewpoint of a stone. To communicate with a plant, you must see through the eyes of a plant."

Marcus half smiled. "Plants have eyes?"

"Of course," the fox said. "Everything does. They may not look like what you think of as eyes, but every plant, animal, mineral—every speck of dust—can see in its own way."

Riph Raph snorted. "I don't think so."

The land elementals looked at each other. "Would you like to see through the eyes of a fern?"

Marcus's mind had been drifting for the last hour or so. It wasn't that what they were saying wasn't interesting. It was just that he couldn't take his thoughts off of Kyja. Even if Graehl changed his mind about leaving, Marcus was escaping tonight. But the idea of seeing what a fern saw suddenly pulled his attention back.

"Yeah," he said, leaning forward. He looked at Riph Raph. "Do you want to see through the eyes of a fern?"

Riph Raph gave his tail a disgusted swish. "No. I. Do. Not. Skytes see the world from the sky. Why would I care what it looks like to a lowly plant?"

Marcus shrugged. "I think it would be cool."

"Close your eyes," Lanctrus said. "Let land magic flow through you while forming the image of a fern in your mind."

Marcus shut his eyes tightly. He tried to picture a tall fern with broad green leaves.

"Let your senses and the senses of the fern become one," Darnoc said. "Feel the rich soil in your roots. Let moisture pump through the veins in your leaves."

Marcus held out his arms. He heard Riph Raph snicker, but thought it might actually be working. He could feel wind blowing across his hair, but it no longer felt like hair. Instead it was a soft fuzz covering his entire body. His arms no longer seemed to weigh anything. They reached up and out for sunlight.

And suddenly, he was in a forest. He could feel the dirt, the sun, the wind. He could see the trees and plants around him—see an ant crawling across him. Only it wasn't exactly *seeing*. It was more like a combination of smell, touch, and taste.

His eyes snapped open, and he was back. "Dude," he cried grinning. "That was so awesome."

Lanctrus-Darnoc smiled. "Become one with your surroundings, and you will learn much."

"Could I do the same thing with an animal?" Marcus asked, looking at Riph Raph.

"Oh no," the skyte said. "Skytes don't become one with anything. And nothing becomes one with me."

"Seeing through the eyes of an animal is difficult," the land elementals said. "It can be done, but only with a creature that has had a profound influence on your life."

Marcus laughed. "With my luck, it would be Chance, and I'd finally learn why he tells all those corny jokes." He stood up. "Listen guys. This has been great, and I'd like to learn more. But right now, I have to go." He glanced up at the sun, estimating the time to be well past afternoon. His stomach rumbled, and he realized he hadn't eaten since the night before. Why hadn't Graehl brought him lunch? What if he'd left already? Marcus couldn't let Graehl leave without him.

Moving as fast as he could, Marcus hurried across the meadow to the dining cabin. By the time he got there, he was out of breath and nearly in a panic.

"What's wrong?" Riph Raph asked flying above Marcus's head.

Marcus slammed open the door. "Graehl," he panted. "Is it time? Are we—" He froze when he saw who else was in the room.

Master Therapass and Tankum were at a table covered with maps, plates, and glasses.

The wizard looked over with a stern expression on his face. "Marcus, it is time for us to talk."

CHAPTER 8

UNWANTED NEWS

Marcus shook his hair out of his face. "When did you get here? Why didn't you tell me? What are you doing?" He had so many questions. Not the least of which was how Tankum and Master Therapass had arrived without his noticing.

The wizard waved him to the table. "Have something to eat."

"Are you kidding?" Marcus said. "I don't care about food. Where have you been, and what have you learned about Kyja?"

"You will be told everything. But first, sit down and get some food in your stomach. Graehl says you haven't eaten all day."

"How can you think about food?" Marcus slammed his staff on the cabin floor. "I'm not eating anything, and

I'm not going anywhere, until you tell me what's going on!"

The wizard's eyes flashed. He started to stand, but Tankum put out a hand.

"Sit down, boy," the warrior said softly. "This is the first meal Therapass has had since you left the city." He handed Marcus a plate. "You may as well get something in you now. I don't imagine you'll feel like eating after you hear what we have to say."

That got through to Marcus. He looked—*really looked*—at Master Therapass and Tankum as if seeing them for the first time. Dark purple circles ringed the wizard's eyes. His skin looked stretched over the bones of his face, and his fingers trembled as he cut his meat. Even Tankum, who was made of solid stone, appeared older and more worn. What could have happened in the last two days to effect this kind of change?

Marcus dropped to the bench and took the plate. "Are you . . . okay?"

Master Therapass gave him a tired smile. "I am here. That will have to do."

Marcus ate quietly, watching the wizard and warrior study the maps and whisper to each other. He'd never seen Master Therapass look so tired or so stressed, and as much as Marcus wanted to know what was going on, he had a terrible feeling that as soon as he knew, he would wish he didn't.

"Have something to drink," Tankum said, sliding a wooden cup of juice across the table.

Marcus downed the liquid quickly. After the day's training, he was parched. Not until the last of the juice had gone down his throat did he notice a slightly bitter aftertaste. He spotted an empty vial near the corner of the table. "Did you put something in my drink?"

Tankum glanced at Therapass. The wizard rolled up the maps and pushed away his empty plate. "Why don't we all step outside."

As Tankum and Master Therapass stepped through the door, Marcus edged up beside Graehl and whispered, "Do you know what's going on?"

"No," the tall man said. "They're holding something back. And whatever it is, it's big. I think at least a few of the elementals know something. But they're not talking either."

Marcus wanted to ask if Graehl had seen either of the men put something into his drink. But before he could, Tankum eyed the two of them. Graehl pulled back quickly, pushing Marcus ahead.

Cascade, Lanctrus-Darnoc, and Divum were all gathered outside the building, as though they'd been waiting. Marcus shot a questioning look toward Cascade, but the water elemental never turned in his direction. It was almost as if they were intentionally avoiding making eye contact with him.

Master Therapass pressed his hands to his lower back and stretched. "I've always liked this place. The peace and quiet gives you time to think—to reflect."

Marcus shifted from one foot to the other.

"Marcus, I know you are anxious," the wizard said without looking at him. "And I apologize for making you wait. Trust me when I say it was necessary. Now I must ask one thing more of you. Then I will answer all of your questions. At least the ones I can."

The last thing Marcus wanted to do was wait a single second longer to learn whatever secret the wizard was holding back. But he gritted his teeth and nodded. "What do you want?"

"Demonstrate what you have learned over the past two days."

Seriously? Kyja was hurt, or lost, or sick, or whatever she was, and the wizard wanted him to perform a magic show? The idea made him so sick, he could actually feel vomit trying to force its way up the back of his throat. He looked to Tankum, hoping the warrior would agree that this was a stupid idea. But the stone face staring back at him was dead serious.

"Fine," Marcus spat. "Divum, throw every weapon you've got at me."

For the next half hour, Marcus avoided weapons, extinguished fire attacks, found hidden items, changed emotions, healed wounds, and viewed the world through the eyes of a tiny insect and the tallest tree in the valley. He answered every question the wizard asked him, and actually managed to surprise the elementals once or twice.

Sweat poured down his face and drenched his aching body, but every time the wizard offered him a break, he shook his head and muttered, "Get on with it. What's next?"

The sky was growing dark by the time the wizard nodded. "Very good, Marcus." He bowed slightly to each of the three elementals. "You have done well."

"*They've* done well?" Marcus gaped. "What about *me*? I'm the one who learned it all."

Master Therapass nodded. "Your progress is fine."

"'Fine,'" Marcus grumbled. He'd waited two days, working so hard his muscles quivered, and all he got was *fine*? What was wrong with the wizard? Before, he'd seemed like a friend—almost like a father at times. Now it seemed as if he didn't want to be around Marcus. Maybe he *did* blame him for Kyja's death. Maybe the whole thing about it not being anyone's fault was a lie.

"Take a seat by the fire," the wizard said, his voice brusque.

Marcus turned to discover a roaring fire behind him, which was surrounded by a circle of smooth, brown logs. They hadn't been there a moment before, but the wizard was already settling himself on a large stump at the top of the circle.

"Watch yourself," Graehl whispered as he walked by.

"What does that mean?" Marcus asked, but Graehl was already past him, taking a seat as far from Master Therapass and Tankum as possible, on the opposite end of the circle.

Marcus limped to the log nearest the wizard and painfully lowered himself to a sitting position.

Once everyone had taken their places, Master Therapass looked around the group. At last his eyes settled on Marcus. "I know you all have many questions."

"Where have you been all this time?" Marcus blurted, unable to bridle his frustration.

Master Therapass nodded to Tankum. The stone warrior unrolled one of the maps he was holding and turned it around so it was visible to everyone in the group. In the dancing light of the fire, Marcus could see that nearly every village and city was covered with arrows or circles.

Marcus leaned forward "What are those marks?"

"The arrows represent cities under attack by the Dark Circle's armies," the warrior said.

But that was impossible. Arrows were all over the map. If each of them represented an army, that meant the undead had spread out across the entire length and breadth of Farworld. Marcus shook his head.

"And what are the circles?"

"Cities that have been destroyed," the warrior said as

calmly as if he were talking about a game of Trill Stones.

Master Therapass rubbed his brow. "We have been doing our best over the last few days to hold off the undead where resistance is possible and to help in the retreat where it isn't. It's clear that the Dark Circle has been preparing for this for some time."

"Wh-why?" Marcus whispered. "Why are they attacking?"

Tankum rolled the map. "They are making a concentrated effort to find and capture *you*."

Marcus had come to live with the fact that he and Kyja were at the center of a battle in which people they cared about both fought and died. But to be the direct cause of something like this . . . He clutched his stomach.

"We knew the forces of darkness would make a push for you," the wizard said. "That is why we planned your escape when and how we did. The only way to assure your safety was to get you out quickly then hide you in a place where their armies couldn't find you."

"You said we were going to Land Keep." Marcus knew that much of his pain was from Farworld's struggles, but he'd assumed the recent worsening aches had been from his training. Now he wondered if they were actually a sign of the carnage spreading all across this world. "Are you telling me that the Dark Circle has defeated the Land Elementals?"

Lanctrus-Darnoc coughed. "No. Land Keep still

stands. But it is surrounded on all sides. Even if we could have gotten you inside safely, escape would have been impossible. With you trapped there, the Dark Circle could have thrown all of their forces at one spot. It is unlikely that the power of all the land elementals combined would have been able to withstand such an attack."

Marcus stared at the faces of the fox and boar, feeling betrayed. They'd known what was happening, but they hadn't told him. "What about Kyja?" he said, turning back to the wizard. "You told me we were going to find a way to rescue her. We can't stay hidden here. We have to do something."

Master Therapass stared into the flames, one wrinkled hand tugging fiercely at the end of his beard. "We've sent dozens of our best wizards to Land Keep, Marcus. It's one of the things we were doing while you were in the dungeon. With the help of the Land Elementals, we've learned everything that is known about Fire Keep."

"And?" Marcus asked. "What did you find? How do we get her back?"

A long silence followed. Master Therapass, Tankum, and each of the elementals looked at him with the same knowing expression—as if they all shared some kind of secret. Graehl was the only one who appeared as confused as Marcus felt. He leaned forward on his log, his body tense, hands fisted on his knees.

Lanctrus-Darnoc flapped their wings slowly, creating

a gentle breeze, which sent the flames swirling. "Of all the elements, fire is the most risky—the most unpredictable. It is capable of creating powerful protections. But at the same time, fire can be used to cause widespread devastation so great that it is all but unthinkable."

Marcus set his teeth. What did any of this have to do with Kyja?

"As you know," the fox and boar continued. "Each group of elementals is known for possessing certain traits. Fontasians are known for their lack of humor and imagination."

"We are known for our logic and judgment," Cascade said.

The fox's whiskers twitched slightly, but it chose not to respond. "The Aerisians are unpredictable and boisterous."

"Instinctive and whimsical," Divum said. "Not to mention able to find humor in any situation."

Marcus slammed his walking stick against the side of his log, the crack unnaturally loud in the quiet night air. "Who cares if you are logical or whimsical or boisterous? The bunch of you could be gaseous, for all I care. What does any of this have to do with finding Kyja?"

Lanctrus-Darnoc looked at each other. "We apologize. Perhaps we are taking too long to get to the point."

"You think?" Riph Raph sniped. "Listening to you

two is like listening to grass grow."

"Which would be a more educational pursuit than you might expect," the land elementals said together. "But the point is that of all elementals, the Pyrinths—the fire elementals—are the most emotional, the most aggressive. By their very nature, the most dangerous. Which is why Fire Keep was created to be . . . inescapable."

"What's that supposed to mean?" Marcus looked from Lanctrus-Darnoc to Master Therapass. "There has to be some way out. Why would Divum have sent her there if she couldn't return?"

Flocks of tiny red and yellow birds chirped laughter. "I'm afraid that, as embarrassing as this is to admit, apparently now and then, even Aerisians make mistakes."

Marcus jumped to his feet, his body shaking as he leaned on his staff. "What are you saying? That we're giving up? We're going to leave her there? I won't do it. Never!"

Graehl was on his feet as well. "This is unacceptable. Explain yourself, wizard. Are you suggesting we abandon Kyja?"

Master Therapass dropped his head into his hands. "I am saying that it's already too late. Kyja is dead."

CHAPTER 9

BETRAYAL

Marcus felt as if the ground had abruptly shifted beneath his feet. His legs wouldn't hold him up. He tried to reach out to catch himself but his arms refused to obey. Right before he blacked out, a pair of strong hands caught his shoulders, and he looked up to see Graehl's face staring anxiously at him.

Sometime later, Marcus woke to the sound of raised voices.

"How could you say a thing like that?"

"What choice did I have? He needed to know the truth."

"He *needed* to have *hope*. You killed that."

From somewhere nearby came a series of heavy thuds and the sound of clashing metal. Marcus opened his eyes to see the star-filled sky. He turned his head and found Tankum and Graehl standing chest to chest. Both had their swords drawn, and though the warrior was surely the stronger of the two, he was clearly using all of his strength to force back Graehl's blade. Master Therapass stood a few feet away, looking confused and unsure.

"Stop . . . it," Marcus said. His mouth and throat were filled with a sour, acidic taste, and he wondered if he'd thrown up.

Graehl and Tankum turned to look at him, although neither lowered his weapon.

"You heard him," Riph Raph said at Marcus's side. "Stop fighting."

Slowly the two men stepped away from each other. Tankum slid his twin curved swords into the sheaths on his back. A moment later, Graehl put away his weapon as well—although it was clear by his upper lip, pulled back over his teeth in a tight snarl, that he was ready to draw it again at a second's notice.

Marcus turned to Master Therapass and tried to sit up, his head wobbling like a top about to fall over. He reached out to touch Riph Raph's scaled back. "Is it true? Is Kyja really . . . dead?"

The wizard tugged at his beard, his face looking like he'd spent the last two days taking one blow after another.

"The *truth*," Graehl hissed, his right hand hovering above the hilt of his blade.

Why were they fighting? Graehl and the wizard were friends. At least Marcus had always thought so.

Master Therapass sighed. "No. Kyja is not dead. Not yet."

Marcus tried to push himself to a sitting position, but a wave of dizziness hit him again, and he dropped back to the grass.

Riph Raph flapped to the wizard's side and landed on the stump where he'd been sitting. "Then we have a chance. To bring her back."

"No." The old man's beard waggled as he slowly shook his head. "I'm sorry. I should have spoken more clearly before. Only . . . I am so tired." He gestured toward the stump. "May I?"

"Oh . . . right." Riph Raph hopped to the ground while the wizard sat.

Master Therapass rubbed his eyes. "It seems Kyja was rash in her decision to attempt entry into Fire Keep."

"Are you saying it was the *girl's* fault?" Graehl asked, his voice cold and tense.

"Of course not." The wizard leaned forward. "She was doing what she thought was right, based on the information she had. If I blame anyone, it is myself for not thinking ahead. I should have researched sooner. Only I never thought . . ." He waved his hands before him.

Lanctrus-Darnoc stepped forward, firelight illuminating the land elementals' nearly transparent wings. "You cannot blame yourself," the fox said softly. "The information was nearly as old as the library itself and scattered throughout hundreds of documents."

Marcus gritted his teeth. "Stop beating around the

bush. What did you find? What are you hiding?"

Tankum stepped toward Marcus, and Graehl tensed. But the warrior only knelt on the ground at his feet. Marcus had never seen Tankum's eyes look so sad. "There's no easy way to say it. When the elementals first came to be, the water elementals had no desire to leave their home; they hid themselves behind a wall of water. The land elementals were left free to collect and gather knowledge. Because of their love of mischief, the air elementals were barred from leaving Air Keep until they learned to trust and earn the trust of others. But the fire elementals were deemed too dangerous to be set free— ever. They are locked behind four gates: one of water, one of land, one of air, and one of fire. It was the perfect way to keep the Pyrinths from escaping. But because she has no elemental magic, Kyja cannot escape either."

"Which is why we have to help her," Marcus said.

Riph Raph flapped his ears. "Tell us what to do. How do we get her out?"

Tankum slammed his fist into the ground, leaving a deep depression in the dirt. "We've explored every possibility. But the truth is that, despite our best efforts, rescue is impossible. The connection between Farworld and Fire Keep is different from the connection between Farworld and Earth. She cannot pull you over from there. And her physical body can last only so long before her death becomes permanent. That time has either passed, or is so close that it might as well have."

Marcus forced himself to sit, ignoring the way it made his head spin. He searched for his staff and used it to leverage himself to his feet. "I'm going to find her."

Riph Raph spat a fireball into the air, illuminating his determined gold eyes. "I'm going with you."

"That is the one thing you cannot do," the wizard said.

Marcus blinked, sure he must have heard wrong. "Are you saying you're going to stop me from looking for Kyja?" He grabbed his wand. He'd fight his way out if he had to.

"Put that away," Master Therapass said. "Our research didn't reveal the truth only about Fire Keep. It revealed something about you, too. Something that should have occurred to me long ago." His shoulders slumped. "When Kyja's body is no longer capable of being returned to—that is, when she—when she dies, the part of you trapped in the realm of shadows will return to your body. You will be completely in Farworld at last, capable of fulfilling your destiny here."

Slowly, Marcus crumpled to the ground. "I don't understand. You said the only way I could return to Farworld permanently was by opening a drift."

"The scales of balance brought Kyja here when I sent you to Earth," Master Therapass said. "I'd always assumed that the only way to bring you back was to return her to

Earth. Perhaps the Dark Circle thought the same; we can never know for sure. But it is clear that they know the truth now. That's why they are searching for you so desperately."

"To kill me?"

"No," Lanctrus-Darnoc said. "Your destiny must be fulfilled—to save Farworld or destroy it. Your death would mean only that another chosen one would be born, and the cycle would start again. We believe now that the only reason you are still alive is because the Dark Circle knows that killing you would be futile. Their plan is much more devious. It is why they have spent so much effort defending the Windlash Mountains."

The land elementals' words caught Graehl's attention. He jerked straight. "What do the mountains have to do with any of this?"

"If Kyja dies," Lanctrus said, "Marcus will be returned to Farworld."

"Except under one condition," Darnoc added. He turned to Marcus. "The realm of shadows is a portal between Earth, Farworld, and other worlds, as well. It is a place of . . . *between*. We do not understand much about it other than that it is the spawning ground of snifflers, Unmakers, and filth unimaginable. The part of you trapped there is on the Earth side. If you are inside the realm of shadows when Kyja dies, then instead of returning here, you would be pulled back to Earth and trapped there permanently. All the Dark Circle would have to do is capture you there and keep you alive. Farworld would be theirs to do with as they pleased."

The whole idea was too much for Marcus. He rubbed his eyes, exhausted and confused. "How could I possibly end up in the realm of shadows?"

"Through the cavern of the Unmakers," Graehl said at once. "That's it, isn't it? The cavern is some kind of, what? Opening to the realm of shadows?"

Tankum stood and pulled a sword from the sheath on his back. He sharpened the metal against his palm, shooting sparks into the darkness. "It's the only explanation. That's how they brought the nightmare creatures here in the first place."

Master Therapass approached Marcus. "Now you see why we can't let you leave here. The Dark Circle would do anything to capture you and trap you in the realm of shadows until Kyja's death. I've developed a potion which should allow you to remain here until your other half is pulled over. I put it in your drink earlier."

"So that's your great plan?" Marcus demanded, looking from the wizard to Tankum and finally to the land elementals. "I stay here—hiding—until you say it's safe to go out, then, bam! I save Farworld, and everything's better. Never mind that Kyja dies, Earth is destroyed, and I could never live with myself."

Cascade, who had been sitting quietly through the

entire conversation, spoke up for the first time. "When Kyja dies, a new child will be born on Earth to take her place. It is only the logical conclusion."

"Oh, right!" Marcus burst into hysterical laughter. "That makes it all better, doesn't it? Sign me up." He raised his wand in one shaking hand. "I'm sorry, but that isn't going to happen. You may all be a bunch of cowards, but I'm not giving up. If the Dark Circle wants Kyja dead, they'll have to kill me first." He pointed the wand at Master Therapass and Tankum. "I'm leaving now. Try to stop me, and you'll be sorry."

Riph Raph flew onto his shoulder and spread his wings. "I'll turn you all to ashes if you get in our way."

"Don't make this harder than it has to be," Tankum said, stepping toward him.

Marcus began to cast a spell, but before he could, a hand pulled his wand out of his grasp and a steel-like arm lifted him into the air.

"I'll take him back to his room," Graehl said.

"Let go of me!" Marcus screamed. "You can't keep me here!"

Graehl hefted Marcus over one shoulder and carried him toward his cabin.

"Sleep on my words," Master Therapass called after them. "Sometimes you know the right thing to do but you have to put your finger on it."

"I'm not sleeping on anything," Marcus yelled.

Riph Raph screamed overhead, firing one fireball after another, but Graehl simply shoved Marcus's wand into his pocket, ducked from the streams of blue fire, and grabbed the skyte out of the air.

"How can you do this?" Marcus's body shook with wracking sobs. "Don't you care about Kyja at all?"

"People have to do what they have to do," Graehl said. "Stop struggling."

"Never!" Marcus kicked at Graehl and managed to catch him on the front of his thigh. He didn't need his wand to cast spells. He reached for land magic, planning to pelt Graehl with rocks, but found nothing there. It was as if his land magic had been taken from him. Air and water were gone too. He tried creating a fireball, but the flames hadn't left his fingers before they snuffed out. "What did you do to me?" he screamed.

Graehl glanced over his shoulder toward the circle of elementals. "I didn't do anything."

Marcus understood. The elementals were blocking his access to air, land, and water, combining them to quench fire. Kyja was going to die, and he was helpless to do anything about it.

A pair of guards were posted outside his cabin. As Graehl approached, they reached for their wands.

"Need a hand?" one of the soldiers asked.

Graehl tucked Marcus under one arm like a bag of laundry and laughed. "I think I can handle one boy." He kicked the door open and threw Marcus onto his bed. "Are you two on shift here for the rest of the night?" he asked the soldiers.

"Until sunrise," the younger of the two said, stifling a yawn.

Graehl grabbed the man by the front of his tunic. "Stay sharp. He may look like a boy, but the future of Farworld rests on him."

"He won't get past us," the man said, clearly offended.

"See that he doesn't," Graehl snarled. "Unless you want to deal with Therapass and Tankum."

The guards nodded.

Graehl fished Marcus's wand out of his pocket and showed it to the guards. "They're blocking his magic, but that won't keep him from trying to escape." He turned to Marcus. "Remember what I told you before, boy."

Marcus glared at him. "About what?"

Graehl's dark eyes bored into him. "People have to do what they have to do." Without another word, he turned and walked out the door, calling to either Marcus, the guards, or both, "I'll be back."

As soon as the door closed, Marcus turned to Riph Raph. "We have to find a way out of here."

CHAPTER 10

PAYING THE PRICE

I t was all Marcus could do to force his eyes open
every time they slipped closed. The day had been
exhausting both physically and emotionally, and his
head ached with everything he'd learned. On any
other night, he'd have been snoring like a chainsaw.
But tonight he had to find a way to get out and save
Kyja.

Every few minutes, he slipped out of bed and
peeked through a crack in the door to see if anything
had changed. Each time, the only thing he discovered
was a guard's fat behind pressed against the solid
wood. If he had a long twig, he could have slid it
between the boards and given the man a poke.

Not that it would have helped. He'd tried

bribing, pleading, and threatening the men, but the only response he'd received was, "Go back to bed."

Lying flat on his back, staring up into the darkness, he tried again to think of some way to escape. Every plan he devised fizzled. The fact of the matter was that he was trapped. The best he could do was wait for the guards to let him out in the morning and look for a chance to run.

"I can't stand waiting," he whispered to Riph Raph.

"Poached beetle eggs on toast," the skyte answered groggily.

Marcus pushed himself onto one elbow to glare at the dark, long-eared shape perched on the back of a chair. "Did you fall asleep?"

"What? Yes. I mean, no. I was resting my eyes so I can use my excellent night vision." Riph Raph stretched his wings and flew to the bed, where he landed beside Marcus. "Is it time? Are we escaping?"

Marcus reached down to touch the bundle on the floor under the bed. His clothes, books, and papers were wrapped tightly inside a robe so he could leave at the first opportunity. "I've tried to come up with a plan, but I can't think of anything."

"Leave it up to me," Riph Raph said, a little too loudly.

"Shh," Marcus whispered, putting a finger to the skyte's beak. It might have been late, but whenever Marcus so much as stepped on a squeaky board, the guards opened the door to check on him. "What can *you* do? In case you hadn't noticed, it's not like there's an easy way out."

Not until he needed to escape did he realize that his cabin was the only one without windows. Until tonight, he'd assumed that the guards had been there for his protection. What if the plan all along had been to keep him trapped? He didn't know for sure whether Master Therapass and Tankum had been fighting like they said. For all he knew, that story could have been a stalling tactic to keep him from asking questions.

In the dim light, Riph Raph examined the cabin. "I could claw a hole through the boards. Skytes have razor-sharp talons. But that would make too much noise." He snorted. "There's only one choice: my fireballs. I'll burn the place to the ground."

Marcus nearly laughed. "With us inside? We won't be much help to Kyja if we're crispy critters."

"Then you'll have to protect us. Use air magic, or

water magic. Whatever you learned from those grotesquely shaped monstrosities."

Marcus tried to use magic again, even though he already knew what he'd find. "It's no good. They've got me completely blocked." If only he'd tried to escape earlier. Maybe if he knew more powerful fire spells—ones the elementals couldn't block so easily. He'd seen Master Therapass do them. But all he'd ever been taught were simple things like making light and fireballs that were little more than Riph Raph could shoot out.

He glanced at the chair and an idea came to him. "Maybe we *can* use fire. Burning the cabin would be crazy. But if you lit something like the chair on fire, it would create a diversion. When the guards see flames, they'll have to open the door, and the smoke might hide us enough to help us slip out. Do you think you can use your fireballs? Or have the elementals put those out too?"

Riph Raph huffed. "Those freaks of nature couldn't stop a skyte from blowing streams of billowing flames in their wildest dreams. I'm a fire machine."

Marcus ran through the plan in his head. They'd have to stay low to avoid the heat and smoke. Once the door opened, there would only be a second or two to get out, so they'd have to move quickly. The plan was risky—they still might end up cooking themselves like Thanksgiving turkeys. But it could work.

He looked at Riph Raph and whispered "You don't think I'm making a mistake do you? Master Therapass has never given me a reason not to trust him."

Riph Raph gave an irritated flick of his tail. "Do you want to rescue Kyja?"

Marcus nodded.

"Does the wizard have a plan to save her?"

"No," Marcus admitted.

Riph Raph nodded. "Then I say we get her."

"All right," Marcus said. "Let's go for it." Sliding quietly out of bed—careful to avoid the noisy spots on the floor—he rolled up his blanket and put it on the chair, then put the pillow on top to resemble a head and body. "If we're lucky," he said in a hushed voice, "when they come in, they'll think that's me."

"But we'll be waiting inside the door to hit them over the head." Riph Raph licked his beak. "It'll be like smashing flashworms with a mallet."

Marcus frowned. He didn't want to know what that meant. "No. We'll be hiding under the bed so we can crawl out in the confusion."

Riph Raph nodded. "That could work too."

Squeezing under the short-legged bed with his bundle was a tight fit for Marcus, and it got tighter when Riph Raph squeezed in beside him. Marcus turned to the skyte. "Is there something you're forgetting?"

"I don't think so," Riph Raph answered, completely oblivious to the problem.

Marcus shook his head, not sure whether he was more amused, annoyed, or nervous. "I'm pretty sure one of us is supposed to light the chair on fire. The one of us who can blow fireballs out of his mouth."

"Right. Right. I was, um, preparing myself." Riph Raph scuttled out from under the bed.

Outside the cabin, there was a soft thump.

Marcus tilted his head to listen. "What was that?"

Riph Raph must not have heard him, because at that moment, there was a flash of light as the chair and blanket crackled into flame. Riph Raph crawled in beside him. "Did you see that?" the skyte piped in an excited voice. "I was all 'wrath and destruction on your head.' And that chair was like, 'Oh, no! I'm on fire.'"

"Yeah. You were great." Marcus's stomach

tightened. If this didn't work, they would be in big trouble. If it *did* work, they might be in bigger trouble. Once they got out of the cabin—if they did at all—there was the issue of how to escape the valley. As soon as the guards realized they were gone, every man, woman, and elemental here would be searching for them. And if they managed to get out of the valley where would they go?

All of that might have been something he should have given a little more thought to before putting things into action. But it was too late now. The fire was growing. Even from under the bed, beads of sweat formed on his face, and he glanced toward the door, wondering when the guards would notice the fire.

Riph Raph coughed "So, uh, is this the part where we get out?"

"I hope so." Smoke was beginning the fill the room. It was thickest toward the ceiling, but getting lower quickly. If the guards didn't see it soon, he'd have to yell before the whole place was on fire.

He heard voices outside. Thank goodness. Any moment, the door would fling open. Marcus pressed his face to the floor, trying to avoid the heat and smoke while still being in a position to escape.

More than a minute passed, and still the door remained closed. What were they doing out there? Smoke swirled in front of his face. It was getting hard to breathe, and the flames were licking the walls.

"You know that whole thing you said about crispy critters?" Riph Raph asked, his tail wrapped around his face to block the smoke.

"I know," Marcus gasped. He was beginning to feel lightheaded. He had nearly decided to shout for help when the door banged open. A gust of blessedly cool air entered the room. With plenty of oxygen, the flames leaped from the chair to the walls and bed, engulfing the room in fire and smoke.

"What in the demon's breath is this?" a soldier exclaimed, stepping through the door.

"Now," Marcus whispered. Grabbing his things, he scooted across the floor toward the door. He reached the grass and headed for open ground, but a hand grabbed him by the back of his robe and lifted him into the air.

"Where do you think you're going?" the guard asked above the roar of the fire, which was growing louder by the second.

A soot-stained Riph Raph crawled through the doorway behind him, coughing and gagging. "Let him go," the skyte croaked.

Marcus tried to bite the man's arm through his thick cloak. The guard lifted him up so high, they were almost face to face. It wasn't a guard holding him. It was Graehl.

"Trying to get away?" Graehl asked.

"So what if I am?" Marcus spat. "Someone has to save Kyja."

"True." Graehl nodded. "But perhaps your chances of success would be better if you made your escape without sending up a signal for the entire camp to see." On the ground at his feet, one of the guards groaned softly.

Marcus turned his head and saw the second soldier lying unconscious on one side of the cabin. He looked back at Graehl. "What . . ."

"I told you," Graehl said, lowing Marcus to the ground. "People do what they have to do. Especially for those they care about."

———◆———

Ten minutes later, the three of them were making their way through a thick grove of trees. Riph Raph, perched on Marcus's shoulder, shivered and whispered, "This place gives me the creeps."

"No kidding," Marcus said. The branches were so thick overhead, he could barely see a thing. And there was no sign of any kind of trail or markings. All he could do was follow Graehl, hoping he knew where he was headed. "It feels like we're going away from the passage through the waterfall,"

"We are," Graehl said. "There's no chance of getting past the guards there." He glanced over his shoulder. "We need to hurry. It's only a matter of time before they realize you're gone. Can you keep up, or would you like me to carry you?"

"I can keep up," Marcus said. His legs were throbbing, and it was hard to breathe at this altitude. But if he was going to rescue Kyja, he couldn't do it being carried around like a baby. "So you were the one who wrote the letter."

"What letter?" Graehl asked, picking up the pace.

If Graehl hadn't written the letter Marcus found on his bed the first night here, who had? "What made you turn against Master Therapass?" he asked, changing the subject.

Graehl shrugged. "I'm not turning against him. I'm doing what I think is right." He paused for a second, as though listening to what he'd said, and nodded. "As he is."

"So am I," Marcus said. "But before, you said it was too dangerous for me to come with you."

Graehl stopped and spun around so quickly that Marcus nearly tripped trying to keep from running into him. Riph Raph flew from his shoulder with a yip of surprise. "Do you want me to take you back?"

Marcus was so shocked, he couldn't speak. He shook his head.

Graehl studied him. "Do you want to save your friend?"

"Of course."

"Would you do anything to save her? Even if it meant doing hard things?" He stared at Marcus as if the wrong word would send them both right back to the burned-out cabin.

"I'd do anything for her," Marcus whispered. "No matter what it takes."

"So will I," Riph Raph said, settling back on Marcus's arm.

Graehl stared at Marcus a moment longer before turning and continuing through the trees. "It's only a little farther."

After a brief but tiring hike, they came out of the trees to find a sheer, gray cliff. Marcus stared up at a stone wall that rose hundreds, if not thousands, of feet above him. Were they going to try to climb that? Was that the "hard thing" Graehl had been talking about?

Graehl reached into his pocket and took out something that glinted in the moonlight. "Therapass is a good man. Tankum too, in his own way. They want what's best for Farworld. Their problem is that they see only one way to achieve their goal. I'm a pragmatist. Do you know what that means?"

Marcus shook his head.

Graehl turned the item in his fingers. It looked like some sort of ring. "It means that when I look at a problem, I examine every potential outcome—all possible solutions. I weigh the costs against the results then come to the best decision. My choices may not be perfect; I may not be the idealist Therapass is. But I get the job done. Sometimes that means doing hard things—things other people shy away from."

Marcus nodded. "I can do hard things." He looked up at the cliff. "How do we start?"

"Start?" Graehl followed Marcus's gaze and laughed. "We're not climbing. I've arranged for a ride."

A shadow blocked the moon for a second, making Marcus look quickly up. But whatever had been there was gone. "How can we get a ride? I thought you said this place was hidden."

"It is," Graehl said. "Protected by magic you and I can only dream of. Which means we need more powerful magic to get past it." He held out a gold ring for Marcus to see.

Marcus leaned forward, and his eyes opened wide. "It has the symbol. The one on my shoulder."

Graehl nodded. "It does. You have no idea how powerful this symbol is."

Something brushed against a nearby tree. Marcus turned to see several figures closing in on them. "The guards found us!"

"Oh, they found us," Graehl said with a dark laugh. "But they aren't the guards."

The figures stepped into the moonlight—six men in dark robes and holding black, forked staffs. They were Thrathkin S'Bae, sorcerers of the Dark Circle. Marcus stumbled backward. One of them lifted his staff, and a bolt of blue light blasted Riph Raph from Marcus's shoulder. Marcus turned to run but found himself looking at curved talons as long as he was tall.

Cold fear froze his feet to the ground as he looked up, into the blood-red eyes of a Summoner.

"People do what they have to do," Graehl said.

"Even if it means doing hard things."

Marcus tried to scream, but a hood was pulled over his head, and something knocked him to the ground.

THE KING'S ARMY

The soldiers finished searching the latest building, with no success.

"Another zero," said the one known as Bones. He picked up a pocket calculator, which had washed up on the edge of the street; he looked it over and stuck in his pocket. You never knew when something like it might come in handy. Whenever one of the engineers needed a circuit board or a battery, he'd be there to provide it. Could be worth a bag of fruit or a video game.

"King won't be happy that we came up empty again," Tuck said. "Word is he thinks the magic level is nearly there. Harness up a couple of powerful Casters, and they could put us over the top."

Bones thought about the harnesses and shivered. He'd been in the dungeon once, and he'd be more than happy to never see it again. All of those blank faces creeped him out. "Sure glad I'm not a Caster."

Tuck gave him a strange look. "'Course you are. Who'd want to be one of them?"

They headed to the next building, both alert for the whistling that meant the beasts had found something. To their right, a bubble rose slowly out of the street, then paused, as though waiting to see if they had any magic before receding back into the blackness. That was a good sign.

"Think it's true what they say about the passages being blocked off?" Bones asked.

Tuck snorted. "How would anyone know? Not like any of 'em's been to the Caster world. They start flapping their gums when nobody shows up for a while."

"True." Bones rubbed his chin. He'd sure have liked to bring King Phillip the magic he was looking for. A Caster with lots of power. Wouldn't he get a reward for that?

PART 2

Fire Keep

CHAPTER 11

AWAKENING

The girl opened her eyes.

Flickers of blue and orange light illuminated the jagged spears of black rock hanging above her head like broken teeth and rotted gums. A faint taste of flowers filled her mouth. Did that mean something? She thought it should, but she couldn't remember why.

She lay, staring up at the shifting patterns, for a period that seemed neither short nor long. Time felt unimportant here—almost unreal. She might have continued to watch the dance of fire and shadow indefinitely if she hadn't been distracted by a steady moaning coming from her right.

It was a rhythmic sound, starting with a quiet *uuuhhhh*, rising to a louder *ah-ah-ah*, and finally ending in an anguished *ohhhhh*, before starting over again. Like the wind blowing through dead tree branches, or waves breaking against a rocky shore.

It was too regular to be the sound of the wind, though—too . . . *human.*

Was someone in trouble? Worry filled her chest—although that emotion had the same unreal feeling as the memories she couldn't seem to dredge up. Her thoughts felt muted, somehow, as if they were no longer important.

She placed her palms on the flat surface beneath her and pushed herself up. She was sitting on a rectangular block of dark stone—the same stone as the ceiling, but, unlike the ceiling, smooth as glass. Her thin, white gown shifted as she moved.

"Hello?" she called, her voice echoing back at her.

The moaning paused for a moment before returning to its regular pattern.

"Is anyone here?" She realized she had no idea where she was or how she's gotten there. She tried to recall anything—her name, where she was from, what this place was. Her mind was as blank and empty as the black rock.

She swung her legs over the edge of the platform, and five or six dancing flames dropped from the ceiling, skipping and twirling toward her. She jerked back, afraid the fire would burn her skin or ignite the gown. But when it touched her, she felt no pain—only a soft tickling against the soles of her feet, like the playful lick of a skyte.

Something about the thought of a *skyte* licking her toes made the girl pause. A memory tried to surface in her mind.

It was . . . It was . . .

Before the thought could become clear, it faded like mist under the sun. Whatever the memory had been, it wasn't important.

She slid forward until her toes touched the floor, which was nearly as smooth as the stone she'd been lying on, and neither hot nor cold. The flames circled about her, drifting forward and darting away.

She glanced around the cavern; it wasn't a single room, as she had first thought, but many rooms seemingly connected by tunnels and passages. Flames cavorted across the floors, walls, and ceilings like fairies.

Laughter came from somewhere behind her, and she followed the sound down a sloping path into a small room with a ceiling so high it disappeared into the darkness. Sitting cross-legged in the center of the room was a man with a tangled, gray beard. For some reason, the beard seemed familiar. But again, the memory—if that's what it was—slipped away like water through her fingers.

"Hello," she said to the man, who wore the same type of robe as she did.

The man gave no sign that he'd heard her. He continued to laugh, staring at a glowing blue ball a few feet away.

She moved closer. "Can you tell me where I am?"

Haltingly, the man's clouded eyes drifted from the pulsing blue globe to meet her gaze. He raised a hand to his mouth, and the laughter cut off abruptly.

She knelt before him and touched his knee with one hand. "I woke up—well, I'm not exactly sure how long ago. But I don't know where I am or how I got here."

The man blinked "A garden. Picking flowers in a garden. The rain. The dirt. The . . . the . . ." His eyes drifted back to the ball, and he began laughing again, his low chuckles growing to lunatic guffaws that made her skin crawl.

Something was wrong with him. She patted him softly and stood. "I'll find my own way. Can I do anything for you? Bring you something?" she asked, before realizing she had nothing to give him.

"Flowers." He coughed out the word between maniacal laughs.

She nodded and drifted away from him. "If I find any, I'll bring you some."

The girl left the room through the same passageway she'd entered from, then heard the moaning again. She cocked her head, trying to place the sound. Either more than one person was moaning, or the chambers made it seem that way. Her feet padded soundlessly across the floor as she explored one room after another.

She nearly missed a skin-and-bones figure pressed so tightly into a crevice that it seemed to be almost one with the stone—a woman, pushed as far back into the wall as she could get. Her arms were wrapped around her knees, drawing them to her bowed head so she was almost a compact ball. Long, brown hair hid the woman's face. But there was no doubt that this was the person—or one of the people—making the moaning noises.

"Are you all right?" She reached for the woman, but a voice spoke from behind her.

"You're new here."

The girl spun around and raised her hands as she took in the creature before her. His lower body was that of a horse, complete with four legs and a tail. His upper half appeared to be somewhat human, with a man's chest and arms. From the neck up, though, he was . . . What? A demon? A serpent? A dragon?

His entire body appeared to be made of raging red and gold fire. Intense heat radiated off of him. The only part of the creature not made of flames was a metal breastplate, which glowed orange as if it were in the center of a blacksmith's forge.

Shading her eyes with one hand, she looked up into the beast's red eyes. "I . . ." she began, unsure whether to speak to the monster or run from it. "I don't . . ."

"Don't know where you are?" The creature grinned. A tongue of flame flickered in and out between his glowing fangs. "Don't know *who* you are? Why you're here?"

"Yes," she said, her pulse beginning to speed up. "I think I've lost my memory. Can you help me?"

"Of course!" The creature cavorted around the room,

his flaming hooves kicking sparks off the floor in a shower of light. "I'm the only one who *can* help you." He flashed a dazzling smile, stuck out one hoof, and bowed before her. "What would you like to know first?"

She studied the creature's face. For some reason she couldn't explain, it didn't bother her that he had the head of a monster and was made of fire. But there was something in his almost insanely cheerful expression and lilting voice that made her uneasy.

On the other hand, he was the first being she'd found here who looked like he might be able to tell her anything. She glanced at the woman who was balled up in the crevice. The woman was obviously incapable of providing any useful information.

She studied the beast. "Where am I?"

"An excellent question." The creature reached inside his armor and pulled out a flaming dagger. He examined the blade and used it to pry a stone out of his front right hoof. "I've asked myself the same thing as long as I've been here—which is ages, I assure you."

She tilted her head, a little annoyed. "You don't know what this place is either?"

He gave a laugh that was half snarl, half whinny. "It depends which answer you are looking for. From a purely metaphysical standpoint, we are somewhere between the celestial realms—the home of the gods—and the fiery furnace of the devils. Although, frankly I admit that I think we're closer to the latter than the former. However, if you're asking about the journey of life, where are any of us? Near our goals? On the brink of failure? At the top of the pile or on the bottommost rung?"

She tapped her foot, and he put down his hoof.

"Not what you were looking for? As far as physical location goes, you are blaze spot in the center of Ignis Deep—the burning abyss, the abode of Pyrinths." He ran a finger along the shimmering blade of his dagger and watched her from the corner of his eyes. "Also known as *Fire Keep*. Does that mean anything to you?"

She thought for a minute before shaking her head. "Should it?"

For an instant, something that looked like anger crossed his face, and she wondered what she said wrong. Then he shook his head and smiled, flames wreathing his scaled features like clouds. "No. Of course not. What else would you like to know?"

"Who are you?"

He bowed again. "My name is Chaos. I am a Pyrinth, a fire elemental."

For a split second, she could have sworn that she'd heard the words *fire elemental* before.

"You've heard of me?" he asked, eyes glowing.

But the flicker of memory was gone. She shook her head. "I'm tired I guess. Who am I? And how did I get here?"

Chaos nodded his dragon-like head up and down slowly, as if that was the question he'd been waiting for her to ask all along. "That's what they all want to know when they arrive."

"*They?*"

The creature pointed a red-hot finger toward the woman sitting on the floor. "Look at her. Poor thing. She has no idea who she is or why's she's here. So she sits there day after day, rocking and whimpering. It seems intolerably unfair to leave her wallowing in her agony, don't you think?"

The girl nodded, watching the woman rock back and forth. "Isn't there something you can do for her?"

The creature's face crumpled into a surprisingly human expression of unhappiness, and he put a hand to his brow. "Alas, I cannot. No matter how much it pains me to see the poor woman that way, I can do nothing for her. Locked in her own ignorance, she'll sit there suffering for all of eternity—or until she fades away to dust." He took his hand from his face and stroked his chin. "Unless . . ."

"Unless what?" The girl looked from the woman to the creature. "If there's some way you can help her, do it."

Chaos sighed. "There's nothing I can do. Human memories are off-limits to my kind. But, if *you* want to help . . ." He pointed to the woman's left, and for the first time, the girl noticed a glowing blue ball like the one the man had been fixated on earlier.

"What is it?" she asked, studying the globe, which was a little larger than her first.

"All of her memories," the Pyrinth said, "are right there. All she has to do is take hold of it, and everything she's forgotten will be returned to her."

The girl walked toward the ball and knelt beside it. She'd thought it was blue, but could see now that the globe itself was clear. Blue mist swirled inside the glassy surface like clouds. Could it be true that the woman's memories were locked in those clouds?

"Pick it up." Chaos said. "It won't hurt you."

She reached for the ball and paused. "Why don't you give it to her?"

"I can't. Fire elementals can't touch human memories."

"Why doesn't she take it herself?"

Irritation flashed in the creature's eyes. "Why does anyone refuse to do the things that are good for them? Why don't people take care of themselves when they are sick? Why do they not talk to those they miss? Why do they refuse their greatest chances at success and instead cling to the very things they know will pull them down?" He shoved his dagger inside his chest-piece. "Do you want to help her or not?"

She was almost sure that there was something more he wasn't telling her. She tried to figure out what he might he hiding, but the woman gave out another anguished moan. Clearly the woman was in pain. If this ball could help her . . . Gently, the girl reached down and cupped the globe in her hands. It was warm and yielded slightly beneath her fingers.

At first she was afraid of the woman's memories entering her own head. The last thing she wanted to do was invade another person's privacy. But apparently, the globe worked only on the person it belonged to.

"Go on," Chaos urged, his eyes bright. "Give it to her."

Cradling the ball in one hand, she brushed back the woman's hair. At her touch, the woman pulled away—eyes dark with surprise, or possibly fear. "Sssssss!" she hissed, baring her teeth.

The girl rocked back, unsure what to do. "Here," she said, holding out the ball. "This is yours."

The only answer was the woman's steady groaning.

Heart pounding, she tried to think. It was hard to concentrate here. The air felt thick, and her mind seemed slow. The flaming creature hovered behind her.

Unsure what to do, but knowing she had to help, she leaned forward. "Please," she whispered. She started to place the ball into the woman's hands, but the fire elemental shook his head. "She must take it from you herself."

The girl took the woman's thin wrist, tugging it away

from her knees until her hand flopped open. "Take it," the girl said, holding out the ball.

For the first time, the woman looked up. Her confused eyes moved from the girl to the swirling, blue globe.

The girl held the ball out to her. "Yes, that's it. Take the ball."

As if in a trance, the woman reached out a pale, shaking hand and touched the ball. A shock shot up the girl's arm. The woman's eyes snapped wide open. Her mouth gaped. Gripping the ball in her hand, she jumped to her feet.

"Why?" she howled. Her face contorted with pain. She held out both hands as though warding off an attacker. "No!" she screeched. "Don't touch me!"

The girl fell backward. What was happening? What was wrong? She looked up at Chaos, shocked to see his face blazing with demonic humor. He was *enjoying* the woman's pain and fear. The girl jumped up and lunged forward, meaning to pull the ball from the woman's grip.

But the wrinkled figure waved her hands, the globe still clutched between her fingers, and backed away from a terror only she could see. "My magic!" she wailed. "What have you done with it?" Her eyes locked on some unseen danger, and she threw out her arms. "Don't! Please, stop!"

Panicked, the girl reached for the ball, but her fingers caught on the neckline of the woman's gown instead. At the same time, the woman threw back her head and screeched in pain.

The girl fell backward, sucking in a shocked breath. She tried to tear her eyes from the sight of what was before her, but couldn't. Her gaze felt locked on the woman's neck.

Stretching across the front of the pale, white skin was a deep, bloodless gash.

CHAPTER 12

No Way Out

A second fire elemental charged into the room so quickly that he was only a blur of flame and a blast of heat until he stood in front of her. "What are you doing?" the creature roared, and the girl found herself pushing her body into a crack in the wall like the screaming woman.

Chaos had looked frightening, but the fiery monster in front of her was truly terrifying. He towered above her, with shoulders as broad as she was tall, and arms that looked strong enough to smash boulders. In one hand, he carried a flaming mace burning so brightly that the spiked ball at the end was like a tiny sun. The beast had the thick neck and head of a bull, with horns that curved wickedly out and up on either side. But his mouth was filled with flaming, dagger-sharp fangs. She thought he might be a minotaur.

His burning, red eyes glared at her as he jabbed the

mace in the woman's direction. "Did you do that?"

The girl opened her mouth, but no words came out.

His lips pulled back in disgust, the minotaur turned to the woman and swung the mace at her hands, which were still clutching the glowing ball.

"No!" the girl shouted. She threw her arms in front of her face, expecting the woman to be crushed by the blazing weapon. Instead, the monster pulled up at the last second, and the mace only tapped the woman's fingers, sending the ball rolling out of her reach. The flames didn't blister her skin. As soon as the ball left her hands, the woman stopped screaming and collapsed back into her crevice.

The minotaur turned to the girl. His massive chest heaved, and his brows bunched over his eyes. "What were you thinking? Why would you do a thing like that?"

The girl gulped. "I didn't . . . I had no idea . . ."

In the back of the cavern, rocks clattered down the sloping floor. The elemental spun around and spotted Chaos trying to slip from the room unnoticed.

"*You*," he snarled.

Chaos broke for the doorway, but the minotaur was too quick. In three leaping steps, he crossed the floor, lifted his mace, and brought it down with a sickening crunch on the fire elemental's back. Flames exploded across the room as if a meteor had struck.

The blow should have crushed the horse-creature's body, but he leaped to his feet as if the weapon had barely touched him. With a shout of his own, he spun around and kicked both rear hooves into the minotaur's chest. As the bull-headed creature stumbled backward, Chaos leaped forward, pulled out his dagger, and stabbed the minotaur's muscular neck.

Soon the two of them were locked in what appeared to be a fight to the death. Rocks splintered and fire shot across the room in blinding gouts as the two beasts howled and clawed at each other. Pressing tighter into her crevice, the woman put her hands to her face and shook.

"Stop it!" The girl jumped to her feet and charged toward the two battling creatures, unmindful of their swinging limbs and weapons. "Leave each other alone."

Neither of the elementals seemed to hear her, so she grabbed the biggest rock she could lift, hefted it over her head, and flung it at them. "Stop!"

The rock bounced off the minotaur without appearing to cause any damage, but it got the fire elementals' attention. With the mace halfway raised, the minotaur turned to stare at her. Teeth opened in a fiery snarl, Chaos stopped fighting as well.

She stomped her bare foot against the floor and pointed to the weeping woman. "Can't you that see you're frightening her to death?"

"She's already dead," Chaos hissed.

"Shut your mouth," the minotaur growled. He raised his mace, and Chaos drew back his dagger, but before they could resume fighting, the girl stepped between them.

She'd seen how the flames of the minotaur's mace hadn't hurt the woman. Still, she clenched her teeth as she approached the fiery creatures, expecting to get burned. Instead, the flames came right up to her skin—enveloped her in a shimmering, orange curtain—then curled away. She could feel the heat, but it didn't harm her.

"Go away." The minotaur shoved her gently, but she threw all of her weight against him.

"I'm not leaving until you two agree to stop fighting." Despite her best efforts, her feet slid across the floor, though she could tell that the elemental wasn't using a fraction of his strength.

"I've got better things to do." The minotaur grunted and got to his feet. He eyed Chaos warily. "You're no match for me anyway."

"Eat smoke, Magma," Chaos said. He bared his teeth and flicked his fiery tongue, but the minotaur seemed to have lost his taste for fighting. He rested his weapon on one shoulder and started for the doorway.

"Wait," the girl called. "Magma? Is that your name?"

"Pyrinths and humans do not speak to one another," the minotaur said without stopping. "I've already said more than I should have."

She hurried after him into a dimly lit passage. "Someone has to tell me who I am and why I'm here."

"That's what I was trying to do when we were so

tactlessly interrupted," Chaos said, trotting up behind her.

Magma stopped. He lowered his head, but did not look back. "That's why you gave the woman her retinentia. Her memories."

At first, the girl had no idea what he was talking about. Then she understood. "The blue ball? Is that what it's called? I didn't know she would react like that."

"You *terrified* her," the minotaur growled.

Chaos placed a fiery hand on her elbow. "Ignore him. You helped a poor woman suffering from amnesia to remember who she is. You gave her back her memories. Is that such a bad thing?"

Magma turned, hands clenched on the handle of his mace. "Memories she'd been trying to forget for hundreds of years."

Why would someone want to forget who they were? The girl looked from the glowering minotaur to Chaos, who covered the smile on his serpentine face with one hand, as though waiting for the punchline of an especially good joke.

Magma growled and slammed his mace to the ground, cracking the stone at his feet. "Three days after she was married, her husband stole her magic, dragged her into the woods, and slit her throat. As he watched her die, he explained that he'd never loved her and had married her only for her money and power. He later blamed her death on thieves and remarried before the end of the year. Can you see why she might want to forget such a traumatizing experience?"

She stared up at Chaos, pushing his hand from her arm. "You *knew*?"

Magma sneered. "That's how he breaks up his pathetic existence. By making humans suffer."

The girl felt sick to her stomach.

Chaos ran a thumb along the blade of his dagger. "You asked who you are. How you got here." He pointed his dagger at the ground behind her, where the blue ball she'd handed the woman lay pulsing on the ground. No, it wasn't the woman's. She could see that one back in the room they'd left. Was this . . . ?

"Your retinentia," Chaos said. "Your memories. Touch it, and all of your questions will be answered."

With her eyes locked on the blue clouds swirling inside the globe, she stepped toward it. Her *memories*. She reached out, and a powerful hand blocked her way.

"Have you learned nothing?" Magma shouted, pulling her back. "Do you want to experience your worst nightmare again?"

She tried to pull away, but the fire elemental's grip was too strong. "What makes you think my memories are bad? Why would . . ." Her voice faltered as Magma and Chaos shared a meaningful look.

The minotaur sighed. "You didn't tell her."

Chaos held up his hands. "Pyrinths and humans do

not speak to each other," he said, mimicking Magma's gravelly voice.

Magma bared his teeth, and Chaos danced nimbly away.

"What?" the girl demanded. "Who am I? Why am I here?"

"You're here because you're dead," Chaos said.

She stared at the fire elemental, thinking that surely this was another of his perverse jokes. But neither he nor Magma were laughing.

The minotaur lifted his mace as if it were no heavier than a piece of parchment and turned it in his hands. "Your magic was taken from you," he said in a voice that sounded old and tired. "You were killed by someone you love."

Something cold and sharp drilled into the girl's chest. She stared at the blue ball with growing horror. "No. You're lying. Both of you. How could you know that?"

"It's the only way to get here," Magma said. "It's bad enough that we're stuck here, but the only visitors we get are sent because they have no magic and their lives were taken by someone they love. It's like some kind of great cosmic joke." He kicked a stone toward the glowing ball. "Be glad your memories were taken from you."

She put her hands to her mouth. Dead. She was *dead*. It couldn't be true, yet she sensed that it was. Not only was she dead, but she'd been murdered by someone she loved. If that was true of all the people here, no wonder they acted like they did.

"Do I have . . . a name?" she whispered.

"Call yourself whatever you like," Chaos said. "Queen, Warrior princess, Master of all. Pick any name you like." He chuckled. "Not that anyone will use it."

He was cruel but right. What did a name matter? Still, she need to call herself something. "Turnip," she said at once. "I'll call myself Turnip."

"*Turnip*." Chaos grinned. "That's unique."

She had no idea why she'd picked that name; it was the first thing that had come into her head. "Now that I know why I'm here, what am I supposed to do?"

"Do?" The minotaur looked genuinely confused. "There's nothing *to* do. Stay with your own kind." He glared at Chaos. "And the Pyrinths will stay away from you."

She couldn't do *nothing*. "There's a man back there," she said, pointing the way she had come. "I think he must have had a garden before he was k—before he died. He asked for flowers. Do you know where I can find some?"

Chaos burst into startled laughter. "Turnip wants flowers. Smoke and embers. Magma, go help her pick some flowers."

The minotaur grimaced. "Look around you," he said. "Do you see any flower gardens? What you see is all there is—fire and rock."

The cold, sharp pain that had been growing inside her turned to panic. She was stuck in a world of rock and fire with these . . . *monsters*? No wonder the people here were the way they were.

"I can't stay here." She grabbed Chaos by the wrist. "Help me get out."

"There *is* no way out," the elemental said.

"No." She turned to Magma. "You're fire elementals, you have magic. Set me free. I'll pay any price."

Magma turned away. "You don't understand. Fire Keep is a prison, for us as much as for you. If there were a way out, we would have used it long ago."

"But your magic. There must be a way."

"We have no magic," the minotaur growled. "It was taken from us the same way yours was taken from you. There is no magic in Fire Keep."

Her heart raced, and her vision blurred as tears streamed down her cheeks. "You're lying! There must be a way out."

A slithering sound came from farther down the tunnel, and the darkness disappeared as a lizard-like creature crawled into view. The long fiery tail dragging behind him made the *shh-shh-shh* noise as his nails clicked on the stone. In one hand, he clutched a thick, flaming book.

"They sssspeak the truth," he hissed with a wise and knowing look on his face. "The only way out of Fire Keep is through magic. But there is no magic here. I'm afraid you are trapped in Fire Keep forever."

CHAPTER 13

A Meeting

Marcus held his breath and listened. Something was in the room with him. He could hear it skitter across the damp floor, pause, then move again. He strained to see into the darkness, but it was no use. Barely enough light came through the crack under the door to suggest a vague outline of the cell he'd been locked in since he was dragged here.

The sound came again. *Clitter-scratch*. The sound of tiny claws on stone. *Clitter-scratch*. It was getting closer. He could imagine something with sharp teeth and furry skin touching his bare feet any minute.

Instinctively he reached for fire to light the room. Instead of magic flowing through him, something slick and revolting attempted to force its way into his body. It was like taking a drink of cool water, only to discover that the glass was filled with vile, black sludge. He choked and tried to spit the taste out of his mouth, but his parched tongue and lips were unable to gather enough saliva.

He had no idea how long he'd been in the cell, but it had been this way since he'd been captured. Every time he called magic, something sick and revolting attacked him instead. He had the feeling that if he kept trying, then eventually whatever was working at getting inside him would succeed.

The sound came again. He rattled the chains stretching his arms above his head and pinning his ankles to the wall. Arcs of pain raced up his shoulders and into his nearly numb hands.

"Help! Someone let me out of here."

Footsteps sounded outside the room, and a moment later, the lock clicked, and a twisted figure with wide eyes and a beak-like nose that made him look like an owl stepped through the door. Light flooded the cell, and Marcus squinched his eyes shut. But not before he saw a spider with a hairy, black body the size of his fist, and spiny legs lifting it a good six inches off the floor.

Less than a foot from Marcus, the spider froze for a second, then scuttled toward a hole in the wall. The owl-faced creature was too quick. It raced across the room on bent legs, snatched up the spider, and crushed it with a sound like breaking egg shells.

Green goop leaked from between the creature's fingers as it shoved the spider into its beak with a muffled crunching and smacking sound.

Marcus's stomach rolled over, and if he'd have eaten anything in the last twenty-four hours, it surely would have come back up.

"Please." Marcus's voice cracked. "Let me out of here."

The hunched creature turned to study him with unblinking gold eyes the size of saucers.

Marcus tried to ignore the line of green spider ichor dripping down the side of its beak. "If you help me, I can get you anything you want."

"*Quarg*," the creature squawked. Was it agreeing to help him, refusing, or just making noise? For all he knew, it couldn't understand a word he'd said. It shuffled to the door, and he braced himself to be plunged back into darkness. Instead, the owl-faced man went outside the cell and returned with a weathered wooden bucket. Water splashed over the rim as the creature carried it across the cell.

Marcus's mouth, which had been too dry to spit a moment earlier, began to salivate at the thought of a drink. It was only as the figure drew the bucket back and swung it toward him that he realized what was about to happen. He barely had time to open his mouth before ice-cold liquid splashed across his face and body.

"*Stik*," the owl-man said in a hooting kind of voice that was difficult to understand.

Marcus licked as much of the water trickling down

his face as he could. The drops felt incredible on his cracked lips, but there weren't nearly enough of them.

"*Stik,*" the creature repeated.

Marcus stuck out his tongue to lick the last of the water from above his chin. "I don't know what you're saying."

"*Stik. Was.*" The owl man pointed to Marcus then rubbed its gnarled hands over its body.

"Stick was *what?*" Marcus asked. If the words held some kind of meaning, he was too tired to figure it out.

With an angry caw, the creature stepped forward, patted a hand in the puddle of water at Marcus's feet, and wiped its palm across its body.

All at once, Marcus understood what the little creature was trying to say, and despite his pain and exhaustion, he couldn't help laughing. "Stink, wash," he said in a hoarse voice. "You're telling me that I stink and need to wash, aren't you?"

"Quarg, *quarg,*" the man squawked excitedly.

Apparently, Marcus had gotten it right. "Try hanging in this stinking wet hole for a few hours then see if *you* stink." Sniffing, Marcus realized the man didn't need to hang around here to stink. The stench of rotted meat flowed off him like some foul perfume.

"*Was,*" the man repeated.

Marcus shook the chains, grimacing at his aching arms. "How am I supposed to wash with my hands chained above my head?"

The expression on the owl face was priceless. Its already big eyes opened wider still, and it cocked its head. It reached into a pocket with bent fingers and pulled out a key ring. With surprising dexterity for someone with such crooked limbs, it unlocked Marcus's arms and legs. The moment the chains were released, Marcus collapsed into the puddled water. Barely able to move his arms, he wet one palm and licked his fingers.

"*Was!*" The owl man darted forward and kicked him in the ribs.

Marcus hissed and jerked away. "Don't touch me." He balled his hands into fists. As weak as he was, though, and with no magic, he might not be able to fight something even as weak as this creature. Marcus scooped what little water remained in the bucket into his hand and used it to scrub off as much of the dirt and sweat from his body as he could.

The owl man watched for a moment before limping out of the room.

Marcus eyed the open door, wondering if his legs were strong enough to make a run for it. Before he could decide, the man returned and tossed Marcus's robe and staff on the floor. No words were needed for Marcus to know what the creature wanted. Using the staff to hold his weight, he forced himself painfully to his feet and pulled the robe on over his head. He had barely gotten his arms through the sleeves when the creature jabbed him in the back.

"Out."

Marcus glared at the bird-like man. "When I get my magic back, Thanksgiving is coming early and you'll be the main course."

The creature hooted what might have a laugh.

The tunnel was lit by only a couple of torches. Still, after all the time he'd spent in the darkness, Marcus was forced to cup a hand over his eyes until they adjusted.

"Did he wash?" a voice asked.

Marcus turned to find another owl man standing beside him. Although this one was as twisted as the first, and its body seemed to be coated in some kind of green mold, it emanated a sense of authority.

"Stik," the first owl man said.

"Yes. It stinks. But no amount of water will wash that off. Its kind all smell that way."

"Look who's talking," Marcus said. "You smell like someone rubbed you down with gopher guts and left you in the sun to rot."

"You would be wise to watch your mouth." The moldy creature snapped its fingers, and a pair of two-headed dogs—each with eight legs—came around the corner. The dogs' ribs stood out like fence posts from their emaciated bodies. Saliva dripped from their twin tongues as they panted hungrily in Marcus's direction. "I was commanded to bring you. Nothing was said about how many pieces you had to be in."

The creature turned and started down the tunnel. With the dogs close behind him, Marcus hurried to follow.

"Who are you taking me to?" Marcus knew he'd been captured by the Dark Circle, but he wasn't sure where they'd taken him.

"You'll find out soon enough," the creature said, swiftly climbing a twisting staircase.

"Hold up," Marcus said. "I can't walk as fast as you." With his bad leg, and after hours in chains, he could barely walk at all, but that wasn't the only reason he wanted the creature to slow down. "Get me out of here, and I'll get you whatever reward you want."

"A reward?" the owl man asked.

"Sure. You don't have to get me out. Show me the way, and I'll go on my own. You can say I hit you over the head and escaped." Marcus eased up next to him, trying not to gag from the smell. "I know an air elemental who can make diamonds and gold out of nothing."

"Do you?" A voice asked from the top of the stairs. "That's quite fascinating. Tell me more of these mystical powers."

Marcus looked up to see a figure made of colorful gemstones. As he watched, the figure changed from gems to gold coins, and then to glittering jewels. It was the same thing he'd seen Divum do dozens of times. But this wasn't her. It was her partner. The one who had sided with the Dark Circle.

Marcus limped up the stairs. "*Calem.*" He muttered the name like a curse. "You're the one who had me captured?"

The Aerisian chuckled merrily. "If this was my plan, I'd have made it much more amusing, like having you delivered one limb at a time, or impaled on the beak of a gryphon."

"I'd have had him drowned the moment I found him," another voice said. A large man with a heavy, gold crown came into view as Marcus reached the top of the stairs.

Marcus hadn't seen Tide in over a year, but his stomach clenched at the sight of the former king of the water elementals, who had tried to have him and Kyja killed. Close behind came Nizgar-Gharat, the land elementals Marcus had taken the scepter from after they'd stolen it and trapped Cascade and the rest of the Fontasians inside Water Keep.

"Drowning is a ssssuperb idea," hissed the purple lizard head. "Then boil him to make sure he's really dead."

All three of the elementals were behind this. He should have known that somehow they were the ones blocking his magic.

"I don't know why we've kept him alive this long," said the green head of Nizgar-Gharat, its tongue flickering.

"He is alive because the Master commands it," the owl-headed man said.

At the word *Master*, icy bumps formed on Marcus's skin. The head of the Dark Circle. He tried not to let his fear show, but how could he not be terrified at the thought of a being powerful enough to control not only an army of dark wizards but Summoners as well?

The elementals must have been as frightened as he was at the mention of their leader's name, because they all went silent.

"You spoke of a reward," the owl man said to Marcus. "A reward is in store. But it will be for you, not for me. The Master has been looking forward to giving it to you."

Marcus couldn't help himself; he turned to run back down the stairs, but the two-headed dogs were blocking his way. Tide grabbed one of his arms, and Calem took the other.

"Let's help you along, shall we?" Calem said, turning his body into a swarm of wasps, scorpions, and other stinging creatures. "I have a feeling this will be more entertaining than spearing you on a gryphon beak would have been."

Locked between the two elementals, Marcus was dragged down a hallway lined with all manner of weapons. Several of the weapons' tips were dark with what looked like dried blood—as though they'd been recently used. Is that what the Master planned on doing to him? Would the

Master kill him right away, or would he be tortured first?

Cold sweat soaked the back of his robe. Why would Graehl bring him here? He still couldn't believe that the man he'd come to think of as a friend had betrayed him. He hoped Riph Raph had managed to escape. Marcus hadn't seen the skyte since one of the dark wizards hit him with a lightning bolt.

At last they stopped in front of a gleaming red door. Tide took Marcus's hand and forced it toward a brass latch. As his fingers neared the metal, a pair of talons that were mounted at the center of the door snapped close on his hand.

Marcus gasped, but felt no pain. A second later, the talons released him and the door swung open revealing a smoky interior. As the elementals pushed him forward and stepped away, Marcus's legs shook so hard that it was all he could do to keep from falling to the ground.

Two red eyes blazed through the smoke, and a dry voice said, "Come in, Marcus. I've been waiting a very long time to meet you."

CHAPTER 14

THE ONLY WAY

Clinging to his staff like a piece of driftwood in a raging ocean, Marcus limped through the doorway. Smoke curled around his head so thickly, it was impossible to make out anything more than a foot away. His thoughts swirled with the smoke.

How many times had Kyja told him that he was too impulsive? How much trouble could he have avoided by stopping to think before taking rash actions? And now, he was here, unable to do anything to help her because, once again, he thought he knew more than anyone else. True, he'd been trying to save her. But what did that matter when he'd failed so miserably—again?

Not only that, but despite his hope that Riph Raph had escaped, there was a good chance that the skyte was dead. Marcus was responsible for that, as well. Whatever happened to him here, he'd failed everyone who'd put their trust in him. He deserved whatever he got—torture, death, unimaginable pain. He deserved it all for what he'd done, but his legs trembled at the thought.

Steeling himself against what waited for him, he pushed deeper into the room. The smoke grew so thick that his eyes began to water, and his lungs burned. What this it? Was he sent here to suffocate? Maybe the clouds were poisonous gas. He thought about turning back but had no idea which direction was back.

Gasping for breath, he stepped forward, and the smoke disappeared. It didn't thin or fade; it was simply gone. He wiped his eyes and stared, unable understand what he was seeing. He'd expected a torture chamber or a dark pit where he'd be beaten and questioned. Instead, he was standing in a candlelit banquet hall. Chandeliers cast a cheery glow, gold mirrors and silk tapestries covered the walls, and a huge table in the center was filled to overflowing with food.

A hooded figure at one end of the table waved a hand. "Please, make yourself at home. Eat. Drink."

This was obviously a trap of some kind. Marcus shook his head and remained where he was. "I'll stand."

"Sit," said a voice to his right. Marcus turned to find Graehl at his side. "You'll need the strength."

"Get away from me." Marcus stumbled from the man, unable to believe that the traitor would dare show his face, let alone act like he was still some kind of friend.

Graehl shook back his long hair and sighed. "It's not

what you think."

Marcus bared his teeth. "You lied to me. You said we were going to recue Kyja. By now she's gone for good, and Riph Raph's probably dead too." He reached for magic but again gagged at the blackness that nearly overwhelmed him.

The man at the table chuckled. "You told me he was a feisty one."

Graehl reached out a hand, but Marcus slapped it away.

"You have every right to be angry with me," Graehl said. "I know you think I lied. But I brought you here because it's the only chance to save Kyja. I would have brought the skyte, too, but he recovered and flew away before we could catch him."

Marcus knew it was all a lie, and yet, as he stared into Graehl's eyes, he was almost positive the man was telling the truth. But how could that be? How could kidnapping him and bringing him to the Dark Circle help Kyja?

"Hear what I have to say," the Master said. "If you still want to leave when we're done talking, I'll let you go."

Marcus glared at him. "How am I supposed to trust a man who won't show his face?"

Graehl sucked in a breath; Marcus wondered if he'd gone too far. He stared at the dark features inside the cloak.

"You can see me. Why can't I see you?"

Graehl began to answer. "It's not—"

But the Master cut him off. "He makes a valid point. A wizard needs to look another wizard in the eyes if he is to take him into his trust." He reached up with two wrinkled hands, grasped the sides of his cowl, and slowly pulled it down.

Marcus stared. He'd expected to see almost anything—a monster, a skull, features twisted into a shape completely unrecognizable. What he hadn't expected was a face almost as familiar his own. "You look just like . . ."

He couldn't complete the sentence, because what he was seeing was impossible. But the resemblance was too hard to miss. Except for the long scar that ran from this man's right eye to the corner of his mouth, everything else—the strong jaw, gray beard, and twinkling eyes— might have belonged to . . . *Master Therapass*.

The bearded face broke into a smile. "I'm afraid he doesn't like to admit that we're related." He took a knife from a silver platter in front of him and cut a leg from the large, roasted bird. "You'd think he'd be proud that his younger brother is the only other living master wizard."

"I don't believe it." Marcus turned to Graehl, who looked as stunned as he felt. "Did you . . . ?"

Graehl shook his head. "I had no idea."

The Master bit into his chicken and smacked his lips. "Come, eat. It's quite delicious."

None of this was what he'd expected. Graehl took

Marcus's arm, and they walked to the table in stunned silence. He and Graehl sat beside one another at the table. Although Marcus didn't trust the wizard, he couldn't stop his stomach from rumbling at the smell of hot meat, fresh bread, and roasted vegetables.

Graehl filled a goblet with water, and Marcus gulped it down greedily.

The Master nodded. "Much more civilized."

Marcus tried to ignore the basket of rolls, which looked as soft and fluffy as clouds. "How can you be brothers? You're enemies."

The Master took a bite of what looked like a spiky yellow melon and patted his chin with his napkin. "That may be true—now. But that wasn't always the case. We were quite close as youths. He taught me some of my first spells."

Marcus didn't understand. After all their time together, why wouldn't Master Therapass have told him this? He knew the wizard had been connected to the Dark Circle a long time ago, but the two men were *brothers*? As if his hand had a mind of its own, it reached for a slice of pink- and orange-swirled cheese. But he pulled back at the last minute. How could he think of eating?

"You said there's a way to rescue Kyja, but Master Therapass would have told me if that were true."

"My brother has misled you about many thing, including the meaning of that mark on your arm."

Marcus found himself reaching for a slice of cheese again; his robe sleeve had pulled up, revealing part of the scar on his shoulder. He yanked it down. "What do you know about my scar?"

The Master stabbed a sausage link with his fork, held it up to his nose, and inhaled. "First we eat. Then we talk."

"No," Marcus said. "I'm not eating anything until you tell me how to save Kyja. Assuming you're not lying about that and everything else."

The Master ladled steaming soup into his bowl. "I promise to tell you nothing but the truth. Whether you choose to believe me is up to you. But I've had a long day, and I'm not saying another word until *I've* eaten. You can sit and watch, or you can eat. It will be the first of several choices you must make soon."

Graehl forked a slice of meat onto Marcus's plate and set one of the delicious-looking rolls next to it. "Eating will help you think straight."

Marcus stared at him, wanting to believe Graehl, but unable to forget his treachery. But Marcus was hungry, and if they wanted to poison him, there were easier ways to do it. Grudgingly, he cut into the meat. Soon his hunger won out over his distrust, and he found himself digging into everything he could reach until his belly felt like it would burst.

At last he put his knife and fork aside. "Okay. We've

eaten. Now tell me how to bring Kyja back."

The Master watched Marcus over the rim of his goblet then set it aside. Graehl, who had eaten very little, rested his hands on the table, his face unreadable.

"First, I must ask you a question," the wizard said. "I'm sure my brother explained that you are destined to save Farworld. But has he ever told you what you are to save it *from*?"

"From *you*," Marcus said at once.

He expected the Master to be offended, but the man only smiled. "Exactly what I would have expected. But think about this: When the prophecy was made, neither he nor I was alive. The prophecy spoke of a divide to be closed. What divide could it possibly have been referring to? No Dark Circle existed at the time."

Marcus guessed he'd known that, but he'd never given it a lot of thought. "I'm sure the prophecy was talking about evil. And the Dark Circle is evil. You want to destroy Farworld."

The Master sat back in his chair. "Let's say that that's true. Say, that for some unfathomable reason, I want to destroy the very world I live in. What about Earth? Your friend is supposed to save it from what? Me again? I admit I've sent a few of my men there, but am I really such a great threat to destroy both worlds that a pair of saviors would be required to stop me?"

Marcus chewed his lower lip. He didn't know enough

about Earth to understand what danger it might be in. But with all the technology there, it seemed unlikely that the Dark Circle could be that much of a threat to it. He turned to Graehl, but the man had no answer.

"Give it some thought," the Master said. "We'll return to the subject later. My second question gets to the heart of the matter: How much do you want to save your friend?"

A lump formed in Marcus's throat, making it hard to speak. "More than anything."

Graehl coughed into his hand, and the Master glanced over at him. "My brother would tell you that she is beyond your reach," the wizard said. "That is not the case."

He waved a hand, and the wall of smoke Marcus had entered through began to swirl and shift. As Marcus stared at the clouds, he began to see something behind them. A cave of some kind came into focus, with dark rock walls. Flames danced on the ceiling and floors. As the smoke cleared, he could discern figures that appeared to be made out of fire—a powerful creature with horns, a monster with the head of a serpent with the body of a horse, and a lizard with a thick book. They all seemed to be listening to someone.

The scene shifted ever so slightly, revealing a girl in a long, white gown. As soon as Marcus saw her, his heart exploded. "Kyja!" he shouted, leaping out of his chair. His leg collapsed under him and he would have fallen if Graehl hadn't grabbed him around the waist and held him back.

It was her. She was really there. He would have known if the Master were pulling some kind of trick. She looked pale, but he thought he'd never seen anything more beautiful in his life. Although he couldn't hear her voice, she looked to be arguing with the fire creatures.

"Let me go!" he cried, struggling to wriggle away. "I have to get to her." His staff had fallen somewhere on the floor, but he didn't care. He'd crawl to her if he had to.

"You reach her," Graehl said, fighting to hang on to him. "She's not here. It's only an image."

Marcus leaned back against the table, panting. "Why didn't you show me before? Why didn't Master Therapass?"

"He didn't because he can't," the Master said. "Or to put it better, he *won't*."

Marcus turned to stare at him. "What are you talking about?"

The wizard smiled, and for a brief second, Marcus saw a flash of red in the man's eyes. "The reason that Farworld and Earth are in danger. It's not because of a man, or a group, or your so-called 'evil.'"

Marcus didn't care about the prophecy right now; all he cared about was rescuing Kyja.

The wizard seemed to read his mind. "You say you want to save your friend. But are you willing to do what it takes? That's the real threat to our worlds—people unwilling to do what is required. To *take* what they want."

"I don't understand," Marcus said. "I'll pay whatever price you want. I'll give my life if I have to."

Graehl's hands tightened on his waist.

"I'm glad to hear that." The Master smiled, and this time, the red flash was clear.

Marcus stared at the wizard's face, which no longer looked quite as much like Master Therapass's. His heart froze as the Master's words sunk in.

To take *what they want.*

The vile blackness that had been trying to force its way into him wasn't *blocking* his magic. No, it was magic of a different kind. The only kind of magic in use here.

His hands and feet felt numb as he shook his head. "Not dark magic." He stared into Graehl's eyes. "There has to be another way. I can't."

Graehl looked away.

"I'm sorry to hear that," the Master said. "I thought you cared about her. But if you don't save her this very minute, it will be too late." He pointed a long, white finger toward the smoke wall.

Marcus turned to see Kyja throw up her hands. She looked from one of the fire creatures to the other, dropped her head, and walked toward a swirling vortex of flames.

CHAPTER 15

THE ONE

The fiery lizard began to slither back down the tunnel, but the girl who now thought of herself as Turnip chased after him.

"Wait!"

The lizard paused. "Do you need something? I'm quite busy."

"Busy with what?" Turnip asked.

The elemental seemed taken aback by her question. He flicked his tail and shifted the heavy volume he was holding from one arm to the other. "I don't understand."

Turnip gave an exasperated sigh and brushed her hair out of her face. "From what I've seen so far, no one here appears to be doing anything worthwhile. What are you busy *doing*?"

The lizard turned to the other fire elementals as though wanting some kind of explanation. The minotaur shrugged his massive shoulders. "Don't blame me, Prudentes. Chaos was the one who first talked to the human."

Chaos kicked a hoof. "At least she was interesting to talk with."

Turnip cocked an eyebrow at the lizard. "You're not busy at all. You want to get rid of me."

Prudentes held out his book with a huff. "As it happens, I *do* want to get rid of you. I have a great deal of studying to do. And you're keeping me from it."

"What kind of studying?" Turnip edged closer to the book, trying to see if she could make out any words on the cover. "Do you have other books? Can I read them? Are there any that explain what Fire Keep is and why I'm here?"

Magma slammed his mace to the ground, fracturing the rock at his feet, and roared. "I told you that already. You're here because you were murdered and your magic was stolen."

Chaos gave a sly smile. "He's got a temper, if you didn't notice."

Turnip stamped her foot on the ground, although the effect wasn't nearly as dramatic as the minotaur's mace. "That's *how* I got here. Not *why*. You're here because you're fire elementals. From what I can tell, all you do is fight, argue, and complain. I can understand perfectly why you're trapped here. No one would want you around them anyway. But *who* sent me here and why? What am I supposed to *do*?"

All three Pyrinths looked genuinely confused and she felt as if she were dealing with a bunch of three-year-olds. She pointed to the book Prudentes was holding. "Can I read that?"

"Absolutely not." He clutched the book to his chest. "It's written in Fire. You couldn't read it if you tried."

Of course it was written in fire. Why did everything here have to be so frustrating? "Then will you tell me what it says?"

"It's instructions, mostly. About fire magic. How it can be used, what it can do, how to grant access or deny it. Being a fire elemental is a great responsibility."

"So you *do* have magic," Turnip said. Now *this* was interesting.

"We don't *have* it," Chaos said. "If we did, we wouldn't be stuck here. We grant it to those who request it. Or we deny their requests." He grinned as if that was his favorite part of being a Pyrinth.

His claim made sense, in a strange sort of way. Fire elementals were the guardians of fire magic. They could choose who used it and for what reason. But they couldn't use it themselves. Is that the way all magic worked? Were water elementals blocked from using water magic? She was almost certain they weren't, but how could she know that when she'd never met one?

Had she?

She tried to remember what she knew about

elementals, but the only thing should could come up with was a poem that, oddly enough, she could still recall:

> *See the Lords of Water—*
> *Behind the waves they leap*
>
> *See the Lords of Land—*
> *Beneath the ground they sleep*
>
> *See the Lords of Air—*
> *Above the clouds they creep*
>
> *See the Lords of Fire—*
> *Around the flames they reap*
>
> *Water, Land, Air, Fire.*
> *Together the balance of Farworld they keep.*

Why did she feel as if she should know more than that? And why did knowing seem so important? Every time she tried to focus on the thought, something blocked her the same way her mind was blocked whenever she tried remembering anything about her past. Could elementals have something to do with why she was murdered? Is that why those memories were out of reach?

"Let's go," Magma said. "This is a waste of time." He and Prudentes walked down the passage.

Chaos patted her back as he went by and whispered, "Find me if you decide to return more memories to the humans. Trust me, it's the only entertainment you'll get around here."

Turnip watched them go. She could ask the Pyrinths questions all day, but she had the feeling that it wouldn't get her any closer to the answers she was seeking. She would look for them on her own. Although she couldn't remember anything about her past, she was almost sure she was the kind of person who wasn't afraid to figure things out for herself.

Only . . . what if there were no answers? Or what if the answer was that she was stuck here for no reason, with nothing to do, and no way out, forever? Is that what had driven the rest of these people crazy?

The first thing she had to do was make up for the mistakes she'd already made. Pulling her gown up to her knees so she could run faster, she hurried back to the woman with the slit throat. Turnip knelt in front of her, being sure to stay well away from the blue retinentia, and leaned close.

"I'm sorry," she said softly. "I didn't mean to hurt you."

The woman gave no indication she saw Turnip at all. Maybe she didn't. Maybe she was so far gone that she had no recognition of anything outside of her own pain.

Turnip stood. What was the point of trying to help?

She'd be better off finding someone who could at least talk back.

But she couldn't walk away, either. This was a real person with real feelings. The fire elementals might not see that, but she did. Even if the woman had stopped communicating, wasn't it possible that somewhere inside, she could still understand what was happening? After all, she had definitely reacted to the return of her memories.

She knelt again and gently took one of the woman's hands in hers. Staring into the woman's eyes, she tried to imagine what it must have been like to be murdered by the man she loved. If there was one thing that made humans special, it was their ability to feel compassion—to try to understand another person's feelings although they might not have experienced the exact same feelings themselves.

"I'm sorry for . . . what happened to you," she hesitantly began. "And I want you to know that you didn't deserve it."

The woman continued to rock and moan.

Turnip tried again. "I don't know if you can hear me, and I know I'm not very old. But I want you to know that no matter what he did to you, no matter what he might have said, you are a good person. He might have taken your magic, but . . ." Suddenly words came into her head as if someone else was saying them. "The real power of magic lies *within* you—it's in who you are, what you do, and most importantly of all, what you may become."

Did she feel the woman squeeze her hand?

Turnip squeezed back. "I care about you, and if you need anything, I'm here for you."

She wasn't sure if the woman had heard her, but she thought that the moans were a little less troubled. And surprisingly, Turnip felt better too, as if she'd found at least a small part of her purpose for being here.

The next task wasn't nearly as easy. For a while, she thought it wouldn't be possible at all. She searched through one cavern after another, often finding herself at a dead end where she had to turn around and start over. She'd nearly given up hope when she came across a sliver of rock twice as long as her pointer finger and so narrow that it looked like it would snap under the least bit of pressure. She thought it might be the tip of a stalactite that had fallen and shattered sometime in the past.

Turning the stone in her hands, she smiled and thought of a way she could use it. Carefully, she took the hem of her gown and tore a length of fabric from it. Then she tied one end of the fabric to the tip of the rock sliver. Adjusting the cloth with her fingers so it curved out at the top like the bloom of a rose, she wound it carefully around the stone until there was barely enough to tuck under the bottom of the fabric—holding it all in place.

She studied the finished work, looking from one side of it to the other. It wasn't perfect, but under the circumstance, it was the best she could do. As she was admiring her work, something clattered behind her. She spun around, but nothing was there.

"Hello?" she called.

No one answered.

Was Chaos up to more of his tricks? Hiding her creation within the fold of her robes, she moved silently to the entrance of the cavern. A few rocks were scattered on the passage floor, but they could have fallen on their own or been there for who knew how long. It didn't matter. What she was about to do wasn't something the fire elemental would be interested in anyway.

It took her a few tries to locate the right passages, but eventually she found her way to the stone platform she'd awakened on. From there it was a short trip to the bearded man.

He was still sitting on the floor, laughing at the blue ball. Was it possible that his retinentia contained happy memories? No, the Pyrinths had been clear on that. Suddenly shy and uncertain, she took what she'd made from her robe.

For a moment, he continued to watch the ball. Then his eyes drifted from the retinentia to what she was holding. His mouth opened.

"It's not exactly what you asked for," she said. "But I thought . . ."

"Flower," he whispered, his eyes gleaming.

She smiled. "I was hoping it would look like one."

His eyes went from the stone-and-cloth flower to her. She held it out to him. "It's for you."

With a gentleness bordering on reverence, he held out his open palms, and she lowered the stone into them.

"Flower," he whispered, holding it up to his face. He sniffed at the cloth blossom, and she felt a pang of sadness, afraid he'd be disappointed there was no scent of flowers. Instead, he broke into a huge grin. He sniffed again and sighed with contentment.

Maybe in his mind, the flower smelled like something from his lost garden. She hoped so.

A clattering sound came from behind her, and she spun around in time to see a flash of fire disappearing from the doorway.

Chaos. She leaped to her feet and ran from the room. If he was planning on causing this poor man any harm, she'd take his dagger and . . . well she'd do something with it that he wouldn't like.

Outside, she saw the fire elemental disappearing around a bend in the tunnel. "Stop!" she shouted, racing as fast as she could. She turned the corner and found the Pyrinth glaring at her.

It wasn't Chaos, though. It was Magma.

"Why were you spying on me?" she demanded, moving so close to the beast that she had to crane her neck to stare up at him.

"Why were you bothering that human?" he snarled. "I

told you to leave them alone."

Turnip felt her face grow hot. "I was trying to help."

"By torturing him the way you did the woman?"

"No. I . . ." Her plan sounded stupid now that she had to say it out loud. "He asked me for a flower. I think because he misses his garden. I couldn't find one, so I made a flower. Out of a piece of rock and some fabric from my gown."

The minotaur looked at her torn hem. He glanced back the way she had come.

"I know it was dumb," she said. "It's just that they're all alone, and no one is helping them. I thought it was the least I could do."

The minotaur stared at her for a moment, slammed his mace into one hand so hard it looked like it would rip his arm from its socket, and spun around. Without another word, he raced out of sight.

Had she done something wrong again? She'd only been trying to help. How had she messed up?

"Wait," she called, running after him. She was tired of being confused. If they didn't want her to cause any more trouble, one of them needed to explain what she'd done. But when she reached the end of the passageway, Magma was gone.

She headed right, but found herself in an empty cavern. Retracing her steps, she went left. Soon she came to another fork. Which should she go? The fire elementals' home was like a huge maze. She had no idea how they managed to avoid getting lost.

With no clue where she was or how to get back to where she'd started, she explored one path after another. More than once, she was almost positive that she was walking the same passage over and over. She had no concept of how long she'd been looking or how far she'd come. Time seemed strange here, and her legs never got tired or sore.

She'd reached an intersection that looked like hundreds she'd already passed when she thought she heard voices coming from her right. Following the sound, she descended a gently spiraling passage to the foot of some stairs she was sure she'd never seen.

Staying close to the wall, she crept up the steps, and the voices came clearer. It sounded like the Pyrinths were arguing. She made out more voices than the three she knew, and some sounded female. Were there female Pyrinths too?

After dropping to her hands and knees, she crawled up one stair at a time.

"There's no reason to bring her here," said a deep voice, which might have belonged to Magma.

"You don't think she'll find us on her own?" a female voice asked. "You said yourself that she's been exploring more than any of the others."

"What if she riles them up?" a third voice asked.

"They could come here themselves."

"Perhaps she is the one."

"There is no *one*."

"The book says—"

"The book says whatever you want it to. You can't read it any more than the rest of us can."

She couldn't keep track of who was speaking, but were they talking about her? Slowly, she climbed to the top of the stairs. As she did, a short section of tunnel leading into a huge, open cavern came into view. Dozens—maybe hundreds—of fire elementals glared and snarled at one another.

A creature that looked more like a plant than an animal, except for the lobster-like pinchers on the ends of its arms, waved a fiery claw. "Throw her in," the creature said in a high-pitched voice. "If she doesn't come out, she isn't the one."

Magma swung a fist that the plant creature barely avoided. "How about we throw you in?" he snarled, to general laughter around the room.

"We aren't throwing anyone in," Prudentes said. "It doesn't work that way. She has to choose to go in."

"Why would she do that?" asked a lumpy dog-looking thing, although it took Turnip a moment to realize that the dog thing was the one doing the speaking, because his words seemed to come from what she'd thought was the dog's tail.

Chaos turned in Turnip's direction. She ducked, but it was too late. He pointed straight at her and said, "Ask her for yourself."

CHAPTER 16

INTO THE FIRE

Turnip slowly rose from her crouch as the eyes of all the Pyrinths turned to her. None of them looked friendly except for Chaos, who wore his typical broad grin. "Didn't I tell you she would come? That's my girl."

She licked her lips, clasping her hands in front of her. "I heard voices."

"She's a baby," someone said.

"They all look like babies," said another. "So do you."

The first elemental jabbed a finger in the other's eye, and the two of them, locked in combat, rolled out of sight.

Turnip took one step forward and then another. The floor had a warped look as if the rock had melted and hardened over and over again in waves.

When she was about to enter the room, Magma blocked her way, his brows lowered like a granite shelf over his eyes. "Go away."

Chaos stepped forward, dagger drawn. "You heard

old scale face. She can do what she wants."

Magma raised a fist. "This is your fault."

Prudentes put a hand on each of the fire elementals' shoulders and studied Turnip with slow, blinking eyes. "Did anyone ask you to come here?"

She shook her head. "I found you myself."

A series of oohs and ahhs came from the room, and Prudentes pushed Chaos and Magma aside. "Let her through."

As she entered the room, all of the fire elementals stepped back. She glanced curiously around the cavern, the largest she'd seen by far—perhaps as big as all of the other rooms combined. At one end, a huge blue-and-orange tornado of fire swirled with loud, crackling flames. The Pyrinths followed her gaze with a kind of awe in their eyes.

She turned to Magma. "You were talking about me, weren't you?"

"Yes," Chaos said.

Magma dropped a shoulder into Chaos's chest, pushing him backward. "No we weren't."

Prudentes held his book beneath his chin like some kind of talisman. "What do you want?"

"To find out why I'm here," she said at once.

"See?" Chaos jabbed his dagger toward her. "She's the one." The Pyrinths standing behind him nodded, and a few even cheered.

"She's not," Magma said. A few of the fire elementals

murmured agreement, but most of them hissed and shook their heads.

Turnip had no idea what they were talking about, and she was sick of veiled references she didn't understand. "What *one*?" she asked. "Tell me who you think I am. What do you think I'm supposed to do?"

Prudentes nodded. "Yes. You deserve to know." He opened the book, and flames spilled out. "According to the Word of Fire, one will come to free us all."

Magma snorted. "You don't know if it actually says that. You're guessing."

Angry murmurs came from the crowd, stopping only when he turned to them and bared his fangs.

"Free you from what?" Turnip asked.

"From this," the lizard said, waving an arm around the room. "From Fire Keep. Our prison."

"Our *home*," Magma muttered. But no one was listening to him.

Turnip nodded. "How do I free you?"

"Enter the vortex and open the gate," Chaos said, his eyes glittering as he glanced toward the spinning tornado of fire.

Turnip looked at the swirling tornado of flames, which rose nearly to the ceiling. Her heart thudded against her chest.

"She doesn't have to—" Magma began.

"I want to know what this is all about," Turnip said,

cutting him off. "Then I'll decide for myself." She looked for a place to sit and found a stone bench. "Tell me everything."

Prudentes stepped forward, and the rest of the elementals moved back. He cleared his throat, thin tongue flicking in and out. "According to the Word, when the elementals were created, they were divided from one another. Water hid from man to avoid his folly. Land went beneath the ground to gather and learn. Air became trapped above the clouds as a punishment for their cruelty, and Fire was locked away . . ." He paused before continuing, not quite as confidently. "Locked away because we were a danger to all."

Turnip sat up straight. "A danger?"

"The book is unclear sometimes," Chaos said. "One word may have a dozen different meanings. *Danger* could mean we were simply unknown or confusing."

"*Now* the book is unclear," Magma said.

Prudentes glared at them both. "It does appear that we were locked away because of our unpredictability—our tempers. But the book says that a time would come when the elements would be gathered to perform a great feat. When that time comes, one from outside our world will arrive to open the gates and free us."

That felt right somehow. That's why she was here. She wasn't sure how she knew, but she did. She stood up. "I'll do it."

As she walked toward the flames, a cheer went up from the crowd, but Magma grabbed her by the shoulder. "Don't."

"Why not?" She twisted to pull out of his grip. "You want me to spend the rest of my life trapped here? Why don't you want me to open the gates?"

He squeezed his Mace until the handle cracked. "Because the vortex will destroy you before you ever get the chance."

———◆———

"What do you mean, 'too late'?" Marcus asked, his eyes locked on Kyja's image.

The Master got up from the table, walked over, and placed an icy hand on Marcus's elbow. "Right now you have a chance to bring her back. You can restore her to full health this very minute."

"So you can *kill* her?" Marcus spat.

"I promise that if you bring her back, I will make sure that not a single hair on her head is harmed. I give you my solemn word."

Kyja, who had been walking toward the flames, stopped and looked up at the horned creature holding the mace. The sight of her made Marcus's heart ache so badly, he thought it would shatter into a billion tiny shards. But *dark magic*? He couldn't.

"If, however, you fail to reach her before she enters that pyre of death, she will be beyond the power of my magic." The wizard squeezed Marcus's elbow like a vise.

Marcus turned to Graehl. "Is it true?"

The man nodded, his eyes locked on Marcus's. "Not even dark magic will not bring her back if she enters the flames."

Magma shook his head, horns slicing the air. "The vortex will destroy you."

"Don't listen to him," Chaos said. "He has no idea what will happen."

Magma slammed his mace into Chaos's chest, sending him reeling across the room.

"What are you doing?" Turnip shouted, slapping at the minotaur's arm. "I'm not afraid of fire. It doesn't hurt me here."

"Don't you think we'd have entered the vortex if that were made of normal fire? It's not. The vortex is a gateway to the outside world. But the gates are locked with magic. You can't get past them."

She turned to Prudentes, a question in her eyes.

"It's true," the lizard said. "The gates are protected by powerful magic meant to keep us in. Without magic . . ." He shrugged his scaly shoulders. "I don't see how you can survive."

She tugged at the sleeves of her gown. "Maybe the book is wrong. Maybe I can get through. If I can't, I'll come back."

Magma snorted. "You can't come back. The vortex is a one-way path. Everyone who has tried to go through has been destroyed. They aren't telling you to enter because they think you'll be any different. They want you to go in because they are stupid and selfish, and they don't care whether you destroy yourself or not."

She balled her hands into fists. "And if I stay? What then?"

He opened his mouth, then closed it.

"Tell me, what I'm supposed to do if I stay here? Tell me where I'll go, what my life will be like."

Magma had no answer for her.

"I'd rather be destroyed than stay locked here forever." She started toward the vortex.

Marcus watched as Kyja turned from the fire elemental and walked toward the flames. "I'll do it," he said.

Graehl looked up.

"You asked if I'm willing to do hard things to save Kyja. The answer is yes."

"*Hard things*," Graehl repeated. Why didn't he look

happy? This was what he wanted, wasn't it?

The wizard grinned and took both of Marcus's hands—the healthy one and the withered. "You will have power beyond your imagining. You will be able to have anything you want. Health, strength, wealth. Nations will bow before you."

"I don't want any of that," Marcus said. "I only want to save Kyja. Show me how."

"Close your eyes," the Master said. "Think about what you want."

Marcus shut his eyes. He thought about everything he'd shared with Kyja. The first time they'd met, the time when he'd touched the Poison Polly and she'd laughed at his mangled attempt to talk with a numb mouth. How brave she'd been when they went up against the Summoner outside Water Keep. Floating down the river together. Helping the woman in Chicago. Kyja's rescuing him in Land Keep. The way she was kind to everyone. He imagined her green eyes and pale skin—the way her hair blew in the wind.

"Focus on what are trying to do." The wizard's voice sounded far away.

Bring her back, Marcus whispered inside his head. In his mind, he saw himself pulling her from Fire Keep and putting her soul back into her body. If he could do that one thing, nothing else mattered. She'd been willing to pay whatever price it took to go to Fire Keep; he'd do whatever it took to bring her back.

A sound like rushing wind filled his ears. He'd done magic before and recognized the power around him. In the past, he'd asked the elementals for help. But that wouldn't work this time. Light magic wasn't enough.

"Hard things," he muttered through gritted teeth.

"Now make it happen!" the Master shouted.

Marcus opened his eyes. Kyja had nearly reached the tower of flames. "No!" he howled. "No. You won't leave me again. Not this time."

Graehl was staring at him, and the Master was laughing, but none of that mattered. The only thing on his mind was saving Kyja.

He reached for magic, and the darkness came again, black and squirming, like a viper trying to force its way down his throat. This time, instead of fighting it, he gave in, and darkness flooded through his body like black ink.

"Hard things," he said, tasting bitterness in his mouth.

"Yes." The master laughed. "Yes!"

———◆———

"You don't have to do this," Magma said, following her toward the vortex. "What you did back there for those two humans, was . . ." He shook his massive head. "I've never seen anyone do something like that before. Who'll take care of them now?"

"*You* could." She stopped and placed a hand against his chest. "It has to be more rewarding than hitting people with that mace of yours."

"But you don't have any magic," he said. "How do you expect to survive?"

Words came to her again. She didn't know where they were from, but for some reason, she heard them in her mind spoken by a voice both wise and gentle. "Everything has magic in it. From the smallest insect to the mighty trees of Before Time."

"No." Magma grunted. "*We* don't."

As they reached the vortex, Turnip could feel the heat radiating off it. Not like the rest of the fires here, but a heat that burned all the way inside her. She wouldn't admit it out loud, but maybe Magma was right. She felt strongly that she needed to enter the vortex—that it's why she was here. But she also felt that she didn't have everything she needed to succeed; something was missing. And because of that, the magical flames would destroy her like they had destroyed everyone else who had tried to enter.

The rest of the Pyrinths had fallen back as they neared the magical flames, but Magma remained at her side, his fire dwarfed by the one in front of them.

Turnip reached up and patted him on chest. "You

have magic inside you. You just don't know it yet. But I think you can learn. If I don't come back, promise me that you'll try and find it."

She paused for a moment and looked around the room. It almost felt like there was someone standing beside her. Not understanding why she said it, she whispered, "This isn't a hard thing."

A sparkling red gem rolled down Magma's cheek. She wouldn't have thought it possible, but she was almost sure it was a tear. He reached out and gently took her hand. "Come back."

———◆———

The more the blackness filled Marcus, the more he was able to take in. The energy rushing into him was the most powerful thing he'd ever felt—pure, raw, and unfettered by conscience, morals, or values. He could see now that he'd been foolish to limit himself. Had he really thought it made sense for the elementals to decide what he could and couldn't do with magic?

"Yes," the Master whispered in his ear. "Do it. Do what you want."

Marcus laughed. He could see how every single thing he'd been struggling for could be accomplished. Saving Kyja would require no more than a command. He'd rip her from Fire Keep, and no one could stop him. If she'd been separated from her body too long, he could fix that, too.

After that, he could . . . he could do anything he wanted. He didn't need to fear the Summoners; he could control them. Their power was his. Same with the undead armies. They'd been torn from their graves with dark magic, and they could be sent back the same way.

Or not.

Why not use them to accomplish good? The Master might not agree with that, but Marcus thought he saw a way that the Master himself could be defeated. The first thing, of course, would be to take control of the four elements then open a permanent drift to Earth. When he'd done that, he and Kyja could go from one world to the other, fixing any problems that got in their way.

Master Therapass had seen this. How could he have given up dark magic, after realizing its power?

Kyja released the minotaur's hand. "Good bye."

She turned and stepped forward into the flames.

"Now," the Master said.

Marcus looked up and saw Kyja stepping into the

vortex. Gathering all of the power inside himself, he commanded the elementals to do his bidding. Distant voices seemed to scream inside his head, but he didn't care. They had to obey his will; they didn't have any choice. Did it hurt them to have their magic torn away? His stomach twisted at the thought, but he ignored it.

Sometimes you had to do hard things to get what you wanted.

You don't have to do this, a voice whispered in his head. It sounded like Kyja, but that was crazy. She was who he was doing this for.

Hard things.

He stared at her face as she stepped toward the flames.

"Get her," the Master said—his voice urgent. "Before it's too late."

Marcus remembered her standing on the cold streets of Chicago, giving a homeless woman their cloaks and money. Would she have accepted dark magic? She'd always wanted magic, but he knew she wouldn't take it. Not this way. He had to, though. It was his only chance to save her.

Hard things.

He reached out his arms and could actually feel his hands touch her shoulders. His heart pounded. Whatever it took. Whatever the price. He was willing to do hard things.

This isn't a hard thing, Kyja's voice whispered.

It wasn't. He'd expected dark magic to be hard, but once he let it inside, taking what he wanted was the easiest thing in the world. Sometimes doing the right thing was hard. But this was easy because . . .

It was the wrong thing.

As much as he wanted to save Kyja, he couldn't. Not like this.

Sometimes you had to do hard things.

He did the hardest thing he'd ever done in his life—he rejected the power. He forced the darkness out of him. He let go of the person he loved most in the world.

———◆———

Kyja stepped into the vortex, and the fire destroyed her.

CHAPTER 17

HARD THINGS

"What have you done?" The Master released Marcus's arm, and Marcus collapsed to the ground. His limbs convulsed, and he couldn't stop gagging. It was like he'd eaten a poisonous meal, managing to cough it back out only seconds before it killed him.

With a wave of his hand, the Master sent the table, chairs, and food smashing against the wall. Mirrors exploded outward, covering Marcus in glass and debris.

The wizard whirled around and advanced on Graehl, his face livid. "You told me he would save her!"

Graehl backed away, tripped over a broken chair, and nearly fell. "I thought he would. She was the most important thing to him."

"She still is," Marcus wheezed. He managed to push himself onto one elbow before the room started to fade in and out. "That's why I couldn't do it."

The Master's face had gone an icy gray, and his eyes

burned like coals. Marcus huddled on the floor, gasping. How had he ever thought the man looked like Master Therapass? "You have made a serious mistake," the dark wizard hissed.

Marcus clutched his stomach and sat up. "You can't get to Kyja anymore. No matter what you do to me, I won't help you." The thought that he'd allowed her to die again, made him sick inside. But he knew it's what Kyja would have wanted.

An invisible fist slammed him to the floor, and his head cracked against the dark tiles. "You think I need you?" the wizard asked, towering over him. He yanked Marcus's sleeve up, revealing the scar on his right shoulder. "What did your precious Master Therapass tell you about this?"

Marcus turned away. With Kyja gone, the dark Circle could go ahead and kill him now. It didn't matter.

The wizard grabbed him by the jaw and forced his head around. "You can talk on your own, or I can make you talk. The second way will be much more painful, I promise. What did my brother tell you about the scar?"

Marcus swallowed. His throat felt raw and bloody. What did it matter if he talked? It wasn't like he'd be telling the Master anything he didn't know. "It means I'm the one chosen to defeat you."

"Does it?" The wizard laughed and shoved Marcus's head back against the floor. He turned to Graehl. "My ring."

His head bowed, Graehl scurried forward. He handed the Master the same ring he'd used to call down the Summoner—the gold band with the symbol branded on Marcus's arm.

The Master slid the ring onto his finger. "Do you find it an interesting coincidence that your arm and my ring share the same mark?"

Marcus didn't know what to say.

"Would you like to know where yours came from?" The Master sat on a jeweled throne, which hadn't been there a moment before.

Did the Master really know about the scar, or was this another trick?

The wizard twisted the ring on his finger. "I'm sure that by now, you've figured out that one of the creatures in the scar is a Summoner."

Marcus nodded. He'd noticed the similarity the first time he saw a Summoner. "What about the other one?"

"The second creature doesn't exist. It's symbolic of the four elements."

He hadn't considered the possibility, but now that Marcus thought about it, he could see how it made sense. The head of a boar like Lanctrus-Darnoc, the tail of a fish to represent water, bird's wings for air, and a flaming sword. Land, water, air, and fire.

"So what? It means that the elements will never give in to you and your creatures."

"On the contrary. If you look more closely, you will see that the Summoner is vanquishing the elements. The symbol is a representation of my control over their magic."

"Whatever." Marcus shrugged, biting back a moan from the pain that the least movement caused. "You'd probably see a symbol of your victory in a bowl of creamed spinach." A weight pressed on his throat, and he barely gasped out, "I'm destined to destroy you."

"Destined by whom?" The Master laughed, and the weight lifted from Marcus's neck. "How do you think you got the mark in the first place? Do you think you were born with it—it's a sign that you are something special?"

Actually, Marcus had sort of assumed that he'd been born with the scar. No one had said any differently.

The wizard stood from his throne. "I'll tell you a secret," he said, gloating above Marcus. "I'm the one who branded you."

Marcus shook his head. That couldn't be.

"Yes. I found you as a baby. You seemed like a likely enough lad. So I snuck into your room in the middle of the night, burned my symbol into your arm, and claimed you as one of my own. I knew that eventually, you would come back to me."

"That's a lie," Marcus said, his face hot. "I'm the one who will defeat you."

"I found it quite amusing the way everyone fawned over you when they saw the mark. *The chosen one. The child from the legend who will save us.* Do you think they would have reacted the same way if they knew you wear the symbol of the one they fear the most?"

Marcus felt sick and exhausted. The Master's claims couldn't be right. Master Therapass had told him that the mark meant that Marcus was Farworld's savior.

"If you marked me, why did you try to kill me?"

"If I'd wanted to kill you as a baby, I would have. I told my armies to destroy each person in the city—every parent, every relative, every friend you had. I had them break your body until you could barely feed yourself. I shattered your spirit. I stole your self-worth. I took anything that might have meaning to you."

He circled Marcus, eyes glittering, and knelt to look into his face. "Of course, I must hand it to my brother. I *thought* I had taken everything from you. But he considered something I hadn't. He took your entire world. I knew that one day you'd come crawling back to it to join me like the worm you are."

"Was that before or after he cut your face?" Marcus asked, pointing at the Master's scar.

It was only a guess, but judging by the wizard's response, Marcus knew he was right. Before the Master could respond, Marcus spat in his face. The Master jerked back in surprise and revulsion.

"I may crawl, but I will never join you." Marcus reached for light magic, fighting past the dark slime that filled the room, and for a brief moment, he felt it find a way in—the smallest of cracks in the dark armor—and power began flowing through him.

Then he was hanging upside down in the middle of the air in a vise-like grip that crushed his chest so tightly he couldn't breathe. His heart struggled against the pressure, and each beat felt like the last.

"Time to finish what I should have done a long time ago," the Master said, pulling the cowl back over his head.

Tide, Nizgar-Gharat, and Calem strolled into the room, smug grins on their faces.

"I've been waiting a long time to see you die," Nizgar-Gharat's two heads said.

Tide plucked a fish from the school circling his crown and popped it into his mouth. "Any bets on whether he suffocates before his heart stops beating?"

Marcus tried to use magic, but it was blocked again. His head felt like a huge rock was smashing it, and his vision began to grow dark. But that was all right. If he was going to die, he'd want it to be while he was fighting against the Dark Circle, not fighting for them. And who knew—maybe he'd be with Kyja in the afterlife.

"Wait," Graehl said. "Don't kill him."

The Master raised a finger toward the man, but Graehl held out his hands. "Kill him, and another savior will be raised up. But there's a way to stop him for good. Something worse than death."

Marcus's eyes widened. Wasn't betraying him once enough? Couldn't Graehl let him die?

"No," he tried to moan, but he didn't have the breath.

"What are you talking about?" The Master demanded.

"Ask him," Graehl said. "He'll tell you everything."

Air filled Marcus's lungs again, and he sucked it into his body, his vision slowly coming back. As soon as he could speak, he said, "I don't know what he's talking about. It's a lie."

Graehl shook his head.

"We'll see." The Master did something then, and Marcus found himself standing on the floor—arms and legs locked stiffly at his sides, like a soldier standing at attention. "What's this about another savior?" the wizard asked.

Marcus tried to clamp his jaws shut, but it was impossible. "If I die, someone else will be born to take my place. The cycle has to be completed. Either I succeed, or someone else will."

The Master squinted. "That's not possible. I chose you."

"Lanctrus-Darnoc said it themselves," Graehl said. "They seemed to think you knew."

The Master turned to Nizgar-Gharat, hands clenched. "Did you know of this too?"

The lizard heads looked at each other uncomfortably. "We didn't spend as much time in the library as some of the others."

"Lanctrus-Darnoc was in the library all the time," Gharat said.

"If anyone knew, he would," Nizgar added.

The Master sucked a frustrated breath between his teeth and turned back to Marcus. "What else did they tell you?"

"That you are a pompous bag of wind," Marcus tried to say, but his mouth betrayed him. "If I am on Farworld when Kyja d-dies, then I return to Farworld completely." He gave Graehl a desperate look. Marcus could understand his ex-friend kidnapping him in hopes of saving Kyja. But why did he have to reveal more?

"Go on," the Master said.

The words forced themselves from his lips. "If . . . I am in . . . the realm of shadows when she dies, I will be trapped on Earth."

Inside his cowl, the wizard's eyes glowed. "For how long?"

They didn't know? How could that be? Marcus tried to hold back the truth, but he couldn't do it. He dropped his head. "Forever."

The Master turned to the spot where the smoke had shown Kyja earlier. "She hasn't been destroyed completely yet, or the boy would have changed." He looked at the elementals. "How quickly can you get him to the cavern of the Unmakers?"

"Get him on a Summoner, and I will put wind beneath its wings," Calem said.

Tide rubbed his chubby hands together. "And I'll make a storm."

Now that Marcus wasn't forced to answer questions, he found that he could talk. "Please," he begged. "Let me die. It could be years before another savior is born."

The Master laughed. "I have no fear of a savior. I have no fear of anything. But the idea of your spending the rest of your life trapped on that disgusting planet is too good to pass up." He waved to the elementals. "Take him." Then to Graehl, "As for you . . ." The Master raised his hand, and a gleaming, black dagger appeared in it.

Graehl stepped away. "I've done everything you asked. Brought the boy. Told you his secrets. I betrayed everyone exactly the way you told me to."

"Yes, you did," the Master said, his voice icy. "But I'm afraid I have little use for traitors." He flicked his wrist, and the razor-sharp blade flew across the room, where it implanted itself in Graehl's chest.

Marcus gasped. Though Graehl had betrayed him, he didn't want him to die.

Graehl grasped the dagger with both hands as if trying to pull it out. A dark stain appeared on the front of his robe, and he moaned softly. As if in slow motion, he turned his head and locked eyes with Marcus. A second before Graehl fell dead to the floor he mouthed the words, "Hard things."

CHAPTER 18

THE REALM OF SHADOWS

Marcus didn't bother struggling against the elementals as they dragged him through the cold, wet caves of the Windlash Mountains. The last time he'd been here, the Unmakers had tried to suck out his emotions. But the Master had done a better job of doing that than the invisible creatures ever could.

He tried to imagine being trapped on Earth, with no hope of seeing Kyja, Riph Raph, Master Therapass, or any of his Farworld friends again. Stuck in a world where his magic made him a freak and people stared at his arm and leg with pity or scorn—and all the while, knowing that Farworld was being destroyed by the Dark Circle. The thought made him want to curl up in a ball and freeze to death on the icy floor.

"Where's your cocky attitude now?" Calem jeered.

"Kind of makes you wish you'd kept your nose in your own business." The Aerisian briefly turned his body into a mass of animal noses, all sniffling and sneezing at the same time.

Marcus looked away. Whether the elementals were blocking his magic anymore or not, the battle was over, and he'd lost. Graehl had talked about doing hard things. Marcus had tried, but look how they'd all ended up because of it.

It wasn't like he had any hope of rescue, either. No one knew where he was. And if they did, the creatures protecting the entrance—ghastly monsters the color of raw meat, with gray, membraned wings and arms like an octopus—could have held off a small army.

As they turned into another passage, all three elementals slowed down. A sucking wind tugged at Marcus's hair, and he raised his head to see that the tunnel ended in an unfocused swirl of grays and blacks. Tendrils of smoke stretched out from the opening like ghostly fingers beckoning them forward. A blue bird—apparently startled by their voices—flapped into the tunnel behind them, fluttered in the wind, and circled away with a frightened chirp.

Nizgar-Gharat flapped their wings and hissed. "Can't we push him forward and let it suck him in?" the purple head suggested.

"Let's kill him and say we put him through the

opening," the green head said. "I don't like this place."

Tide swung at the lizards with the back of his hand. "The Master told us to dump him into the realm of shadows, and that's what we're going to do."

Calem, who had turned his body into a thick-trunked tree, dug his roots into the floor of the tunnel. "You all go ahead. I'm not getting any closer. Don't you feel the way it wants to take whatever it can?"

"All I feel is what the Master will do to us if we don't obey orders," Tide said, rubbing his hands on his robe. "Which one of you wants to tell him you failed?"

Marcus understood their fear. The wind blowing them toward the doorway felt like the inhalation of some great beast, and the more he stared at the rotating circle, the more it looked like a mouth with scraggly gray teeth and a black throat. Back when he and Kyja had fought the Dark Circle together, it would have terrified him. All he felt now was a sense of inevitability.

"We'll do it together," Tide said, taking one of Marcus's arms. "You two grab him."

Nizgar-Gharat snatched Marcus's other arm and Calem reluctantly wrapped a tree branch around his legs. Together the three of them hoisted Marcus into the air. Holding him in front of them like a shield, they edged toward the opening.

"You're all a pack of cowards," Marcus said.

Gharat flicked his tail. "If you're so brave, go on your

own." They took another step toward the opening, and the pull of the wind grew stronger.

The leaves on Calem's body began snapping off and whirling into the portal. The little bird flapped around Calem, as if looking for a place to land, and Marcus silently urged it to leave before it got pulled in too.

Marcus squinted against the bits of rock and dirt battering his face. "I'm not talking about the door. I'm taking about the Dark Circle. Kyja and I did a lot of things that scared us. But we did them because we knew they were the right thing to do. You're only obeying the Master because you're terrified of him, not because you believe in him."

"I believe," Tide said, holding his crown down with one hand. "I believe that it's better to be on the side of the strongest and smartest than to be standing against him."

They edged another step closer to the opening, and Nizgar-Gharat's wings suddenly bent forward like an umbrella snapped inside out by a storm.

"That's it!" Nizgar shouted. "We aren't going any farther."

The land elementals released Marcus's arm. Tide did the same, and Calem flung Marcus toward the portal. His body floated for a moment, like the scene from the Wizard of Oz where Dorothy's house gets lifted into the air, and then an immense force took hold of him.

Right before Marcus was pulled through, the bird

dove toward him. He tried to wave it away, but both of them were spinning and falling—not down, but sideways.

———◆———

"Ge omf mer," a muffled voice said.

"Huh?" Marcus rubbed his eyes, and something moved under him. He jerked away, thinking it was a spider or something worse.

"Get off me," a familiar voice said. Marcus moved his arm, and the bird that been fluttering around the cave hopped out from beneath him and fluffed its wings. "Do you have any idea how much you weigh?"

"Riph Raph?"

Other than the blue color, the bird looked nothing like the skyte, but the voice was unmistakable.

"No. I'm Master Therapass in disguise," the bird snapped. "See the gray beard growing under my beak."

Marcus would have recognized that sarcastic tone anywhere. It was Riph Raph. He thought he'd never see the skyte again. He wrapped the bird in a one-armed hug.

"Stop squeezing me," Riph Raph chirped, "or I'll peck your eyes out."

"How did you get here?" Marcus laughed, releasing the skyte. "How did you know where to look for me?"

"I'll tell you after you turn me back into myself," Riph Raph said crankily. "I keep getting this insatiable urge to sing. Besides, I want my fireballs back. I don't like the look of this place."

Marcus looked around. He was lying near the curb of a large city street. Tall, dark buildings were outlined by a darker sky. A yellowed newspaper flapped in the gutter.

"Are we back on Earth?" How could that be? The Master had meant to send him into the realm of shadows. The only way he could be back on Earth was if . . .

"Definitely not Earth." Riph Raph's blue head bobbed to the right. "Unless Earth has *those*."

Marcus turned to see a large bubble rising out of the middle of the street. The bubble pulsated in and out for a moment, then headed straight toward them like a sea monster swimming through the ocean. He'd definitely never seen anything like that on Earth.

"What is it?" Marcus asked, scooting away.

"No idea," Riph Raph said, flying into the air. "I'm guessing it's not coming to offer a welcome-to-the-neighborhood gift."

Marcus tried to stand before realizing he didn't have his staff. He searched the street for it, but either the elementals hadn't thrown it in after him, or it had landed somewhere else. He glanced over his shoulder, hoping that whatever was moving beneath the street had gone in another direction. But it was close and coming straight toward him. It was bigger now too, stretching the surface of the street like a whale coming up for air.

With trembling arms and legs, Marcus scooted down the street.

"Faster!" Riph Raph shouted from overhead. "It's getting close."

As though sensing its prey was near, the creature sped up, rising higher and higher.

"Try this," Riph Raph said, swooping over something discarded in the street. Sliding himself forward with his good leg and arm, Marcus found a piece of metal that looked like it might once have been a fence post. It was rusted and bent, but it looked solid enough to hold his weight.

He propped it under one arm, and pushed himself to his feet. The creature was right behind him now. He could feel the asphalt thrumming beneath him. How could it push the street up like that without cracking it?

"Cast a spell," Riph Raph called, swooping and diving. "I'd burn it to a cinder, but birds don't have fireballs."

Magic! He'd been blocked for so long that he'd almost forgotten he had it. Did magic work in the realm of shadows? Only one way to find out. Pointing his good hand toward the bubble, which now towered a good ten feet higher than his head, he called for the elements of fire and air to blast it with a bolt of electricity.

Welcome power flowed through his body, and a bright-blue light flashed from the sky, piercing the bubble like a needle through a balloon. Black gunk sprayed everywhere. A drop of it splashed on his skin and burned him before he could brush it off.

Riph Raph did a loop-the-loop in the air, tweeting triumphantly. "That's right. Don't mess with me and my boy. We'll cook you like yesterday's leftovers. We'll batter you, fry you, and serve you up for dinner."

"Riph Raph, we may want to get out of here," Marcus said pointing down the street. He'd managed to zap the creature closest to him, but the noise or the magic must have woken more. Marcus counted two black bubbles, then three, four, five. Everywhere, black shapes rose, and all of them were headed in his direction.

He glanced around and spotted a narrow alleyway between two soot-stained buildings. "Over here," he said, hobbling onto the sidewalk and toward the alley.

As he crossed the sidewalk, he kicked a shattered black-and-gray lump with wires sticking out of one end. He paused for a moment, eyes locked on the piece of junk. It had buttons and a tiny controller—the kind he and his friends had used thousands of times. He could almost swear that this was a broken video game controller—from an old PlayStation maybe, or an Xbox. But what was a game controller that had clearly come from Earth doing in the realm of shadows?

Riph Raph, who had been dive bombing the first bubble, telling it what they'd do to it the next time it dared to mess with them, spotted the rest of the bubbles closing in and squawked. "We're leaving now. But don't think it's because we're scared. We've proved our point, and, um . . . good bye."

Marcus looked behind him, and his throat tightened. The entire street was filled with bubbles like waves on a black ocean. Ignoring the controller, he hurried into the alley. Other than trash and an occasional dirty brick, there was nothing—no place to hide. Cracked and broken windows looked down on them like empty eye sockets, all too high for him to reach. If the bubbles followed them into the alley, they'd be in trouble.

"Over here," Riph Raph said, swooping toward an opening in the building. The bubbles weren't following yet, but that didn't mean they wouldn't.

Marcus reached the opening—a narrow doorway— and paused to catch his breath. "I'm not so sure about this."

The door, no longer attached to its hinges, lay in shattered pieces a few feet inside the dark entrance. Odd graffiti covered the walls and floor around the opening.

> *The reaping comes.*
> *Creepers creep.*
> *You feed me.*
> *No way out.*

What did any of it mean? A foul smell came from the room—a combination of burned wood and something chemical. Marcus created a baseball-sized flame that hovered in the middle of the room. What it revealed was at least as bad as the smell. A dried puddle of something dark stained the center of the floor, the walls were covered with oozing mold, and a metal staircase leading upward was bent and covered with rust.

"Maybe we should look for something a little more . . . welcoming?" Riph Raph suggested.

"My thoughts exactly." Marcus said. He turned to continue farther, when a shrill whistling sound cut through the air. He spun around, sure that the bubbles were coming. The tar-like creatures were still crowded around the entrance to the alley.

The sound came again—a high-pitched whistle. The kind of sound people made at sporting events or to get someone's attention by sticking their fingers in the mouth and blowing. Why did the whistle sound so familiar, and why did it send icy fingers down the back of his neck?

"I've heard that sound before," Riph Raph said.

"I know." Marcus edged back toward the door. "I can't quite remember—"

A insect-like shape the size of a large dog hopped into the other end of the alley, and Marcus felt his legs grow weak. All at once, he remembered where he'd heard the sound before and why it terrified him.

"Snifflers," he moaned.

CHAPTER 19

GLOSING IN

Wrinkling his nose at the stench, Marcus ducked through the doorway into the room, hoping the creature hadn't seen him. He peeked out and looked from one end of the alley to the other. They were trapped between the bubble creatures collecting in the street and the sniffler hopping in his direction. He remembered all too well the way one of the snifflers had attached itself to him and sucked away his magic when he and Kyja had been searching for Land Keep. He couldn't let that happen again.

He pointed to the roof of the building across from them. "Fly up there and wait for me."

Riph Raph landed on Marcus's shoulder and pecked his ear. "After what happened last time, you think I'll let you go? I don't think so."

"What are you going to do against a sniffler? *Sing* it to death?"

Riph Raph puffed out his feathers. "Just because I don't have my fire doesn't mean I don't know a dozen other ways to kill. I am a living weapon."

Marcus didn't have time to argue. "Fine. But if you end up getting baked in a pie or something, don't blame me." He tried to memorize the layout of the room before putting out his flame.

"As the room was plunged into darkness Riph Raph squawked, "Are you crazy? How are we supposed to get away if we can't see where we're going?"

Marcus tapped his metal pole in front of him, heading in the direction of the stairs. Outside, the whistling was getting louder. Was there more than one sniffler?

"They can sense magic," he whispered. "I think that might have been what attracted whatever was under the streets. The less magic I use, the better chance we have of losing them."

His pole clanged on the metal staircase at the same time his hip banged against the railing. Putting his weight on the pole, he raised his left foot onto the first step and dragged his bad leg behind him. The stairs gave an ominous groan under his weight. "I really think you should go on your own," he said, trying the next step. "This whole thing could collapse beneath me at any time."

Riph Raph's talons tightened on Marcus's shoulder. "All the more reason for me to stay. Who else will drag you out of the rubble?"

Marcus smiled at the thought of the tiny bird trying to lift him. With his good hand clutching the pole, Marcus had no way of holding the rail. Instead, he leaned against the wall, trying not to think about the wet green coating he'd seen earlier.

They'd barely reached the first landing when clicking sounds came from below. "It's here," he said, so softly he could barely hear his own voice. He felt the bird's body shift in acknowledgment.

He tried to keep his footsteps silent as he turned and started up the next staircase, but his bad foot clanged against the riser, echoing in the darkness. Immediately, the sniffler's high-pitched call filled the air. Worse, the whistle was followed by a wet smacking and a deep voice that said, "I smell magic."

"Unmakers," Marcus muttered through gritted teeth. He tried to push himself harder, but he was already gasping for breath, and his legs shook. Below them, the metal stairs clanged.

Ignoring the sweat pouring down his back, he focused on keeping his legs moving. Pain burned in his calves and thighs. Maybe the creatures would have a hard time climbing the steps.

The stairs clanged again—closer this time. So much for that hope. Reaching the second landing, he banged his pole to the side, hoping for a door, but the wall continued uninterrupted. As he started up the next set of steps, something thudded below, and the entire staircase shuddered.

"You can't escape," the Unmaker's voice called.

Marcus's strength was rapidly disappearing, and although he couldn't see the creatures, the clanging was growing louder and louder, and the excited whistles were so close that he imagined he could reach out and feel the sniffler's tentacles stretching toward him.

"Change me back to a skyte," Riph Raph said.

"No time." Marcus wiped his sweaty face on the sleeve of his robe and gasped for air.

"*Change me.*" Riph Raph gave Marcus's shoulder an urgent peck. "They haven't seen us yet. They only sense magic."

Marcus felt a chill as he realized what they skyte was suggesting. "I won't let you act as bait."

"I'm going one way or the other," Riph Raph chirped angrily. "Will you change me back so I at least have fire to protect myself?"

"I'll try," Marcus said. "But I might screw it up." He wasn't sure he knew how. He thought back to everything he'd learned from the elementals. Maybe a combination of land and air magic would work?

"Master Therapass told me you'd be able to do it," Riph Raph said. "Just don't turn me into a lizard, or I'll never forgive you."

Was Master Therapass the one who'd sent Riph Raph to find him? How did the wizard know where he'd be? And why send the skyte? Marcus was missing something— something big. But he didn't have time to figure it out now.

Closing his eyes, he focused on remembering exactly what Riph Raph looked like as a skyte—how he moved and flew. The sniffler sounded like it was right on top of him, but he didn't dare look.

Hoping he was doing it right, he touched Riph Raph and let magic flow through his hands. Instantly, the texture under his fingers changed from feathers to scales, and the weight on his shoulder increased.

The talons, now larger and sharper, released his shoulder, and he opened his eyes in time to see three blue fireballs burst down the stairs.

"See me and be afraid!" Riph Raph screamed, diving straight at the eyes of the sniffler. Blinded by the unexpected attack, the creature leaped backward on its insectile legs.

Something thudded against the wall, and the Unmaker cried out, "Get off me. Seek the magic."

"You want magic?" Riph Raph shouted. "I'll give you magic."

Celebrating his return to skyte form, he spat out so many fireballs that it reminded Marcus of a fireworks show. Using the glow of the explosions to light his way,

Riph Raph flew over the creatures and down the stairs.

"Hate to tell you, you spell-sucking simpletons, but magic has left the building!"

Marcus wanted to protect Riph Raph, but the best thing he could do for them both was to escape while the shadow creatures were distracted by the skyte's exploits. He waited until he heard the sniffler charge back down the stairs, then began climbing again. Every step was torture, but he couldn't afford to stay put if the creatures came back.

As he reached the third landing, he noticed a sliver of gray light. A metal door was propped a few inches open. He pushed his shoulder against it. With a low whine, the door swung outward. Flakes of rust and dirt showered onto his head, but he didn't care. The important thing was finding somewhere to hide.

The hallway beyond the door was dimly lit, which might have been for the best. Some kind of creatures had been here, gnawing the wood and metal of the floors and walls into jagged shards. Their dried droppings were scattered around in little faintly glowing piles, which smelled like motor oil. He heard scurrying in front of him and behind. He suspected that if he created more light, he'd see things that made the spider in his Dark Circle prison cell look like a fuzzy bunny.

Halfway down the hall, he found another door, this one mostly intact. The room beyond it had a solid floor and walls that were only *mostly* covered with mold. Given the other options he'd seen so far, this might be the best he could hope for. He used a plank of wood from a corner to jam the door closed.

There was no need to open the room's single window; it only had a few dirt-grimed spears of glass in one corner. Keeping far enough back that he hoped nothing outside could see in, he peeked out to the alley below—no sign of the sniffler or Riph Raph. Which didn't mean it was safe. An entire army of Unmakers could be down there, and he wouldn't have any idea until they sucked away his magic.

He leaned a little more forward, when a dark shape hurtled through the window and plummeted straight into him. He was reaching for magic when the shape landed on the floor and glared at him.

"Are you *trying* to give yourself away?"

Marcus collapsed to the floor and grinned. "Riph Raph."

"Don't 'Riph Raph' me," the skyte said, sniffing the walls with clear distaste. "Do you have any idea what's out there?"

Marcus shook his head.

"No, you don't. Because you can't fly. But I can. You're lucky to have me around."

Marcus tapped the skyte gently on the head with his knuckles. "Are you going to tell me what's out there? Or should I take a nap until you're done bragging?"

"You want to know what's out there, waiting to devour you like a boy burrito?"

Marcus waited.

"Kyja appreciated me," the skyte said. He scratched behind one of his ears. "Fine. I'll tell you. Five or six snifflers, and at least a couple of Unmakers—you can sort of see glimmers from them when the light is right—plus a couple of dozen soldiers in black leather uniforms."

Marcus sat up straight. "What kind of soldiers?"

"The kind that carry weapons and run around looking like they want to hurt somebody. I led them a couple of blocks in the other direction before flying into a building and circling back out the other side. They should be searching in the wrong place for at least a little while."

"Good thinking," Marcus said, rubbing a hand between the skyte's wings. The realm of shadows was nothing like he'd expected. In the past, all he'd seen of it was a gray mist. But these buildings looked almost like Earth skyscrapers. And then there was the controller, which he was almost sure had come from an Earth video-game console. "When you say *weapons*, are you talking about magical weapons or ordinary swords?"

Riph Raph flicked his tail. "They aren't Farworld weapons. They're the kind we saw in the Earth shop where Kyja sold the gem."

Marcus remembered the pawn shop where he, Kyja, and Riph Raph had gone to raise money on her first trip to

Earth. It had been almost completely filled with power tools and guns. "If they have guns, we need to find a way back to Farworld. Master Therapass sent you here; he must have given you some kind of clue to how we can escape."

Riph Raph spotted a beetle-like insect crawling along a floorboard and stalked toward it. "No. He turned me into a bird, said you could change me back, and told me to fly to the place in the Windlash Mountains where Graehl had captured us when he was a cave trulloch."

That didn't make any sense. If the wizard sent Riph Raph to the Unmakers cavern, he obviously knew that the Dark Circle would be taking Marcus there. But why not send a rescue party or plan an escape? What good was a single skyte?

Riph Raph snatched the bug in his beak, crunched it, and immediately spat it back out. "What kind of bugs do they have here?" he asked, making a face. "I've tasted better things scraped off the soles of shoes."

Marcus made a gagging noise.

"What? We skytes are known for our amazing fighting skills—not our taste buds." Riph Raph wiped his tongue on the back of one leg. "There was something else he mentioned, though."

"What?" Marcus leaned forward.

Riph Raph flapped his ears in concentration. "Hmmm. A note, maybe."

"He gave you a note? Why didn't you tell me?"

"He didn't give me a note. Or if he did, I must have lost it." Riph Raph studied the bug again before turning away regretfully. "Maybe he mentioned one. Maybe not."

Marcus slammed his hand on the floor, sending up a plume of dust. "Which is it? Did he give you a note, or didn't he?"

"I don't remember. It was hard to think as a bird. Their brains are so tiny, and all they think about is seeds and worms." Riph Raph ran his tongue over the tip of his beak. "Of course, now that I think of it, a worm does sound pretty good."

Marcus put his head in his hand. He was trapped in a world of creatures that ate magic and men that carried guns, he might be pulled to Earth at any second, and his only hope of escape was a lost note that might or might not have ever existed. What could be worse?

In the distance, a high-pitched whistling floated on the air.

CHAPTER 20

TOO MANY QUESTIONS

Turnip stepped into the vortex and the spinning fire ripped her into a hundred pieces—a thousand. Her body, mind, and soul were split into millions of fragments that combined with millions of other fragments from all the creatures that had entered the flames before her. Voices screamed and she was overwhelmed by the shared sense of shock and fear of those who had disappeared into flame. Like them, she could never be gathered and put back together after the flames had pulled her apart.

And then she was.

Whole again.

But how? She *knew* the vortex had destroyed her as soon as she entered it. That's what its magic was designed to do. She'd heard the voices of everyone and everything the fire had eaten, had felt their pain, experienced the terror that had welled up within them when they realized there was no way out.

She looked down, expecting to find her limbs broken and bruised. But there wasn't a mark on her. She felt no pain, no fear. Heard no voices. How had she survived when they hadn't?

"Hello?" She tried to look around, but couldn't make out anything beyond the light.

She tugged on the sleeves of her gown. "What am I supposed to do now?"

Marcus watched a pair of soldiers enter one end of the alley. They glanced at the doorway he and Riph Raph had come through, but didn't go inside. When they walked out of sight, he gave a sigh of relief. But it was only a matter of time before they'd be back. Riph Raph was right; they definitely had Earth guns strapped to their shoulders.

"Have you come up with a plan yet?" Riph Raph asked from a spot on the floor where he was sharpening his talons. "Or are you going to stand there looking out that window until someone discovers us?"

Marcus turned and limped across the room. "If *you* could remember what was in the note, maybe *I* could come up with a plan."

"I told you. I'm almost positive there wasn't a note."

"Then why did you mention one in the first place?"

The skyte dug a furrow in the floor. "The wizard said something about a note. I think. I don't remember what."

"How am I supposed to figure out anything from a note you can't remember?" Marcus ran his fingers through his hair. "Maybe you lost it,"

"I didn't lose it," the skyte snapped.

"Well whatever you did with it, it's not here. Which means I can't read it."

Riph Raph looked up, gold eyes wide. "*That's* what he said. He asked if you'd read the note."

"How could I have read something I don't have?"

The skyte blinked. "I have no idea."

Marcus paced around the room, the rusty pole thumping with each step. "We've gone over this so many times, I don't know what else to ask. He didn't give you a note. He didn't give me a note. So neither of us has read any note."

"Except for the one you found under your pillow."

Marcus froze, left foot in the air. The note Graehl had left him in the cabin. The one that had turned to ash after he'd read it. "Do you think *that's* what Master Therapass was talking about?"

"Could be."

What had it said? "Something about not trusting the wizard, I think."

"Because he wasn't telling you everything," Riph Raph added.

Marcus stared at him. "*Now* you can remember?"

Riph Raph flicked his floppy blue ears. "You told me about it when I was a skyte. Skytes are far more intelligent than birds, remember? I told you, our brains are, like, twenty times bigger."

"Okay, okay, good." Marcus lowered himself to the ground to think. "So the note said not to trust the wizard because he wasn't telling me everything. Master Therapass must have heard about the note, and he wanted to make sure I didn't fall for it. Because . . ." He pinched his lower lip, trying to think. "Because he knew Graehl had left it, and since Graehl was the one who kidnapped me, Master Therapass wanted to make sure I realized that Graehl was a liar and a traitor."

"Yeah, I don't think so."

Marcus stared at the skyte. "What?"

"I don't think that's it." With the tip of his tail, Riph Raph flicked the dead bug he'd tried to eat earlier, as if he were a cat playing with a ball of yarn. "It doesn't make sense."

After three hours of *Gosh, I don't know. Maybe there was a note or maybe there wasn't*, Riph Raph was suddenly some kind of master detective? Marcus tried to hold his temper, but it wasn't easy.

"*What* doesn't make sense?"

Riph Raph flicked the bug into the air and speared it with the tip of one talon. "For one thing, by the time the wizard talked to me about the note, Graehl had already taken you. Everyone knew he was a traitor. Therapass would only have needed to tell you that if he thought you were, um, not so sharp in the reasoning department."

Marcus had to admit he was right.

"For another thing, how would Therapass have known about the note? We were the only ones who read it."

True. The note had been hidden under his pillow. If someone else *had* discovered the paper, it wouldn't have meant anything to them, because the words hadn't appeared until Marcus had touched them. And it had burned up right after.

"Since you and I didn't tell Master Therapass, the only one who could have told him about the note was the person who wrote it. Why would Graehl tell me not to trust Master Therapass, and then tell Master Therapass he wrote the note?"

Had Graehl been trying to make the wizard trust him? Had he confided in someone else at the camp who then gave away his secret? Were more people than Graehl involved in the deceit? So many possibilities, but so few clues. Marcus tried to think, but it was hard with the threat of being discovered at any moment.

Riph Raph sniffed at the bug. "Maybe Graehl didn't write the note." He touched the bug with the tip of his tongue, made a face, and flicked it into the corner. "That's disgusting. It tastes like boogers."

Marcus looked up. "Say that again."

"That bug tastes like boogers. You know, the long, green kind you pull out of your nose when you have a cold and it's all backed up until—"

"Hush." Marcus stood up. "I asked Graehl about the note when he was taking me into the woods. He claimed not to know anything about it. I've been thinking it was another one of his lies. But what if it wasn't? What if . . ."

Like a match struck in a dark room, making everything clear, Marcus remembered something else that had happened the night he'd been kidnapped. Graehl had been carrying him back to his cabin. Marcus had screamed at the wizard, and the wizard had told him . . .

"*Sleep on my words,*" Marcus whispered. "He told me to sleep on his words, that sometimes you know the right thing to do, but you have to put your *finger* on it." He stared at Riph Raph, all of the pieces that had confused him finally coming together. "*Sleep on my words. Put your finger on it.* He was talking about the note. Master Therapass wrote me a note telling me not to trust what he said."

Holding her hands in front of her, Turnip stepped into the blinding light. She still thought she could hear traces of the voices that had filled her head moments before, but now they were only distant echoes, fading with every passing second.

Why hadn't the fire destroyed her? It should have. It was made to destroy those without magic, and clearly she had none.

Except . . . something was different about her. Turnip had felt the vortex try to react with her body, and then . . . pull back. In some way, it couldn't tear her apart the way it had done to everyone else. She felt like she should know why, only the reason was lost with everything else she couldn't remember.

She walked through the light for what seemed like a very long time. Unable to see in any direction, she might have been passing through deserts, mountains, or forests. She might have been within arm's reach of monsters, traps, or unknown dangers of any kind. She might have been walking in circles. But she wasn't. She felt an odd assurance that she was going the right way.

At last, the light began to fade—or maybe her eyes had finally adjusted to the brightness. In the distance, a dark rectangle came into view. As she drew closer, she made out a door—twice as tall as she was and nearly as wide as it was tall—made from the same black stone as Fire Keep.

In the center of the door was a flaming symbol, which again tugged at the memories she couldn't recall. Standing on tiptoes, she traced her finger along the shape, which had a loop on one end and a sort of curlicue on the other. For some reason, the word *water* came into her head—although there wasn't any water to be seen.

She stepped back and studied the door. Was this one of the gates the fire elementals had told her about? If so, trying to enter it without magic might be the most dangerous thing she could do. She could still go back. Now that she knew the vortex wouldn't destroy her, she might be able to learn more that would help her here. Maybe she could convince the lizard to let her read his book. And there were plenty of other people she could help.

She looked back the way she had come, and something on the floor caught her attention. It was a blue ball—her retinentia. It must have followed her into the vortex. But something was different about it. The magical flames, which hadn't affected her, had cracked the surface of the globe in so many places that the clouds inside were only blue blurs. It was a wonder the ball was still holding together at all. Even now, it shivered slightly, and another crack, larger than the others, ran across one side.

Those were her memories. The Pyrinths had warned her against viewing them. That her nightmares were better left alone. But what if the globe contained something she needed to know? So many times since she'd awoken in Fire Keep, she'd felt on the verge of some important revelation.

Could touching the retinentia—even if doing so caused her unbearable pain—help her to understand why she was here?

Yellow light flashed on the globe, and another crack formed across the top.

———◆———

"Stop fooling around and help me think," Marcus said.

Riph Raph, who was lying on his back, scratched his stomach. "I think best when I'm getting a belly rub. What are we thinking about again?"

Marcus banged his pole on the wall, knocking loose a carpet of green mold. "What was Master Therapass warning us not to trust him about? It has to be something important, or he wouldn't have gone to all this trouble."

"Um-hum. Um-hum." Riph Raph nodded thoughtfully. "I never trusted that beard of his. Scraggly and full of weird things. Kind of freaked me out, if you want to know the truth. I definitely didn't trust him when he turned into a wolf—all those sharp teeth. And remember that flying cookie jar with . . ."

Marcus tuned him out. He needed to know what the wizard had said to him that wasn't the truth. But more than that, he wished he could understand *why* Master Therapass had lied to him. The idea that the wizard might not trust him stung. What hurt worse was that Marcus hadn't trusted the wizard. The only reason he'd gone with Graehl in the first place was because he'd thought Master Therapass and Tankum had failed Kyja.

"His beady eyes," Riph Raph said—still listing things about Master Therapass he didn't trust. "And that robe. Did you ever notice how many things he pulled out of it? And Kyja. How he said we couldn't rescue her. It also occurs to me that I've never seen him eat cheese. Not a single slice. Do you think he could be hiding some sort of allergy?"

"Kyja," Marcus muttered. He'd been so sure that there had to be a way to save her, but the wizard had insisted it was impossible to . . .

Wait. What if *that's* what the wizard had lied about? Marcus had been so disappointed when Therapass and Tankum appeared to have given up. What if they hadn't? Marcus walked slowly around the room.

"Let's say that Master Therapass thought there might be a way to save Kyja. What's the first thing he'd do?"

Riph Raph stopped scratching himself and rolled over. "Rescue her."

"Right." Marcus wanted to think the wizard would have come to him about a rescue, but most of the time Kyja had been trapped, he'd been moping in a prison cell. "Since he didn't save her, we have to assume he couldn't for some reason. But why wouldn't he say so? Why pretend that he'd given up?"

"Because . . . that was part of the plan?"

"Yes, but part of *what* plan? All they had to do was tell me that they had a plan to rescue Kyja, and I never would have gone with Graehl. I never would have gotten captured, and the Dark Circle wouldn't have learned that I couldn't be sent to the shadow realm, and—"

Marcus stared at Riph Raph. Riph Raph stared at Marcus. What if Master Therapass's plan was for Marcus to end up in the shadow realm all along?

"We're here to save Kyja!" they both said at once.

CHAPTER 21

So Close

Turnip looked from the door to the ball. She shuddered, remembering how the woman in Fire Keep had reacted to seeing her memories. Turnip brushed her hair back from her face. Did she really want to see the person she loved the most murdering her? Did she want to find out how she'd lost her magic? She liked to believe the best about people. What would seeing something like that do to her?

On the other hand, she'd come here for a reason. If her suffering allowed her to discover that reason—to understand a little bit more about her background—wasn't there a chance that her memories could help her find a way to get through the gate?

The globe cracked again, and a tiny blue drop of liquid—of her memories—leaked out. There was no more time. She had to decide now. Biting her lower lip, she reached for the retinentia.

"I don't know how to do this," Marcus said.

Riph Raph, who was perched by the window, looked over his shoulder. "You'd better figure it out fast. I think they're closing in. Four more soldiers in the last five minutes, and lots of snifflers."

Marcus placed his hands flat on the ground. Master Therapass had claimed that the Dark Circle was protecting the realm of shadows because they wanted to put Marcus into it. But it wasn't until the Master forced Marcus to reveal what he knew that the Dark Circle sent him here. Which meant that either the wizard was wrong, or he'd told the story as an elaborate trick to get the Dark Circle to send Marcus to the realm of shadows.

What if, in their search for Kyja, Master Therapass and Tankum had discovered that there was only one place Marcus could reach out to her from? The army outside the Unmakers' cavern had been too strong to get past. Maybe that's what Therapass and Tankum had been trying to do while Marcus had been training. With no way to get him into the realm of shadows on their own, they had to trick the Master into doing it for them.

If that was true, it meant . . . Marcus's throat tightened until he could barely breathe.

Graehl had been in on the plan the whole time.

Master Therapass had sent him to the Windlash

Mountains. Having spent more time there than anyone, he would have known that there was no way in. Had he contacted the Dark Circle to convince the Master he was on their side? With as much time as Graehl had spent around the Master, he had to be aware that there was a good chance that returning to the Dark Circle was a death sentence.

Marcus remembered the way Graehl had looked at him when the Master's dagger had plunged into his chest.

When he'd talked about doing hard things to save someone you loved. He hadn't been talking about what Marcus was going to do. He'd been talking about what *he* was doing.

At the very moment Marcus had labeled Graehl a traitor, he'd been giving up his own life.

Tears dripped from his eyes and down his chin, then splattered on the dirty floor.

"Hurry," Riph Raph whispered. "Someone's coming."

Marcus closed his eyes. When they'd been sitting around the campfire, Darnoc had said that the realm of shadows was a portal between Earth, Farworld, and other worlds. At the time, Marcus had assumed that the land elemental was talking about other planets. But maybe, just maybe, he was saying that the realm of shadows had some kind of connection to the elemental keeps as well. If so, and if Marcus could use his magic to find Kyja the same way she had used the Aptura Discerna to find him, he might be able to contact her to see why she hadn't pulled him over.

Focusing on what she had looked like the last time he saw her, and what Fire Keep looked like, of the magical flames she'd step into, Marcus drew on all four elements and called out, "Kyja, where are you?"

Nothing.

He tried again. "Kyja! It's Marcus and Riph Raph. We're trying to bring you back to Farworld, but we can't find you. Why haven't you pulled me over?"

For a moment, he saw nothing. Then a yellow light—so bright it made him squint, although his eyes were closed—filled his vision. A second later, she was there, looking straight at him.

"Kyja!" he cried "You're alive."

———◆———

"Kyja, where are you?"

She was about to touch the retinentia when a voice came out of nowhere.

Turnip looked up from the ball and glanced around the room. "Hello?" She checked the door, but was almost positive that the voice hadn't come from beyond it. She stared into the light. "Is someone there?"

The voice came again. It was a little unclear and she

couldn't make out all of the words. Something about a *kyja*—whatever that was—and a *riff raff* and something called *Farworld*. The voice sounded like a boy's.

"Kyja!" the voice called again.

This time the voice was so clear, it could have been coming from right beside her. She looked into the light and saw a boy with messy, brown hair. Something was wrong with one of his arms, and his right leg was bent in an odd way. Behind him, outlined against a gray square of light, seemed to be some sort of winged creature.

She reached out to the boy. "Hello?"

———◆———

Kyja didn't sound nearly as excited to see Marcus as he was to see her, but he didn't care. It was Kyja. She was alive and speaking to him.

"Pull us over!" he shouted. "Find the rope and pull us over so we can—"

The door of the room slammed open and Riph Raph shouted a warning. Marcus looked up to see four men in dark uniforms storming toward them.

"Hands on your head," the one in the middle yelled. "Do not try magic, on the penalty of—"

Marcus created a fireball and blasted it toward them. The fire bounced off the men's shields and singed the walls, but didn't appear to hurt them at all.

One of the soldiers fired a shot, and Riph Raph gave a squawk of pain.

As Marcus reached for air magic to blast the men away, one of them flung a silver wire at him. The wire wrapped around his wrists and legs, cutting off the flow of magic like turning off a water faucet.

He looked for Riph Raph, but the skyte was gone.

"Pull us over!" he screamed to Kyja. But when he closed his eyes again, she was gone too.

After the boy turned away, Turnip heard shouting and a loud bang. His voice cut off and an instant later, he was gone. She looked around the room. Who was he, and what happened to him? He'd said something about a rope, but she didn't see one anywhere.

"Where are you?" she shouted. "How do I pull you over?"

No response.

Clearly, he'd been frightened and needed her to do something. He looked sort of scruffy and maybe not all that trustworthy. But if he needed her, she wanted to help him—if only to find out where he'd come from and how he'd managed to talk to her.

"Hello?" she shouted. "Boy, where are you?" Wherever he'd been—*whoever* he'd been—he was gone.

Something popped, and she looked down in time to see her retinentia burst open. She reached for it, but the moment the liquid inside touched the glowing yellow air, it disappeared. Nothing was left but hundreds of tiny glittering shards.

TAKING CHANCES

Master Therapass was poring over his maps when Tankum walked into the study. "Have you heard anything?" the wizard asked starting to stand up.

The warrior waved him back to his seat. "Only what we already knew. They were spotted heading into the Windlash Mountains. Since then, nothing."

Master Therapass rubbed his temples. "Maybe all of this was a mistake. I should go after him."

"And alert the Dark Circle to what we've discovered? Besides, we both know that the Unmakers cavern is too well protected. It's why we had to send him that way in the first place." Tankum tried to sit in a chair, but as soon as he put any weight on it, the wooden legs cracked and splintered. "Sorry about that," he said, tossing the mangled furniture aside.

Therapass rolled up the map. "You don't know what's in there—what could happen to him in the realm."

"You've told me," Tankum said. "And we both agreed that the risk was one we had to take. Trust me—if you had told the lad what he was up against, he'd have made the same decision."

"He may never come out," the wizard said, slamming his fist on the table. "The things they're rumored to do in there . . ." He shook his head.

"And if he didn't go in, there was no chance of saving the girl." Tankum walked around the table. "If you want my personal opinion, I think he'll make it. The boy's got spunk and heart. He's done more than I could've done at his age."

Master Therapass nodded. "I know. If anything happens to him, though, I'll never forgive myself."

Tankum tapped the rolled map. "My men are two days out from the target, a day and a half if they push it. But I need to join them."

The wizard stood up. "I don't like your chances."

Tankum grinned. "Have you ever? The day *you* like the odds of a battle I'm in is the day I retire my swords."

"Take care of yourself," the wizard said. "I'll let you know when we're on our way."

Tankum nodded and slapped Master Therapass on the back so hard, the wizard's teeth snapped together. "He'll be back. You can count on it."

Master Therapass watched Tankum walk out the door with a strong feeling that it might be the last time he'd see his friend alive.

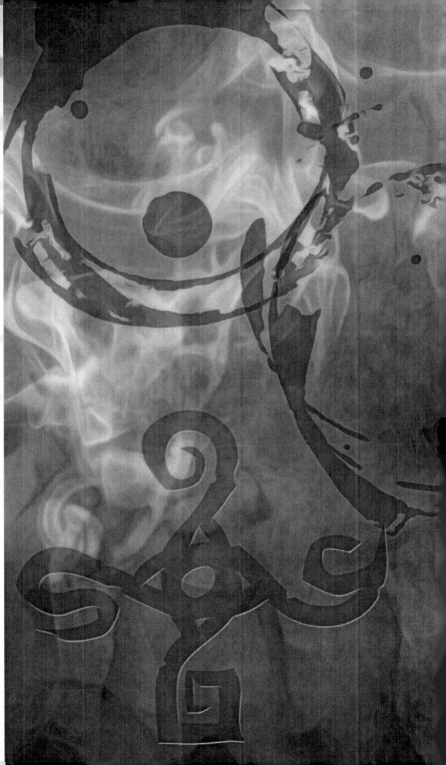

PART 3

Three Worlds

CHAPTER 22

PAIN

He tried to keep up with the soldier who was dragging him by a silver wire, but without his pole, Marcus could barely walk.

"Didn't know the Spell Casters had crips," the soldier said, picking Marcus up and flinging him over one shoulder. "Thought you'd all magicked yourselves perfect bodies."

"I didn't know the realm of the shadows had dimwits," Marcus said, trying not to moan from the pain of being bounced him around as he walked downstairs.

A soldier behind them laughed. "Kid's got you there. I've been telling you that you're a dimwit for years."

As they stepped into the alley, the soldier carrying Marcus "accidentally" banged him against the doorway and chuckled. "Oops. Sorry about that."

The one who seemed to be their leader turned with a frown. "Damage the livestock, and you'll be on crap detail so long, even your girlfriend won't remember your name."

"Tuck don't have a girlfriend," cracked the soldier behind him. "She left him for a geo-vacuum. Said he sucks rocks more than it does."

Two soldiers laughed, but their leader knelt and touched a spot of blood in the street a few feet from the building. "Looks like we hit the flying lizard. Racker, you and Lii track it. Tuck, throw the Spell Caster in the wagon. King Phillip wants him brought in ASAP."

"You have a king?" Marcus asked. The realm of shadows kept getting weirder and weirder.

"You'll learn all about him soon enough." Tuck carried Marcus out of the alley to a vehicle that looked like a mix between a car and a covered wagon. The back was clearly made from an Earth car, which Marcus guessed to be from the late fifties, with tall lights on the back almost like the fins of a fish. The roof was gone, and the vehicle appeared to have been chopped in half right about where the front seats should have been. In their place were a wooden seat and reins. The whole thing was covered with a piece of white canvas cloth held up by curved rods.

Tuck threw Marcus roughly onto the back seat, and springs sticking up through the ragged leather jabbed his side. "You think you're special 'cause you've got magic," the soldier said under his breath. "But trust me. Once the King has you harnessed, you'll wish you were nothing but a grunt."

When the leader climbed onto the wooden seat and picked up the reins, the vehicle began rolling down the street, although Marcus couldn't see anything pulling it. Watching them go, Tuck gave a sarcastic wave and mouthed the word, "*Crip*," before walking away.

With the driver looking straight ahead, Marcus tugged at the wires wrapped around his ankles and wrists. He couldn't see any kind of clasp, but there had to be a way to release the bindings.

"You seem like an okay sort, for a Caster," the driver said without turning around. "Recognized Tuck for the piece of digger dung he is right away. So I'm going to give you some advice."

Marcus tried to slide his fingers under the wire, but the harder he pushed, the tighter it dug into his flesh. He tried rubbing the wire against the edge of a spring, but it didn't appear to do any good.

The soldier pulled the reins to the right, and the wagon turned in that direction. "The silver stuff you're yanking at right now is called conductor wire. It not only blocks any magic you try to use, but also the more you mess with it, the more it clamps down. Pull hard enough, and you'll cut your own hand clean off. Even then, it don't let go. You'll walk around with a wire-tied stump that looks kind of like a sausage."

Marcus stopped tugging at the wire. "How did you know I was trying to get it off?"

The soldier shrugged. "That's what you all do. I'd do the same thing if I were on my way to be harnessed. But it won't do you no good. Once you're wrapped, no one gets away."

Marcus shifted, trying to find a position that kept him from getting poked by the springs so much. "When you say *all*, are you talking about other . . . *Spell Casters*?"

"They're the only ones conductor wire works on. Supposed to be because their magic is what makes it work in the first place."

They turned right off of the road they'd been on, and Marcus noticed that the farther they went, the less ragged the buildings got. "Do a lot of Spell Casters come here?" If he could team up with a few other wizards, they might be able to fight their way out of wherever this King Phillip was keeping them.

"Not as many as there used to be," the driver said. "That's why it was such a big deal when you showed up. Power's been getting a little low."

Marcus didn't hear the last of the soldier's words because at that moment, they drove past a 7-Eleven. Not something that *looked* like the convenience store, but the real deal, complete with a poster of a blue Slurpee.

"This looks exactly like Earth," Marcus gasped. There were gas pumps out front. Even a propane tank.

"Parts of it do," the soldier said. "Other parts look like the Caster world, from what I've been told. Then there're parts that . . . well, let's just say you don't ever want to experience them yourself. Some nasty things out there. You're lucky you holed up where you did. If you'd crossed to the other side of the street from the diggers, you might never have come back."

"Diggers?" Marcus asked.

The soldier nodded. "The things that look like big black bubbles."

"But how is this all possible? How can you have cars and guns and video game controllers?"

"Ask King Phillip," the soldier said. "When he's in a good mood, he can talk for hours. When he's not . . ." He shook his head. "You don't want to be anywhere around him."

They pulled up in front of a five-story building, which looked like a mix between a high-tech office building and a fairytale castle. Conical spires of gleaming chrome and dark glass rose high into the air. As the wagon approached, a drawbridge with flashing multi-colored neon bulbs lowered, and a couple of dozen fairies flew out, scattering handfuls of sparkling dust as they soared overhead.

A man and woman dressed in maroon robes came out of the building. They reached into their sleeves and pulled out what looked like metal wands. Marcus felt a surge of air magic freeze him in place and lift him out of the car.

"Are you wizards?" he asked, feeling a surge of hope.

"Do you see any harnesses?" the woman sneered. "We're engineers."

The two of them floated him toward the building. As he was carried across a moat filled with rollercoaster cars, he saw something white and furry peek up out of a sewer grate. He could have sworn it was an Ishkabiddle.

Inside, the building was as odd as it was outside. One entire wall was covered with cuckoo clocks of all shapes and sizes. None seemed to be set to the same time, and when one went off, instead of a little bird popping out, tiny fireworks exploded. They passed an ordinary-looking receptionist typing on a modern computer. Hanging above her on the wall was the head of a dragon and a pair of crossed long swords.

They turned down a hallway lined from floor to ceiling with microwave ovens. Through a window on the left, Marcus saw a colored fountain outside. Beautiful creatures with fish-like bodies and human faces frolicked amid blasts of colored water shooting into the air through white plastic sprinkler pipes.

At the end of the hallway, the robed pair stopped in front of what looked like a piece of medical equipment. "This will measure your magic capacity," the woman said, plugging the other end of Marcus's silver wire into the machine.

"It may hurt a bit," the man said, right before he flipped a red switch.

Marcus had lived his whole life with chronic pain, but until that moment, he had never understood how intense pain could be. His arms and legs shot out to the sides. Every hair on his body stood on end, and each nerve-ending screamed as though it had been hit with a blowtorch. His teeth slammed together, and his body convulsed. He felt as if blunt nails had been driven through every inch of his flesh into the bones beneath. He tried to scream, but the pain locked his muscles so tightly, he could barely breathe.

His response was completely instinctive. Knowing he couldn't take that kind of agony for more than a second or two, he slammed magic through the silver wire and into the machine. The pain stopped at once and he gasped with relief.

A digital readout on the front scrolled rapidly through a series of numbers, and the man and woman nodded their heads and smiled.

"Very good," the man said, turning off the machine. "The king will be quite pleased."

"The highest I've ever seen," the woman said, patting him on the back.

Trembling with exhaustion, Marcus lost track of where they were after that. His entire body shook like a kite in a hurricane, and his brain kept trying to convince him that this was all a dream. Not until they stepped out of a crystal-and-stone elevator that had no cables or pulleys, did he finally come back to his senses.

He had a feeling that they were deep underground now. Light came from a combination of torches and electric bulbs, which seemed to be randomly distributed. The man and woman carried him through a brightly lit room where more robed figures hunched over computer screens, tapping keyboards and waving metal wands.

"New one?" asked a man with steel rimmed glasses.

"He may be the last one we need," said the woman floating Marcus, and everyone looked up from their computers with interest.

They passed through the room and into a downward sloping hallway. The air took on a sour smell, which for some reason reminded Marcus of a zoo. He could hear a rumbling, as if heavy equipment was running nearby. The walls and floors seemed to be vibrating, and the air pounded against his eardrums.

They entered another room, and the sour smell intensified. The vibrating was so powerful that he could feel it all the way to his bones. He turned his head, and at first thought he was seeing hundreds of acrobats—the kind that did tricks in a circus—hanging from silver trapeze bars on the ceiling.

He blinked and realized that they weren't trapeze bars. They looked more like swings. And the people hanging from them were definitely not acrobats. The wires holding them in the air were connected to their arms, legs, chest, back, and neck, like the strings on a marionette. The people might as well have been puppets, with their lifeless expressions, and slack limbs. Tubes pumped clear liquid into their arms, and several of the people had drool leaking from the corners of their mouths.

"What are you doing to them?" Marcus asked, terror making his voice shake with the same vibration as the air.

The man and woman stopped and released the air magic holding Marcus. As his body began to drop, two muscular guards stepped forward and caught him. One of them had metal hands with robotic fingers, which clicked as he opened and closed them. The other had normal hands, but the lower half of his face was gone, replaced by what looked like the bucket of a steam shovel.

"Welcome to the harnesses," said the one with the metal hands. "We're going to get a charge out of you."

The second laughed, his mechanical jaw clanking open and shut. "Good one." He held Marcus upright, and the first guard started to take off Marcus's robe.

"Won't be needing this here," the first guard said. His metal fingers clicked like a sewing machine as he grabbed Marcus's sleeves. "What's this?" He leaned down to look at Marcus's right arm, then ran an icy metal finger over the scar there. "Think the king's gonna want to see this."

CHAPTER 23

PHILLIP AND AURORA

The man and woman who had floated Marcus into the castle wanted to take him to see the king. But the guards argued that the prisoner was theirs now, and they'd be the one's getting the credit. Carrying him between them as if he weighed no more than a pillow, the guards took him back up the elevator to the top level of the building.

There they waited outside elaborately carved double doors until a robotic voice granted them permission to enter. Once the doors had swung open, they carried Marcus along a red rug, which ran down the center of a room piled high with every kind of electrical equipment Marcus could imagine. Ovens, toasters, computer monitors, air conditioning units, DVD players, video game systems, and some things Marcus didn't recognize, were stacked floor to ceiling. Thousands of displays, panels, and lights blinked in a kind of surreal mosaic.

At the end of the rug, they stopped and knelt before a raised pedestal. They lowered Marcus until he knelt beside them.

"Your majesty," the guard with the metal jaw said, eyes locked on the floor. "We present the newest Spell Caster."

Footsteps sounded on the podium, and Marcus tried to look up, but the guard with the metal hands forced his head to stay down.

"You may arise," said, a pleasant-enough sounding voice.

Considering what he'd seen so far, Marcus expected the king to look like something out of a fairytale—wearing a jeweled crown, a long fur-lined robe, and lots of rings. Except in this world, maybe his scepter would be a car antenna or a blender.

But the man who entered and sat on the throne looked like an older and slightly less heavily armed soldier. His disheveled hair was gray on the sides, and his neatly trimmed beard and mustache had traces of salt and pepper in them. He wore a black leather jacket and boots, with no trace of a crown, scepter, or any other symbol of royalty.

The king sat on the throne, crossed his legs, and waved a hand. "You may rise."

The guard on Marcus's right pulled him to his feet, and Marcus had to wrap an arm around the man's waist to keep from falling.

"What's wrong with your leg?" the king asked, staring down at him.

"It's been this way since I was a baby," Marcus said. "I was attacked by . . . by some bad guys." Until he had a clearer idea of what was going on, it might be better not to give too much information.

"Bad guys." The king raised an eyebrow. "I've been informed you bear the mark of some rather *bad guys* on your right arm. I want to know who you are and how you got the mark."

Marcus folded his arms across his chest. "I'll answer your questions if you answer mine."

The guard on the right clamped his steel hand on the back of Marcus's neck, and the guard on his left raised a fist, but the king laughed. "You have more spirit than the typical Caster. Perhaps you don't understand your current situation."

Marcus knew he was taking a big risk. But unless he could figure out what was going on and find a way to escape, he had no chance of saving Kyja. "I understand that you want to hook me up to a machine that will turn me into some kind of living battery."

King Phillip's leather jacket crackled as he folded his arms. "The realm of shadows is a harsh place. We all do our part. However, being hooked to a harness should be the least of your worries at the moment. The penalty for consorting with the Dark Circle is death. The penalty for being a *member* of the Dark Circle is a very slow—and very painful—death."

"I'm not *part* of the Dark Circle," Marcus said. "I'm fighting against them."

The king leaned forward, hands on his knees. "How?"

Marcus licked his cracked lips. He couldn't back down now, or he'd lose any leverage he might have gained. "Like I said, I'll answer your questions if you answer mine. I want to sit down. My leg hurts."

"What if I choose not to grant your requests?" King Phillip asked. "I can order the guards to torture you until you're ready to answer."

"You can torture me. You can kill me. But that would mean losing the strongest battery you've ever seen, and you still wouldn't get what you're looking for. Or, you can answer my questions, which won't cost you a thing, and I'll tell you whatever you want to know."

The king snapped his fingers. "Get the Caster a chair."

The guard with the metal jaw hurried out of the room and came back with a wooden chair which Marcus gratefully dropped into.

The king leaned back in his throne, eyes fixed on Marcus. "Lie to me, and you'll regret it. Now, how many of you came across from Farworld?"

Marcus didn't know if the soldiers had managed to

track Riph Raph. If not, he didn't want to say anything that might help them. "Only me."

A metal fist slammed into his side, and pain burst across Marcus's ribs and back. The king waved a hand, and a soldier carried Riph Raph into the room. The skyte's right wing was bloody, and he was wrapped, head to talons, in conductor wire.

"Riph Raph," Marcus cried. "Are you okay?"

Riph Raph winked a swollen left eye. "You should see what the soldiers who caught me look like."

"Lie to me again, and I'll have you killed without further discussion," the king said.

Marcus pressed his arm to his side. Every breath brought pain. "I thought you meant *people*. I was the only person who came through. Riph Raph came through as a bird, but I changed him back."

The king nodded, as though satisfied with that answer. "Where did you enter, and why?"

Marcus had no idea how much they knew, and he now believed that the king would have him killed if he lied again—even if it meant losing a powerful battery.

"I was pushed through a portal in the cavern of the Unmakers by three elementals at the command of the Master—the leader of the Dark Circle."

At the mention of the Master, King Phillip's face visibly darkened. "What do you know about the Master?"

"My turn to ask a question," Marcus said. "How do

you have so much Earth stuff here? Microwaves, computers, video games."

The king blinked. "How would a Caster know about microwaves?"

Marcus rolled his eyes. "I've heated up plenty of frozen dinners in them. Now answer my question. Please, your majesty."

The king was obviously confused, which delighted Marcus. Maybe the man didn't know as much as he thought he did. As he studied Marcus more carefully, his eyes narrowed. "You know of Earth?" he said, holding up one hand.

Marcus nodded.

"And you know of Farworld." The king held up his other hand. He moved them together until the thumbs overlapped. "The realm of shadows is the place where the two worlds touch. Think of this place as an island between two oceans. Things . . . wash up on our shores. Some from one world, some from the other."

That sounded a little hard to believe. "You're saying that one day, a 7-Eleven appeared here out of nowhere?"

"Sounds like a big fat lie to me," Riph Raph said, and Marcus put a finger to his lips.

The king lowered his hands. Marcus was almost sure he was holding something back. "We may have ways of encouraging things to come here. Now tell me how you know Earth."

Marcus wondered how much he should reveal. Eventually, he went ahead and told it all. How he'd been found in the desert by monks, raised by various fosters families, and pulled over by Kyja. He told of his past with Master Therapass. The more he talked, the more interested the king became, until at last, the man was leaning forward on the edge of his throne.

When Marcus finished the story, the king shook his head. "Fascinating. This Therapass, the wizard who sent you to Earth—he wasn't, by any chance, related to the leader of the Dark Circle?"

The question caught Marcus off guard. "The Master claimed that he and Master Therapass were brothers. How could you know that?"

"Yes." King Phillip waved to the two guards and to the soldier who'd carried in Riph Raph. "Wait outside until I call you." The guards reached for Marcus, but the king shook his head. "Leave the boy and the skyte."

"Are you sure?" the soldier asked. "The flying lizard can't be trusted. He bit an ear off one of my men."

"I'm *not* a lizard," Riph Raph said, struggling against the silver wire. "And I would have bit the other ear off too if the first hadn't tasted so nasty."

"I'll watch my ears," the king said.

As the men left the room, he studied Marcus. When they were alone, he folded his hands and rested his chin on his fists. "Did Therapass say anything about the rest of the people in the city that was attacked when you were a baby?"

Marcus lowered his eyes. "Only that they were all killed."

The king blew out a long, slow breath. "Your parents?"

"Killed." Marcus rubbed his right shoulder. "By the Dark Circle. Because I'm the one who is supposed to save Farworld."

King Phillip leaned back again. He ran his fingers through his graying hair and crossed his legs. "What if I told you that you are not why the city was destroyed? What if I told you the reason you were attacked, why everyone around you was killed—was because of me?"

Marcus slid forward on his chair. "I don't understand. What could any of this have to do with you?"

"It has everything to do with me," the king said. "Because unless I am mistaken, you are my son."

"Don't believe him," Riph Raph said. "He doesn't look anything like you."

Except that Marcus thought that he and the king did look a little alike. The resemblance wasn't something you'd notice right off, but once you were looking for it, you saw small things. Like the way their ears stuck a little too far, the way their hair looked like it needed to be cut and combed, the way they both sighed when they were thinking.

"Is it true? Are you my father?"

King Phillip drummed his fingers on the gilded arm of his throne. "You told me a story. Now I'll tell you one. I haven't always lived in the realm of shadows. I was born on Earth. But I never really felt like I fit in. I preferred reading to the company of other children. My father called me a daydreamer and said I'd end up living on the streets if I didn't learn how to work."

Marcus nodded. Many of his foster parents had said the same things to him.

"When I was not much older than you are now, I left home. I don't know exactly what I was looking for—something different, I guess. A place where everything didn't already feel claimed, used, and worked to death. Whatever I was looking for, I didn't find it. Soon enough, my father's predictions came true. I was living on the street, begging, stealing, doing whatever I could to satisfy appetites that continued to grow more and more base. I probably would have died there if I hadn't met a man with baggy clothes and a long, dirty beard."

"A wizard," Marcus said. "You met a wizard. Was it Master Therapass?"

The king chuckled. "No. He wasn't a wizard, at least not in the traditional sense. Just another homeless man I'd come across in a bus station. But he must have seen something in me, because one rainy night, after I shared my dinner with him, he said that he could tell I was a dreamer. He said that if my dreams were still alive, he knew a place they might come true.

"He sent me to an abandoned house, which didn't look any different than the hundreds of other places I'd holed up in. Only it *was* different. I knew it was different the moment I walked through the rusty screen door. There was a feeling." He closed his eyes and rubbed his chin with one hand. "The floors were warped. The linoleum looked like someone had gone after it with an axe. The whole place smelled like cat urine. But as I stepped inside, I felt hope, a return of purpose, a sense of adventure. I remember thinking that it felt like . . . magic."

"It was a passageway," Marcus said. "A door between Earth and here." Ever since he'd realized there was a portal between Farworld and the realm of shadows, he'd wondered if there might be more of them. And if there were doorways to here from Farworld, why not from Earth?

"It was," the king said. "I found myself drawn toward a closet with a nest of rats in the corner. One minute I was walking across rotted boards. The next minute I was stepping into . . . a new world."

Marcus looked around at the appliance filled-room. "And this was all here?"

"No." King Phillip laughed. "The realm was nothing

like the magical world I'd pictured. Most of it was gray and empty. There were monsters I'd never imagined, plants that made me so sick I thought I'd die, and odds and ends I recognized as coming from Earth. Other things I didn't recognize at all. It was cold and depressing and dangerous."

"If it was so bad, why did you stay?" Marcus asked.

"I probably wouldn't have. After weeks of nearly dying from one thing after another, I figured that the old man had sent me here as a joke, or maybe a punishment. I was ready to return through the portal and tell my father that he'd been right. But then I met the most beautiful girl I'd ever seen."

CHAPTER 24

THE LAST PIECE

Turnip knelt on the floor and gathered the shards of the globe. She hoped that by touching what was left, she might regain some fragments of her memories. But whatever had been in the retinentia, it was gone now. She'd never know who she was or where she'd come from. Letting the pieces fall to the ground with a tinkle like fairy wings, she stood up and looked from the black door to the golden light.

Go back, or go forward? There were good reasons for choosing both of them, and maybe if she'd been able to regain her memories, the decision would have been clear. But now, with nothing pushing her one way or the other, she felt as if she had to continue on. Who knew—if she opened the gate, maybe freeing the fire elementals would somehow help her figure out who she was along the way.

She looked around the room, wondering again who the boy was and what he'd wanted. Would he come back, or had contact been a one-time thing? Like her memories, that might be something she'd never know.

Steeling herself against whatever would come next, she reached out with both hands and pushed the door.

Nothing happened.

She pushed harder. It didn't budge. She searched for a knob or button—some kind of hidden lock. But other than the flaming symbol, the door was completely blank, no edges to grab or cracks to pry into.

She banged on the door. "Hello? Is anyone there? Let me in." But if anyone heard, they didn't respond. She tried pressing the symbol, running her fingers over it forward and backward. None of it made a bit of difference. She picked up a sliver of the broken retinentia and tried scratching the door's gleaming black surface It didn't leave so much as a mark.

Defeated, she collapsed to the ground. The fire elementals were right. Without magic, she couldn't open the gate. Her efforts had been for nothing.

———◆———

"My mother?" Marcus asked.

The king nodded. "Neither of us was much more than a child at the time, but our stories were very similar. I was born on Earth and went in search of magic. She was born into a world filled with magic and went in search of . . . I'm not sure exactly—predictability? Reliability? A place where people actually worked for what they wanted instead of casting a spell? We each found a portal, and apparently we each found what we were looking for in the other."

"Did she come back to Earth with you?" Marcus asked, remembering the first time Kyja had jumped from Farworld. He wondered if his mother had been as excited by chocolate milkshakes as Kyja had.

"She couldn't come to Earth. And I couldn't go to Farworld. As it turned out, while we could both pass through the portals between our worlds and the realm of shadows, neither of us could go through the portals to the other's world. Once we realized that the only way to be together was by staying here, we decided to make the best of it. She told me all about her world, and I told her about mine. Obviously, I was thrilled when I discovered that magic was real, and she was equally fascinated by technology. She got such a kick out of anything electrical.

"Once day, I told her the story of Sleeping Beauty. She loved the idea of love's first kiss so much that we changed our names to Phillip and Aurora, after the prince and princess in the movie. We decided to create our own kingdom by combining magic and technology."

"It sounds great," Marcus said. "What went wrong?"

The king clenched his jaws so tightly that Marcus could hear his teeth grinding. "We met a couple of wizards with a plan."

With nowhere else to go, Turnip walked back into the light. She hoped that once she returned to Fire Keep, Magma, Prudentes, and the other fire elementals could come up with a way to get through the door. But the truth was, now that she'd seen what was inside the vortex for herself, she was afraid there *was* no way out. Maybe that was for the best. The fire elementals did have fierce tempers, and perhaps they were locked up for a reason.

Moving deeper into the brightness, she thought about the boy again. Had he seen her as clearly as she'd seen him? He seemed to recognize her, to reach out to her. Could that mean he knew her? And that, therefore, she'd known him? She pictured his face as hard as she could, and for a second, she saw a flash of something.

The word *turnip* came into her mind. The name she'd chosen for herself. But nothing else.

The boy might not have been real. He could have been a random bit of memory brought to life by the leaking globe. She'd been walking for quite a while when she realized that the light was growing dimmer. Hurrying forward, she looked for the passage back to the vortex. But when she stepped out of the blinding brightness, she was at the door again.

"It seemed like a great idea at the time," the king said, resting his chin in his hand. "The wizards wanted to open a permanent doorway from Farworld to Earth, and we wanted to explore each other's worlds. At the time, I never thought to question their motives. I believe that Therapass genuinely thought the two worlds should meet each other. His brother, who went by his rank of Master Wizard even then, had other plans, which I didn't learn about until much later."

Marcus picked Riph Raph up off the floor and set the skyte in his lap, trying to see how bad the injured wing was. He knew all too well why the Master wanted to open a permanent doorway between Earth and Farworld. "He wants to use Farworld's magic and Earth's weapons to rule both worlds."

"Yes," King Phillip said. "But we didn't find that out until it was too late. The wizards never actually came into the shadow realm themselves. They knew about Unmakers, snifflers, and a dozen other creatures that could steal their magic, so they weren't willing to take the risk, although by then we'd figured out how to keep the creatures in check. Therapass and the Master requested items from Earth, and I'd get them. Some things changed when they passed across, and others wouldn't cross at all. But that only made the wizards more intrigued."

He got up from his throne and paced around the pedestal. "In exchange for getting the items they requested the brothers did magic for us." He waved his hands as though taking in his realm. "The buildings you see here. This palace. It all came from Earth via their magic. They were both positive that with the right combination of technology and magic—parts of both worlds—a doorway could be opened. But the more we built, the stronger the magic it required. Neither Aurora nor I knew anything about dark magic—about what the two of them had done to obtain the power they needed. When we learned of it, we put a stop to the building at once.

"They were furious, of course, especially the Master. They threatened to take away everything we had. In turn, we refused to work with them anymore and began blocking the portals. That's when I found out that Aurora was pregnant. I was afraid of bringing Earth doctors here, and I couldn't take her to a hospital on Earth."

He clenched his hands, fingernails digging into his palms. "I agreed to let a couple of wizards into the realm from Farworld long enough to deliver the baby. She knew both of them; they were family friends."

Marcus didn't need to hear the rest to know what had happened. "They worked for the Dark Circle."

The king pressed his palms against his eyes. "The Master, who was running things by then, convinced Aurora's family that I was keeping her prisoner here, that she was in danger. He planned to steal her and our baby right after the birth. Moments before the baby—you—

were born, they used magic to knock me out. When I woke up, my wife and child were gone."

Marcus stroked Riph Raph's back. "I can't believe that Master Therapass would go along with something like that."

"He didn't; he was gone by then. I think he and his brother had parted ways over using dark magic. I'm quite sure he had no idea that the child he sent to Earth was my son."

Marcus thought back to how the wizard had warned him to stay out of the realm of shadows. That one of Marcus's parents might be from there. "I think he might know now."

The king cocked an eyebrow, but didn't ask for any more details. "The rest of the story is fairly short," he said. "I did everything I could to rescue my wife. I recruited wizards from Farworld, weapons from Earth. I built up an army using both technology and magic to get her back. By then, the Master had realized that I was no use to him. He told me I'd never see my wife again, and that my son would be raised as his. I made it my goal to reach Farworld and return to my wife and child."

"Now that I'm here, and you know that my mother is . . ." Marcus shrugged. "You can stop trying."

The king walked back to his throne and lowered himself into it. He reached inside his jacket and took out a gleaming metal pistol. "I gave up all hope of rescuing

Aurora years ago. I assumed she must be dead or she would have gotten word to me. Now that I know for sure, it changes nothing."

"Then what's all this for?" Marcus asked. "What are you doing with the wizards and soldiers?"

King Phillip gripped the arms of his throne. "Earth is corrupt and getting worse by the day; I was right about that part. I never fit in because it wasn't a world worth fitting into. All anyone cares about is getting more power and stronger weapons. It's only a matter of time before they destroy themselves.

"I'd searched for magic all those years, but I was wrong about that, too. Magic is just another kind of power—another weapon. I never did discover a way to make a passage between Earth and Farworld. But I found something much better. I discovered a way to use each of the worlds' power to destroy the other."

Marcus's stomach went cold. He'd always thought he was fighting against the Dark Circle. That's what everyone had thought. He'd never understood what Kyja was supposed to save Earth from.

What if this was it—what if the danger to Earth and Farworld was coming from the realm of shadows? From Marcus's own father? The thought that he could be related to this man—that a member of his own family might be the danger they had been fighting all along—made him feel like throwing up.

"What do you need me for?" he asked.

"You're my son," the king said. "It's only right that together we avenge your mother's death."

Marcus shook his head. "You expect me to help you destroy Earth and Farworld? That will never happen."

"I'm afraid you don't have any choice." The king smiled a little sadly. "I've been close to completion for a while now. All I need is a little more energy—a sort of super-charged magic battery. And you're it."

CHAPTER 25

THE ROPE

Marcus pushed himself out of the chair, but there was nowhere to go. Without some kind of staff, he could barely crawl, and he definitely couldn't escape from the castle. Riph Raph continued to struggle against the silver wires, and they sank deep into the skyte's flash.

"Stop struggling," Marcus said, propping himself up against the back of the chair. "They'll cut into you if you keep fighting."

"I don't care if he's your dad or not," Riph Raph said. "We can't let him destroy Farworld."

"I know." Marcus turned to the king. "You don't have to do this. If you let me go, I can finish opening the drift between Earth and Farworld. That's what I've been working on—but with light magic, not dark. You could visit Farworld for yourself and see that most of the people there are nothing like the Dark Circle."

"I don't need to see them," the king said. "I know

what they're like." He clapped his hands. "Guards!"

The two burly men came into the room.

"Take the Spell Caster and hook him up to the harness immediately," the king said. "Tell the engineers to meet me in the control room."

The men grabbed Marcus by the arms and lifted him off his feet.

"What should we do with the flying lizard?"

"Take it to the kitchen to see if the cook has any recipes for skyte."

"How can you do this to your own son?" Marcus shouted as the men dragged him away. "What kind of a king are you?" How could he be related to this man?

"You should brush up on your history," the king called. "Royalty have a long reputation of not treating their relatives very well."

<hr />

Turnip sat on the floor, staring at the black door. She'd tried three more times to get back to the vortex, but each time, she'd returned here. What if there was no way back, if she was trapped here alone, with no one to talk to and nothing to do—not even bad memories to keep her company? She'd go as crazy as the people in Fire Keep.

This had all been a huge mistake. She had thought that life with the Pyrinths was so bad that anything would be an improvement. But being trapped here alone made Fire Keep look like a paradise. She let her eyes follow the fiery symbol on the door, and again the word water filled her mind.

What did that mean?

A thought came to her. What if the symbol stood for water? What if *water* was a password? She got up and hurried to the door. "Water," she said.

Nothing happened.

She tried shouting. "Water, water, water!"

It wasn't a password. The door required magic that she didn't have. Sinking to the floor, she put her head in her hands. Why didn't the boy try contacting her again? He had once—at least for a little while. Why not try again? Unless he couldn't. Maybe the shouting and the bang she'd heard meant he was in trouble. Could he have been trying to contact her because he needed her help?

The thought gave her an uncomfortable feeling. She didn't understand what he wanted, but if he'd come to her for help, he'd been disappointed. Not that there was much she could do to help him. She couldn't even help herself.

She tried to remember his face. He'd seemed surprised at first, then happy. He'd wanted her to pull a rope, which didn't make sense; there were no ropes down here. Then, when the shouting had started and she heard the bang, his face had looked . . . She tried to remember. Scared. She was almost positive that he'd looked scared.

If only he'd contact her again, she could at least tell him she wasn't in any position to help—explain that there was no rope. But she thought he'd used magic to contact her, and as her failure with the door clearly demonstrated, she had none.

Still, she thought, even if he had used magic to speak to her, hadn't she seen him and spoken to him too? Was it possible for her to contact him? Part of her didn't want to try, sure that it would end in failure, like her attempt to open the door had. Then again, it wasn't as if she had anything else to do.

Shutting her eyes tightly, she tried to remember every detail of the boy's face. Scruffy hair, dirty robe, the sort of smile that looked like he might get into trouble, kind eyes. She especially liked his eyes. They reminded her of someone.

Magma. They reminded her of Magma, which seemed silly; the two of them appeared so different. But something about the way they looked at you made you believe that they would go through walls to be there if you needed them.

With the boy's eyes locked in her mind, she called out, "Boy! Are you there?"

As the elevator descended to the bottom level of the castle, Marcus managed to put just enough weight on his good leg so the guards didn't completely carry him. Holding Riph Raph against his chest, Marcus let his head droop until his mouth was next to the skyte's ear. "When I yell, do anything you can to distract the guards. Bite, claw, scream."

Watching Marcus with his good eye, Riph Raph nodded ever so slightly.

"I've never eaten flying lizard before," the guard with the metal jaw said, as the elevator stopped and the doors slid open. "Wonder what it tastes like."

"With those chompers of yours, I'm surprised everything don't taste like scrap metal," the other guard said. They dragged Marcus into the hallway.

As the elevator doors began to close behind him, Marcus screamed and twisted in the guards grasp. "Ishkabiddle on the loose!"

The man with the metal hands turned to look behind him, and Marcus bit him on the inside of his elbow. At the same moment, Riph Raph jumped up and snapped his beak shut on the earlobe of the metal-jawed guard.

"Aargh!" the man screamed, blood spouting from his ear. "Get him off me."

The robotic hand holding Marcus loosened ever so slightly, and Marcus pulled away. Still holding Riph Raph, he dove into the elevator as the door closed behind him.

"Get outta there!" howled the man with the metal jaw.

Marcus punched the L button on the elevator.

The other guard smashed a steel fist through the crystal door, but the elevator was already rising, and he had to pull his arm back before it got cut off at the wrist.

"Nice work!" Riph Raph said, spitting blood out of his beak. "I thought you'd given up for a minute."

"Not a chance," Marcus said. As soon as the doors opened, he hopped out, balancing on his good leg.

Sirens sounded as he jumped over to the receptionist's desk, which was now empty. Stretching as high as he could, he grabbed one of the swords from the wall and yanked. The weight of the sword knocked him off-balance as it ripped from its mounting, and he and the weapon fell to the ground with a clang.

"Prisoner escape," a voice called over the sound system. "Prisoner escape."

Using the sword as a staff, Marcus hobbled toward the doors. Before he could get there, four soldiers rushed in from outside. Another pair came running down the hallway.

Marcus backed up against the wall, holding the sword out. But what good was a blade against soldiers already lifting rifles to their shoulders?

He looked down at Riph Raph. "I won't let them take me alive."

Riph Raph nodded his battered face. "I'll see if I can bite off another ear."

⸺◆⸺

"Boy," Turnip called again. No answer. "Boy, are you there?"

What was the point? She didn't have any magic, and she never would. More than likely, he'd been trying to reach someone else and had contacted her by mistake.

She opened her eyes. She guessed she'd wander through the light again. Maybe she'd find the way back to Fire Keep. Or maybe she'd wander forever, until she constantly moaned like the woman, or laughed like the man. Maybe one day, someone would come across her, and she'd ask for a flower.

If only she had a rope, like the one the boy has asked her to pull. She could climb it and go somewhere else.

A rope. What an odd request. Why would you contact someone magically and ask them to pull a rope? And what kind of rope would it be? A climbing rope could take you somewhere. But if he wanted her to pull the rope, he would have to be below her, needing to be lifted up like a bucket from a well. Maybe he meant the kind of rope that rang a bell when you pulled it.

She tried to imagine what the rope might look like, and a picture came to her as clearly as if the rope were really there. It wasn't brown and rough the way she'd first imagined, but gold and nearly as thick as her wrist. It would be easy for someone to hold onto if you were pulling them with it. She could almost imagine she saw the boy hanging onto the other end.

What would happen if she reached out with both hands and tugged?

"Get out of the way, and I'll put a bullet in his head," said a man with sideburns and a pockmarked face.

"You aren't shooting nobody," said the soldier in front of him. "King Phillip wants this one alive and in the harness."

Marcus swung his sword at the nearest soldier, and the man had to step back quickly to avoid being cut. "You want us?" Marcus said. "Come and get us."

Standing there fighting against unbeatable odds reminded him of the time he'd held off four bigger kids with only a mop. He didn't think he'd be as lucky this time.

"Come on, Caster," a soldier said. "Don't make this harder than it has to be." He darted forward, trying to grab the end of the silver wires attached to Marcus's hands and feet, but Marcus stabbed him in the palm with the point of the sword.

The soldier howled as blood streamed down his wrist. "He cut me."

"Good one!" Riph Raph said. "Slice his nose off next."

Another soldier raised his rifle.

"Go ahead and kill me," Marcus said. "You won't take me to the harness alive."

"Not gonna shoot *you*," the soldier said, edging to the right. "But I think I can get a clear shot at the scaly bird."

Marcus turned to keep Riph Raph between him and the rifle, and another soldier stepped forward. Before Marcus could turn back around, the man slammed the butt of his weapon against the sword, knocking it out of Marcus's hands. Instantly the soldiers dove on top of him, pinning his arms and trying to wrestle Riph Raph away.

"No!" Marcus screamed, holding onto the skyte as tightly as he could and biting at anything within reach.

Riph Raph closed his beak on someone's ear and pulled until the man screamed in pain.

But it was no good. The soldiers pinned Marcus against the walls. One hit Riph Raph with his rifle.

"I'm sorry," Marcus said, closing his eyes.

"Boy!" a voice called. "Are you there?"

Marcus's eyes snapped open. That sounded like . . .

He felt as if his body were being yanked inside out, and then he was falling.

The next thing Marcus knew, he and Riph Raph were

lying on the floor bathed in golden light. Kyja was a few feet away, staring at him in surprise and wonder.

He dove toward her and wrapped his arms around her neck. She was *real*—and she was right here. He could feel her. "Kyja," he said, pulling back. "It's you!"

Carefully she disentangled herself from his grip. "Um, thank you for the hug. It's uh, nice to meet you." She held out one hand. "My name's Turnip. What's yours?"

CHAPTER 26

ALL OVER AGAIN

Riph Raph flipped his ears so hard, they landed on top of his head like a little blue bonnet. "Did you say your name was *Turnip?*"

"Yes," Kyja said, smiling uncertainly. "And you're a skyte, aren't you?"

"Kyja, what's wrong with you?" Marcus asked. "Why are you calling yourself *Turnip?*"

She pressed her lips together. "Do I know you?"

Marcus and Riph Raph looked at each other. "She *is* Kyja, isn't she?" Marcus asked.

Riph Raph—still bound in conductor wire—hobbled over to her and sniffed. "Smells a little different, but it's definitely her."

"Can I help you with that?" Kyja asked. She reached down and casually unwound the wire from the skyte's body. "You should be careful where you fly."

"How did you do that?" Riph Raph asked, stretching his wings.

Marcus pulled at his own wire, and the bindings immediately tightened.

Kyja leaned down and studied the silver loops. "How did this happen?" She slid a finger under the wire, and it all simply fell from his wrists and ankles. She touched his withered arm gently. "Did the wire do this to you?"

Marcus and Riph Raph stared at her.

She shifted from one foot to the other. "Why are you two looking at me that way?"

"You really don't know who we are, do you?" Marcus asked.

She pointed to a small pile of what looked like broken glass. "The fire burned my memories."

Marcus looked from the glass to her with his heart lodged in his throat. To have come all this way, to have worked so hard to find her, only to discover that she didn't remember him was almost like losing her all over.

She must have seen at least part of his thoughts on his face, because her chin quivered and her eyes misted over. "I'm s-s-sorry. I wish I could remember who you are."

"No." Marcus pulled her down and hugged her with both his good arm and bad one. "Don't do that," he said, although he could feel tears streaming down his own face. For the next few minutes, all of them shook with crying.

Even Riph Raph dripped great salty drops onto the floor.

At last, Kyja pulled back and wiped the sleeve of her gown across her eyes. "You were my friends, weren't you?"

"We *are* your friends." Marcus sniffed, trying to get himself under control. "We've been looking for you since the day you . . ."

"Died?" she finished. When he nodded, she studied him with her deep-green eyes. "The fire elementals said that everyone in Fire Keep was sent here because we were killed by the person we loved the most. Is that true? Is that how I died?"

Marcus couldn't bear to look at her. He studied the indentation on his wrist where the wire had dug into his skin. "Yeah. It is. There was this poison drink at a big dinner and—"

She put a hand to his mouth. "No. I don't want to know. I was hoping it wasn't true. But since it is, that's a memory I don't want back. It would hurt too much."

Marcus glanced at Riph Raph, but the skyte appeared to be intently studying something on the ground. "Listen, the important thing is that we need to get you back to your body before it's too late."

She smiled a little as if he'd made some kind of joke. "How can I go back to my body if I'm dead?"

He tugged at the collar of his robe. The situation was complicated. "Okay, here's the thing. We—that is, you and me—"

"And me," Riph Raph said, flapping over to join them. "I've been part of this from the beginning. You could call me the brains of the operation."

Kyja smiled and nodded.

"The three of us," Marcus corrected, "are trying to save Earth and Farworld from being destroyed. At first, we thought we had to save them both from the Dark Circle. But now I think it might actually be my father we have to protect them from. Anyway, to do that, we need to create a drift between the two worlds, which sounded a lot easier when Master Therapass told us about it than it really is."

Kyja nodded uncertainly. "Um . . ."

"You're making it too complicated," Riph Raph said. "All you need to know is that first, we went to the water elementals, where Marcus got turned into a fish. Then we went to find a land elemental, but it turned out that there is no such thing as a land elemental because there are only land *elementals*. After that, we went to the air elementals and almost got killed by a giant pair of frozen teeth. Get it?"

Kyja bit her lower lip and shook her head. "Could you tell me what a *Farworld* is?"

Riph Raph flicked his tail. "This is gonna take a while."

"Okay," Marcus said. "Let's take this all the way back to the beginning. First of all, your name is Kyja."

"I like Turnip," she said.

He sighed. "It all started when I was at a boys' school and got in trouble for fighting." He told her about the dreams he'd had on Earth and continued on to how she'd pulled him to Farworld the first time, where he'd fainted after hearing a horse tell a joke.

She liked the story of how they'd battled the Mimicker. But when he got to the part where Master Therapass had told them of their true origins, she stopped him. "Do I know who my parents are? Do I have brothers or sisters? Any relatives at all?"

He couldn't stand to see pain in her eyes, but he couldn't lie to her either. "No."

"And I *never* had any magic?"

He studied a fold in his robe.

"What about potions or charms?"

Marcus shook his head. "Magic doesn't work on you. You're immune to it because you're from Earth. I think that's why you were able to take off our wires. But you're really smart."

"And you're a great sword fighter," Riph Raph said. "Plus you tell good jokes, and you're an amazing snail rider."

Kyja forced a smile, but Marcus could tell she was fighting not to cry again.

"*We're* your family. Me and Riph Raph. Master Therapass and Tankum." He reached out and took her hand. "You're the nicest person I know." He went on to tell her about all of the people he'd watched her help in their time together.

By the time he finished, she sighed. "Well at least it's good to know I don't steal from babies or kill old ladies."

Marcus laughed. "Not that I'm aware of. But I've only known you the last three years."

That won him a real smile.

Quickly he and Riph Raph caught her up on the rest of their adventures, stopping only when she insisted that she didn't want to know how she'd died.

"Anyway," he finished, "right now your body is in a glass coffin waiting for you to be put back into it."

She nodded. "And we would do this . . . how?"

"You push me back to Terra ne Staric, and then I yank on the rope, pulling you behind me, and *bam,* you're alive again."

"But I don't know where Terra ne Staric is. I don't know where Farworld is."

Marcus scratched his head. He hadn't thought of that. "I'll describe it to you, and you do your best. If we're off by a little, you can pull me back and try again."

The plan was cut and dried to him, but she didn't seem convinced. "I don't know . . ."

"He's not very good with explanations," Riph Raph said. "Let me try. You push him back to Terra ne Staric, and he pulls you over, and you get put back in your body, and *bam,* you're alive."

Marcus glared at him. "All you did was repeat what I said."

"But I said it so much better. Skytes are great at explaining things. We're known as the explainers of the sky."

Marcus balled up the coil of silver wire and threw it at him. "You aren't known as anything of the kind."

Kyja stepped between them. "You both did an excellent job of explaining. And I thank you." Marcus and Riph Raph gave each other dirty looks. "But didn't you tell me," Kyja continued, "that we decided for me to come here to free the fire elementals?"

"Technically, *you* chose that," Marcus said. "We weren't exactly included in the decision. Besides, that was before any of us understood how dangerous it would be for you to come here."

"All right," she said. "Then I choose not to leave here."

Marcus stared at her. She wanted to *stay?*

Riph Raph spread his wings like a professor about to give a speech. "I think that what Turni—that is, Marcus—failed to point out is that if you don't go back now, you might not be able to return to your body at all."

Marcus opened his mouth, but Kyja stopped him. "I understand that part. But unless I'm mistaken, once we leave here, we might not be able to come back."

"Well . . ." Marcus began.

"I'm not . . ." Riph Raph sputtered. "That is . . ."

Kyja set her jaw in the way Marcus was all too familiar with. She might have lost her memories, but she hadn't lost her stubborn streak. "Do you or do you not have magic?" she asked.

"I do," Marcus said.

"And unless we open the gates to Fire Keep, the Pyrinths won't be able to help us, which means that we can't open a drift, which means that Farworld and Earth will both still be in danger."

"But if we don't get you home immediately, *you* will be in danger," Marcus said. "And right now, I care about you more than anyone or anything."

She smiled, and his heart sang. "That is *so* nice." Her smile disappeared. "But I'm not going back until we open the gates."

Marcus took a deep breath, trying to calm himself. "I know spells that can make you do what I say." Actually, he had no idea how to cast such spells, and if he did, they were probably dark magic. But she didn't need to know that.

She smiled her sweet smile again. "Since I'm immune to magic, none of them would work on me, would they?"

He turned to Riph Raph. "Tell her."

Riph Raph coughed into his wing. "I don't want to tell you what to do, but . . ."

She patted him on the head. "I don't remember

rescuing you when you were a baby, but since I did, I'm sure that this one time, you'll do what I ask."

Riph Raph gave Marcus a sheepish look and shrugged his wings. "Yes."

She wrapped her arms around both of them in a group hug. "Then it's decided."

Marcus didn't know what to say. Apparently losing her memory didn't make her any less bossy. It didn't appear that he had any choice. "Fine, but if we run into any kind of trouble at all . . ."

"Perfect," she said, helping him to his feet and walking him to the door. "The fire elementals said that we have to open a series of gates to set them free. I think this door is either one of the gates or it leads to them." She pointed to the flaming symbol in the center of the black surface. "Do you know what that symbol means?"

He nodded. "It's the elemental sign for water."

"And can you open the door?"

He looked at Riph Raph, still hoping to find a way to change her mind, but the skyte waggled his ears. "I think we'd better do what she says."

Marcus shook his head. It was great to be back with Kyja again, but that didn't mean he'd let her push him around. "I'll try. But first you have to promise me one thing."

She blinked her green eyes and waited.

"Stop calling yourself Turnip. Your name is Kyja."

She flipped back her hair and smiled "I'll think about it."

He grunted and faced the door. Since the symbol was water, water magic was probably needed to open it. He knew lots of water spells, but the easiest was a simple extinguishing spell. He called on the water elementals for help, then held out his hand. A splash of water put out the flaming symbol and the door swung open.

"Great," Kyja said. "Let's go."

CHAPTER 27

NOT A TEST

A narrow trail on the other side of the door wound down into the darkness, lit only by the faintly luminescent blue moss on the stone walls.

Kyja, she thought as she helped the boy along the trail. The name would take some getting used to, but she had to admit that it was probably a better name than Turnip. Other things would take a lot more getting used to.

Like the fact that she was apparently quite close to the boy and the skyte.

Not that she had anything against them. They both seemed nice enough, if a little bossy. It was just strange to have someone who claimed to know you so well when you couldn't remember meeting them. Like playing a game of tag where you were blindfolded but everyone else could see.

She thought she could trust them—they'd come to

rescue her, hadn't they? But a part of her couldn't help questioning whether they were such good friends; how had they let her end up here in the first place? And their stories of jumping between worlds, fighting monsters, and solving quests was a little hard to take in.

"Is everything okay?" the boy asked.

Marcus, she reminded herself. His name was Marcus. And the skyte had the silly name of Riph Raph.

"Yes. I was only . . ." She glanced into the descending tunnel. "I was wondering what's down there."

"I'm hoping for bugs," Riph Raph said, flying slightly above them in the tight passageway. "I'm starving." Marcus had used water magic to heal the skyte's wing, and he seemed as energetic as ever.

"*Bugs.*" She glanced up at the ceiling and shivered.

"In Land Keep, there were these things called Harbingers," Marcus said. "They had super long claws, and they sang songs about death. They kidnapped me, but you couldn't see them."

"Claws?" She shivered.

"Those were nothing compared to the Frost Bite," Riph Raph said. "Remember how it almost bit your leg off? That was amazing."

Marcus laughed, although Kyja didn't see how that could be funny.

"You never got to see the swimming monkeys that nearly drowned us," Marcus said.

"You think it's *funny* that you've almost been killed?" Kyja stopped walking and stared at them.

Marcus's smile disappeared. "Well . . . it wasn't funny at the time."

"It was *kind* of funny when the air elementals hit you in the head with that melon." Riph Raph snickered. "

Kyja couldn't believe they were having this conversation. "Did *I* think it was funny?"

"Actually," Marcus said, "you were pretty mad at the air elementals. You got up in their faces and called them monsters."

"I did?"

"Totally," Riph Raph said. "You're no one to mess with. Remember that time you spit in a Summoner's face?"

"No." This was a side of herself she didn't know at all. "So, I'm . . . *brave?*"

"Heck yeah." Marcus snorted. "One time you took on a bunch of undead with a sword. You were all ducking and slashing." He turned to look at her. "Don't *you* think you're brave?"

She hadn't given the idea a lot of thought before. She knew she liked to help people. But sword fighting and spitting on monsters weren't things she would have expected to find in her past.

Marcus put a hand on her shoulder. "Why do you think you were so determined to go through the door?"

"Because it was the right thing to do," she answered

at once. "The fire elementals need our help. And it sounds like the people of Earth and Farworld do too. I couldn't give up when I knew something like that."

"Even though it was probably dangerous?"

She tugged on a length of hair. "It's not like I *want* to do anything dangerous. I definitely don't see any of this as some kind of amazing adventure the way you two seem to. But if I have to take a risk to help the people who need us. . ." She stuck out her chin. "Then yes. I will face monsters or sword fights or—or —flying melons. Whatever it takes."

Marcus leaned forward and gave her an unexpected kiss on the nose. "That's why we love you."

She felt heat spread all the way from the top of her head to her toes, and was glad for the darkness of the passageway.

◆

They'd been walking for what felt like thirty minutes, and Marcus found himself leaning more and more on Kyja as his leg got worse.

They stopped to catch their breath. "Am I too heavy?"

"No," Kyja puffed. "Well, maybe a little. Do I always help you get around like this?"

Marcus laughed. "More than I'd like to admit. You

dragged me through a desert once, and you drove me across the country on a motorcycle—you probably don't remember what a motorcycle is. But normally, I have a stick or a staff or a pole to support myself with."

"We'll try to find you one then," she said. "Until we do, I don't mind."

It was great to be back together again—even if he could tell that she didn't completely trust everything they'd told her. Would he have acted any differently if it were him in her shoes? He tried to imagine Kyja and Riph Raph coming up to him at the old boys' school and attempting to convince him they'd all been friends for years.

"Hey," Riph Raph called from ahead. "I found the end of the trail. And there's fish!"

Marcus glanced at Kyja. "We better catch up with him before he gets into trouble."

"Does he do that a lot?" Kyja asked as the two of them shuffled along again. "Get in trouble?

"More than I'd like to think about."

They rounded a sharp turn and emerged in a large domed chamber. At the center of the room, a perfectly circular pool glowed the same blue as the walls.

Riph Raph dove into the water and came out holding a green and gold fish. The fish's scales shimmered as it flopped back and forth. Riph Raph threw back his head and gulped the fish down in one bite. "Delicious," he called, going in for another.

"Are you sure you should be eating those?" Kyja asked. She lowered Marcus to the ground, and the two of them knelt at the edge of the pool. "They could be poisonous."

"Skytes have stomachs of iron," Riph Raph hooted, scooping up another fish.

Marcus looked into the water, but it was impossible to see more than a foot or two down, past the hundreds of fish swimming lazily near the surface. He had no idea how deep the pool was, or what might be lurking near the bottom. "We may want to move back a little," he said, remembering the frog-monkeys that had tried to drown him when he and Kyja had gone through the land-elemental tests.

As though his voice had conjured up the very danger he had been remembering, bubbles started rising to the surface. Kyja leaned over the water, but Marcus quickly pulled her back.

"Get out of there!" he called to Riph Raph. The skyte flew back to land behind Marcus and Kyja.

The fish disappeared, and the number and intensity of the bubbles increased until the entire pool was roiling like a pot of hot water.

"Have you—or *we*—ever seen anything like this?" Kyja asked, clutching Marcus's arm.

"No." Marcus began planning what kind of magic he might need to defend them. Air to block an attack? A fireball to fight off whatever was coming?

"Look," Riph Raph said, poking his head out between them.

A shape rose toward the surface of the pool, much larger than the fish. Marcus started forward, ready to attack or defend at the first sign of danger. Kyja's fingers dug into his arm.

Kyja leaned forward and smiled. "It's a woman." She started toward the pool as a figure with flowing, green hair and pale skin came into focus beneath the water, but Marcus tugged her back.

She did *look* like a woman. As he'd quickly discovered, though, things in Farworld weren't always as they appeared. The figure rose almost to the surface then stopped. Hair that was either intertwined with, or possibly made of, water plants floated in a nimbus about her face. Her body was wrapped in a flowing, green gown.

His first thought was that she was young, but as the woman's dark eyes met Marcus's, he realized that wasn't the case. There were no wrinkles on her skin and he saw no other physical signs of aging. Yet he sensed in the being a presence so old as to be almost timeless. If she were a tree, her rings would have gone back to before civilization existed.

"She's not dangerous," Kyja said, sliding toward the edge of the water.

"No," Marcus agreed. He didn't know what the

woman was exactly, but he felt no threat from her. Instead, an almost overwhelming impression of peace emanated from her expressionless face as her gaze took in the three of them. He moved to the side of the pool and looked down on the figure.

"Why have you come here?" Although the woman's mouth was still under water, her voice echoed in the chamber without distortion.

"To free the fire elementals," Kyja said.

The woman waited, limbs floating with a casual elegance, which, for some reason, reminded Marcus of lily pads.

"We're trying to open a drift," Marcus said, "between Earth and Farworld. We have the help of a water elemental, a pair of land elementals, and an air elemental, but we still need fire."

The woman's gaze drifted toward the ceiling. "The Fontasians have chosen to interact with the rest of the world," she said in a musing tone of voice. "The"—she said something Marcus would never have been able to pronounce, but which he was sure meant land elementals—"have at last decided to *do* something instead of only documenting events, and the Aerisians have been freed."

Marcus nodded, although it wasn't a question.

"The time has come at last. Danger presses from inside and out. Darkness eclipses light. Evil overcomes good." Her eyes shifted from the ceiling to give Marcus a penetrating stare. "*He shall make whole that which was torn asunder. Restore that which was lost. And all shall be as one.*"

Marcus recognized the words of the prophecy.

"*Or he shall bring chaos,*" the woman said. "*Pull down that which was built up. Destroy all, so that none may restore it.*"

Marcus went cold. He'd heard that there was another version of the prophecy in which he failed. But he'd never heard the words.

Her eyes burned into his soul. "You come to undo that which was done much longer ago than you can imagine," she said. "Do you understand the risk?"

His voice shook as he said, "I'm not sure."

The woman's head bobbed ever so slightly, as if that was the correct answer. "I am one of the four," she said. "Those for whom time and distance have no meaning. We are they who locked away the elementals at the first breaking. We who swore to protect, and wait. Now the time of breaking has come again. You alone stand to restore that which was torn asunder, or to destroy it once and for all."

Marcus didn't know what to say. He had the power to destroy Farworld forever? The Master of the Dark Circle had said that *he'd* been the one to put the brand on Marcus's arm. His own father had all but confirmed the truth of the claim. Did that mean he was only some random kid the Master had picked? If so, putting Farworld's future in his hands would be crazy.

"He doesn't stand alone," Kyja said. "I'm here to help him."

The woman's eyes moved to Kyja. "Two. That is as it should be."

"Three," Riph Raph said, and pushed forward. The woman stared at him, her eyes glittering beneath the dark water, and he eased away from the pool. "I mean, I'm just, you know, kind of tagging along. You can forget I'm here."

She turned back to look at Marcus at Kyja. "Once you choose to open the gate, there is no turning back. What you do here cannot be undone. Do you still wish to proceed?"

"Yes," Kyja said, softly.

Marcus's throat felt almost too dry to speak, but he croaked out a "Y-yes."

Riph Raph nodded.

"Very well. To free those who have been locked away and restore their magic, you must pass through four gates. At each gate you will be . . . evaluated."

"Like a test?" Marcus asked, thinking about the trials they'd had to pass through in Land Keep.

"Do not think of them as tests," the woman said. "Think of them as opportunities to learn. If you learn what is required, you may pass to the next gate."

"And if we fail?" Kyja asked.

"Then you are not the right ones to open the gates," the woman said. She lifted a hand out of the water. "If you are ready . . ."

Marcus looked at Kyja. It wasn't fair to get her into something like this with no memory of how hard it had been to gain the help of the other elementals. He was about to ask her if she wanted to wait here, but Kyja took his right hand in her left. Before he could say anything, she reached out and grabbed the woman's hand.

"It is done," the woman said, and she pulled them into the water.

CHAPTER 28

THE FIRST GATE

They were standing at the end of a dimly lit alley. Trash overflowed from dumpsters teeming with flies. The air smelled like raw sewage and exhaust, and somewhere above them, music pounded.

Kneeling on the asphalt, Marcus felt dirty water seep through his robe.

Kyja looked around and wrinkled her nose. "Is this Farworld?"

"No," a voice squeaked. "It's not."

"Riph Raph?" Kyja bent over to look at a sharp-nosed rat. "Is that you?"

"For some reason, he doesn't travel very well between Farworld and Earth," Marcus said. "He's turned into a lizard, a chicken, and a frog."

Riph Raph wiggled his whiskers as Kyja scooped him in her hands. "Why don't I ever get turned into something powerful? Like a fire-breathing dragon?"

"No dragons on Earth," Marcus said. "Although you'd probably make an adorable kitten."

Kyja petted Riph Raph's furry head. "What are we supposed to do now?"

"I have no idea," Marcus said. "It's not like that woman gave us instructions or anything."

A faint whimpering came from somewhere nearby. Marcus grabbed a dented trashcan and pulled himself up. "Do you hear that?"

"Yes." Kyja tilted her head, and the whimpering turned into all-out crying. She handed Riph Raph to Marcus. "It sounds like a baby."

The two of them started down the alley, Kyja walking, Marcus scooting through the debris.

"Over there," he said, pointing to a sheet of newspaper that shook and rustled. The crying sound came from beneath it.

Kyja lifted the paper. Lying on the ground, wrapped in a pink blanket, was a baby who couldn't have been more than a month or two old. Kyja picked up the baby and cradled it her arms. "Ohh," she cooed, rocking it. "You poor little thing. Who could have done this to you?"

A group of shadows appeared from the open end of the alley, and Marcus turned to see four men walking toward them. They looked to be anywhere between sixteen and twenty years old—dressed in jeans, t-shirts, and jackets. One of them carried a length of pipe, and Marcus caught a flash of metal under the hoodie of another.

Remembering what he'd learned about deflecting weapons from Divum, Marcus reached for air magic, but found nothing. It was as if his magic had been cut completely off again. He tried to ready a fireball, and the same thing happened.

"Give me the kid," said the biggest of the four—a muscular man with red hair buzzed short.

"You can't have him." Kyja stepped away, clutching the baby to her chest.

The teenager with the pipe swung it back and forth like a pendulum. "Give him the kid. Now."

"Leave us alone," Marcus said, clutching the edge of a dumpster to pull himself upright. "We'll call the police."

A tall guy with a bald head grabbed Marcus and threw him against the wall.

After that, everything happened fast. Riph Raph jumped out of Marcus's hand and ran at the men, squeaking, "Nobody messes with my friends!"

"A rat!" the bald man squealed, backing up against the wall.

Kyja broke for the end of the alley, holding the crying baby in her arms. The man with the pipe grabbed her and spun her around. Marcus felt the ground for anything he could use as a weapon. His fingers closed on a chunk of concrete. He picked it up and threw it at the man with the pipe, hitting him square in the back.

The man with red hair darted forward and pulled a knife from under his hoodie. Before anyone could respond, he leaped at Kyja and stabbed her in the stomach.

She looked at the man, in shock, before slumping against the wall. He snatched the baby from her, and the four men raced out of the alley.

"Kyja!" Marcus screamed as a red circle bloomed on the front of her gown and she fell to the ground.

⸻◆⸻

At first Kyja felt nothing at all—a flash of metal and a sense of surprise. The pain came a second later, sharp and tearing. She fell against the wall and watched in shock as the man yanked the baby from her arms. The strength went out of her legs, and wetness spread down the front of her gown.

She heard the boy shout to her. *Marcus*, she reminded herself woozily. *His name is Marcus.* She put her hands to her gown, and they came away red. "Why?" she tried to ask, but the only thing that came out of her mouth was a wet clicking sound.

"Do something!" Riph Raph squeaked. "Use magic."

"I can't." Marcus was at her side, taking her hand, talking to her. "You're going to be okay. We'll find someone to help you. I'm so sorry. I tried to stop them, but I couldn't touch air or fire or . . ." His words began to slur together.

Was he having a hard time talking, or was she having a hard time hearing? She looked up. The stars seemed especially bright. Like fairies watching over her. Her head slumped to the side, and she couldn't see them anymore.

"She's dying," Riph Raph said.

"I don't know what to do," Marcus cried. "What kind of test is this? Why did you take my—" He stopped yelling, and Kyja felt his hand tighten on hers. "Water," he said, his voice rising. "I have *water* magic."

He leaned over her, whispering something that sounded like a poem All at once, the pain was gone. The weakness was gone too. She sat up and touched the spot where she'd been stabbed. It was completely healed. She stared up at Marcus.

"Are you . . . okay?" Marcus asked.

"Yes," she said, unable to believe it. One second she'd felt her life draining away, and the next, she'd never felt better. "How did you do that?"

Marcus beamed. "Water is the strongest healing magic. I learned about it from Cascade while waiting for Master Therapass and Tankum."

"Way to go," Riph Raph said, pink rat tail swishing trash behind him like a broom.

Kyja tentatively stood up and didn't feel wobbly at all. She felt good. Strong. "What about the baby? We can't let them take it."

"We won't," Marcus said.

He seemed so confident and determined. He stared at the brick walls, although there didn't seem to be anything to see in them. "There," he said, pointing at a spot a little to her left. "They're about a block away, heading east on foot."

Kyja stared from Marcus to the wall. "How can you know that?"

"Water's good for more than healing," Marcus said. "Fontasians can see for miles."

Riph Raph's whiskers quivered as he crawled up Kyja's arm. "We'll never catch them. And even if we do, how are we supposed to get the baby back?"

Kyja petted his gray fur. "We'll figure that out once we've found them. This has to be what we were sent here for. Recusing the baby will prove that we are the right people to save Farworld and Earth." She reached out to Marcus. "I'll help you walk."

"Thanks, but I've got this." Marcus pointed at a puddle of dirty water, and a glittering ice staff rose from it. "Water magic has lots of uses. I'll bet that's the test—to show that we know how to use magic that fire elementals can't."

He and Kyja walked out of the alley to the street. "What kind of magic do those use?" she asked, pointing to metal carts rolling by in both directions.

"They're called cars," Marcus said. "And they use engines, not magic. But don't even think about it."

"*Cars*," she repeated, eyeing them hungrily. "We have to find those men before they hurt the baby," she said.

Marcus nodded. "Leave it to me."

———◆———

Sprawled in the filthy alley, watching Kyja get stabbed, Marcus had never felt more helpless. All of his years of being picked on, the many times his damaged body had let him down, the weeks he'd spent with no idea whether Kyja was dead or alive, with no way to help her— it all come back in a wave of anger and despair.

He didn't understand why the other elements were blocked, but now, with water magic surging through him, he'd never felt more powerful. He planned to use every ounce of that power to stop the men who'd stolen the infant. How dare they attack Kyja? How dare they steal an innocent child? Anger throbbed in his temples and made his muscles shake. If the thugs wanted a fight, he'd bring them one.

"The first thing we need to do is slow them down," he said. He raised his withered arm, and thick, gray fog billowed from the clear sky. "Let's see them try to find their way through that." The kidnappers would be the helpless ones, while he was more powerful than ever.

Next they needed transportation, but he could do a lot better than a car. He pointed to a sewer grate. Water streamed up between the metal bars, freezing into shape as it hit the sidewalk. An ice-scaled body with crystal wings formed in front of them.

Riph Raph blinked his beady rat eyes. "Since when can you make a frost pinnois?"

The ice creature wasn't as big as the real thing, and Marcus probably wouldn't be able to hold it together for long—especially not if the weather were warm. But on a cold, damp night with only a few blocks to cover, it would work.

Kyja looked at him with wonder in her eyes, and he stuck out his chest a little. "You didn't say you were such a powerful wizard."

He shrugged as they climbed onto the miniature pinnois. "I've been practicing."

"Where do you wish me to take you?" the pinnois asked in what sounded like a rather bad French accent.

Marcus pointed in the direction the men were walking, and the pinnois took off.

"Whooooo-weeee," Kyja whooped as they flew through the foggy night air, zipping above taxis, under stoplights, and around phone poles. Her dark hair blew back from her head, fluttering like a cape. "This is incredible."

"Please tell me he has a license for this," Riph Raph said, flattening himself against her palm.

With his water-magic-enhanced vision, Marcus

watched the men with the baby walking cautiously through the swirling mist. They seemed to be headed toward a nearby apartment building, but he would make sure they never got that far. His hand tightened on the ice staff. After years of being bullied, it felt great to have a way to fight back.

In minutes, they landed in front of the building the men were walking toward.

"Stay quiet," he whispered as they climbed off the pinnois. It melted back into a puddle. "The men will be here any second."

"Should we try talking to them?" Kyja asked.

Marcus shook his head. "Talking didn't work."

Huddled together, the men stepped into the light from the building entrance. The baby had stopped crying, and it seemed to be okay—for now.

Marcus leaned casually against the wall. "Look who it is," he called, startling the group.

"How did you get here?" asked the man with the infant. His eyes went to the red stain on Kyja's gown; he was clearly wondering how she was still standing.

"That's none of your business," Marcus said. "Give us back the baby, and we won't hurt you too much." Kyja glanced at him, and he winked.

The red-haired man clutched the child to his chest. The teen with the pipe stepped forward, brandishing his weapon.

Marcus tapped the end of his ice staff on the ground, and steaming hot water gushed from the end of the man's pipe.

"Ahh!" he screamed, dropping his weapon as hot water soaked his jeans. Marcus thought it looked comical—like something from a movie.

The man with the baby pulled a knife, but Marcus made it wet and slick in his hand. The handle slipped through his fingers, and the knife fell to the ground.

Clearly spooked, the men backed away. "We don't want no trouble."

"Then you shouldn't have messed with us," Marcus said.

"Maybe we should—" Kyja began.

But Marcus was already tapping his staff again. The rage he'd felt before thudded in his temples. Bullies like these needed to be taught a lesson. Just because they were strong didn't mean they were allowed to hurt other people. What they needed was a taste of their own medicine.

Water magic flowed from Marcus's staff, and something with bunched muscles rose out of the water; its claws and teeth glinted in the fog. Spikes rose from the back of its twisted neck. Marcus smiled at the terror that replaced the men's earlier confidence.

The water creature lifted a clawed hand. One of the men turned to run, but Marcus froze his feet to the sidewalk. He'd let the creature go at them for a while and then—

"Stop it!" Kyja yelled, stepping between Marcus's creature and the men.

"What are you doing?" he demanded, struggling to contain the monster he had created.

She spun to glare at him. "What are *you* doing?"

"Getting back the baby." Why was she getting in his way? Isn't this what she wanted? He'd thought she'd be impressed by what he could do, but she looked mad.

She put her hands on her hips. "You're getting the baby back by hurting these men the way they hurt me? You don't care about the child. You're trying to get revenge."

The water creature hesitated, awaiting Marcus's command. This wasn't revenge, he argued with himself. He was saving the baby, saving Kyja. And, okay, maybe he wanted to let them experience the helplessness he'd felt, but what was wrong with that?

Kyja turned to the man holding the baby. He clutched the infant to his chest in a way that Marcus realized looked more protective than he'd expected. The child should have been terrified, but it cooed and gurgled against the man's jacket.

"Do you know who the baby belongs to?" Kyja asked.

He nodded, looking from her to the water creature. "She's my sister's. Her boyfriend broke up with her and took little Lizzie. He said she'd never see her again. We thought you guys were helping him."

His *sister's* baby? Marcus's grip on the ice staff loosened, and the water creature began to melt back into the puddle.

"I'm sorry I stabbed you," the man said. "I guess I panicked. Are you okay?"

Kyja nodded. "I'm fine. Take Lizzie home to her mother."

Fog swirled around them, and Marcus and Kyja were no longer in the street. Instead they were standing on a grassy clearing in the middle of a forest. Riph Raph was a skyte again, and the blood was gone from the front of Kyja's gown.

What had happened? Why were they here? Had they passed the test, or failed it? Marcus didn't understand. He'd felt so sure he'd been doing the right thing—sticking up for the weak. Now he realized he'd probably made a huge mistake.

CHAPTER 29

THE SECOND GATE

Kyja's heart was still pounding. She couldn't believe Marcus had made that, that . . . *creature*. Hadn't he seen how the man obviously cared for the child? Had he really been about to let the monster he'd made attack them?

What if the man had dropped the infant? What if the monster had accidently hurt the baby? It was exactly the way Chaos would have reacted if he ever got loose.

"What were you thinking back there?" she demanded.

Without his ice staff, Marcus's bad leg wobbled. He grabbed the branch of a nearby sapling to hold himself upright. "I wasn't thinking," he said. "I was doing what had to be done."

"Really?" she balled her hands into fists. "You *had* to make that man scald himself? You *had* to freeze the other one's feet to the ground? You *had* to threaten them with that *thing?*"

Marcus's face slowly went red. "Maybe not. And maybe I didn't have to save your life, either. Or did you forget about that part?"

"Hey, kids," Riph Raph said. "How about we look for some tasty bugs? Or explore the forest? This looks like a great place for a picnic."

Kyja and Marcus ignored the skyte. She turned on him. "You think that saving my life excuses the way you acted afterward?" Kyja asked. "I would rather have bled to death than take a chance of hurting that baby. You terrified those men." Marcus had seemed so nice at first, but now she was seeing his real side.

"They. Tried. To. Kill. You," Marcus shouted, spit flying from his lips.

"Because they thought I was trying to take their child," Kyja shouted back.

"Which you wouldn't have discovered if I hadn't found a way to catch up to them and scare them so bad that they had to talk to us."

Riph Raph's head followed the argument back and forth like the ball in a ping pong game. Suddenly the skyte's eyes went wide. "Um, if you two could put your argument on hold for a minute . . ."

"You were a brute," Kyja said.

Marcus sneered. "And you think you can talk your way out of any situation."

"Guys!" Riph Raph shouted.

Marcus and Kyja glared at him. "What?" they yelled together.

"There's, um, someone else here," the skyte said, looking to his left out of the corner of his eyes. "So maybe you could, you know, save the argument for later?"

The sapling Marcus had been holding bent as though caught in a strong breeze. Kyja barely had time to think that there was no wind when the tree turned, and she realized it wasn't a tree at all, but a man with brown skin and thick, leaf-like hair. He raised from a bow and studied the three of them with nut-brown eyes set in a deeply wrinkled face.

"What did you learn?" the man asked.

Kyja looked at Marcus. Had the tree man been there all along? Had he heard everything they'd said? She had a strong feeling that they hadn't made the best impression.

"You're one of the . . ." Marcus said. "You're like the lady in the pool?"

"I am one of the four," the man said.

Marcus quickly let go of him, and the man conjured a root out of the ground. The root turned into a beautiful polished staff, which he handed to Marcus. "This should help you."

"Thanks," Marcus said. "It's the perfect length."

Riph Raph studied the man with big, round eyes. "Are you a person, or a . . . plant?"

"Riph Raph!" Kyja said. "That's rude."

The man only smiled. "I am a living thing. Like each of you. I have watched you three since you began your quest." He spoke slowly, as if choosing his words with care. "So far I have been impressed. But now I must determine if you have learned enough to continue your journey."

"We've learned that talking is better than fighting," Kyja said.

The man intertwined his branch fingers and looked at Marcus.

"Maybe that's what you leaned," Marcus said. "But that's not what *I* learned. We didn't start the fight, and talking didn't help when those men first showed up. Maybe I went overboard, but if we hadn't chased them down and threatened them, we never would have discovered the truth."

"That's only because they wouldn't talk to us in the first place," Kyja said. "If they'd told us the baby belonged to that one man's sister, we wouldn't have needed to fight."

Marcus frowned. "The problem is, we didn't have that choice. They chose to attack us. We tried to talk, but they didn't listen. They forced us to act, and until we did, talking wasn't an option."

Kyja turned to the tree. Surely arguing wasn't helping their cause. "Marcus is right. As much as I hate to say it, sometimes you have no choice but to react."

"You're right too," Marcus said. "I was trying to help, but I got carried away."

The tree man studied them, the leaves of his branches fluttering ever so slightly.

"I guess we don't know what we learned," Kyja admitted. "Sometimes using logic and common sense is best. But at other times, it seems like you have to follow your emotions. Maybe we aren't ready after all."

The man's bark-like face crinkled into a smile. "Very good. You may continue on the path." He pointed a twig finger toward the woods, where Kyja saw that a path had opened up.

"I don't get it," Marcus said. "How can you send us on if we don't know what we were supposed to learn?"

"It's not important that you know what you have learned," the man said slowly. "Only that you learned it." He turned and started toward the woods, his root feet sinking into the ground and pulling back out with each step. Behind him, the grass looked a little greener.

"Can you give us any advice?" Kyja called after him. "Something to help us going forward?"

"Be wise," the tree called back before vanishing into the woods.

"A lot of help he was," Marcus said. "He might as well have told us something like, don't make mistakes, or make the right choices."

Kyja laughed. "Don't believe lies. Pay attention to important things."

"Don't let birds poop on your head," Riph Raph added. "And try not to eat poisonous mushrooms."

Together the three followed the path into the woods. The trees were so high and thick that it was like walking into a tunnel. The brightness of day changed to a gloomy twilight gray, and the air took on a chill.

"From now on," Marcus said as they walked along the winding dirt path, "I promise to talk first and do magic second."

Glancing around the woods, Kyja had the distinct feeling that something was watching them. She edged a little closer to Marcus. "Maybe you should keep your magic ready. Just in case."

They continued silently along the trail. Every so often, one of them stopped to look around, thinking they had seen movement from the corner of their eyes. But when they turned to look, there was nothing around.

Riph Raph, who had been flying ahead, returned to land on Kyja's shoulder. "Do you smell that?"

Kyja sniffed. The air smelled like swamp water or eggs that had gone bad.

"Stinks like dirty diapers," Marcus said.

The farther they walked, the stronger the odor grew. Another smell appeared too, beneath the rotten-egg smell. Kyja wasn't able to identify it until Marcus suddenly stopped and looked around.

"Is something burning?" he asked.

That was it; she smelled smoke. Kyja looked around, trying to identify the direction it was coming from. "Do you think the forest is on fire?"

"I don't *see* any flames," Marcus said. "But I definitely smell smoke. And notice how there aren't any more bird or insect sounds. The woods were full of cheeps, and chirps, and buzzes when we started out. But now it's like we're standing in the middle of a cemetery."

Kyja patted Riph Raph's head. "Maybe you could fly around and take a look."

Riph Raph wrapped his tail tightly around himself. "When birds and bugs disappear, skytes tend to stay put. It's a self-preservation thing."

"Hang on," Marcus said. "I have an idea." He knelt on the ground, clasped his staff in his hands, and closed his eyes.

"Praying isn't a bad idea," Riph Raph said. "But I'm thinking running might be a little more useful at the moment."

"I'm not praying," Marcus said. "I'm *seeing*."

Kyja nodded. "Like when you used water magic to find the baby."

Marcus continued to close his eyes. "There's no water magic here. They've blocked it off like they did with land and fire magic before. The only magic I can reach here is land, so I'm using it to look through the eyes of a tree."

Kyja thought she must have misheard. "Trees have eyes?"

"It's one of those yoga witchdoctor things," Riph Raph said. "Become one with nature and eat a pine cone."

"Shhh," Marcus whispered. "Okay, I can see the sky, a lot more trees, and a mountain with a cave in the side."

"Any smoke?" Kyja asked. "Or flames?"

Marcus shook his head. "There has been, though. I can see lots of burned trees near the mountains, but nothing recent. The forest is worried; I can sense it. They know more fires could come at any time. And . . . wait, what's that?" He put his hand to the side of his head, brow wrinkling in concentration.

"Well?" Riph Raph asked. "What is it? Plague? Pestilence? Please don't tell me you see starvation."

Marcus opened his eyes and stood. "Come on, we have to go."

"What did you see?" Kyja asked as Marcus limped quickly along the trail. "Are we in danger?"

"Not *us*," Marcus said.

They walked over a low rise, and a small cabin came into view. A neat garden was planted on one side, and as they got closer, Kyja noticed that the dirt in front of the porch was neatly raked. The shutters and door had been painted a cheery green, and smooth river rocks had been used to build a chimney and garden wall. But what caught her eyes right away were the scorch marks on the roof and walls of the cabin.

"Hello," Marcus shouted, hurrying toward the building. "Is anyone home?"

There was no answer.

"Maybe they moved," Riph Raph said. "That's what I'd do if I lived in a place that smelled like this."

As they reached the cabin, Kyja noticed something discarded on the side of the porch. She walked over and picked it up. It was a rag doll with blonde yarn hair and blue button eyes. No child would willingly leave a beloved toy like this behind.

Marcus banged on the door. "Is anyone there?" When no one answered, he tugged on the leather pull and pushed the door open. Cautiously they stepped inside. The room was in disarray, with belongings strewn all over the floor and food spilled everywhere.

"What is it?" Kyja asked. "Did robbers attack?"

"I don't think so." Marcus looked slowly around the room before walking back outside. "See the flame marks?"

Kyja nodded. It was as if someone had tried to burn the place down—and nearly succeeded. "What could have caused that?"

"The same thing that took the family," Marcus said. "The trees were trying to warn me, but I couldn't understand." He turned and pointed to the cave in the side of the mountain. "They were taken by a dragon."

CHAPTER 30

TALKING IT OUT

"Tell me again what we're trying to do here," Riph Raph said as they climbed the side of the mountain. "Because it seems to me that we're on our way to face a creature that could destroy an entire village. Yet we have no weapons, no spells, and no plan."

"That's pretty much it," Marcus said. "I've been giving a lot of thought to what happened when we tried to save the baby. Like Kyja said, if we'd talked to the men in the first place, we could have worked everything out."

Raph Raph's eyes began to twitch. "So you want to ask the dragon to give us back the family—assuming it hasn't already eaten them? What are you going to give it in trade? Dragons aren't exactly known for the high number of favors they do."

"We won't know what it wants until we ask," Marcus said. He'd been crawling the last hundred feet, and now the mountain was so steep that Kyja had to crawl too.

"Who knows?" Marcus went on. "Maybe it's a nice little baby dragon."

"Are you sure this is a good idea?" Kyja asked. "I'm wondering if this might be a situation where we use magic first and talk second."

Marcus stopped to catch his breath. They were almost to the cave entrance, and he could see faint swirls of yellow smoke drifting into the air. "Wasn't the idea of the thing with the baby to teach us the logic and reasoning of water elementals?"

Kyja raised an eyebrow but didn't say anything.

He pointed to the cave. "We negotiate with the dragon. We ask how it's doing. What kind of dragon it is. Have a little casual chitchat to get things started. Then we happen to mention how we're looking for a family. Maybe it's seen them. Is there something it would trade them for? It tells us it wants some magical gem, a special sword, blue slippers, or whatever. We find what it wants, make the trade, and the next member of the four moves us forward."

"Sounds too good to be true," Kyja said.

Riph Raph flapped his ears. "That's because it *is*. Here's how the conversation will go. We say, 'How are you doing?' The dragon eats us. No more conversation. No more us."

"You've learned nothing from this experience," Marcus said. "This is why I'm in charge."

"Excuse me?" Kyja said. "*I'm* the one who made *you*

come here in the first place. What makes you think you're the one in charge?"

Above their heads, an especially large plume of yellow smoke rose from the cave entrance, and a roar shook the entire mountain.

"Who invades my home?" a terrifying voice bellowed.

"Remember, *you're* in charge," Riph Raph said, ducking behind a rock.

"Did you prepare any spells?" Kyja asked. "In case logic doesn't work?"

Marcus shook his head. "Land magic doesn't have a lot of weapons. It's mostly used to study and learn things."

A large, green snout emerged over the ledge. The mouth had several rows of teeth as tall as Marcus.

"I think we're about to learn something," Riph Raph wailed, his blue body shaking. "We're about to learn why nobody tries to negotiate with dragons."

Marcus craned his neck to look up at the dragon. "Hello!" he shouted. "How are you today? Nice weather we're having."

A burst of flame shot down at them, and they all ducked.

"No more chitchat," Kyja said. "Get to the point."

Marcus agreed. Arms and legs trembling, he pushed himself up on a boulder to address the dragon "We're looking for a family and—"

The dragon stretched out its neck and gazed down at

them. The creature's head was as big as the entire cabin the family had been taken from. Each of its eyes was the size of a tractor tire.

"That's no baby," Riph Raph yelped.

The dragon shot another burst of flame down at them. Marcus used land magic to create a barrier of rock and dirt, but the heat still singed the top of his hair. With another roar, the dragon lunged and opened its mouth to eat them.

"Run!" Marcus screamed. He cast a spell to pull as many rocks onto the dragon as he could—creating a minor avalanche that was a distraction at best—and rolled down the side of the mountain.

———◆———

"Did that go according to plan?" Riph Raph asked, nursing a badly sprained tail. They were back in the cabin, each of them banged up and bruised.

"I told you before; I didn't have a plan," Marcus said, holding a wet cloth to his eye. "I assumed the point of this quest was to show what we'd learned from the last one."

"I think we can safely conclude that that's not the case," Kyja said. She turned a carving knife left and right, wincing at the reflection of an egg-sized lump on her forehead. "Are you sure you can't heal this? It looks like I have a second nose."

"Sorry," Marcus said. "Land magic doesn't have any healing spells. At least none I've learned."

Kyja sighed and put down the knife. They'd searched the entire house, but found no weapons to fight a dragon with. Which made sense. If the people who had lived here owned weapons that could have destroyed a dragon, they'd still be here.

"What kinds of things can you do with land magic?" she asked. There had to be something they could cast that would give them an advantage.

Marcus sighed and leaned back in his chair. "Digging holes. Filling up holes. Moving rocks and stuff. Seeing through the eyes of plants and animals."

"Seal its cave off," Riph Raph said. "We could suffocate it."

"I don't have that kind of power," Marcus said. "That little avalanche was pretty much the limit of my abilities, and it barely gave us enough time to escape."

"Besides," Kyja said. "Suffocating the dragon would kill the family, too."

Marcus found a couple of apples under the table and offered one to Kyja. She shook her head. "Ever since I died, I'm not hungry."

Marcus took a bite of his and wiped juice from his chin. "If you're already dead, how did you almost die when you got stabbed?"

Kyja shrugged. "I've been thinking about that ever

since it happened. I shouldn't have been able to get stabbed any more than I should have this lump on my head. I think this is all some kind of illusion."

Riph Raph licked his bent tail and sniffed. "Feels real to me."

"What about that seeing thing?" Kyja asked. "Is there any way you could look through the dragon's eyes and get an idea of what's going on in its lair? Or maybe look through one of the family members' eyes?"

"I'm pretty sure dragons are immune to magic," Marcus said. "Even if they weren't, that wouldn't work. Plants are easy. But Lanctrus-Darnoc said that you can only see through the eyes of animals who have had a profound influence on your life."

Kyja got up and began looking through the belongings of the family who had lived in the cabin. She found a big bed and a little bed. Clothing in adult sizes and a child's sizes. Adult books and children's stories. All of the items were pointed reminders that a family needed help, and they had no way to give it.

"You said that water elementals are known for logic and reason. What are land elementals known for?"

Marcus lay back on the floor, resting his head in his hands. "Having giant wings and arguing with each other." He laughed. "I don't know. Wisdom, I guess. Learning things and teaching them to others. They have this huge library in Land Keep with, like, every book in the world."

"*Books?*" Kyja went back to the stack of thick leather volumes she'd glanced at earlier. Was there a chance one of those might help? She skimmed through each of the titles. She found books about trapping, skinning, and cooking. She opened one on mining, and the pages flipped to a section covered with handwritten notes.

"Look at this," she said, studying the pages. "It says that the cave where the dragon lives used to be a gold mine. According to these notes, the people who lived here have been exploring the mine for a while. They discovered several air vents leading into the mountain."

Marcus pushed himself to his feet and limped to her side. He studied the pages over Kyja's shoulder. "Air vents won't help us. See, the miners were hoping to use the vents to get into the cave. But the openings are too small to climb through."

"They're too small for us," Kyja said. "But not for Riph Raph."

———◆———

"Maybe negotiating wasn't such a bad idea," Riph Raph said. "We probably got off on the wrong talon last time."

Marcus sat with his eyes closed. "Be quiet and let me concentrate." Seeing through the eyes of plants had been easy, but seeing through the eyes of an animal was proving to be much more complicated. It was like trying to make his way through a maze with millions of possible doors. Every time he thought he was getting close, he'd take a wrong turn and end up having to start over.

"I need you to help me," he told the skyte. "You have to guide me to your eyes."

"No thanks," Riph Raph said. "We skytes don't like things inside us unless we ate them. Why don't you try looking through the eyes of a bird or a bug?"

Marcus ground his teeth. "I told you, it has to be something I've been influenced by. And a bug won't help us. I need something that can go down the air shaft and free the family."

"There are so many problems with that plan," Riph Raph said, counting them off on his talons. "One, I don't want anyone or anything in my head. It gives me the jim-jams. Two, I am not going into a dragon's lair. No way, no how. Three, no. Just, no." He put his wings over his head and shuddered.

Kyja scratched the skyte behind his ears. "Marcus promised he would create a distraction once you're inside."

"And if the dragon doesn't get distracted?" Riph Raph asked. "You two are safe out here, and I get cooked."

"What do you want to do instead?" Marcus asked, slamming his fist against his leg. "Leave them to die?"

"I thought you said you trusted each other," Kyja said. "You both took chances to save me."

Marcus and Riph Raph looked at each other.

"I trust Riph Raph as much as anyone I know," Marcus said.

The skyte waggled his ears. Kyja waited. "Fine," the skyte said. "I trust him."

Kyja nodded. "From what you two told me about land elementals, it seems like there is something else they must have in common besides wisdom and learning. Can you imagine how much trust it would take to commit to spend the rest of your life attached to another creature? It's the same kind of trust family members need to have in one another."

"You don't have to let me look through your eyes," Marcus said. "I trust that you'll get to the family. We can work out a signal, or a count, or something."

"No, I'll let you see through my eyes." The skyte sighed. "But if that dragon singes a single one of my scales, I'm holding both of you personally responsible."

Marcus closed his eyes and again tried to find his way to seeing through Riph Raph. This time it was like having a friend take his hand and guide him through the maze's twists and turns. A moment later, the world came into sharp focus.

"Wow!" He gasped. "I've never seen things so clearly before. Even water vision didn't have this kind of detail." He opened his eyes but continued to see through the skyte.

"Of course," Riph Raph said. "Skytes have the

greatest eyesight of any creature who soars above the ground."

Marcus had gotten used to Riph Raph's constant boasting. But this time he thought the skyte's claim might actually be true. "Remember," he said, "once you find the family, wait for our diversion. Then free them and find a way to get them out of the cave entrance."

As Riph Raph soared into the sky, Marcus felt his stomach lurch. Trees, rocks, and grass raced by below him in detail great enough that he could see a furry, white creature peek out from beneath a rock, a tiny purple flower nod in the wind, and a pine cone drop from a tree branch then bounce its way to the ground. What must it have be like to spend every second of every day with this kind of sensory input?

"Is he there yet?" Kyja asked.

"He's spotted the air shaft," Marcus said. "He's going down now."

The sky disappeared and, he found himself in a dark tunnel. Even with the skyte's keen vision, it was difficult to make anything out. Riph Raph glanced up toward the opening, and Marcus whispered, "Don't give up."

"What's he doing?" Kyja asked, squeezing his hand.

With his vision coming through Riph Raph's eyes, Marcus couldn't see her, or anything around him. He would be completely reliant on Kyja to guide him when the time came for him to do his part.

Marcus held his breath. Riph Raph glanced toward the light above him one more time, then began crawling down the tunnel. "He's doing it," Marcus said. "He's going in."

For several minutes, he couldn't see anything at all. It was a strange sensation to see no light or color, despite the fact that his eyes were open, and he knew that it was the middle of the day—a small taste of what it must feel like to be blind. He spotted a glow ahead.

"I think he's almost there." The glow grew brighter. It was a room, a huge cavern filled with piles of treasure, weapons, armor, shields, and . . . *bones*. Was it too late? Had the dragon eaten the family?

Riph Raph looked left and spotted the dragon, who was searching suspiciously around the room as though he sensed someone nearby.

"Now," Marcus said, gripping Kyja's hand. "Point me toward the cave entrance."

Taking Marcus's shoulders, Kyja turned his body slightly to the left, and he held out his hands. He'd said that land magic was mostly good for things like digging and filling holes. That was true. But digging could be done quite rapidly. And when it was . . .

A boom rattled the air, and Marcus felt the ground shake beneath him. He blasted another hole, and another. *Boom. Boom.*

Kyja squeezed his hand. "That's incredible."

Inside its lair, the dragon's head spun around. It roared and shot a plume of flame toward the mouth of the cave.

"It's working," Kyja said. "Here it comes."

Watching from Riph Raph's eyes, Marcus saw the dragon disappear through the cave entrance. "Go," he urged the skyte.

Riph Raph launched himself out of the vent and soared around the dragon's lair. The skyte darted around the cave, searching for the family. For a second, Marcus was afraid that the family really had been killed, but then he saw them in the back of the cavern, locked in a large cage. Riph Raph flew down and began working the lock with his talons as the family crowded around the door. The mother and father said something, but, with no sound, Marcus couldn't tell what.

The key now was to keep creating diversions. Marcus used every bit of land magic he knew—blasting holes, dropping rocks, creating walls of dirt.

"Hurry," he whispered.

Kyja's grip tightened until she was crushing Marcus's fingers. "The dragon sees us. What do we do now?"

Marcus hadn't thought that far.

"It's coming!" Kyja yelled.

Riph Raph had the cage open, and the family was climbing out. But escaping would take a couple of more minutes.

A roar shook the air, and Marcus felt a blast of fire inches above his head.

"Look out!" Kyja screamed.

Marcus wanted to see what was happening, but he couldn't take his eyes off the family until he knew they were safe. He had no way to fight the dragon, and they'd never be able to escape from it with him being unable to see and having a bad leg.

Doing the only thing he could think of, Marcus dug a hole right under them. They fell through the air and hit the ground hard enough to knock the breath out of them

"What are you doing?" Kyja shouted. "It's right on top of us."

Marcus smelled the dragon's sulfuric breath and gave them the only cover he was able to—piles of rock and dirt flew over them. He did his best to provide a little breathing space, but he wasn't that skilled with land magic. Dirt filled his mouth, nose, and ears. He clung tight to Kyja, hoping she understood what he was doing.

Over his head, the dragon's roar shook the ground, and he could feel it clawing its way through the dirt and rocks toward them. The family was running for the entrance. They were almost free, but he had no idea what he'd do after they'd escaped. Rocks and dirt tumbled around him. Something banged against his head, and he instinctively pulled his vision back to his own eyes.

The dragon was right above them, its razor teeth close

enough to touch. It drew back its head, sucked in a breath, and blasted a wall of flame toward them. He dove on the top of Kyja, knowing it wouldn't do any good, and—

They stepped through a doorway into a crystal room.

CHAPTER 31

THE THIRD GATE

Kyja threw her hands up, waiting for the flames to turn her and Marcus to ash, before realizing that the dragon was gone. They were no longer in a hole covered with dirt. Her lumps and bruises had disappeared. They stood inside the door of a huge room with walls and a ceiling that glittered like ice.

"I am *so* sorry," Marcus said, throwing an arm around her. "I nearly got you killed. What was I thinking?"

"Are you kidding?" Kyja squeezed Marcus in a bear hug so tight it made him gasp for breath. "You were amazing! I would *never* have thought to bury us in a hole. I'll bet that stupid dragon had never seen anything like that in its life."

"I was pretty amazing too," Riph Raph said. "Did you see the way I flew right past that dragon? I was like, 'Please, you don't scare me. You're nothing but a big flying lizard.' And he was like, 'I'm getting out of here.' Then I picked the lock on the cage—an impossible task if it wasn't for my superb talent and brains. And the family was all, 'You're incredible. Thank you for saving us. What can we ever do to repay you?' And I was all—"

"You were both great," Kyja said. "And we did it. We saved the family."

She looked slowly round the room they'd entered. It was like something out of a storybook. Glittering floors, beautiful pools with dancing fountains. The ceiling curved into a majestic dome, and glowing, pastel-colored globes lent the space a feeling of peace and tranquility.

A thick mist coalesced before them until it formed the image of a beautiful woman. "Welcome," she said.

Kyja felt that she was in the presence of a higher being. She held out the sides of her gown and curtsied.

Marcus must have felt the same way, because he bowed as low as he could while holding his staff. "We did it, Your Majesty," Marcus said. "We saved the family. We passed the test."

"You need not address me as Your Majesty," the woman said in a regal tone that made Kyja think of goddesses and queens. "It was not a test. Whether you succeeded in saving the family does not matter. What *is* important is what you learned in the attempt."

"Hang on," Riph Raph said, perching on the edge of

a fountain. "Are you saying that we risked our lives for nothing?"

"Riph Raph," Kyja scolded. Had the skyte always been this annoying? If so, how had they stayed friends all these years?

Instead of being offended, the woman only smiled. "Life is full of trials. Sometimes you succeed. Other times, you fail. In the end, it is not the count of successes and failures you take with you, but the knowledge gained in the pursuit."

Marcus scratched his head. "Did any of that really happen? Did we save a family from a dragon? Or was it, like, some kind of super-realistic 3D movie?"

The woman laughed, and overhead, the crystal globes tinkled in response. "You may choose to believe whatever you like."

"I believe I was the most heroic skyte in the history of skytes," Riph Raph said. "And that's saying something, because there have been some seriously heroic skytes."

The woman nodded, her eyes twinkling. "What did you learn?"

Kyja thought carefully. She didn't want to get her answer wrong. "I learned that working together is important. None of us could have accomplished what we did alone."

"I learned that logic and magic aren't the only way to solve a problem," Marcus said. "If we hadn't read the book and learned from other people's experiences, we wouldn't have come up with the plan we did."

"I learned that dragons have way too much treasure," Riph Raph said. "Talk about greedy."

"Good lessons all," the woman said. "They will serve you well in your ultimate quest. And now it is time for another lesson." The mist the woman was made of began to thin. Looking at her was like looking at a slightly out of focus picture.

"Wait," Marcus said. "Before you go, have *you* been watching us too, while we've been trying to open the drift? Do you know about our quest to open a doorway between Farworld and Earth?"

"I watch all." The woman's silver eyes glinted with hidden knowledge. "I know much."

Marcus stepped toward the mist, his hand wrapped around his staff. "I have a question. If we open the drift—*when* we open the drift—what happens next? Kyja can go to Earth, and I can come here, but does the door stay open? Can we always go back and forth through it? And what's the danger we're supposed to save our worlds from? What are we supposed to do? It seems like no one is willing to talk about what comes after."

"The doorway may open but once," the woman said. She was so insubstantial now it was like looking at a painting that was almost completely washed away by the rain. "What goes through it may not return. If you open it, all will become clear."

"What does that mean?" Kyja asked. "Are you saying that if Marcus comes here and I go to Earth the drift will close? We'll never see each other again? That's not fair. How could you do that to us?" She hadn't known the boy for long—at least not in her current memory—but already she couldn't bear the thought of being separated from him forever.

"All will become clear." The woman was nothing but bits of washed out color. "Choose the right door," she said as she disappeared, "and learn from your success. Choose the wrong door, and learn from your pain."

Ten shimmering doors appeared on the other side of the room, and the mist was gone.

———◆———

Marcus and Kyja studied each of the ten doors. They were all the same size and shape—made of frosted crystal just opaque enough that they couldn't see through. The only notable difference between them was that each door had a unique symbol on it. The problem was that the symbols were a bunch of complicated lines and curves. Marcus had no idea what any of them meant.

"Maybe they're Aerisian writing," Kyja suggested.

"Maybe. But if there is such a thing, Divum never taught it to me." It seemed like there had to be an explanation of the symbols somewhere in the room. The last quest had taught them that if you didn't know something, you could seek out knowledge from another source. They searched the entire room from top to bottom, but found no books, scrolls, translations, or writing of any kind. They'd had Riph Raph fly to the top of the dome. All he came back with was a juicy spider.

"I guess you can't use water magic to see what's on the other side?" Kyja asked.

"It's blocked," Marcus said. "Along with land magic and fire magic. The only element I can touch is air."

Kyja reached out to touch one of the doors.

"No," he said, stepping in front of her. "We have no idea how these doors open. There aren't any knobs. Touching one could set something off."

"What other choice do we have?" Kyja asked, studying the symbol on the door closest to her. "Eventually we have to try one."

"Count me out," Riph Raph said from across the room. "Did you miss the part about learning from pain? The only thing I've ever learned from pain is that I don't like it."

Marcus sighed. "You two stand as far away as you can get, and I'll try one of the doors."

"Good plan," Riph Raph called.

"No," Kyja said at once.

"Why not?" Marcus asked, a little offended that she'd

shot down his suggestion so quickly.

"This is as much my quest as it is yours," Kyja said. "You stand on the other side of the room, and *I'll* open a door."

"You *want* to get hurt?" He knew she could be stubborn at times, but this was ridiculous.

"Of course not." She folded her arms across her chest. "But if someone has to get hurt, I have as much of a right for it to be me as you do. Is this because you're a boy?"

"No," he said at once. If it had been—at least a little—he wasn't going to admit it. "It's because I have magic. I can protect myself." How could she argue with that?

"What if we have to fight?" she asked. "You both said I'm a better sword fighter."

Marcus glared at her. Sometimes she could be so annoying; it was amazing they'd stayed friends.

"We'll do it together," she suggested. "We open the door at the same time. If whatever is on the other side requires magic, you take over. If it's something we have to fight, I'll handle it."

Marcus didn't like the idea of Kyja being in danger, but there didn't seem to be any other choice that would satisfy them both. He randomly picked the fourth door from the left. "When I count to three, we both push that one at the same time."

"All right," Kyja said, eying him with obvious suspicion.

Riph Raph flew across the room and landed on Kyja's shoulder. When she gave the skyte a curious look, Riph Raph said, "Someone has to be here to protect you two."

Gripping his staff with his good hand, Marcus held his left hand up near the door. Kyja did the same. Riph Raph put his head under his right wing and peeked out with one eye. "One," Marcus said. "Two . . ."

Before he could say three, they both touched the door. It slammed open with such force, it threw them across the room, knocking them into the far wall, then banged shut.

Marcus sat up and rubbed his head. It felt like he'd been punched by a giant. "I thought we agreed to wait to three."

"I knew you wouldn't, so I didn't either," Kyja said, rubbing her shoulder. "That really hurt."

Riph Raph flapped his ears. "You two are incorrigible."

Wincing, they crossed the room. The door they had picked was closed again, and neither of them had seen whatever was behind it.

"This time, I pick," Kyja said. "Let's stand off to the side so we're out of the way."

Marcus agreed.

"On two," Kyja said. "One . . ."

They both touched the door. Marcus stepped back, expecting to be slammed again. Instead, a dozen gleaming daggers shot through the doorway. Kyja ducked away from one coming at her face. Riph Raph flew, screaming from a knife that chased him across the room. A blade cut through the sleeve of Marcus's robe before he remembered to create an air shield.

Every time the knives tried to stab one of them, Marcus knocked it away, until at last all twelve daggers flew back through the door, and it slammed shut. "Did you see what was inside?"

Kyja shook her head. "The light behind it was too bright."

Riph Raph flew back from the top of the dome, where he'd been circling to stay out of range. "Another second, and I would have melted those daggers to piles of slag."

Marcus inspected the cut in his robe. At least the blade hadn't reached his skin. "Divum said that air elementals are instinctive. They do what they feel is right, even if logic tells them something different. Maybe we should pick the door that *feels* right."

Kyja pointed to the door at the far left. "That one. I have a feeling about it."

They walked to the door, and Marcus studied it, waiting to see if he had a feeling one way or the other. His right ear itched a little. Maybe that was a sign. "Okay, I've got an air shield ready. When I count to—"

Before he could begin to count, both he and Kyja

touched the door. It swung open, and a huge crab scuttled into the room. It was nearly the size of a car, with claws big enough to cut off an arm in one swipe. How had something that large had made it through the door?

"Use air magic," Kyja yelled dancing away from the giant pincers.

Marcus tried to blast the crab away, but it was too heavy. His air magic moved it no more than a few inches and then it was at her. The crab backed Kyja toward a corner. Marcus blasted it again. Trying to drive it back was like trying to lift a tank with his bare hands.

Riph Raph pelted the creature with fireballs, but they bounced harmlessly off its armored back.

Kyja attempted to get around the crab, but it could move faster than she could. "give me your staff," she called.

Marcus threw his staff like a javelin. She caught it with one hand and used it to jab the crab in the eyes. Every time it tried to cut her, she dodged and jabbed again, making the creature give an angry hiss.

She couldn't keep holding the creature off for long though. It was only a matter of time before she'd miss, and the crab would take off her hand or foot.

Marcus searched the room for something to use against the monster. How could he stop it? He wasn't strong or fast enough to fight it, and his air blasts and shields were completely ineffective.

"Do something!" Riph Raph shouted. "It's going to kill her."

The skyte was right. Sweat poured off Kyja's face, and her jabs were getting slower and slower. Marcus searched his memory. What else had Divum said air magic was good for?

Emotions. The air elemental had taught him how to use air to control emotions. The crab had a big body, but Marcus guessed it probably had a small brain that would be easy to control. He blasted air magic at the creature's heavily-armored head, enveloping it with fear. Nothing happened.

Kyja's next jab missed, and the crab's pincers slashed the back of her arm, drawing blood above the elbow.

Was it possible that crabs had no emotions? They had to be scared of something. What if it was attacked by a creature that was bigger and stronger? He imagined the green dragon in the mountain. If it were to come after the crab, it would definitely feel fear then. Using that image to guide him, Marcus projected fear at the crab one more time.

The response was immediate. The monster threw up its claws, gave a high-pitched scream, and scuttled back through the door, which slammed closed behind it.

"Are you okay?" he asked, scooting across the floor to where Kyja had collapsed against the wall.

"I'm . . . fine," she panted. "It's only . . . a . . . little cut."

Marcus tore a length of fabric from the sleeve of his

robe and wadded it against her wound. "I've had enough. I'm not opening any more doors. Air elementals have the strangest sense of humor; I'm sure they'd think this was hilarious."

"What should we do?" Kyja asked.

Marcus didn't know. He was sick of jokes and pranks. Other people could learn from their pain, but he would . . .

He glanced across the room. "Their sense of humor," he whispered.

Kyja stared at him. "What's wrong?"

"Nothing," he said. "Nothing at all." He picked up his staff and walked back across to the side of the room where they'd first come in. "The woman said we needed to open a door. She didn't say it was one of those *ten* doors."

He reached out to touch the door they'd entered through. It swung open, revealing a dusty, book-filled office. A familiar figure doffed his top hat and bowed.

"Congratulations," Mr. Z said. "What have you learned?"

RAISING THE STAKES

Killing Graehl had been a mistake; the Master was nearly positive. The more he thought about it, the more sure he became that the man had been keeping secrets. The dark wizard ran a cold palm across his face. Why hadn't he used the truth magic on Graehl the same way he'd used it on the boy? Because he'd been so sure of himself that he'd overlooked the fact that he might have been duped.

The question was, what secrets had Graehl been keeping? Surely nothing too important. If the man had been trying to goad him into throwing the boy into the realm of shadows, so be it. Either the whelp would be stuck on Earth, if that story had been the truth, or he'd end up in the harnesses. Either way was fine.

Still, it bothered him that he'd missed something.

Footsteps in the hallway interrupted his thoughts, and

someone knocked rapidly. He considered sending a bolt of ice straight through the door, teaching the fool to think twice before arriving unbidden.

Instead, he shook his head and called, "What is it?"

Tide opened the door and hurried into the room. "The stone army has been spotted heading northward."

"North? To where?" What was his brother up to, sending away his most powerful army?

Tide rubbed a pudgy hand over his cheek. The Fontasian was a fool, but a powerful fool. "My best guess would be Icehold."

That made no sense. They'd already fought over Icehold. His brother had won that battle, which still rankled. The city was useless. The only other place of significance in the area was . . .

His eyes snapped open wide. It all made sense now. They'd wanted the boy in the realm of shadows because they hoped he would be able to contact the girl. The one in Fire Keep. And if they were sending an army to Icehold, they had to think the boy had a better than even chance of bringing her back.

The Master turned the gold ring on his finger. Was it possible that they thought they could free the fire elementals? If that happened, they'd be giving him exactly what he needed to accomplish something he'd only dreamed about. He turned to the Fontasian. "I want a legion of undead and as many of my wizards as you can get waiting for the stone fools when they arrive. I want my brother's pathetic army outnumbered ten to one. Make that a hundred to one. Leave me the Summoner, but take everyone else—including the other elementals."

Tide nodded. "At Icehold?"

The Master cackled. "No you fool. It's not Icehold they're headed for." As he told the Fontasian what he had in mind, Tides eyes began to gleam.

"What shall we do when we get there?"

"Kill any enemy who shows up," the Master said. "Tell the leaders of Icehold I'll destroy their city if they come against me. Now go." As the Fontasian scurried toward the door, the Master raised a hand and called him back. "I also want you to come up with a way to destroy those living statues once and for all. They've been a thorn in my side for too long."

Tide smiled and nodded. "It will be my pleasure."

PART 4

The Drift

CHAPTER 32

THE LAST GATE

"You're . . . one of the *four?*" Marcus could barely get the words out. After the grace and dignity of the woman in the water, the wisdom of the tree man, and the majesty of the woman in the mist, the idea that this little man, with his purple vest, lensless eyeglasses, and silly top hat could be one of them, was too hard to accept.

Kyja pushed forward, nearly toppling a stack of books. She stared at the little man and turned to Marcus. "Do you know him?"

"Zithspithesbazith at your service," the man said, brushing lint off the shoulders of his long, black coat. "But if that twists your tongue into torturous turns, you can call me Mr. Z."

Kyja grinned, but Marcus put a hand to her ear and whispered, "He's the crazy guy I was telling you about who drove us to Air Keep on a racing snail."

"The racing snail." Kyja looked around the office. "I've never seen one before. Is it here?"

"I'm afraid Drymaios is in bed with a bad case of slug sniffles." Mr. Z pulled out a silk handkerchief and blew his bulbous red nose into it. "I fear I may be coming down with a case of it myself."

"Don't get him started," Marcus said. Mr. Z might have helped them in the past, but as far as Marcus was concerned, the man had been nearly as much trouble as he was help, talking nonsense and disappearing at the most important times. He glared at Mr. Z. "What are you doing here? Sending us on more confusing quests? Offering rides on a snail that supposedly travels faster than a race horse? Whatever it is, we don't want it."

"I agree," Riph Raph said. "You can keep your racing snail. Far away."

"Why are you two acting like this?" Kyja asked. "What's this man done to either of you?"

"He hasn't done anything," Marcus said. "I just don't trust him." He turned back to Mr. Z. "I thought you said you wouldn't help us anymore."

Mr. Z, whose head barely came up to Marcus's waist, climbed onto a stack of books and crossed his legs. "I'm not here to help you. In fact, I'm afraid you won't like the things I must tell you. Which raises the question, why would I tell you at all?" He put out one pudgy palm. "On the one hand, if I don't say anything, you'll probably go ahead with your plans. On the other hand, if I do tell you, you won't listen to what I say, which will lead you to do what you would have done if I hadn't told you in the first place."

"See?" Marcus said. "He always talks in riddles that make no sense."

Kyja looked around the office. "You must read a lot."

"More than my friends think I should, but less than I'd like. Given the choice, I'd rather read than eat, sleep, or breathe. After all, stories are more nourishing than soup, and the dreams inside them more invigorating than those of sleep."

"I agree," Kyja said. "I can't remember for sure, but I'm almost positive I love to read. Have you read *all* of these books?"

"These?" Mr. Z looked around the room. "I never read my own work. That gives you a big head and small stomachache. Or is it a small head and big stomachache? Either way, I highly discourage writers from reading their own work more than absolutely necessary."

"You wrote all of these?" Marcus asked. There had to be at least a thousand volumes, and the little man had never mentioned anything about writing books once. With Mr. Z's constant babbling, he'd hadn't been entirely sure the man could read at all, let alone write.

"Certainly," Mr. Z said. "If reading is like breathing, then writing is what provides sweet, pure air."

"I'd like to read your books sometime," Kyja said. She picked up a volume, flipped through the first few pages, and set it back on the pile. "You asked us what we've learned."

Mr. Z shifted, sending the stack he sat on wobbling dangerously left and right. "Have you *learned* anything? No offense, but in my experience, one of you is more than a little hardheaded."

"I know," Marcus and Kyja said at the same time, turning to look at each other.

"In the rooms with the doors," Marcus said, "I learned that air elementals are nothing but a pain in the neck, and that air blasts are almost useless against giant crabs."

Kyja sniffed dismissively. "I learned that humor and trusting your instincts are sometimes the best way to make a decision."

Mr. Z rubbed his glasses on the sleeve of his jacket, though Marcus knew for a fact that there wasn't any glass in the frames. "Surprisingly astute answers from both of you." He pulled a quill pen from his vest pocket, opened a nearby journal, and scribbled inside it. "I may need to write a volume on the topic. *Instincts, Air Magic, and Neck Pain: Why Humorless Crabs Make Notoriously Bad Decisions.*"

Marcus shook his head. "So, did we pass? Can we move to the next test?"

"There are no tests here," Mr. Z said. "I'm surprised my associates didn't inform you of that. Or perhaps they did, but you suffer from a case of wax-in-ear syndrome. In any case, if these were tests, you'd have failed them miserably."

"Failed?' Kyja asked. "But we got the baby to its mother, saved the family from the dragon, and opened the right door. I think we've done pretty well."

Mr. Z laughed so hard that his top hat fell off, and he was barely able to catch it before it hit the floor. "You think you've done *well?* You took a child who didn't belong to you—a felony in most worlds—terrified the child's uncle, aided and abetted a group of thieves who'd tried to help themselves to the legally gotten gains of an honorable dragon, and frightened a poor crustacean so badly it will need years of therapy to carry on a normal life. No, if this were a test, you would have earned an F for *flounder*, *fizzle*, and *flop*."

"I told you," Marcus said to Kyja. "He's a full-on lunatic."

"Crazy as a fuzz worm in a pond full of biter fish," Riph Raph said.

Kyja looked crestfallen. "So we can't go on? We can't open the gate to free the fire elementals?"

Mr. Z tilted his hat forward nearly to his nose and scratched the back of his head. "Why would you think that? You've learned the importance of balancing emotion with logic, wisdom, and instinct. What more would you need to know?" He pointed a finger behind them. "You may open the last door any time you wish."

Marcus and Kyja turned to see a black door with a flaming symbol on it—a curlicue loop with what looked a little like a claw at the end—the magic symbol for fire.

"That's it?" Kyja asked. "All we have to do is open it?"

"That's all," Mr. Z agreed.

Marcus wasn't buying it. He'd seen this kind of flimflam from Mr. Z before. There was always a hidden meaning to whatever he said. "What about the quest—or test or experience, whatever you want to call it? Don't we have to learn something before we can open the last door?"

Mr. Z pressed a finger to his chin. "If you choose to go through that door, you will have learned everything you need to know."

He *knew* there was a catch. "You said *if* we choose to open the door. Why wouldn't we?"

"That brings me back to the thing I have to tell you that I'd rather not tell you. But if I *don't* and you *do* what you do, then you might come to the conclusion that I intentionally—"

"Say it!" Marcus shouted. "Why wouldn't we want to open the door?"

Mr. Z took off his top hat and placed it over his heart. "If you open the door, freeing the Pyrinths, I'm afraid you will be unable to return Kyja to her body."

Kyja thought she'd misheard. "It's too late for me to go back? I'm dead?"

Mr. Z pulled his hat back on his head and tugged it into place. "Stringently speaking—that is, in the most factual format—you *are* dead. Poison will do that to you."

"But . . ." She patted her arms and legs. "If I'm dead, why can I be seen and touched and heard?"

"Consider it a glitch in the system, if you will." Mr. Z waggled his fingers. "A situation unique to Fire Keep. Those who have the dubious privilege of ending up there are given a sort of temporary physicality. As long as you remain here, you have a body—although not one of flesh and bones."

"She's not staying here," Marcus said. "Master Therapass magically preserved her body so she could return to it."

"A fantastic bit of magicating for a mortal. Should you return her to her body using your little rope trick, she will be fit as a French horn. Although perhaps a bit peckish. Long time with no food will do that, you know."

Kyja didn't understand. "I thought you said it was too late for me to go back to my body."

"Not precisely." Mr. Z blew his nose again. "If you go now, or in the close proximity to now—say in the time it would take to skim one of my books—Marcus can return you to your body. Not snail surgery by any stretch of the imagination, but an impressive feat nonetheless. However, should you choose to open the last door, I'm afraid that returning you to your body will be beyond the ability of even a master wizard."

"Then we won't open it," Marcus said. He grabbed Kyja's hand. "Come on. Push me to Terra ne Staric now, while we can still get you back."

And make all of this for nothing? Kyja unconsciously chewed on a strand of her hair. "If we did open the door, what would happen to me?"

Mr. Z wobbled the stack of books again. "Nothing. You would remain as you are—in Fire Keep, in a sort of limbo. If you should leave . . ." He waved his hands. "You would lose your corporeal nature and move on to wherever mortal beings go when they leave their bodies."

"Why are you asking that?" Marcus demanded, grabbing her arm. "Kyja, you have to come back. We can't lose you. *I* can't lose you."

Kyja didn't want to lose him either, but she had to know everything before she could make a decision. "If I return to my body now, will Fire Keep ever be opened?"

Marcus stared at her, and she tried to avoid the hurt in his eyes.

"Not likely," Mr. Z said.

"And without the fire elementals, Earth and Farworld . . . ?"

The little man with the big nose and floppy hat tugged at the front of his vest. "Think of Earth, Farworld, and the realm of shadows as three kegs of explosives attached to one burning fuse. The fuse is . . ." He held his thumb and forefinger so close there was barely any space between them. "At this point, an explosion is inevitable. What that explosion will be, and who it will affect and how—I'm afraid all of that is now up to you and you alone."

Kyja slid her hand from Marcus's grip.

"Forget it," Marcus said. "The door can't be opened without magic, and I won't open it for you. I know you want to help people. But I'm sorry, I will not let you sacrifice yourself."

Kyja whirled on him. "I don't have any choice."

Marcus stepped toward her until they were bare inches apart, his face twisted. "I . . ." He swallowed. "I'm the one who killed you."

She stared at him. Was he joking? No, she could tell that he wasn't. Was this some kind of trick then, to stop her from freeing the fire elementals? She might not remember their past, but she knew him well enough to know he could never do what he was claiming.

His chin trembled. "There isn't enough time to explain it all, but I'm the one who gave you the poison that sent you here. I've never forgiven myself for that, and I never will if you don't come back. If you won't return for yourself, do it for me so I don't have to have this guilt eating me up for the rest of my life."

He was telling the truth. She didn't understand why or how, but she realized that it didn't matter. She'd been so terrified to discover how she'd died, but now that she knew, it didn't hurt at all. She'd been so foolish to believe that living without her memories could ever be good. The woman in the mist was right. You did learn from your pain.

She would never want to make Marcus hurt any worse than he did. But she couldn't choose to spare him pain at the cost of the lives of millions of innocent men, women, and children any more than she could choose to save her own life instead of theirs.

How could she face herself for a single day if she allowed the Dark Circle, or the realm of shadows, or anyone to hurt innocent babies like the one she and Marcus had found in the alley? If she had any way to stop it, she couldn't turn her back on them. She wouldn't.

"No," she cried, tears streaming from her eyes. "I forgive you for whatever you've done, and if I could save you from another second of guilt, I would. But I'm not going back to my body if it means abandoning the people who need me. I. Will. Open. Fire. Keep!"

She slammed her fist against the door, and fire leapt from the symbol down her arm. Flames enveloped her whole body.

"The last lesson," Mr. Z said. "Sometimes logic, wisdom, and instinct are overruled by emotion."

Fire Keep burst open.

CHAPTER 33

NOT ENOUGH MAGIC

"**K**yja!" Marcus reached out for her, but she was gone. He spun around. The room with the books was gone, too. "Mr. Z!" he screamed.

What had happened? Where was he?

Riph Raph flew to his side. "I'm, I'm s-sor-sor—" The skyte couldn't finish its sentence. Tears dripped down his blue-scaled face.

Marcus knew this room. The fireplace, the shelves of bottles and potions. He was back in Master Therapass's study. How did he get here? And why wasn't Kyja with him? The last thing he'd seen was her reaching for the door, and—

Realization of what must have happened hit him like an anvil to the back of the head. She shouldn't have been able to open the door without magic. But somehow, she had. She'd opened the door, and with it, she'd opened Fire Keep.

He crumpled to the ground. "No!" he screamed. "No. No. No."

Master Therapass stepped into the room. His eyes went wide. "You're back. Does that mean—"

Marcus pushed himself to his feet and raced past the wizard without a word. Ignoring the pain in his leg, he ran faster than he ever had to the stairs, then down them. Slipping, stumbling, scraping skin off his arms and legs as he fell and got back to his feet. Behind him he heard Master Therapass calling his name. But he didn't have time to answer. He reached the bottom of the stairs, and Riph Raph flew beside him.

"Stop," the skyte said, trying to land on his shoulder. "There wasn't anything you could have done."

"I have to get to her," Marcus panted. "I have to save her." He shoved Riph Raph away then ran out of the tower and down the hill. Skipping the winding path, he tripped and rolled most of the way down the grassy slope. It was a miracle he didn't break an arm or a leg. But he didn't care. Ramming his staff into the ground with a burning fury, he raced through the western gate.

There it was—the glass glittering in the afternoon sun. "I'm coming," he cried as he stumbled to the coffin. "I'm coming."

She was there, lying on the white satin pillow exactly

the way he'd remembered. The wizard's magic had kept her body safe and protected from the Dark Circle. Now he needed to bring her back. Pressing his forehead against the glass lid, he grasped the coffin's gold handles and reached for her with his mind.

"The rope," he moaned, focusing all of his energy on finding her. "Send me the rope, and I'll pull you over."

Nothing happened.

He tried again. He'd found her while he was in the realm of shadows; he could do it from here, too. All he needed was enough desire. "I won't leave you," he said, tears running down his cheeks and onto the glass.

If she couldn't come to him, he'd find her. Calling on every ounce of magic he could pull into his body, he drew in water, land, air, and fire. Combined, there had to be a way to bring her back. Mr. Z's words echoed in his head.

You will be unable to return Kyja to her body. But he didn't believe it. There had to be a way. He couldn't go on without her. No one and nothing would take her away from him.

Pounding his hand against the glass, he screamed at the elementals. "Give her to me! Bring her back! I don't care what it takes. Please. Please. Please. Please."

Arms closed around him, and Master Therapass lifted him up. Cascade was there, along with Lanctrus-Darnoc, Divum, and most of the town.

"It's all right," the wizard said, cradling Marcus against his beard.

"No," Marcus sobbed. "It's not. You have to bring her back, Master Therapass. You have to. My magic's not strong enough. But yours . . ."

The wizard shook his head, his old eyes wet. "I'm sorry. If I could do anything, I would."

Marcus turned to the elementals. "Please. I'll do anything you ask. Take my life. Only save her."

Cascade stared at the ground.

"We're sorry," Lanctrus-Darnoc said.

Divum placed a cool hand on his burning cheek. "If there were any way, I would do it for you."

Marcus stared at the townspeople surrounding him. Surely with all of their combined knowledge, all their magic, there had to be a way.

High Lord Broomhead shook his head. "We can't."

Riph Raph landed on Marcus's shoulder, and this time Marcus clutched the skyte to him, drenching Riph Raph with his tears. She was gone. She was really gone. And there was no one who could bring her back.

There was a rustling in the crowd, and Marcus lifted his head to see men and women falling over each other to get out of the way as someone approached the coffin. Two curved horns appeared, and then a face that would send children crying to their mothers. The creature had bulging biceps and shoulders broader than Tankum's. A flaming mace rested on one of them.

It was the fire elemental he'd seen Kyja arguing with

before she went into the vortex. The flaming creature approached the coffin and looked down at Kyja with a clear expression of tenderness. He slammed the head of his mace into the ground and everyone stepped back—even the other elementals.

The Pyrinth turned to Marcus and said in a deep voice, "*I* can bring her back."

———◆———

Kyja dropped her head. She knew she'd made the right decision. So why did she feel so terrible?

"What happens now?" she asked.

Mr. Z took off his gold spectacles, tucked them into his pocket, and pulled out a pair with thick, purple frames. "That was a brave decision you made."

Kyja sighed. "I only did it because I was mad. I didn't use anything we learned in those tests or whatever they were."

"On the contrary, you used everything you leaned." He balanced the purple glasses on his nose, opened a book, and squinted at the pages. "Logic told you that the only way to complete your quest was to open the final door. Wisdom told you that the fate of many often outweighs the pain of one. Intuition told you to follow your heart, even if it might cause pain for one you love. And your emotions were what gave you the strength to do what you knew was right."

She squeezed her hands together. "I wish I could get my memories back. I think they would have made whatever comes next easier to bear."

Mr. Z shut the book and tucked the glasses in his pocket. "Once you've lived a thousand years, your eyes are never the same." He put the book back on the stack. "Perhaps, as a reward for your sacrifice, I could share one memory with you."

He waved his hand, and Kyja saw herself and Marcus standing on an Earth street. It was nearly twilight, and they were standing beside a boy with beautiful brown skin and curly hair. He was holding a basketball.

Kyja saw herself notice a women and a baby in a metal cart—what Marcus had called a *car*—but it had no wheels. The Kyja on the street gathered up their money and cloaks and gave them to the woman in the car.

"She was about to give up," Mr. Z said. "When you noticed her, she'd been considering leaving the baby in the back seat of the car and taking enough pills to stop her heart."

"No," Kyja whispered.

"She'd had a hard life," Mr. Z said. "Her first child was stolen years before and never found. She searched for years without success. She was never quite right after that. Eventually she had another baby, hoping it would make things right. But her husband left soon after, and she found herself homeless and hopeless."

"She didn't, did she?" Kyja asked. "Kill herself?"

Mr. Z shook his head and smiled. "The money you gave her was enough for her to find temporary housing. But the hope you gave her was much more important. It helped her realize there were still good people in the world. In fact, you reminded her of someone. She didn't realize it until later, but something about you reminded her of the child she'd lost all those years before—a little girl with lots of dark hair."

Kyja looked up. It took a moment to understand what he was saying. When she did, her mouth dropped open. "You mean . . .?"

Mr. Z nodded. "The woman you saved that night was your mother."

Kyja took Mr. Z's hand. "Thank you. Thank you so much." She squeezed his fingers. "I'm ready to go now—to that place you talked about where mortals go when their bodies are gone."

Mr. Z blinked. He grinned. He began to chuckle, and the chuckle turned into all-out guffaws. He waved both hands and fell over backwards off the stack of books, which made him laugh all the harder.

"What's so funny?" Kyja asked.

"You'll go there one day," the little man said, his feet sticking straight up in the air. "But that day is not for a long while. You have a perfectly fine body waiting for you to return to it."

She didn't understand. "But you said . . . Marcus couldn't . . ."

"*He* can't," Mr. Z said. "He could have before you freed the Pyrinths, because that magic was available. But once the fire elementals got their magic back, they were the only ones with that power. In fact . . ." He pulled his watch out of his vest pocket. "I should think right about . . ."

Kyja felt odd. The flames which had been circling her body since she opened the door, swirled around her and tightened like a cloak. The fire lifted her into the air as though giant, invisible hands were picking her up.

"Good bye," Mr. Z called. "And good luck with the drift."

The flames roared around her, and for a moment everything went black. Then she opened her eyes and found herself lying on her back, her head resting on a white silk pillow. Magma was looking down at her. She tried to sit up and banged her head on clear glass.

"Kyja!" Marcus was there. He threw open the lid of what she realized was a glass coffin and hugged her so tightly she couldn't breathe. Riph Raph hopped onto the edge of the coffin and licked her face. Sitting up, she saw Cascade, Lanctrus-Darnoc, and Divum. Most of the town was there too. Char Everwood raised her youngest child above her head and the babe opened and closed a chubby hand. Bella the cook waved a large metal ladle. They were all looking at her and cheering.

Bella, Char, Cascade—she realized she knew the names of everyone there. She had her memory back. All of it.

She reached up weakly to Marcus, taking one side of his face in her left hand. He leaned toward her. She pulled him closer, until his lips were only inches from hers, and . . . whacked him on the head with her right hand. "I can't believe you blamed yourself for my death."

CHAPTER 34

DARING PLANS

Kyja couldn't stop eating. She was trying to keep up with the conversation, but every time she quit putting food in her mouth, her stomach began growling again. She was seated in the great hall of the tower of Terra ne Staric with Marcus, Riph Raph, Master Therapass, the elementals, and the city council.

She finished off the last of a pin fruit tart that was nearly as big as her head, and Riph Raph flapped his ears. "If you ever look at me the way you're eyeing that roasted goose, I'm flying for my life."

Kyja elbowed him. "Shush. I can't help it. I'm starving."

"Tell me again about the Dark Circle's headquarters," High Lord Broomhead said.

Marcus shrugged. "There's not much to tell. I never saw where they took me. It seemed to be underground. But I'm not sure about that."

"Tide was there?" Cascade asked, his expression grim.

"Tide, Nizgar-Gharat, and Calem. I don't think they believe in the Master's cause, but they're convinced that his side is the strongest."

High Lord Broomhead put his head in his hands. "All they need now is a fire elemental, and they'll be able to open the doorway."

"That won't be hard to find," Magma growled. "If Chaos hasn't joined them already, he will soon enough. He has always been drawn to evil."

Master Therapass tugged on his beard. "Graehl?"

Kyja put down her fork, realizing Graehl wasn't there. "Where is he?"

Marcus stared at his hands and shook his head.

Kyja looked around the table. Graehl and Master Therapass had been like fathers to her. "Someone tell me. Where is Graehl?"

"I would have said something before," Marcus said. "But you didn't know who he was. He died making sure the Dark Circle didn't know what we were doing."

"*Died?*" Kyja suddenly felt far too full. Her stomach lurched. "How can Graehl be dead? What did he have to do with any of this?"

All eyes in the room went to Master Therapass. The wizard blinked slowly. "Even before you freed the air elementals, it became clear that getting into Fire Keep would be a problem. Lanctrus-Darnoc had been

373

researching it and had discovered that there was no direct path from Farworld to Fire Keep."

He glanced at Kyja. "This was before Divum revealed the way you took. Not knowing that it was an option—and unwilling to ask either of you to take that risk if I'd known about it—I sent several of my trusted associates to scout out other options. Graehl asked to explore the Windlash Mountains. He was almost sure that a portal to the realm of shadows was there, and we'd heard rumors of the barrier between the realm and Fire Keep being thin.

"Once he saw how heavily the Dark Circle was guarding the portal, he came up with a plan to get one or both of you inside. I thought it was far too risky for the two of you, and for Graehl. But when we realized that Kyja was trapped . . . we didn't seem to have much choice."

She put a hand to her mouth. "I'm to blame for his death."

"No." Marcus took her hand, blinking away the tears that filled his eyes. "He loved you, and he would have done anything to help us. But he did it because he believed in fighting against everything the Dark Circle stands for. The last thing he said to me was, '*Hard things.*' He did what he did because it was right, even if it *was* hard."

Kyja squeezed her eyes shut, but tears leaked out anyway. Sometimes she wished she could block the memories again. The pain was too much. Too many people were getting hurt. They had to stop the Dark Circle once and for all.

"About the realm of shadows," Marcus said. He glanced toward Master Therapass, clearly uncomfortable about something. "I met a man who claimed to be my . . . my father. And he told me a story about you." He bit his lip. "And your brother."

The wizard's face tightened. "What did he tell you?"

Marcus told them what happened between the time he'd entered the realm of shadows and the time he'd arrived in Fire Keep. Kyja had heard parts of the story after she'd pulled him over, but it took on a new meaning now that she had her memories back.

His story was almost impossible to believe. Master Therapass and the head of the Dark Circle—brothers? How could that be? And how must Marcus have felt to discover that his mother was dead and his father was a, a *monster*? She'd remembered discovering that her mother had loved her and had been searching for her. To learn that your only living parent cared about you only as a means of destroying two worlds? She couldn't imagine the pain that must have caused him. Must still be causing him. She squeezed his hand.

When Marcus had finished, he asked, "Is it true?"

Master Therapass nodded slowly. "A few of the facts are wrong, but for the most part, yes. The man you know as the Master is my brother. We discovered a link of some kind between Farworld and Earth. We became obsessed with finding a way to travel between worlds. I had no idea where my brother's interests lay until it was too late."

"And he is—my *father*?" Marcus could barely say the word. He was embarrassed and disgusted that such a sick individual could be related to him in any way.

"When I realized you were tied to the realm of shadows, I began to suspect who your father might be."

Marcus stared at his hands. It was true then. His only living parent was a monster. "I always hoped my parents were—I don't know—noble. Or at least good. How can you trust the son of a man like . . . well, like he is?"

Master Therapass pointed a finger at him. "You parents *were* noble. Do not doubt that for a second. Your mother and father had a grand dream of uniting two worlds. Your father's mind has been warped by pain and anger, but that does not change the fact that once upon a time, he was an honorable man with a noble goal. And no man or woman is ever completely beyond hope."

"But he wants to destroy Earth and Farworld," Marcus said.

The wizard nodded. "Yes. And we must stop him."

Kyja stood up. "Mr. Z said that Farworld, Earth, and the realm of shadows are like powder kegs about to explode. What can we do about it? We have all of the elementals; why haven't we opened the drift? Let's do it now, before they get the chance."

"It's not that easy." The wizard rolled a map out

across the table. "Based on our research, the drift can be opened in only one place—a gate located here." He pointed to a spot near the forest of Before Time, slightly outside a city called Windshold.

Marcus sucked in his breath.

"Isn't that—" Kyja began.

Marcus looked pale. "The city where I was nearly killed. Where I lost my mother."

"I don't think it's a coincidence," Master Therapass said. "My guess is that at the very least, your mother was aware of the gate's existence. I think she was trying to find a way to get you to Earth."

"What are we waiting for?" Divum asked. "If we know where it is, let's go."

Cascade stared intently at the wall. "The Dark Circle must know too. They've assembled a massive army. I count at least five hundred Thrathkin S'Bae and ten times that many undead."

Master Therapass nodded. "I sent the stone warriors and wizards as soon as I confirmed the location. That's one of the places Tankum and I scouted while Marcus was training. But they won't arrive until late tomorrow. By then, it may be too late."

Magma slammed his mace on the floor, sending a crack all the way up into the stone wall. "I'll gather all of the fire elementals that I can, and we'll take the fight to their doorstep."

Lanctrus-Darnoc shook their heads. "Too risky," said the fox.

The boar spoke next. "If the Dark Circle manages to open the drift, they will have the power to destroy any elementals in the area."

Kyja leaned forward. "What do you mean? I thought it was only a door."

The fox and boar looked at the wizard. He nodded and said, "Go ahead. It's time everyone knew."

"A great power source lies between the two worlds," Lanctrus said. "We discovered it when we were looking for a passage to Fire Keep. The source appears to have existed for a very long time."

"It may be what your father is planning on using to blow up Earth and Farworld," Darnoc said. "If the source is accessed with light magic . . . We are not entirely sure what will happen. But if it is opened with Dark Magic, the Dark Circle will have power we can't imagine. It may have been their plan all along to have you free the elementals to give them access."

"What's our plan then?" Marcus asked.

Master Therapass waved his wand, and a line raced across the map from Terra ne Staric to the forest of Before Time appraching the gate from the west. Another line moved more slowly, coming toward the gate from the east. "All of the elementals except for those at this table and a small group of Aerisians will barricade themselves in their keeps. Should the Dark Circle prevail, it will be up to the elementals to find a way to stop them. The air elementals will fly those of us here who are willing—along with a contingent of our best wizards and warriors—to the forest tonight, hopefully avoiding detection. After taking us to the forest, all the Aerisians but Divum will return to Air Keep We will launch a surprise attack at dawn, attempting to engage the Dark Circle long enough for the stone army to arrive."

"A few dozen against thousands?" Cascade asked.

"We've also asked Icehold for all the help they can send," Master Therapass said. "They have the only army close enough. But we haven't heard from them yet."

"And we will have elementals," Divum said.

High Lord Broomhead tapped his fingers on the table. "We have to assume that they will have elementals too, as well as the Master and at least one Summoner. Attacking them now may be the only chance we have, but the odds are still strongly against us."

Magma slammed his mace head into the palm of his hand. "When do we leave?"

<hr />

Marcus lingered in the room until he and Master Therapass were the only ones remaining.

"You have a question?" the wizard asked, carefully

rolling up the map and tucking it and the wand into his robe.

Marcus wasn't sure how to approach the subject, so he just went ahead and said it. "The Master told me that he was the one who put the brand on my shoulder."

Master Therapass nodded slowly. "I hadn't heard that before."

"Then it's a lie." Marcus slumped against the back of his chair with relief.

"I didn't say that. My brother and I discovered the prophecy at the same time we were researching Earth and Farworld. We found many versions of the story, but the one constant was the mark. The amulet I gave to Kyja was found on the other side of the forest of Before Time. Tankum and I went to see you because we'd heard about your mark. I can see how it might have been placed on you when you and your mother were kidnapped, without her being aware of it."

"Then for all you know, I'm not the savior that was prophesied. This might all be for nothing."

The wizard smiled. "And the fact that you have managed to free all four elementals is coincidence?"

"That only makes it that much worse." Marcus sighed. "We've managed to gather all of the elementals, start a worldwide war, have people give their lives for us, and it all might be a mistake. I may be nothing more than a kid who had a brand put on his arm by the most evil man in the world. I may be a complete fraud."

Master Therapass walked around the table and sat by Marcus. "Everyone has to decide for themselves who they are. I once heard a saying that went something like, 'A man is born with lips and gums, nose and ears, fingers and thumbs. It's not what he's given that makes his sums, but where he goes and what he becomes.' There's one thing I never heard in any of the versions of the prophecy. Do you know what that is?"

Marcus shook his head.

"How the chosen child got the mark in the first place."

CHAPTER 35

THE FINAL BATTLE

Marcus hadn't seen a lot of forests, but those that he had usually started out thin, with sparse smaller trees, bushes, and grass turning into thicker trees, and eventually full-on woods. The forest of Before Time was nothing like that. One minute there was grass and newly bloomed flowers, and the next minute, grass was replaced by trees so big around that twenty men with linked arms would have been unable to circle one of their massive trunks.

The last time he and Kyja had been this far north, Icehold had been bitterly cold and blanketed with snow. In the last two weeks, the weather had changed. The snow was gone, but its melting had left the ground wet and swampy, and the early morning air was so cold that both he and Kyja shivered under their leather armor and heavy cloaks.

"Any sign of the Icehold army?" High Lord Broomhead asked.

"They have not left their city walls," Cascade said.

The high lord sighed and paced across the pine-needle-covered ground. "We can't put this off any longer."

As Master Therapass and Lanctrus-Darnoc entered the clearing, the high lord tensed and asked, "Has the fire elemental joined the rest of the Dark Circle army?"

"No," Lanctrus said. "We were able to get quite close, viewing them through nearby plants, and though the other three elementals are gathered together, there is no sign of the Pyrinth."

Master Therapass pulled out his wand. "My brother and the Summoner are missing as well, which leads me to believe that they have gone to get Chaos. They could return at any moment, and we will be too late."

Magma bared his teeth in a fiery grin. "I'm ready to go now. I can't wait to try my mace on a few dark wizards."

High Lord Broomhead stared from the trees to the open field beyond, where close to a hundred campfires burned. "I can't ask my friends to go their deaths."

"You won't have to," Master Therapass said. "I believe they've made that decision for themselves."

Out of the woods came the fifty men and women who had flown in with the air elementals the night before.

Eden, the short but fierce red-headed captain of the

guard, held her sword out. "My lord, it is almost dawn. We are ready to fight."

The high lord looked over the men and women. Even to Marcus, the group looked tiny compared to what they were going up against.

"Do you all make this decision of your own free will?" Broomhead asked.

"We do," the group said as one.

"I would not think less of any of you who would rather stay back," he said. "If you do not wish to fight, you may leave with honor." When none of the men and women left, he nodded. "Very well. Prepare for battle."

"That's what I like to hear," Magma said, flexing his fiery muscles.

The high lord turned to Divum. "Were you able to set any traps?"

The Aerisian laughed and turned herself into hundreds of tiny weapons, swinging and stabbing. "They will have a few surprises when they wake up."

As the group began moving out of the forest, Marcus and Kyja headed forward too. Master Therapass caught them before they reached the tree line. "I'm sorry, but you're too valuable to risk. I need you to stay here."

"We have to fight," Marcus said. "We're shorthanded enough as it is."

Kyja drew her sword. "I can fight, and Marcus's health has improved so much. With my sword and his magic, we could be a big help."

Riph Raph flew down from a nearby tree. "I think you'd better listen to the wizard. I'll stay behind to look after you. In case anything breaks through the lines."

"I'm sorry," Master Therapass said. "I can't let you into the battle. We'll try to clear a path to the gate. It's a flat stone circle raised slightly off the ground in the center of the camp. When we do, we'll gather you and the four elementals and attempt to open the drift. Do not leave here unless you can see the gate has been cleared. Will you promise to do that, or must I need to leave someone behind to keep an eye on you?"

Marcus and Kyja looked at each other.

"Fine," Marcus said.

"We'll stay behind," Kyja agreed.

The wizard appeared skeptical.

"We promise," Kyja said. "We won't leave the woods unless we see a clear opening to the gate."

"Very well. Be safe. I hope we meet again soon." Master Therapass turned and joined the rest of the warriors and wizards.

Marcus and Kyja edged up to the trees so they could get a better view of what was happening. High Lord Broomhead divided the people into four groups, each with a combination of wizards, warriors, and one elemental.

"Group one will go to the right, to flank the camp. Group two will circle to the left. Draw as much of the army toward Icehold as you can. Hopefully the city will come to your aid. The third group will strike at the center, and the fourth will take and hold the gate. Any questions?"

When there were none, he lowered his voice. "We are going to try a stealth approach," he said. "Get as close to the tents as you can before attacking."

"Right flank, attack!" Magma raised his mace and charged toward the camp, screaming at the top of his lungs. The flaming creature was impossible to miss in the dark; alarms sounded, and men came running from their tents.

As if someone had lit a string of firecrackers, explosions sounded from all over the camp. Tents burst into flame, and charred clothing and supplies flew into the air.

Divum grinned. "So much for stealth."

———◆———

Standing with their backs pressed against a tree as big around as a house, Kyja and Marcus watched the battle begin. Even from where they stood, the fight was clearly one-sided. Magma swung his mace as he charged into the mass of dark creatures and wizards. Every swing sent bodies flying, but each space he cleared quickly closed around him, filled with more of the Dark Circle's soldiers. It was like watching a spark floating in the middle of an endless black sea.

Explosions shook the ground as Master Therapass and Lanctrus-Darnoc used land magic to blow chunks of rock and dirt into the air. But for every one of their spells, dozens of Thrathkin S'Bae wizards returned fire.

Kyja couldn't stand waiting and watching as her friends fought without her. She could tell that Marcus felt the same way; his hands fidgeted on his staff, and he kept moving his foot as if it was all he could do to keep from racing into the fight.

"We can't stand here," Marcus said. "They need all the help they can get."

"You promised you wouldn't go unless the gate had been cleared," Riph Raph said.

Marcus was right. Kyja clenched her fists watching the battle that even from this distance looked futile. They had to find a way to help. "We promised not to go unless we could *see* the gate." She cupped her hands to her eyes. "Do you see that?"

Marcus looked at her and grinned. "Yeah, a flat circle right in the middle of camp I see it clear as day."

"I don't see the gate," Riph Raph squawked. "And I have better eyes than either of you."

Kyja gripped her sword tight, adrenaline making her heart race. "I'm pretty sure I see an opening."

Riph Raph thrashed his tail. "There. Is. No. Opening."

"I see it too," Marcus said. "It's definitely a clear

opening to the gate. And you heard what Master Therapass said."

Kyja grinned. "If we see a clear opening . . ."

"We have to go."

"No. No. Noooooo!" Riph Raph cried.

Side by side, Marcus and Kyja entered the battle. As soon as they reached the nearest of the Dark Circle soldiers, Kyja cut both heads off of a two-headed dog. Three skeletons came at her, armed with spears. She had to back up quickly to avoid getting turned into a pin cushion.

With a blast of fire, Marcus turned the skeletons to ash, but dozens more closed in behind them.

"There are too many," Kyja said backing away. She looked for a spot to retreat, but dark creatures surrounded them. It was clear normal fighting tactics wouldn't work.

"Have you ever used a magic sword?" Marcus yelled.

"You know I can't use magical items," Kyja shouted back.

Something that looked like a giant sponge rolled toward them, and she punctured it with a quick lunge.

"Swing at those," Marcus said, pointing at a pair of undead Mimickers approaching.

The creatures were too big for two or three skilled swordfighters to take on alone, but Kyja had no other option. The Mimickers were almost on top of them, and they had no room to retreat.

She swung at the nearest monster, and a flash of blue

lighting shot from the blade, frying both monsters with one blow. Kyja stared at her sword. "How did I do that?"

Marcus grinned. "You handle the sword, and I'll send magic out from it. It's not a magic sword, exactly, but no one needs to know that."

Working together, they were able to hold off enough of the dark creatures to keep from being overrun. Kyja fought until her arms shook, but she kept on swinging. Marcus switched the magic he sent, changing between fire, air, ice, and electricity, depending on the creature.

Overhead, Riph Raph did the best he could, calling out instructions, shooting tiny blue fireballs, and reminding them that they were crazy for doing this.

Right when Kyja was beginning to think that she couldn't hold up her sword a minute longer, Riph Raph shouted, "The Icehold soldiers are coming."

Kyja and Marcus spun around to see a wall of warriors and wizards attacking the Dark Circle from the north with heavy axes and a stream of magic. Unprepared for their charge, the Dark Army fell before them.

They might actually have a chance to win.

Kyja grabbed Marcus's arm. "Look," she called, pointing to a white circle in the not-too-far distance. The gate. With the sudden attack, the Dark Circle had left it completely unguarded.

"Let's go," Marcus said.

Together they ran for the gate, blasting any creatures

in their way. But mostly it was a clear shot. The entire Dark Circle army seemed focused on the Icehold attackers.

Marcus and Kyja reached the gate and came to a circle that measured somewhere between ten and twenty paces across. It was divided into four parts, clearly one for each type of magic, each marked by its symbol. In the center of the circle was the image on Marcus's arm—a Summoner doing battle with a creature formed of water, land, air, and fire.

"What now?" Marcus asked, kneeling to examine a keyhole in the center of the image.

Kyja looked for the elementals, hoping they could open the drift, but none of them were in sight. "I guess we wait for the Dark Circle to run."

"I don't think that's going to happen any time soon," Riph Raph called down.

Kyja looked north to see that the battle had turned. The Icehold army, which had been making steady progress before, had since taken heavy losses. Worse, every Icehold soldier who fell was rising again as an undead warrior for the Dark Circle.

"There must be a Summoner nearby," Marcus yelled.

Kyja looked up, and sure enough, a dark shadow was silhouetted by the rising sun. On its back were a cloaked figure and a fire creature that could only be Chaos.

"We have to go," Kyja said. But it was already too late. The dark army was closing in from all sides, and there was no way to escape.

"Swing your sword," Marcus yelled.

Forgetting the ache in her arms, Kyja slashed in every direction. The combination of her steel and Marcus's magic was lethal. But it wasn't enough. The wall of creatures advanced relentlessly.

In the distance, Master Therapass spotted them. "Hold on, children," he shouted. "I'm coming." The wizard blasted his way toward them. But he wouldn't arrive in time; too many undead were coming too fast.

"I . . . can't . . . hold . . . them off," Kyja panted.

Marcus slumped to the ground, his arms and legs shaking. He tried using more magic, but his best spells barely made a ripple in the ocean of undead flowing toward them. Kyja stepped in front of him. Holding her sword as best she could, she waited for the army to tear them apart.

A blur of motion blew past her. Dark creatures flew in every direction. Twin blades flashing, a massive figure forced back the horde.

"Tankum," Kyja sobbed.

The warrior took a quick moment to bow before charging back into the battle. "You looked like you had this under control, but I was feeling left out of the party." Behind him, dozens of warriors and wizards charged forward.

The stone army had arrived at last.

CHAPTER 36

GOODBYE

"What are you two doing here?" Master Therapass panted, blasting the undead around them. "I told you to stay back."

"We saw an . . . an opening," Kyja said, blushing at the obvious lie.

Getting his second wind, Marcus stood up and began fighting again. "We made it to the gate. Isn't that what matters?"

"Only if you survive long enough to open it," the wizard said. He shot a beacon of light over their heads, and one by one, the other groups joined them at the gate. Of the fifty men and women who had gone to battle, less than half of them remained. And of that number, most of them had injuries of one kind or another. The thought of so many dead and hurt made Marcus feel like throwing up.

Cascade had set up a sort of onsite hospital, using water magic to heal as many as he could, moving from one wounded to the next as the person he'd just healed charged back into battle.

Magma was a tank, drawing the heaviest of the attacks. His mace mowed down enemies by the dozens. Lanctrus-Darnoc built up a berm of rocks and dirt, which provided some protection, and Divum changed air currents, forcing the Summoner to keep its distance. But with all that, it was only the stone army that kept the enemy at bay.

Tankum matched Magma blow for blow. Marcus watched the two warriors compare themselves to each other and nod with appreciation of the other's skills.

"Maybe we should try opening the gate now," Kyja suggested.

"No time," Master Therapass said, hurling fireball after fireball into the horde. The old man seemed to have limitless endurance. "As soon as we take our elementals out of the battle, the Dark Circle will close in." He nodded toward the circling Summoner, emphasizing his point.

The battle raged all day. Every so often, the Dark Circle would make progress, and then the stone army would drive them back. The problem was that no matter how many creatures the stone army slayed, the Summoner continued to raise more. And while the elementals and stone army could fight forever, the humans were running out of strength. Even with Cascade's healing, another soldier collapsed every few minutes.

High Lord Broomhead limped to Master Therapass's side. "We can't go on like this," he panted. "Icehold has closed their gates, and our people are exhausted. The stone army is taking heavy damage as well."

Therapass blew up the ground under fifty dark creatures and nodded. "We have to run for the forest."

"I'm not sure the injured can make it that far."

The wizard pressed his lips tightly together. "I'm afraid they don't have a choice."

Broomhead nodded. "I'll tell them to prepare for retreat."

Therapass waved down Riph Raph. "Carry the word to the elementals and the stone army that on my command, they must open a path to the woods."

"Consider it done," Riph Raph said, circling into the air.

"How's your leg?" the wizard asked Marcus.

"Good enough to get back to the woods. But once we retreat, the Dark Circle will open the gate."

"Once we get the people safely to the woods, we'll send the stone army back to hold them off until we come up with another plan."

"How are you doing?" Kyja asked. "You must be exhausted."

The wizard smiled. "I'm an old man. Exhaustion is part of life."

Riph Raph flew back. "I've passed the word."

Master Therapass nodded. "Get ready," he told Marcus and Kyja. Pointing his staff in the air toward the woods, he fired off three quick blasts of green fire.

Instantly the stone army changed course. Fighting in two columns, they forced a path through the battle. Limping and stumbling, a few soldiers carried by others, the humans started toward the woods.

Without a central spot to defend, holding off the dark creatures became twice as difficult. Not only did the stone army have to defend their spots, but they also had to keep moving forward at the same pace as the humans. Cascade and Divum were forced to join the battle.

They were almost halfway to the woods when Riph Raph screamed a warning. Marcus looked up as a dark shadow passed over them. Divum tried to divert the Summoner, but Calem flew right behind it, keeping it aloft with his air magic.

Magma turned and flung a bolt of fire, which the Summoner easily dodged.

"Is that all you've got?" Chaos laughed from the back of the Summoner. "Looks like you picked the wrong side this time."

"Faster!" Therapass shouted. But with the combination of the Summoner, the Master, elementals, and the dark creatures to deal with, progress slowed to a halt.

"Give up now, and I might let you live, brother," the Master shouted.

Therapass fired off a bolt of ice, which sent the Summoner circling away. "We've got to get to the woods," the wizard shouted.

Marcus never saw where Tide came from. It was as if the elemental had been hiding in the middle of the undead army, waiting for the right moment to attack. With everyone's attention on the Summoner, he stepped forward and cast a spell at the stone army.

Ice encased the stone wizards and warriors. Before any of the human wizards could react, the Summoner swooped low and blasted the frozen soldiers with a stream of superheated fire, which acted like a sledgehammer on the stone warriors and wizards, cracking their bodies into a million pieces.

Beneath the layer of ice, Tankum's eyes moved to give Marcus one last look. Marcus thought he saw the stone warrior attempt to wave goodbye, and then the man who had saved his life at least twice crumbled to dust.

◆

Kyja stared in shock as Tankum and the rest of the stone warriors and wizards were destroyed in front of her eyes.

With no one to stop them, the dark army next fell on the helpless humans. The elementals moved in to protect them, but they were too outnumbered. Even Magma seemed to realize that he didn't stand a chance as he went from attack mode to a defensive posture. The humans and elementals backed together, surrounded on all sides by blades, teeth, and fangs.

"Stop!" Master Therapass shouted. "We surrender."

"No," Kyja whispered. They couldn't give up. Not after the stone army had given their lives. Not after Graehl, Rhaidnan, and so many others had died so the rest of them could be here and fight.

The undead creatures and Thrathkin S'Bae cleared space as the Summoner soared slowly overhead then landed at the head of the dark army. The Master and Chaos climbed from the creature's back.

The Master walked forward until he was nose-to-nose with Master Therapass. "What's that, brother? I'm not sure I heard you."

The old wizard dropped his head. "We surrender. Allow these people to live, and you may do whatever you want with me."

"Never," Marcus said. He began to raise a hand, but the Master clamped his cold fingers around Marcus's wrist. "I told you that you'd come crawling back. Should I make you do that now—squirm on your belly to save your life? Grovel in the mud so I won't hurt you?"

Chaos laughed.

"Kill me if you like," Marcus said. "But I'll never crawl for you."

"No?" The Master turned to Kyja. "You're the one who's caused me so much trouble. On the other hand, you also gave me everything I needed to take complete control of Farworld and Earth. I suppose I should thank you. Would you like to be my serving girl—clean my toilets and wash my laundry?"

Kyja had never wanted to spit in anyone's face so much, but she had to hold her temper or risk endangering the rest of the group, so she bit her tongue and said nothing.

"Touch her, and I'll make you pay," Marcus snarled, and Kyja silently begged him to be quiet. Didn't he understand they were at this monster's mercy?

The Master's red eyes flared. "You fancy her, do you? Good to know. If you want to save her, kneel down and lick my boots."

Marcus's entire body shook with shock and anger.

"Lick my boots, or I'll flay her here and now in front of you."

Marcus began to lower himself, but before he reached the ground, Master Therapass dropped instead. He pressed his face to his brother's feet and licked first one boot and then the other. Marcus tried to pull him back by his robe, but Cascade and Divum locked their arms around him.

"You are the greater wizard," Master Therapass said. "I am not worthy to be your brother. Please let us live."

Hot tears of shame and fury filled Kyja's eyes. She

couldn't stand to see her mentor humiliated like this.

The Master laughed and pushed Master Therapass down in the dirt. "I always said you weren't cut out for anything more than shining shoes."

Tide, Nizgar-Gharat, and Calem stepped forward. "Would you like us to kill him?"

"Give horn-head to me," Chaos said. "I've always wanted to slit his thick throat."

"I'd like to see you try," Magma growled.

The Master patted Chaos on the back. "I've got plans for each and every one of them. Plans that involve weeks of torture and humiliation. And I do believe that you are the right person to help me in that work. But first, I want them to see my complete and final victory."

He looked around and pointed to a hill about a half mile away. "Take them there. Make sure they have a good view of what is about to happen. Set the Summoner to guard them, and if anyone turns away for so much as an instant, kill them."

As they were being marched toward the hill, Marcus looked back. "You won't succeed," he said. "No matter how much you accomplish now, in the end, you will fail."

"On the contrary," the Master said. "I will succeed beyond anything you imagine. I will take the lives of innocent men, women, and children in numbers beyond counting. And I will make sure you and your girlfriend see each and every death so you can blame yourselves for them over, and over, and over. Now get back there with the rest of the cowards." He shoved Marcus forward, knocking him into the dirt.

Kyja ran to pull him up. "It's okay," she said. "We'll find some way to fight back. This isn't over."

"Of course," Marcus said, scraping mud off his knees.

But despite her own words, Kyja wondered if maybe their quest was over. If they'd been too slow. And if so, how many people would end up paying for their mistakes.

CHAPTER 37

OPENING THE GATE

"I'm sorry," Marcus said. "I should have been the one licking his boots.

Master Therapass shook his head. "There are worse things than a little humiliation now and then. In fact, humiliating oneself can be good for the ego. When you start to think you that are incapable of failure, failure has a way of reminding you that it's still around."

"Is this it, then?" Kyja asked. "Isn't there any way left to stop them?"

The wizard smiled down at her, and it warmed Kyja's heart to see that he was still capable of smiling. She felt as if she'd never be able to smile again.

"Good men and women do their best to stop evil when they see it," the wizard said. "But the truth is, sometimes that isn't possible. Sometimes, as much as we want to see justice done, bad people do bad things, and we cannot stop them."

Kyja felt like weeping.

"That doesn't mean evil will win out," Master Therapass continued. "While we can't always stop people from doing evil things, bad decisions tend to lead to bad consequences."

No matter what words he used, what he said still sounded like failure to Kyja. But she couldn't say so. Instead, she put an arm around his waist. "I'm sorry about Tankum. That must have been hard for you."

The wizard smiled and patted her on the back. As they continued up the hill, Master Therapass gazed wistfully up at the sky, which was beginning to turn orange as the sun dipped behind the trees of Before Time. "When I lost him many years ago, it was hard. He was my best friend. Having him back for the last year has been a joy I never expected to have. I'm sure he was glad to leave this world defending others, the same way he did the first time."

He climbed up the hill by himself, and Kyja wandered over to join Marcus. "Thanks for defending me back there," she said.

Marcus shrugged. "It was dumb. I shouldn't have let the Master's words get to me."

"True," Kyja said. Marcus gave her a look that said he hadn't expected her to agree. "But it was still sweet."

"You were pretty good with your sword back there," Marcus said.

"And you were pretty good with your magic. We made a great team."

"Move along," a pair of dark wizards said, jabbing them in the back with their staffs.

Marcus and Kyja hurried to catch up with the others. At the top of the hill, the Thrathkin S'Bae formed them into a line. The Summoner landed at the base of the hill, and Kyja remembered the time it had plucked her off the wall of Icehold. She wondered if it remembered that time too.

"Face the Master," one of the Thrathkin S'Bae ordered. "Do not drop your heads or look away in any fashion. Disobedience is punishable by death."

Was this how the rest of their lives would be—taking orders from the Dark Circle? She had to live this way, but that didn't mean Marcus did. She edged up to him and whispered, "I can push you back to Earth."

"Would you come with me?" he asked.

She thought for a moment. "The Dark Circle might take it out on the rest of the group."

"It doesn't matter," he said. "Once they force open the gate, there won't be any escape from them on Earth or Farworld."

Below, the Master lined up Tide, Nizgar-Gharat, Calem, and Chaos in front of the gate. "Behold!" he shouted, looking up the hill. "The beginning of a new world!"

A world of terror, Kyja thought. *A world of madness.* Despite knowing that she and Marcus had tried their best, she felt guilty.

———◆———

Marcus watched the Master move each of the elementals into place at the circle. "How does it work?" he whispered to Master Therapass. "How do they open the gate?"

The wizard shook his head. "I don't know any more than you. I'm not sure my brother knows either. But you can be sure he won't quit until he figures it out."

From where they stood, it was hard to make out what the dark wizard was saying, but it looked like he was instructing each elemental on what to do. Marcus found himself both terrified and fascinated. Opening a doorway would give the Master more power. But after all this time, Marcus wanted to see what the drift would look like—how it worked.

Chaos was the first to act. He held out his arms, and a line of fire traced the symbol in his quadrant then rushed to the middle of the circle.

Nizgar-Gharat went next. Marcus watched a dark line fill the symbol for land magic, and meet fire in the middle.

For a moment, the land magic seemed about to put out the fire, and the two elementals shouted something at each other. But the Master quickly quieted them.

Tide went next, then Calem. Lines of water, land, air, and fire magic met in the middle of the circle. Marcus leaned forward with anticipation.

Nothing happened.

"What's going on?" Kyja asked. "Why isn't it opening?"

Master Therapass shook his head. "Combining magic is a difficult task at the best of times, and elementals of different types do not typically work well together. Remember what I said long ago about fire and water magic?"

Marcus remembered the wizard explaining how two powerful forms of magic could offset each other, like a bucket of water dousing a candle.

"More magic!" the Master shouted, and the lines on the circle flashed brighter. Intent on what was happening below, the Thrathkin S'Bae moved down the hill and closer to the action.

The Master held up his staff, and a low whine came from the gate. Blue, brown, silver, and orange pulsed to the sound.

"Something's happening," Kyja whispered.

At the center of the circle, all four colors wound themselves into a thick, black vine stretching high into the air. The whining grew louder, and the ground began to vibrate.

Standing on the circle, Calem appeared to try to move away, but the master pointed his staff at the air elemental, and Calem's head snapped up—his spine bowed as if someone were stretching him backward over a barrel.

Divum smirked. "I wonder if he's questioning his choice to join the Master now."

Power filled the air, and the entire dark army moved toward the circle. Marcus felt the hair on the backs of his arms and neck stand straight up.

The whining sound grew louder still as the black vine thickened into a pillar of solid magic that rose high into the sky. The clouds seemed to be affected too, swirling around the pillar like a tornado about to touch down.

"Harder!" the Master shouted, and the entire circle began to pulse. Orange, brown, blue, and silver lit the Master's face, giving the wizard the appearance of an insane clown. All of the elementals writhed in their spots on the gate.

The sound grew louder and more high-pitched. Cracks spread across the ground as the land vibrated. It was happening. Darkness now made up nearly half of the circle. The colored lines flashed so brightly that Marcus had to shade his eyes. He started forward with the rest of the dark army, but Master Therapass grabbed him by the shoulder.

"Get down," the wizard said to Marcus and Kyja. "Put your hands over your heads and press your faces to the ground." He turned to the rest of the group. "Everyone get down. Take cover."

Hand in hand, Marcus and Kyja lay face down on the ground, with Riph Raph tucked between them. Magma knelt over them, shielding their bodies. The wizards and elementals flattened themselves against the hard-packed dirt.

The whining reached a pitch that sounded like a drill about to snap its bit.

"What's happening?" Marcus shouted, cheek pressed to the ground.

Even though Master Therapass was right beside him, he could barely hear the wizard over the shrill scream. "They're pushing the gate too hard. There's too much magic going in. With no way for it to escape—"

The twilight sky, which had been a purplish-gray suddenly flashed white—as though a thousand lightning bolts had struck at the same place. Marcus squeezed his eyes shut against the glare, but he could still see the image imprinted on the insides of his lids.

At the same time, the ground rolled like a ship on a raging ocean. Marcus and Kyja were flung upward, and it was only the weight of the fire elemental that kept them from being tossed like a rock from a slingshot.

Explosions and screams filled the air. The ground

continued to shake, and lights flashed. Chunks of rock and dirt flew into the air, and the ground felt like part of the hillside had broken completely away. As the quake went on and on, Marcus began to wonder if it would ever stop, or if Farworld was shaking itself to pieces.

At last the rumbling slowed, then shuddered to a halt. The screams stopped, and Marcus opened his eyes. The sky had taken on a strange, greenish-yellow hue, as if the very atmosphere had been bruised. His ears rang, and his head throbbed.

Kyja released his hand and shakily stood up. "Look," she said. "Look what happened."

Marcus pushed himself to his knees. Despite the fact that the ground had stopped shaking, his body still swayed. He couldn't be seeing what he thought he was. He rubbed his eyes, but the view remained the same.

All of the colors were gone, along with the black pillar that had reached up to the sky. The gate looked exactly as it had before, with no sign of change or damage. But everything around it had been flattened. The entire army of the Dark Circle had been completely destroyed.

CHAPTER 38

WATER, LAND, AIR, AND FIRE

All around, people were bleeding and grasping limbs twisted at odd angles. Wizards had been thrown as far as a hundred feet or more from their original positions, and several had been hit by flying rock and debris.

Cascade and Master Therapass hurried from one person to the next, healing the most grievous injuries, and moving on. Marcus realized that he should be doing the same. His staff was nowhere to be found, so he asked Kyja to help him move around the hill.

Together they began tracking down the hurt, often by the sounds of their moans or screaming, and doing what they could to help. Riph Raph flew about the hill, finding supplies and scouting for more injured. Kyja had the perfect bedside manner, encouraging everyone as she tore sheets of cloth, tied bandages, and cleaned wounds.

"It's okay," she said to a woman whose arm had nearly been torn off by a flying branch. "You make dresses don't you?"

"That's right," the woman said, her face pale and clammy.

"You do amazing work. I saw one of your gowns in a shop window." Kyja comforted the woman, as Marcus stopped the bleeding and carefully reattached the limb.

"Really?" the woman asked, perking up.

"It was green with puffy sleeves. You'll be making them again in no time." Kyja pointed at the woman's arm.

The woman looked down and her eyes went wide as she saw that the wound was completely healed. "Thank you," she said, hugging Marcus and Kyja. "Come by my shop when this is over and I'll make you anything you want."

They found a wizard with a deep gash above one eye cowering on the ground. "It's all right," Kyja said, taking his hand. "They're gone. The entire dark army has been destroyed."

The man clasped her hand with shaking fingers. "Is it true?"

She helped him stand so he could see for himself, and the man wept with joy.

Marcus, who had never healed so many people at one time, was beginning to feel faint, so Riph Raph flew off to get him some food. Each wizard they healed began healing others, and soon everyone still alive was at least stable.

Looking at the number of bodies no longer moving, though, Marcus felt sickened and shocked by how many of his friends and neighbors hadn't survived. Thousands of bodies from both sides lay scattered across the field beneath a lingering cloud of yellow-gray smoke. Both good and evil looked the same in death.

"Victory has come at a terrible cost," a voice said from beside him. Marcus turned to find Divum there. She was dressed in all black, and he had never seen the Aerisian looking so somber.

Kyja wiped her eyes. "I didn't want them to die for us."

"They didn't die for you," Cascade said. "They died for what they believed in, and so that others could continue to have the freedom to choose their own beliefs."

Magma rested his mace on his shoulder and surveyed the damage. "Until this day, I had no idea humans could be so . . . heroic."

"For years to come, stories will be told of the sacrifices made here," Lanctrus-Darnoc said.

Marcus looked up at the fox and boar. "Tide, Calem, and the other elementals. Are they . . . ?"

"Destroyed," Lanctrus said with a nod. "They were at the center of the explosion. I believe the force of dark magic flowing through them was the catalyst that set it all off."

Kyja touched the land elementals' wing. "Master Therapass said that if dark magic opened the gate, all of the elementals would be destroyed. But you're all still here."

Master Therapass limped up the hill to them. He had deep-purple bags under his eyes, and his skin had a glossy sheen Marcus didn't like the look of. But the wizard also looked satisfied.

"They did not open the gate. The power is still there." He looked at Marcus, Kyja, and the elementals. I believe that task is now up to you."

<hr>

Kyja stood at the edge of the great white seal, afraid to actually step onto it. They had worked so long to get here—to reach this moment—that she felt a sort of superstitious dread. As if the moment she set foot on the gate, something terrible would happen to destroy everything they'd worked for.

"Why did the others explode when they tried to open it?" she asked.

Master Therapass shook his head. "What they were doing wasn't working. I don't know why, exactly. But instead of backing off, my brother kept driving them, kept pushing—until something snapped."

"Like an engine running at high speed until it throws

a piston," Marcus said. When the others stared at him, he shrugged and smiled. "Earth analogy."

Kyja looked at the wizards gathered around them. "Shouldn't they move away? In case it . . . happens again?"

The wizard shook his head. "They were using dark magic in an attempt to force the doorway open. My brother has always been convinced that the best way to get what you want is to take it—to push and push until it is yours. Light magic doesn't work that way. I can't say if you'll be able to open the gate any more than they did. But I am quite sure that there will not be another explosion."

"I agree," Divum said. "Us being here now, this way, feels right to me."

Kyja nodded. This was it, then—the time to finish the quest Master Therapass had told them about so long ago, when she and Marcus barely knew each other.

She lifted one foot to step onto the gate, but Marcus grabbed her hand. "Wait."

Kyja, Master Therapass, and the elementals turned to look at him. Leaning on his staff, he licked his lips. "What if we don't open it?"

Kyja didn't understand. "You mean, what if we *can't?*"

He shook his head. "Think about it. The Dark Circle is gone. Even if there are a few Thrathkin S'Bae remaining somewhere, they'll scatter now that the Master is gone. There's no one left for us to fight. What if we left the gate alone?"

"What about your father?" Kyja asked. "Isn't he trying to get the power?"

"He'll probably end up destroying himself the same way the Dark Circle did. Now that we know how to enter the realm of shadows, we can keep an eye on him. Why risk trying to open the gate ourselves when we don't really have to?"

"Turnip Head has a point," Riph Raph said. "And that's a pretty rare thing. Maybe we should listen to him."

Master Therapass dropped to one knee in front of Marcus. "You've worked too hard to stop now. What is it? What are you afraid of? Are you still concerned about the origin of your mark? Because by now—"

"No," Kyja said, suddenly understanding. "It's what the woman in the mist told us, isn't it?"

Marcus stared at his feet and nodded.

Master Therapass scratched his beard. "The *woman in the mist?*"

Until this moment, Kyja had completely forgotten about the woman's words. But now that she remembered, her heart began to pound. "She was one of the four—the beings who asked us questions when we were opening the gate to Fire Keep. Marcus asked her what would happen if we created a drift and went through. She said that the doorway would only open once, and that what goes through can't return. If Marcus and I go to our own worlds, we'll never see each other again. I'll go to Earth and never see Riph Raph or any of you."

"You didn't tell me this," Master Therapass said. "Who were these four? Can you trust them?"

Marcus nodded slowly, looking a little sick. "I think they may be the ones who created the elements in the first place. The ones who locked Fire Keep and Air Keep."

Magma glowered. Divum and Cascade looked distinctly uncomfortable. Lanctrus and Darnoc whispered back and forth.

"Here's the thing, Kyja," Marcus said. "I've nearly lost you twice, and I don't want to take that chance again. If we don't open the drift, I'll never be able to come here completely, and you won't be able to stay in Farworld. But with the potion Master Therapass made, we can stay longer than before."

"And maybe we could find a way to stop your father, and then we can live in the realm of shadows," Kyja said. "Like your parents did." That wouldn't be so bad. There was no rule that said they had to open the gate as soon as they'd freed the elementals. If it looked like anything bad would happen, they could always do it later. Maybe much, much later, when they were older than Master Therapass.

"I know you two want to stay together," the wizard said, laying his hands on their heads. "And I can't say that I blame you. You share a bond I've never seen the likes of. I still don't understand how you were able to pull Marcus here from Earth in the first place, little one. But I think you both know that this is not something we can put off. Fire Keep was opened for a reason. Until the drift is opened and the prophecy fulfilled, Earth and Farworld will never be safe. It's time for you to do what you know you must, even if it means never seeing each other again."

Marcus sighed and stared at the ground.

Kyja wiped away a stray tear.

Riph Raph swished his tail angrily. "Well, this stinks!"

"You know what we have to do," Kyja said.

Marcus nodded. "I guess I knew it all along. I just . . . I'm going to miss you so much."

Kyja pulled him into her arms, and for several minutes, they hugged silently while everyone else found something to look at. Sniffs and choking gasps could be heard through the group of wizards and warriors.

At last, Marcus pulled away. He wiped his nose on his sleeve. "Are you ready to do this?"

"I guess so," Kyja said, trying to smile.

Hand in hand, they led the elementals to the gateway. Each of them took their place on the symbol representing his or her magic while Marcus, Kyja, and Riph Raph stood at the center of the circle, where the image of the two creatures remained locked in deadly combat.

"Remember to take it slow," Master Therapass said. "Feel your way."

Kyja took one long last look around, wanting to lock Farworld into her memories in case she never saw it again.

She gave Riph Raph a hug. "Take care of Marcus for me."

Riph Raph nodded his head and glistening tears dripped from his big golden eyes. "I'll n-never for-for . . ." The skyte couldn't finish what he was trying to say and instead tucked his head under one wing.

One by one, each elemental fed magic into the symbols. Water flowing from Cascade filled the carvings in his fourth of the gate. Rock and soil filled the next. Wind gusted from Divum, and fire erupted from Magma. Lines of blue, brown, silver, and orange pulsed with energy.

The four elements flowed together at the center of the circle, and for a brief second, a glowing key formed there. Marcus reached out, whispering something Kyja couldn't hear. But before he could touch the key, Magma's flames flared, and Cascade's water evaporated.

"Careful," the Fontasian said. "You're using too much. Calm your emotions." Cascade refilled his section of the circle, but his water washed away part of Lanctrus-Darnoc's soil.

"Watch what you're doing," the land elementals said. "Haven't you studied the proper amount of magic for combining land and water?" They added more soil to replace what they'd lost but ended up extinguishing Magma's flames.

Divum burst into delighted laughter as the Pyrinth gave a frustrated snarl.

"You think this is funny?" Magma asked.

"Very much so," Divum said with a grin. "You look like a child who has lost its toy."

Magma gave a blast of flame, which burned up her oxygen with a whoosh. "Now *that's* funny."

"Keep your balance," Master Therapass called.

"More fire over there. Not so much air!' Marcus pointed from one element to another, trying to get the perfect mix. Occasionally the key would appear, wavering, but every time he reached for it, one of the elements snuffed out one of the others.

"Stop blowing out my flames!" Magma roared at Divum.

"Stop washing away our soil," the land elementals complained to Cascade. Soon all of the elementals were spending more effort on stopping each other's magic than creating their own.

Was this what had happened when the Dark Circle had attempted to open the gate? The elementals were getting more and more frustrated, channeling greater and greater energy into the gate. Slowly, the whining that had started before began. Those standing outside the circle backed away.

"Stop!" Kyja shouted. The elementals pulled back their magic, and the whining cut off. The circle changed back to white. "We can't fight each other. Don't you understand that the reason you were all separated in the first place was to avoid this very thing? I hate to tell you, but none of your magic is powerful enough to do this alone."

"What are you thinking?" Marcus asked.

Kyja looked from one elemental to the next, trying to figure out a way they could all help one another instead of canceling out others' magic. She pointed to Lanctrus-Darnoc. "Fill your section of the circle until it reaches the center."

"But fire—" Magma began.

With a raised hand, Kyja cut him off and watched as the land elementals followed her order. She pointed to Cascade. "Add enough water to make the earth elementals' soil soft and moldable."

"This makes sense," Cascade said. "Much more orderly."

As soil and water mixed, Kyja looked to Magma. "Can you add enough fire to harden the soil into stone?"

Magma sneered. "I can melt it to a puddle."

"No!" Kyja said. "That's exactly what we don't want. Increase the heat gradually but consistently. Cascade, continue to feed enough water to keep the stone from cracking, but not enough to put out the flames. Lanctrus-Darnoc, keep feeding enough soil to give the stone more mass."

"The flames aren't hot enough," Lanctrus said.

"The stone won't hold its shape," Darnoc said, his face furrowed with concentration.

"That's where you come in," Kyja said to Divum, who still wore an amused grin. "Fan the flames higher without putting them out."

Blue, brown, silver, and orange filled the circle and flowed together.

"More flame!" Kyja shouted. "More air. Keep the water and soil coming."

In the center of the circle, the key formed. It wavered, almost disappeared for a moment, then glowed brightly.

"That's it," Marcus said. "Hold it right there."

He knelt on the circle, grasped the key in his right hand, and tried to turn it.

The key didn't move.

"What's wrong?' Kyja asked.

"It won't budge." The muscles in his good arm stood out as he used all his strength to twist. Sweat beaded on his forehead.

"We can't hold it," Lanctrus-Darnoc yelled. "The key's about to break."

"Try harder," Kyja called. Leaning over Marcus, she wanted to help him turn the key, but she couldn't help, not without magic.

They'd done everything right. Why wasn't it working?

Marcus grunted. He gave one last heave, and the key disappeared from between his fingers. Water, land, air, and fire magic disappeared as well.

"Did we do it?" Kyja asked. "Did we open the gate?"

"No," Marcus said. "It didn't work."

CHAPTER 39

THE DRIFT

"**M**aybe you weren't turning hard enough," Kyja suggested. "Maybe part of you doesn't want to open the gate."

"I *was* trying," Marcus snapped. "I gave my word that I'd open the drift, and I won't break a promise."

"I wasn't suggesting you would," Kyja said. "But if part of you isn't completely committed—"

"I'm committed!" he yelled.

Kyja pulled back, her face crumpling, and he felt like a complete jerk.

"I'm sorry," he said. "I shouldn't have yelled." He stared at his twisted left arm. "Maybe I'm not strong enough. Maybe it takes two arms." He looked at Master Therapass and the rest of the wizards, who were sitting dejectedly around the gate. "Why don't one of *you* try?"

The wizard shook his head. "Opening the gate does require strength, but it's the kind you possess more of than anyone else here—strength of heart, strength of will. Lack of strength is not the problem."

"Than what is?" Marcus's face went red. Kyja had been so amazing with how she'd gotten the elementals to work together. It was the kind of thing she did all the time—making peace, helping those in need, figuring things out. She'd done *her* part. She'd managed to create the key, which even the Dark Circle hadn't been able to do. All he'd had to do was reach down and turn it. And he'd failed, spectacularly, in front of everyone.

"I don't know why the key didn't turn," Master Therapass said. "But you are the one to turn it, and I'm sure you'll figure it out."

"What if I'm not?" Marcus whispered. He pulled up the sleeve of his robe. "What if this scar is fake, and I'm not special at all?"

The Wizard met his gaze with a steely stare. "It is not the mark that makes you special."

Maybe, but what else did he have? Without the mark, he was nothing but a kid with a bad leg and arm, a dead mother, and a psychotic father. What did he have to offer? He stared at the image of the Elementals battling the Summoner—the Master's last and greatest joke, continuing even after his death.

What was the stupid mark supposed to mean anyway? There never had been a battle between the elementals and a Summoner. The explosion had killed Bonesplinter, not . . .

Marcus looked around the field of dead bodies. He pushed himself to his feet.

"What?" Kyja asked. "What are you looking for?"

Marcus hurried back to the hill. He searched through the piles of bodies. It had been here, at the base of the hill when the explosion went off, surely it was still there; it couldn't have disintegrated.

"Can I help you find whatever you're looking for?" Kyja asked.

Master Therapass watched them both with a raised eyebrow.

"I think he's finally lost his crackers," Riph Raph said. "One too many bangs to the melon."

Marcus looked left, and there it was—farther away than he had expected, but clearly identifiable by its bright-red body.

"The Summoner?" Kyja asked. "What do you want with that?"

"I'm just glad it's dead," Riph Raph said. "I don't ever want to see another one again."

Marcus approached the tattered creature. One of its wings was completely blown off, and the other was in shreds. Gashes covered its scaled body, and several large chunks of flesh were missing. Yet somehow, its chest raised and lowered slowly.

"It's still alive," Kyja said.

Marcus searched the bodies around the monster until

he found a sword, which he dragged back to the creature. "This is why the gate won't open. There's still one thing left to do. The elementals have to slay the Summoner. *That's* what the mark on my arm means. Only then will the prophecy will be complete, and we'll be able to make the drift.

He held the sword out to the elementals. "Do you want to do it?"

Magma took the sword. "With pleasure."

Kyja tilted her head as though listening. Her lips moved, but Marcus couldn't make out what she was saying.

Cascade, Lanctrus-Darnoc, and Divum each all took hold of the sword with Magma. The elementals raised the sword above their heads, and the Summoner weakly opened one eye.

As the elementals began to plunge the sword downward, Kyja leaped in front of them. "Wait," she cried. "Don't kill it."

<hr />

"What do you mean, we have to let it live?" Marcus yanked up his sleeve and showed her his scar. "You have one of these on your amulet. Master Therapass says they are everywhere. Have you looked at it? The elementals have to kill the monster. It's the end of the quest."

"The boy is right," Magma said, holding the sword in

one hand and his mace in the other. "The creature must die."

Kyja stood squarely between the Pyrinth and the Summoner. "There's a person inside there. He's been tortured and hurt. But deep inside, he is still a person."

"I know who he is," Marcus spat. "Bonesplinter has been trying to kill us for years. Now it's our turn."

"He can't hurt you anymore," Kyja said, unwavering.

"I don't care whether the monster can hurt me. It's the last remaining piece of the Dark Circle. Until it's destroyed, we can't open the gate."

She knew she was being stubborn, but she didn't care. Killing the creature didn't feel right, and if there was one thing she'd learned over the course of their adventures, it was to trust her instincts. Back in Icehold, when the Summoner had snatched her off the city wall, she'd sensed that there might be a way to free the poor soul trapped inside the creature. She felt that way now.

She took out her amulet and studied the image. "What if this doesn't mean what you think it does?"

Marcus looked at Riph Raph. "Is she making any sense to you?"

The skyte waggled its ears. "Not really."

"You see two creatures trying to kill each other," Kyja said, holding the amulet directly in front of Marcus's face. "But what if they aren't fighting? What if they are embracing?"

Marcus's mouth dropped open. "Uhhhh . . ."

Magma looked just as flummoxed. "You want me to . . . *hug* the creature?"

"You don't have to hug it," Kyja said. "But think about it this way: What do Earth, Farworld, and the realm of shadows all have in common? War. Fighting. Unhappiness. Is one more death what it takes to connect our worlds? Or do we need to prove that we've finally managed to find peace?"

Master Therapass grinned. "I knew there was magic inside you."

Marcus eyed the Summoner dubiously. Its body, which the wizards had floated to the center of the gate, covered the keyhole completely. He had no idea how he was supposed to get at the key—if it would form again at all.

But Kyja didn't seem to share any of his doubts. She squeezed his hand and grinned. "This is going to work."

"If you say so." He glanced at the elementals, who all seemed as unconvinced as he was, except for Divum, who still appeared amused by the whole thing. Marcus rubbed the back of his neck. "What do you want me to do?"

"Exactly what you did before," Kyja said.

He shrugged. "Okay. Places everyone. And . . . lights, camera, action."

As they had done the first time, Lanctrus-Darnoc

filled their section of gate with soil. Cascade added water, Magma produced flames, and Divum fanned them with air. Except this time, the spot where the elements met was hidden by the Summoner's body.

Standing with Marcus next to the Summoner, Kyja shouted, "Everyone together!"

"Are you sure this is going to work?" Marcus asked.

Kyja pointed down.

Something was happening to the Summoner. It was twisting, changing. Its body began to shrink. Wings turned into arms. Talons into feet. Fire, air, land, and water magic swirled around the figure in a pillar of twisting colors.

Then Bonesplinter was standing in the center of the gate. He looked around, clearly confused.

"It's all right," Kyja said. "We won't hurt you."

The key flared in its hole. Marcus dropped and clasped it between his fingers. He tried to turn it but still couldn't. Another hand closed over his. He looked up to find Bonesplinter leaning over him. Kyja added her hand on top of theirs.

Kyja and Marcus met eyes, knowing it might be the last time they would see each other. She waited as though, giving him a chance to stop the drift from opening. But Master Therapass was right. This was about so much more than the two of them. It was the hardest thing Marcus had done in his life, but he smiled at her and nodded.

Together, the three of them twisted, and the key turned.

On an early Chicago morning, a boy was shooting baskets into a rusty hoop. As he stepped back to take a free throw, the ball suddenly blazed in his hands. Lines of color shot out from it like fireworks. He should have been terrified, but he wasn't. He clutched the ball to his chest, looked up at the cloudy, gray sky and shouted—not entirely understanding his own words, but knowing they were true. "They did it!"

In an underground room deep in the center of the realm of shadows, King Phillip and his engineers were working feverishly on a bank of computers. It was almost time. He looked up at a screen showing hundreds of Spell Casters feeding his system. Suddenly, the screen in front of him blew out, shattering glass across the room. Then another and another.

"What's going on?" he screamed.

His engineers backed away from their computers. One of them pointed at the screen on the wall, and the king looked over to see every one of the Casters wrapped in a glowing cocoon of color. The silver wires attached to their bodies snapped like short-circuited electric cables, and the Casters floated to the ground. Two guards, one with metal hands and the other with a metal jaw, raced toward the Casters, weapons drawn. A silver cable touched them, and they were thrown across the room, unconscious.

The King ground his teeth, much the way Marcus did when he was angry, then clenched his fists and muttered, "My son."

In a small but neat apartment, a woman was feeding her baby before going to work for the day. Pink light filled the room, and the baby floated up out of its highchair, giggling. The woman froze with the spoon of baby food in her hand. She stared at the ceiling, but it wasn't the cracked panels she noticed. In her mind, she saw the girl who'd brought her money and cloaks when she'd been about to give up. The girl who'd felt . . . *different*, somehow. In the world, but not of it.

All at once, as though someone else's memories had been put in her head, she knew. Who the girl was, where she'd gone, where she was, and what she'd done. The woman dropped the spoon to the ground. "My daughter!"

A woman who had left her abusive husband was watching her son's first horseback riding lesson when the old nag he rode turned into a unicorn.

Three women playing cards burst into tears of joy for no reason then hugged each other. "The children," one of them said, although she wouldn't remember doing so later. "The children are safe."

Strange things happened all over Earth. In Africa, a beggar realized he could fly. A pair of starving children in Bangladesh discovered that they could make as much food as they wanted. Volcanos that had been dormant for a thousand years erupted. Los Angeles skyscrapers turned into castles. People driving to work stared in shock as their cars changed into carriages pulled by winged lions. A man running through Central Park skidded to a stop as a group of white ball-shaped creatures with pink antennas scurried across his path.

Every elemental on Farworld looked up from what they'd been doing as requests for their magic came flooding in.

Mr. Z shook hands with two women, and with a man who looked more like a tree—or was he a tree who looked more like a man? The little man threw his tophat in the air and whooped with joy.

"I knew they could do it all along! Never doubted it for a minute." He pulled a tiny whistle out of his pocket and blew it loudly. "Drymaios, get over those sniffles and come here. We have places to go."

* * *

Magic blasted into the air like the spout of a fire hydrant filled with rainbows, and Marcus and Kyja both felt something roaring up from the gate. At the same time, something was sucked past them into it. Power like neither of them had ever imagined shook them from head to foot.

Around them, the elementals stood frozen in shock. Even Cascade—who was never surprised by anything—

stood with his mouth hanging open.

Bonesplinter, who had once been a boy with a dream of becoming a great wizard so he could care for his ill parents, burst into tears for everything he'd lost, then realized that maybe he hadn't lost quite everything.

The ground, which had been shaking like an earthquake to end all earthquakes, finally stopped rumbling. The pillar of magic subsided into the gate once more.

Kyja looked around. She was still here, in Farworld.

Marcus looked for a door, but there wasn't one. The entire gate had disappeared.

Riph Raph checked to make sure he was still in one piece.

"What happened?" Kyja asked. "Why am I still here?"

"Where's the door?" Marcus asked. "Did we fail?"

"I don't think so." Master Therapass's eyes were filled with wonder as he stared up at the sky. "No. I don't think so at all."

Marcus and Kyja looked upward together and stared at a long white line that had appeared in the evening sky.

It was the vapor trail from a plane flying overhead.

CHAPTER 40

A NEW WORLD

Marcus and Kyja waited outside the door to Master Therapass's office. It had been six months since Earth and Farworld had combined, and he still couldn't get over the weird combinations of magic and technology he ran into every day, like the elevator that went from the top of the tower to the dungeon while chatting about the weather, local politics, and the chances of fire elementals defeating water elementals in an upcoming debate.

After a minute, a fairy with a postage-stamp-sized wireless tablet opened the door and ushered them inside. In some ways, the room looked like the wizard's study Marcus remembered. Shelves still covered the walls from floor to ceiling. Only now, they were as likely to hold a digital music player or a charging station as a jar of bat's eyes or a vial of powdered frog tongue.

As soon as they came in, Master Therapass jumped to his feet and hugged them both. "It's good to see you. I was starting to think you might have outgrown the town. It doesn't seem nearly as big as it used to."

Kyja shook her head. "Terra ne Staric will always be home. We've been spending some time visiting friends—and family." Her eyes twinkled. "I have a baby brother. Did you know that? He's only three years old, and already he can do magic better than my mom.

The wizard smiled. "And you? Are you still . . . ?"

"Immune to magic?" Kyja raised her hands. "So far. No one's sure why. Cascade thinks it could be because I'm from Earth but was on Farworld when the worlds combined. Some weird combination that doesn't seem to have affected anyone else."

"I'm sorry," the wizard said.

"I'm not." Kyja laughed. "Maybe that will change some day. But for now, I'm kind of enjoying being the way I am. So many Earth things don't require magic. Also, it's kind of neat to know that I'm the only person in the whole world magic doesn't affect. Besides, someone told me once that the most powerful magic isn't spells or wands or potions."

"But what's inside you," the wizard finished. "Who you are, what you do, and most importantly of all, what you may become. You've certainly lived up to that." He turned to Marcus. "With Farworld well, I see that . . ."

"My leg and arm aren't healed?" Marcus asked.

The wizard nodded. "Opening the gate should have

broken the link between your health and Farworld's. With the new combinations of magic and medicine, it would appear that you have plenty of options."

"I do," Marcus said. "I could be like everyone else tomorrow. But . . ."

"I used to want magic more than anything," Kyja said. "Not because of what I could do with it, but because it would make me like everyone else."

Marcus nodded. "And I wanted to have my arm and leg healed because I thought it would make me whole. But I realized I'm not a broken version of someone else. I'm a perfect version of me."

Kyja took Marcus's hand in hers. "The things we were able to accomplish weren't *in spite* of our differences but *because* of them. Our differences make us who we are."

Marcus patted his magic wheelchair. "Besides, you should see what this thing can do. I won't be able to get a driver's license for a couple more months, but I'm not sure I need one anyway. Divum fixed this thing up so I can go faster than most cars and soar from zero to a thousand feet in less than six seconds."

The wizard laughed. "You've learned everything I could have hoped for." He looked around. "I don't see Riph Raph."

Marcus grinned. "He's still a little bit freaked out about coming here. He says skytes never intentionally enter a wolf's den."

"Besides," Kyja said. "He's been a little preoccupied ever since meeting Sasha."

The wizard raised an eyebrow.

"A girl skyte," Marcus said. "Who apparently has a thing for little blue fireballs."

"I see." Master Therapass chuckled. "Love in the skies."

Marcus raised his wheelchair a few inches and moved close enough to take Kyja's hand. "When you asked us to come visit today, you said something about finding a clue as to why Earth and Farworld combined when we opened the drift."

"*Do* you understand why it happened?" Kyja asked. "Was it something we did wrong?"

"One moment." The wizard pulled a lightweight laptop out of his robe and waved his wand at the screen. "This device is fascinating. Did you know I can access every record in Land Keep without ever leaving my office? It's like magic."

Marcus grinned. The internet had always seemed a little bit like magic to him too. And now, it definitely had some magical elements added to it.

"Here we are." The wizard waved his hand again, and a mass of text flew through the air. Marcus tried to read it as it scrolled by, but he didn't recognize the characters. "Ever since I began researching Earth and Farworld, the links between them seemed unusually large in number."

"Like the fact that when we moved on one world, we moved on the other," Kyja said.

"Or how many places in both worlds seemed unusually similar," Marcus added. "And that some of the animals and plants in both worlds were the same."

The wizard nodded. "I found many more similarities that I won't bore you with now. Suffice it to say that the coincidences made me reexamine things. It seemed far too unlikely that two worlds would randomly combine when a door was opened between them. Not to mention that the combination could occur so seamlessly. I went back to the oldest records I could find. I believe that it is not a mistake, or a coincidence. I think that once, long ago, Earth and Farworld were the same planet."

Marcus and Kyja stared at him.

"How could that be?" Kyja asked. "They were so different. Until we opened the drift, Earth had no magic at all."

"It did once," the wizard said. "Look at the oldest Earth records, and you'll discover stories of dragons, alchemy, and spell casters. Things that until recent events, had been viewed as fantasy. I believe that a cataclysm of some kind—most likely manmade—split the world in two, leaving one half with magic and the other with technology. I believe the four you spoke of meeting in Fire Keep may know more about it, and that they were waiting for the right time to reunite the worlds."

Kyja sat up straight. "The prophecy!"

"What about it?" Marcus asked.

"We always thought we were supposed to save Farworld and Earth from some force threatening to tear them apart. But it makes so much more sense if they were once the same world. *He shall make whole that which was torn asunder. Restore that which was lost. And all shall be as one.* It was talking about bringing Earth and Farworld back together all along."

Marcus shook his head. Of course. How could he have missed that? It seemed so obvious now. "That's why Kyja and I were supposed to save our own worlds. We were never trying to open a doorway. And the gate wasn't a portal; it was a lock. When we turned the key, we brought our worlds back together."

"What about the realm of shadows?" Kyja asked. "Was that a third world?"

The wizard shut his computer. "I don't think so. I don't have any proof for my theory, and I can't find anything about it in the writings I've searched so far. But my best guess is that when Earth and Farworld split, it wasn't complete. A small bit of overlap remained. Like when the two of you jumped to each other's worlds, a small part of you remained behind. I think the realm of shadows was the intersection of the split—a place where technology and magic could coexist."

Marcus nodded. That made sense too.

"What now?" the wizard asked. "What are the two of you up to next? I've heard there are a lot of people who'd like to meet the boy and girl who brought their worlds together. You could both be quite famous."

"No thanks," Marcus said. "I've had enough of fame."

Kyja nodded. "Now that Earth people have magic and Farworld people have technology, it seems like so much good can be done," she said. "A lot of people need help, and we thought who better to help them than a couple of kids who've been to both worlds?"

Marcus rubbed his thumb across the arm of his wheelchair. "Also, this may sound crazy, but no one seems to know what happened to the people in the realm of shadows when Earth and Farworld combined. And I was thinking . . ."

Kyja squeezed his hand and nodded encouragingly.

Marcus blew out a long slow breath. "What you said when we were planning the attack on the Dark Circle, about no one being beyond hope. I've thinking that even though my dad kind of went off the deep end, that maybe there's still a part of him—the part my mom fell in love with—that is still a good person."

"Like the good part of Bonesplinter that was inside the Summoner," Kyja said.

"I'd like to see if I could maybe find him and bring him around." Marcus stared at his hands, feeling his face burn. He was sure the wizard would tell him it was a terrible idea—that the man was definitely dead, and that if he wasn't, that he was still too dangerous to try and help.

"That doesn't sound crazy at all," Master Therapass said. "In fact, it sounds like a wonderful plan." The wizard looked at Marcus and Kyja and beamed. He tugged at his beard and nodded. "Even after meeting all of the elementals I have, after spending my whole life learning spells, and after seeing technology I couldn't have imagined in my wildest dreams, I have to say, the most powerful magic I have ever seen is inside the two of you."

"Double or nothing," Folium said, leaning over the log. His leaves shook with excitement, and his dark eyes gleamed.

"If you insist," Mr. Z said. "But I'm telling you, I have the best jousters in the world."

"What is it with men and snails?" Naiad asked from a nearby pool, where she floated serenely.

Mr. Z was so surprised by her words that he nearly tumbled off his log. "Surely you jest. Snails are the pinnacle of athletic achievement. Smooth as a glacier. Graceful as a dancer. Nimble enough to climb a perpendicular surface while carrying their houses on their backs."

"And slow as the movement of continents," Nebula added from a swirl of silvery fog. "To be perfectly honest, I'm not sure the one on the left is alive. It hasn't moved for as long as I've been watching it."

Mr. Z winked and put a finger along the side of his nose. "It's thinking. Plotting. Waiting for the right moment to strike. Snail jousting is not a game of speed. It's a game of cunning."

"Besides," Folium said, his wrinkly brown skin breaking into an infectious grin, "it's not as if we're in a rush. What are a couple of hundred centuries among friends?"

"Do you think they'll get it right this time around?" Naiad asked. "Will they finally use the power of magic and technology for good instead of using it to destroy each other?"

"They haven't before," Nebula said. "What is this, the seventy-eighth time we've let them try?"

"Seventy-ninth," Folium said. "But who's counting?" He flicked a twig toward the green-and-black snail. "Go on. Make your move while he's looking the other way."

"No fair," Mr. Z said. "That's cheating."

Naiad reached out a languid hand and brushed a couple of fish swimming around her head. "I have a good feeling about the boy and girl. I bet they can actually keep their worlds from blowing apart again."

Folium ran his twigs through his leaf hair. "I'll take that bet. Double or nothing."

ACKNOWLEDGMENTS

Over five years ago, I started writing this series to prove to myself that I couldn't do it. The fact that you are now reading the final book is testament to the facts that a) you should always give yourself permission to try things you don't think you can do, b) I have been blessed by many incredible people who made these books a reality, and c) I have the best readers in the world. If I tried to list everyone whose encouragement made these books possible, it would easily add another hundred pages, but I would like to recognize the following.

The great people at Shadow Mountain who believed in these books and in me. The series would never have happened without you.

The people who edited, drew, formatted, and did all the hard work that turns words into a book, including: Brandon Dorman, Annette Lyon, Lisa Mangum, Richard Erickson, and Mikey Brooks.

My amazing critique group, the Women (and Men) of Wednesday night. Your feedback has been invaluable to my writing success, but your encouragement has meant even more.

My wonderful wife Jennifer and our amazing family Nick and Erica Thurman, Scott and Natalie Savage, Jacob, Nicholas, Graysen, Lizzie, and Jack-Jack. Thanks for

ACKNOWLEDGMENTS

understanding when I disappeared into my office so many nights and for loving this series as much as I did.

And most of all to the readers who believed in my books, loved the characters, and told me in no uncertain terms that Fire Keep was being anxiously awaited.

I hope you love the end of this story as much as I do.

—J Scott Savage

Author of *Farworld*, *Case File 13*, & the new *Mysteries of Cove* Series coming Fall 2015

ABOUT THE AUTHOR

J. Scott Savage is the author of fifteen published novels including Farworld, Case File 13, and Mysteries of Cove. He lives in a windy little valley of the Rocky Mountains with his wife Jennifer. He has four children, and three grandchildren. He enjoys reading, writing, camping, games, and visiting schools. He loves hearing from his readers, who can e-mail him at scott@jscottsavage.com